Pierre Lemaitre

ALL HUMAN WISDOM

Translated from the French by
Frank Wynne

MACLEHOSE PRESS
QUERCUS · LONDON

First published as *Couleurs de l'incendie*
by Éditions Albin Michel, Paris, in 2018
First published in Great Britain in 2021 by

MacLehose Press
An imprint of Quercus Publishing Ltd
Carmelite House
50 Victoria Embankment
London EC4Y 0DZ
An Hachette UK company

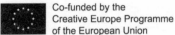

Co-funded by the
Creative Europe Programme
of the European Union

This publication has been funded with support from the European Commission. This publication reflects the views only of the author, and the Commission cannot be held responsible for any use which may be made of the information contained within.

ISBN (HB) 978 0 85705 899 7
ISBN (TPB) 978 0 85705 900 0
ISBN (ebook) 978 0 85705 902 4

2 4 6 8 10 9 7 5 3 1

Designed and typeset in Sabon by Libanus Press Ltd
Printed and bound in Great Britain by Clays Ltd, Elcograf S.p.A.

MIX
Paper from
responsible sources
FSC® C104740

Papers used by Quercus Books are from well-managed forests
and other responsible sources.

To Pascaline,

For Mickaël,
with my affection

1927–1929

There were, strictly speaking, not good people and bad, honest and dishonest, lambs and wolves; there were only those who had been punished and those who escaped.

Jakob Wassermann

1

Although the funeral rites of Marcel Péricourt were disrupted, and indeed concluded in utter disarray, at least they began at the appointed time. From early morning, the boulevard de Courcelles was closed to traffic. Gathered in the courtyard, the band of the Republican Guard discreetly tuned their instruments while, out on the street, automobiles disgorged ambassadors, members of parliament and foreign delegates, who greeted one another gravely. Members of the Académie Française arranged themselves beneath the silver-fringed black canopy bearing the monogram of the deceased, according to the hushed guidance of the master of ceremonies tasked with marshalling the vast crowd while they waited for the ceremony to begin. There were many recognisable faces. For people of a certain rank, a funeral of such importance, like the wedding of a duke or the presentation of a new collection by Lucien Lelong, was a place to be seen.

While she was devastated by the death of her father, Madeleine nonetheless dealt with everything, murmuring instructions, efficient and self-possessed, attentive to the slightest details. All the more conscientious since the Président de la République had let it be known that he would personally come to pay his respects to "his friend Péricourt". Once this was announced, everything became much more difficult, since codes of behaviour in the Third Republic were as exacting as those of a monarchy. There was not a moment's peace in the Péricourt household, overrun as it was by members of the security service and civil servants responsible for protocol, to say nothing of the throng of ministers, sycophants and counsellors.

The head of state was like a fishing trawler, constantly followed by flocks of gulls that fed in his wake.

At the appointed hour, Madeleine was standing at the top of the steps, her black-gloved hands carefully clasped in front of her.

The car pulled up. The crowd fell silent. The president emerged, gave a little wave, climbed the steps and briefly took Madeleine in his arms, saying nothing: the greatest griefs are silent. Then, with an elegant, fatalistic gesture, he stepped aside and ushered her towards the chapel of rest.

The presence of the president was not merely a sign of his friendship with the late lamented banker: it was a symbol. The circumstances, it should be said, were exceptional. With Marcel Péricourt, "a leading light of the French financial world has been snuffed out," according to the headlines of the newspapers with some sense of decorum. The gutter press preferred to run with: "He survived the dramatic suicide of his son Édouard by only seven years . . ." It hardly mattered. Marcel Péricourt had been one of the towering figures in the financial world and his death, everyone vaguely realised, marked the beginning of a new era, one that was all the more unsettling as prospects for the looming 1930s seemed grim. The economic crisis that had followed the Great War had never truly ended. The promise made, hand on heart, by the French political classes, that the defeated German nation would pay for the damage they had caused down to the last centime, had been debunked by events. The country enjoined to be patient while houses were rebuilt, roads repaired, crippled soldiers compensated, pensions paid, jobs created – in short, while France was restored to its former glory, or even greater glory still, since it had won the war – was now resigned: the miracle had failed to happen, France would have to cope alone.

Marcel Péricourt had been a symbol of the former France, one who had managed the economy like a benevolent father. No-one quite knew what was being buried today, an important French banker, or the bygone era he personified.

In the chapel of rest, Madeleine gazed at her father's face for a long time. For months now, his chief occupation had been growing old. "I have to be constantly vigilant," he would say. "I worry that I smell like an old man, forgetting my words; I'm afraid of being a burden, of being overheard talking to myself, I watch myself, it occupies my every waking minute, growing old is exhausting . . ."

On a hanger in his wardrobe, Madeleine found his best suit, a freshly starched shirt, his immaculately polished shoes. He had prepared everything.

The night before, Monsieur Péricourt had dined with Madeleine and his grandson Paul, a boy of seven with an angelic face, pale, timid and prone to stammering. But, in contrast to other evenings, he did not ask the boy about his studies or how he had spent his day, did not suggest that they continue their game of draughts. He sat deep in thought, not worried, but almost wistful, something that was not usual. He barely touched his food, but simply smiled to show that he was present. And, when dinner dragged on too long for him, he folded his napkin, I'm going up, he said, you stay and finish without me, he had pressed Paul's face to his chest, sleep well. Though wont to grumble about his aches and pains, he walked towards the staircase with a light step. Usually, as he left the dining room, he would say, "Behave yourselves." That evening, he forgot. By morning, he was dead.

As the funeral carriage pulled into the courtyard of the hôtel particulier, drawn by two caparisoned horses, as the master of ceremonies gathered close friends and family, ensuring they were arranged according to protocol, Madeleine and the president of the Republic stood side by side, staring at the oak coffin on which gleamed a large silver cross.

Madeleine shivered. Had she made the right choice all those months ago?

She was a spinster. More precisely, she was a divorcee, but at the time there was little difference. Her former husband, Henri d'Aulnay-Pradelle, was languishing in prison after a sensational trial. The plight of his daughter being without a husband worried Marcel Péricourt, who was thinking of the future. "At your age, people marry again!" he would say. "A bank with vested interests in a number of major companies is no business for a woman." In fact, Madeleine agreed, but on one condition: she was prepared to take a husband, but she had no need of a man, I had my fill with Henri, thank you very much. Marriage, fine, but I have no interest in the rest. Although she often claimed otherwise, she had invested much hope in her first calamitous union, so now, she was candid: while she was prepared to remarry, it would be a marriage of convenience, especially since she had no intention of having more children, Paul was enough to make her happy. It was in the autumn of the previous year that people had begun to realise that Marcel Péricourt was not long for this world. It seemed prudent to make plans, since it would be many years before his grandson, Paul the stammerer, would be able to take the reins of the family business. And, even then, it was difficult to imagine such a succession; little Paul could scarcely get his words out and often found it so difficult that he refused to speak, he was hardly company director material . . .

Gustave Joubert, a childless widower who was senior executive at the Banque Péricourt, seemed the ideal match for Madeleine. At fifty, Joubert was a serious, prudent man, disciplined, self-possessed and forward-thinking. His only true passion seemed to be for machines: automobiles (he loathed Benoist but adored Charavel) and aeroplanes (he despised Blériot but worshipped Daurat).

Monsieur Péricourt had vigorously argued the case for this solution. And Madeleine was agreeable, but:

"Let me be clear, Gustave," she had warned him. "I understand that you are a man and you have needs, and I will not prevent you from . . . well, you know what I mean. But on condition that you are discreet. I refuse to be made a laughing stock a second time."

Joubert was all the more receptive to Madeleine's demands since the needs she spoke of were urges he rarely felt.

Then, some weeks later, Madeleine suddenly announced to her father and to Gustave that the marriage would not take place after all.

The news was like a thunderclap. It would be something of an understatement to say that Monsieur Péricourt became enraged with his daughter and her ridiculous arguments: it could hardly come as news to her that she was thirty-six and Joubert fifty-one. Besides, surely marrying a man of mature age and sound judgment was a good thing? But no; apparently, Madeleine could not "resign herself" to the marriage.

So that was that.

She had closed the door to any further discussion.

In the past, Monsieur Péricourt would not have been content to accept such a response, but now he felt weary. He argued, he insisted, but, in the end, he capitulated, and it was such capitulations that made him realise he was no longer the man he had been.

Today, Madeleine was anxiously wondering whether she had made the right decision.

Outside, everyone was waiting with bated breath for the president to emerge from the chapel of rest.

In the courtyard, the guests had already begun to count the minutes, they had come here to be seen but they did not want to take all day about it. The worst of it was not the cold, that was inescapable, but trying to conceal their impatience for it to be over. There was nothing to be done, even muffled up, their ears, their hands, their noses began to freeze, they discreetly stamped their feet, soon they would begin to curse the deceased unless he emerged. They were eager for the cortège to set off, at least then they would be walking.

A rumour trilled through the crowd that the coffin was about to be carried out.

In the courtyard, the priest, wearing a black and silver cope over his alb, led the altar boys dressed in their violet cassocks and white surplices.

The funeral director surreptitiously checked his watch, slowly mounted the front steps to get a better view of the situation, and looked around for those who, moments from now, were to lead the cortège.

Everyone was present, except for the grandson of the deceased.

This was vexatious as it was expected that little Paul and his mother would lead the procession, walking a few paces ahead of the rest of the cortège; it always made for a striking image, a child walking behind a hearse. All the more so since young Paul, with his moonlike face and his slightly sunken eyes, had a certain frailty that would add a very poignant touch to the scene.

Madeleine's dame de compagnie, Léonce, walked over to Paul's private tutor, André Delcourt, who was feverishly scribbling in a notepad, and asked him to inquire after his young charge. He looked at her, affronted.

"But, Léonce . . .! Can't you see I'm busy?"

There had never been any love lost between the two. The rivalry of domestic servants.

"André," she said, "I don't doubt that one day you may be a great journalist, but right now you are still a private tutor. So, go and fetch Paul."

Furious, André snapped shut his notebook, angrily pocketed his pencil and, amid profuse apologies and rueful smiles, pushed his way through the crowd towards the front door.

Madeleine walked the president back to his car, which pulled out of the courtyard, the crowds parting as he passed as though he were the deceased.

To drum rolls from the Republican Guard, Marcel Péricourt's

coffin was carried into the entrance hall. The doors were thrown wide.

In the absence of her uncle Charles, who was nowhere to be found, Madeleine, supported by Gustave Joubert, walked down the steps behind her father's remains. Léonce looked to see whether little Paul was with his mother, but there was no sign of him. André reappeared, throwing his hands up in a gesture of impotence.

The coffin, carried by a delegation from the École Centrale des Arts et Manufactures, was laid upon the openwork bier. The wreaths and the bouquets were placed around it. An usher stepped forward with a cushion on which rested the Grand-Croix of the Légion d'Honneur.

In the middle of the courtyard, the crowd of dignitaries was suddenly seized by a swaying motion.

All eyes turned to look up at the facade of the building. A communal cry was quickly stifled.

Madeleine in turn looked up and her mouth fell open: on the second floor, little Paul, aged seven, was standing on the window ledge, his arms flung wide. Staring into the void.

He was wearing his black mourning suit, but his tie had been ripped off and his white shirt was open.

Everyone stared into the heavens as though anticipating the launch of an airship.

Paul bent his knees slightly.

Before anyone had time to call to him, to run, he let go of the shutters as Madeleine screamed.

As it fell, the child's body fluttered wildly like a bird hit by a shotgun pellet. After a swift, hectic descent, he landed on the black canopy and disappeared for a moment.

The crowd suppressed a sigh of relief.

But he bounced off the taut canvas and reappeared, like a jack-in-the-box.

Once again, the crowd watched as he was catapulted into the air, over the curtain.

And landed with a crash on his grandfather's coffin.

In the suddenly silent courtyard, the sickening thud of his skull smashing against the oak sent the hearts of the mourners lurching into their throats.

Everyone was dumbfounded; time stood still.

When they rushed over to him, Paul was sprawled on his back.

Blood was trickling from his ears.

2

The master of ceremonies was at a loss. When it came to funerals, he knew a thing or two, he had handled the funeral rites of countless members of the Académie Française, of four foreign diplomats, he had even buried three serving or former presidents. Renowned for his sang-froid, here was a man who knew his business, but a child plunging from the second floor onto his grandfather's coffin was beyond even his expertise. What was to be done? He stood staring into the middle distance, his arms hanging limply by his sides. He was completely out of his depth. In fact, he died a few weeks later, and was, one might say, the François Vatel of funeral directors.

Professor Fournier was the first to react.

He climbed onto the funeral carriage, brusquely tossed the wreaths onto the cobblestones and, without moving the child, undertook a swift medical examination.

He was wise to do so because, by this time, the crowd had begun to stir and were making a dreadful racket. The dignitaries in their Sunday best were suddenly transformed into ghoulish onlookers, quivering with curiosity at the accident; there were gasps of Oh! and Ah! and Did you see that? Of course I did, it was Péricourt's son! Ridiculous, his son died at Verdun! Not that one, the younger one! What do you mean "out the window", did he jump? Did he slip? Personally, I think someone pushed him . . . Oh, well, really! It's true, look, the window is still open! Ah, you're right, shit . . . Michel, please, mind your manners! Each recounted what he had seen to others who had witnessed the same thing.

Standing by the hearse, clutching the slatted side, her nails like talons digging into the soft wood, Madeleine was howling like a damned soul. A sobbing Léonce gripped her mistress's shoulders, trying to pull her away. No-one could believe it, a child falling from a second-storey window, it was scarcely possible, but they had only to look up from the scattered wreaths to see, despite the milling crowd, the body of Paul lying like a recumbent effigy atop the oak casket, with the doctor, Fournier, bent over him, listening for a heartbeat, for some sign that he was breathing. He sat back on his haunches, his dress suit and his shirt front daubed with blood, but he was not looking at anything or anyone, he took the child in his arms and struggled to his feet. A lucky photographer caught the image that would be seen around the country: Professor Fournier, standing on the funeral carriage next to the coffin of Marcel Péricourt, cradling the child whose ears were gushing blood.

Someone helped him to climb down.

The crowd parted.

Clutching young Paul to his chest, he raced through the throng, followed by a distraught Madeleine.

As he passed, all chattering stopped, this sudden moment of silence even more heart-rending than the funeral. A motor car was requisitioned, a Sizaire-Berwick belonging to Monsieur de Florange, whose wife stood by the door of the vehicle, wringing her hands because she was afraid the blood would stain the seats – you can't get that out.

Fournier and Madeleine got into the back seats, the child's body lying limply across their laps. Madeleine turned and shot Léonce and André a pleading glance. Léonce did not hesitate for an instant, but André wavered for a moment. He turned and surveyed the court-yard, the scattered wreaths, the coffin, the horses, the uniforms, the fine suits . . . Then he bowed his head and climbed into the car. The doors slammed shut.

They sped towards the Hôpital Pitié-Salpêtrière.

Everyone was dumbfounded. The altar boys had been robbed of their starring role; their parish priest clearly could not believe his eyes. The Republican Guard hesitated about whether to play the programmed funeral march.

And then there was the matter of the blood.

A funeral is all well and good, but it invariably involves a closed casket, whereas blood is organic, it frightens people, it reminds them of a suffering that is worse than death. And Paul's blood was every-where: on the cobblestone courtyard and even on the pavement, a trail of droplets that could be tracked as though across a farmyard. Seeing the blood reminded the mourners of the little boy, his limp body, it chilled them to the marrow, making it difficult to participate calmly in a funeral that was not their own.

Thinking they were doing the right thing, the servants of the house scattered handfuls of sawdust, but this merely set everyone coughing and looking the other way.

Then it was decided that one could not decently set off for the cemetery to bury a man whose coffin was dripping with a child's blood. The servants searched for a black sheet, but there was none to be found. A maidservant climbed onto the funeral carriage with a bucket of steaming hot water and tried to wash down the coffin with its large silver cross.

Gustave Joubert, a decisive man, ordered that the blue curtain in Monsieur Péricourt's library be taken down. Madeleine had fashioned it out of a heavy, dark fabric so that her father could doze during the day even in the blazing sun.

From the courtyard, through the second-floor window from which the boy had hurled himself only moments earlier, the crowd could see servants climbing on stepladders, reaching up towards the ceiling.

At length, the hastily rolled curtain was brought downstairs. It was laid reverentially over the bier, but the fact remained that it was simply a length of curtain and the impression was of burying a man in his dressing gown. Especially, as it had not been possible to remove the three copper curtain rings which, with every breath of wind, clattered against the sides of the coffin.

Everyone was eager for things to return to normal and for the conventional – not to say banal – rites of the official funeral to resume.

As the car sped through Paris, little Paul, lying across the lap of his sobbing mother, did not move. His pulse was slow and faint. The driver honked the horn continually, and the passengers were jostled and jolted like livestock in a cattle truck. Léonce looped her arm through Madeleine's and squeezed it tightly. Professor Fournier had wound his white scarf around the boy's head to staunch the wound, but blood seeped through and dripped onto the floor.

André Delcourt, seated uncomfortably facing Madeleine, kept his face turned away as much as possible, sick to his heart.

Madeleine had met André in the religious institution where she had planned to send Paul when he was of age. He was a tall, thin youth with curly hair, almost an archetype of his time, with dark, somewhat mournful eyes but lips that were fleshy and eloquent. He tutored the boys in French, it was said that he spoke Latin like an angel, and he could even turn his hand to drawing when required. He could talk endlessly about the Italian Renaissance, his great passion. Since he thought of himself as a poet, he affected a feverish expression and an impulsive manner, brusquely tossing his head, a gesture he believed signalled that he had just been visited by some inspired thought. He was never without his notebook; even in company, he would take it out, turn away, frantically scribble down some deathless thought, then turn back to the conversation with the air of someone afflicted by an agonising disease.

Madeleine was immediately attracted by his hollow cheeks, his long fingers, and a smouldering air that seemed to hint at passion. This woman who wanted no more to do with men found in him an unexpected charm. She tried her hand, and he proved equal to the task.

In fact, he was more than equal to the task.

In André's arms, Madeleine rediscovered memories that were far from disagreeable. She felt desired, he was very attentive, even if it took him some time to get down to business, because he invariably had impressions he wanted to share, visions to describe, ideas to explain, he was so loquacious that he would still be reciting poetry in his underwear, but in bed, once he shut up, he was perfect. Readers familiar with Madeleine will know that she was never particularly pretty. Not ugly, certainly, but plain, the sort of woman who goes unnoticed. She had married a handsome man who never loved her and so it was with André that she discovered the pleasure of being desired. And a sexual pleasure that she had never imagined she would feel. Being older, she felt obliged to make the first moves, to demonstrate, to explain; in short, to initiate things. This proved entirely unnecessary. Although André thought himself a doomed poet, he had frequented many a bawdy house, and had participated in a number of orgies at which he showed himself to have an open mind and an unquestionable versatility. But he was also a realistic young man. When he realised that Madeleine, though she had little experience, enjoyed the role of initiator, he revelled in the situation, and his pleasure was all the greater since she pandered to his predilection for passivity.

Their relationship was singularly complicated by the fact that André lived at the institution and was forbidden from receiving visitors. At first, they would meet in hotel rooms, and Madeleine would arrive hugging the walls and leave with her head bowed, like a thief in a vaudeville sketch. She gave André the money to pay the owner of the hotel, resorting to various ruses so that it did not feel as though she were paying to be with a man. She would leave the money on the mantelpiece, but that made it feel as though it were a brothel. She would slip the money into his jacket, but when he arrived at the reception desk, he would have to rummage through his pockets to find it, which was hardly discreet. In short, she needed to find another solution, a need that was all the more pressing since Madeleine had not simply taken a lover, she had fallen in love. Before long, André proved to be everything her former husband had not been. Cultivated, attentive, passive but virile, available, never vulgar, André Delcourt had only one failing: he was poor. Not that Madeleine attached any importance to this fact, she was rich enough for both of them, but she had her position to consider, and a father who would not have taken kindly to the idea of a son-in-law ten years his daughter's junior and utterly unsuited to the world of business. To marry André would be unthinkable, so she hit upon a pragmatic solution: she would hire him to tutor Paul. The boy would benefit from private tuition and a close relationship with his teacher, and, most importantly, he would not have to be sent to boarding school – a notion that terrified her, given the rumours of what went on in even the finest institutions. As schoolmasters, the clergy had long since earned a reputation in this field.

All in all, Madeleine found that her scheme had many advantages.

And so André moved into an attic room of the Péricourt mansion.

Young Paul was delighted at the idea, imagining that this meant he would soon have a playmate. He was sorely disillusioned. For the first few weeks, all went well, but over time Paul seemed less and less enthusiastic. Children are all alike, Madeleine thought, no-one enjoys studying Latin, French, history, geography. And André took his responsibilities very seriously. Paul's gradual loss of interest in his private lessons did nothing to temper the enthusiasm of Madeleine, who could see many advantages: now, there were only two flights of stairs to go up. Or down, if André was visiting her boudoir. Despite this, in the Péricourt household their relationship quickly became an open secret. The servants laughed as they imitated their mistress furtively tiptoeing upstairs with a sultry expression. When they mimicked André going back to his room, he was stumbling and exhausted. There was much amusement in the kitchens.

For André, who dreamed of being a man of letters, who imagined spending a short time as a journalist, publishing his first book, then his second, and being awarded a prestigious literary prize – why not? – being Madeleine Péricourt's lover had undeniable advantages, but honestly, living in an attic room next to the servants' quarters was a bitter humiliation. He saw the chambermaids giggling, saw the chauffeur smirking. In a sense, he was one of them. The service he provided was sexual, but it was a service nonetheless. What would have been rewarding for a gigolo was mortifying for a poet.

Thus, extricating himself from this degrading situation seemed to him imperative.

Which was why he was so unhappy on the day of Monsieur Péricourt's funeral: it was to have been a glittering opportunity, since Madeleine had personally contacted Jules Guilloteaux, the editor of *Soir de Paris*, to request that André write the account of her father's funeral.

Just imagine: a lengthy article, with front page billing in the newspaper with the highest circulation in Paris.

For three days, André had thought of nothing but the funeral, more than once he had walked the route the funeral carriage was to take, he had even written a number of passages in advance: *The myriad wreaths that weigh down the hearse confer upon it an air of grandeur that recalls the familiar, calm, authoritative gait of this giant of French finance. It is eleven o'clock. The funeral cortège is about to set off. In the first carriage, quivering beneath the weight of so many dignified mourners, one can easily make out . . .*

What a stroke of luck! If the article were a success, the newspaper might take him on . . . Oh, to earn his living decently, to be free of the demoralising obligations imposed on him . . . Better yet: to succeed, to be rich and famous.

And now this accident had ruined everything and left him back where he had started.

André stared determinedly out the window so he did not have to look at Paul's closed eyes, at Madeleine's tearful face, at Léonce's tense, inscrutable expression. Or at the dark pool spreading across the floor. For at the sight of the dead child (or almost dead, the boy's body was limp, his breathing now imperceptible beneath the blood-soaked scarf) he felt a pain that cleaved his heart, but it was thinking about his own plight, about the hopes and dreams that had so suddenly faded, that brought tears to his eyes.

Madeleine took his hand.

And so Charles Péricourt found that he was the last remaining member of the family at his brother's funeral. He had finally been tracked down near the steps, surrounded by "his harem" (the man was not a sophisticate, he used the term to describe his wife and his two daughters). He firmly believed that his wife, Hortense, had too great an antipathy towards men to bear him sons. His two daughters were growing like weeds, with spindly legs, knock knees and flourishing acne. They were constantly tittering, bringing their hands to their faces to hide the dentition that was the despair of their parents; it was almost as though, when they were born, some disconsolate god had scattered a handful of teeth in their mouths. Dentists were dismayed. Short of having everything extracted and dentures fitted as soon as they were old enough, the young women would spend the rest of their lives hiding behind fans. A considerable sum would be required for the dental work, or the dowry to be given in its stead. It was a problem that harried Charles like a curse.

A large paunch born of spending his life at table, a shock of prematurely grey hair scraped back from his forehead, heavy features, a prominent nose (the sign, he believed, of a resolute character) and a walrus moustache: this was Charles Péricourt. Add to this the fact that two days spent grieving for his brother had left him with a red face and puffy eyes.

As soon as his wife and daughters saw him emerging from the lavatory, they raced over to him, but in their hysterics, not one of them could clearly tell him what had just transpired.

"Eh? What?" he said, turning from one to the other. "What do you mean 'jumped'? Who jumped?"

With a calm, authoritative hand, Gustave Joubert parted the crowd and, taking him by the shoulder, come, Charles, led him through the courtyard, explaining clearly that, as the sole remaining representative of the family, he had certain responsibilities.

The distraught Charles glanced around, struggling to make sense of a situation that was utterly different from the one he had left behind when he excused himself. The anguish of the crowd was not that of a funeral, his daughters were whimpering, their hands held in front of their mouths, his wife was racked with sobs. Joubert held him by the arm, in Madeleine's absence, you will have to lead the cortège, Charles.

But Charles was all the more flustered because he found himself facing a painful moral dilemma. His brother's death had been profoundly saddening, but it had also come at just the right moment to extricate him from some serious personal difficulties.

He is not, the reader will have realised, a particularly intelligent man, but he had a brute cunning that in certain circumstances would prompt some unexpected ruse, leaving his brother Marcel to bail him out.

Dabbing his eyes with his kerchief, Charles stood on tiptoe, and, as various people were draping the blue curtain over the bier and arranging the wreaths, as the altar boys were falling back into line and the Republican Guard was striking up a funeral march to fill the awkward silence, he slipped from Joubert's grasp, rushed over to a gentleman and seized his arm. And this is how, amid a general disregard for protocol, Adrien Flocard, deputy secretary to the Ministre des Travaux Publiques, found himself at the head of the cortège, wedged between the brother of the deceased, his wife Hortense, and his daughters Jacinthe and Rose.

Charles trailed behind Marcel by thirteen years, which tells the reader everything she needs to know. He trailed behind his elder brother in most aspects of life. He was less intelligent, less hard-working, less forward-thinking, less fortunate; he had been elected to parliament in 1906 thanks to his elder brother's money. "Thing is, it costs an arm and a leg to get elected," he commented with consummate naivety. "It's astonishing how much you have to pay out to constituents, newspapers, colleagues, opponents . . ."

"If you are going to fight for a seat, there can be no question of you losing," Marcel had warned him. "I will not allow a Péricourt to be beaten by some obscure radical socialist candidate."

The election had gone well. There were numerous advantages to being a député, the Third Republic was a benevolent mistress, not grudging, indeed generous to wily old souls like Charles.

Many députés worried principally about their constituency. Charles worried only about his re-election. Thanks to the talents of a handsomely paid genealogist, he had unearthed some very old, very vague roots in the district of Seine-et-Oise which he presented as solid facts, claiming, without a whit of irony, to be a son of the land. He had absolutely no political talent; his sole mission was to pander to the electorate. More by instinct than cunning, he hit upon an issue that was extremely popular, one that spoke to voters outside his own party and appealed to rich and poor, liberals and conservatives alike: the battle against income tax. This proved to be fertile territory. From the moment of his election in 1906, he vehemently opposed Joseph Caillaux's proposal for a tax on income, stressing that it alarmed "those who own, those who save, those who work".

Every week, he made a laborious tour of his constituency, glad-handing and railing against the "insufferable financial inquisition", he presided over prize-givings, agricultural shows and sporting tournaments, and he showed his face at religious festivals. He kept a series of colour-coded index cards on which he scrupulously noted anything and anyone that might be important to his re-election: local dignitaries, ambitions, sexual proclivities, the income, debts and vices of his opponents, anecdotes, rumours – in fact, anything that he might use to his advantage. He submitted written questions to ministers pleading the cause of his constituents, and, at least twice a year, he even managed to speak for a few minutes in the Assemblée Nationale on some issue of local importance. These interventions, scrupulously detailed in the *Journal official*, made it possible for him to hold his head high with his electorate, proof that he had bent over backwards, that no-one could have done more.

All this energy and effort would have been useless had he not had money. He needed it for campaign posters, for meetings, but also, while in office, to pay the electoral agents who sustained his campaigns, principally curates, town clerks and a few café owners, and to prove to voters that electing the brother of a prominent banker had its advantages, since he could subsidise sporting clubs, provide books for prize-givings, prizes for tombolas, flags for war veterans, and could secure medals and decorations of all kinds for almost anyone.

The late Marcel Péricourt had put his hand in his pocket in 1906, in 1910, and again in 1914. He was spared the cost in 1919, since Charles, having served in the Supply Corps near Chalon-sur-Saône, was swept to victory as part of the so-called "blue wave" that resulted in many ex-servicemen being elected to the chamber.

To ensure his re-election in 1924, Marcel had had to spend considerably more, because the Cartel of the Left seemed destined for victory and getting a right-wing député with a poor track record re-elected was a little more difficult.

Marcel had always kept Charles and his political career afloat. Even in death, if things went as Charles hoped they would, Marcel might once again get him out of a rather catastrophic situation.

This was precisely what Charles wanted to discuss with Adrien Flocard as soon as possible.

The cortège set off. Charles blew his nose loudly.

"Architects are a greedy lot . . ." he began.

The deputy secretary (a bureaucrat to his bones, weaned on the Code Civil, and liable to recite the Loi Roustan on his deathbed) simply knitted his brows. The hearse glided forward with slow majesty. Everyone was still choked with emotions after witnessing the sudden defenestration of young Paul, emotions Charles did not feel because he had witnessed nothing, but also because, in that moment, his own concerns were of greater import than the death of his brother and the – possible – death of his young nephew.

When Monsieur Flocard did not respond as he had expected, Charles, tolerably irritated by the nature of his own thoughts and the failure of the civil servant to respond, added:

"Honestly, they take advantage, don't you agree?"

Caught up in his own frustrations, he had fallen behind the hearse and had to quicken his step in order to catch up with his interlocutor. He was already beginning to feel winded, he was not accustomed to walking. He nodded his head . . . At this rate, he thought, there won't be a Péricourt left in Paris by nightfall!

Charles' default mood was one of indignation: life, he felt, had never been fair to him, the way the world turned had never favoured him. His experience with the H.B.M. project was merely further proof.

To deal with the vast housing crisis afflicting the capital, the département had launched a programme to build low-cost housing: "Habitations à Bas Prix". This was a godsend to architects, construction companies and building providers. As well as to the politicians who controlled planning permissions, land concessions, expropriations, eminent domain . . . Undisclosed commissions and backhanders flowed like wine in paradise, and amid this secret yet bounteous bacchanal, Charles had been unable to avoid getting splashed. As a member of the departmental planning commission, he had manoeuvred for the company of Bosquet et Frères to be granted the magnificent site on the rue des Colonies, an expanse of two hectares on which one might erect a number of elegant buildings providing affordable homes. So far, so unremarkable: Charles received his "commission", like everyone else. But he used this windfall to buy shares in a major builders' supplier, Sables et Ciments de Paris, and then insisted they be awarded the contract to supply the construction company. From that point on, it was no longer a question of niggardly bribes and symbolic backhanders. Between the commissions on timber, ironwork, concrete, frameworks, tar, plaster and mortar, Charles saw spectacular sums rain down on him. His daughters expanded their wardrobes and increased their visits to the dentist, Hortense replaced every stick of furniture in the house, even the carpets, and spent a king's ransom on a pedigree show dog, a hideous little mutt that was constantly yapping and, within weeks, was found lying dead on the carpet – doubtless of a heart attack – and was tossed by the cook into the rubbish bin with the potato peelings and the fishbones. As for Charles, he presented his current mistress, a comic actress with a taste for members of parliament, with a diamond as big as a grape.

At long last, Charles' life measured up to his expectations.

But after this financial boon, which lasted almost two years, life once more began to chastise him. And chastise him severely.

"All the same," Adrien Flocard murmured, "the builders' supply company was seriously . . ."

Charles closed his eyes. By dint of having to pay commission to all and sundry, Sables et Ciments de Paris had been forced, in order to protect its profits, to deliver cheaper materials, timber that was not dry, mortar that was three parts sand, concrete that was less well reinforced. A first floor had almost become the ground floor, a bricklayer had fallen through the floorboards, everything had been quickly shored up. And the site had been closed.

"A broken leg, a few fractures!" Charles pleaded. "It's hardly a national disaster . . ."

In fact, the workman had now been in hospital for eight weeks and the doctors still had not managed to get him on his feet. Fortunately, his family was humble, even in their demands, and had been sworn to silence for a paltry sum, a mere bagatelle. For the modest sum of thirty thousand francs in cash, the officials in charge of the H.B.M. programme found the injured worker to be unwittingly responsible and ordered the site reopened, but not before echoes reached the Ministry of Public Works, where, despite pocketing twenty thousand francs, a senior officer proved unable to block a bid by two architects each demanding twenty-five thousand francs to rule that the accident was truly accidental.

"Do you think there's anything to be done . . . with town planning or the ministry? What I mean is . . ."

Adrien Flocard knew exactly what Charles meant.

"As to that . . ." he said evasively.

For the moment, the matter was confined to a closed circle of well-disposed officials, but Charles had already expended fifty thousand francs and Flocard's evasive response made it clear that before the matter was resolved other go-betweens would value their duty and their sense of integrity at exorbitant sums. If a scandal were to be avoided, five times the usual number of envelopes would have to be distributed. And it had all been going so well.

"I just need a little time. That's all. A week or two, no more."

All of Charles' hopes rested on his expectations: in a day or two, the lawyer would announce Marcel's testamentary dispositions and Charles would be given his share.

"I'm sure we can stall things for a week or two . . ." Flocard ventured.

"Excellent!"

With his inheritance from his brother, he would pay whatever was asked, and that would be an end to it.

Business would return to normal, he would put this horrid memory behind him.

A week or two.

Once again, Charles began to weep. He had just lost the best brother a man could wish for.

3

When they arrived at the courtyard of La Pitié, Madeleine ran behind Professor Fournier, clutching her little boy's lifeless hand. With infinite care, the child was laid on a stretcher.

Fournier immediately took Paul to the examination room, which Madeleine was not permitted to enter. The last thing she saw was the crown of Paul's head and the unruly wisps of hair she complained about so often.

She went back to Léonce and André, who were sitting in silence.

The prevailing mood was one of disbelief.

"I can't . . ." she faltered. "How could this have happened?"

Léonce was disconcerted by this question. She had only to picture what she had seen to realise "how" this had happened, but visibly Madeleine had not yet made the connection. She stared at André – surely it was his responsibility to explain the situation to Madeleine? But although the young man was physically present, his mind was elsewhere. Perhaps the hospital setting made him ill at ease.

"Was there anyone else upstairs?" Madeleine asked.

It was difficult to say. The Péricourt house had a large staff of servants, to say nothing of those who had been hired for the funeral.

Had someone pushed Paul? Who could have done so? A servant? But why would a servant do such a thing?

Madeleine did not hear the nurse come and say that there was a room at her disposal on the second floor. It was spartan: a bed, a chest of drawers, a chair. It felt more like a convent than a hospital. André remained standing, staring out the window at the cars and ambulances coming and going. Léonce persuaded the sobbing Madeleine to lie down on the bed while she sat on the chair and held her hand as they waited for Professor Fournier. When he did reappear, it hit Madeleine like an electric shock.

She sat bolt upright.

Fournier was wearing a doctor's uniform, but he had not removed his wing-collar, which made him look like a country priest who had strayed into the hospital. He sat on the edge of the bed.

"Paul is alive."

Paradoxically, each of them sensed that this news was not entirely positive, that there was something else they had to prepare themselves for.

"He is in a coma. We believe he will come around in the next few hours. This is something I cannot absolutely guarantee, Madeleine, but the thing is, when he does wake up, you will be faced with a . . . difficult situation."

She nodded, impatient for him to tell her what she needed to know.

"Very difficult," Fournier said.

At this, Madeleine's eyes flickered shut and she fainted.

The cortège was an impressive sight. The hearse moved at a glacial pace that, though exasperating to the mourners, compelled crowds of passers-by to stop and watch. As the carriage passed, eyebrows were raised. In the light of day, the library curtain was of a rather tawdry blue, the wreaths and bouquets looked as though they had suffered as much as the deceased, the curtain rings clacked steadily against the coffin, all these things gave the cortège an unbecoming air that Gustave Joubert was the first to deplore.

Joubert marched solemnly in the second row, a few metres behind Charles and Hortense Péricourt and their gangling twin daughters. Even Adrien Flocard, who had no standing whatever in the circumstances, was walking ahead of him, since Charles had buttonholed the deputy secretary to discuss an affair of which Joubert was fully aware. Joubert knew almost everything about almost everyone; in this, he was an exemplary banker.

Tall and thin with angular features, broad shoulders and a sunken chest, Joubert was all skin and bone and utterly focused on his work, which he considered a vocation, the sort of man one could easily picture in the uniform of a Swiss Guard. His piercing blue eyes rarely blinked, something that was deeply unsettling when he stared at you intently. He was like a medieval Inquisitor. Though not naturally loquacious, he expressed himself well. He had a limited imagination but great depth of character.

He had been hired by Marcel Péricourt when he graduated from the École Normale Supérieur. Having attended the institution himself, Péricourt invariably recruited his staff from the E.N.S. Gustave Joubert was gifted in maths and physics, and had narrowly missed graduating first in his class. With the exception of the war years, when he had been seconded to the military because he spoke fluent English, German and Italian, Joubert had spent his entire career working for the Péricourt Group. Serious, hard-working, calculating, with few scruples, he was ideally suited to being a banker and had quickly risen through the ranks. Marcel Péricourt found his faith in Joubert rewarded and, in 1909, appointed him director general of the group and senior executive of the bank.

He had routinely taken change of business when, after the death of his son in 1920, Monsieur Péricourt's health began to decline. Péricourt had handed over the reins and for the past two years Joubert had had almost complete control.

When, a year earlier, Monsieur Péricourt had raised the possibility of Joubert marrying his only daughter, the man had nodded sagely as at a decision by the board of governors, but behind his apparent detachment he felt an overwhelming surge of joy. Better yet, of pride.

Having scaled the heights of banking by the sweat of his brow, as they say, and won the respect of the business world, he lacked only one thing: riches. Being too scrupulous to make his own fortune, he contented himself with a standard of living made comfortable by his salary, and a few perquisites that were hardly extravagant: a plush apartment and a passion for mechanics that led him to change his automobile more regularly than most, but nothing exorbitant.

Many of his fellow students at the École Normale had succeeded in the business world, but in a private capacity. They had taken over and developed a family business, founded companies that had become successful, made advantageous marriages; Joubert's success was vicarious. The unexpected suggestion that he might marry Madeleine Péricourt triggered something in him that he had hitherto not suspected: he had dedicated his life to the bank and had been waiting for some gesture of appreciation proportionate to his devotion and the services he had rendered, a gesture that had never come. Monsieur Péricourt, who was always slow to express his gratitude, had finally found a way of doing so.

Before the news had been officially announced, all of Paris was buzzing with rumours about the imminent nuptials. Shares in the family bank rose several points, a sign that the market regarded Gustave Joubert as a safe pair of hands. He had felt the delicious air of jealous rumours whirling around him.

In the weeks that followed, Gustave began to view the Péricourt family's hôtel particulier in a very different light. He pictured himself at home there, lounging in the leather armchairs in the library, in the vast dining room where so often he had had dinner with his boss. And after so many years of disinterested effort, he felt that it was not unwarranted.

He built castles in the air. At night, when he went to bed, he planned, he reorganised. Firstly, there would be no more dinners at Voisin, the restaurant where Monsieur Péricourt was in the habit of entertaining; instead guests would be received "at home". He had a list of young chefs he might poach, and was planning on creating a wine cellar worthy of the name. He would keep one of the finest tables in Paris. People would pester for invitations and, from the countless candidates, he would invite to his soirées those who would prove most useful to the business. The epicurean delights and the understated elegance of these evenings would further the fortunes of the bank which Joubert hoped would be among the most important in the country. Right now, they needed to adapt, to develop innovative financial instruments, to be creative; in short, to devise the model for the modern bank that France so desperately needed. He did not imagine little Paul ever taking over from his grandfather. A president who stammered at board meetings would be disastrous for business. Gustave would do as Monsieur Péricourt had done: in time, choose an heir apparent capable of building on his extraordinary success.

As the reader can tell, Joubert felt he was the ideal man for the job.

So when, without the least forewarning, Madeleine announced that the marriage would no longer take place, Joubert was brutally brought down to earth.

The idea that she could terminate such a project merely because she was sleeping with that pitiful French tutor seemed to him completely irrational. Let her take what lovers she liked, why should that imperil their marriage? He was perfectly prepared to accept his wife's extramarital affairs. If one were to waste time worrying about such trifles, what would become of the world? Yet he said nothing, fearing that if he were to allude to her "womanly ways", even in veiled terms, she might take this as a lack of respect and he would thereby run the risk of exacerbating his misfortune, and adding ridicule to humiliation.

In fact, it was the shadow of Madeleine's former husband, Henri d'Aulnay-Pradelle, that loured over the affair. Spirited, swaggering, masterful, virile, dissolute, overbearing, cynical, unscrupulous (yes, I realise that seems a lot, but anyone who knows him will confirm that there is nothing hyperbolic about this pen portrait), Henri d'Aulnay-Pradelle had as many mistresses as there are days in the year. Gustave became aware of this one day when, leaving Monsieur Péricourt's office, he overheard a brief exchange with Léonce Picard in which Madeleine explained how much her first husband had made her suffer.

"I could not do such a thing to Gustave, make him the laughing stock of Paris as I was. We sometimes hurt those we love, but to hurt someone one does not love . . . no, it would be cruel and petty."

Having informed her father of her decisions, Madeleine had felt obligated to say something to Joubert:

"Gustave, please don't see this as a personal slight. You are a man of exceptional . . ."

The word would not come.

"What I mean is . . . Don't take offence."

He felt tempted to say: I'm not taking offence, you're giving it, but he held his tongue. He simply looked at Madeleine, then bowed, as he had done all his life. He did what any gentleman would have done in such circumstances, but took her sudden change of heart as an affront.

His position as senior banking executive suddenly seemed constrained. Before long, he sensed colleagues sneering at him. The delicious breeze of rumour gave way to sardonic silences and mocking insinuations.

Monsieur Péricourt appointed him vice president of a number of companies within the group and Gustave thanked him, but considered the appointments scant damages for the loss he had just suffered. He remembered something he had read as a boy, about d'Artagnan's bitterness when, having been promised a promotion to captain by Cardinal Richelieu, he is left a lowly lieutenant.

Three days earlier, as the body of his former employer was being laid in the casket, he had stood near Madeleine, slightly in the background, like a major-domo. It was enough to look at him to intuit his private thoughts, to discern the strain, that stiltedness so common in slow-burning anger, an anger that is all the more dangerous in cold-blooded creatures.

As the cortège reached the boulevard Malesherbes, a freezing rain began to fall. Gustave opened his umbrella.

Charles turned around. Seeing Joubert, he reached out his hand and, with an apologetic nod in the direction of his daughters, took the umbrella.

The two adolescent girls huddled next to their father for shelter. Hortense, frozen stiff and stamping her feet, tried to steal a few centimetres of shelter. Gustave, for his part, continued the long march to the cemetery, bareheaded. The rain quickly turned into a downpour.

Shaken and unconscious, Madeleine too was admitted to the hospital. Excepting Charles' branch, half the Péricourt family was in hospital, the other half in the graveyard.

It was, in fact, a reversal that chimed with the spirit of the times. Within a few short hours, a rich, respected family had seen the death of the patriarch and the untimely fall of the only male heir. Defeatists might have seen it as a prophecy. It might offer considerable food for thought for an intelligent, educated man like André Delcourt, but, once he had recovered from the terrible shock of little Paul's fall, he began to brood over his bitter misfortune. His article recounting the obsequies of Marcel Péricourt, his hopes of success – all was lost. Here was a subject worthy of disquisition: chance, destiny, providence and contingency . . . Delcourt, with his love of big words, should have been in his element, but he could see only bleak perspectives.

Eventually Paul, still alive after ten hours in a coma, was brought back to the room in the middle of the night, strapped into a sort of rigid jacket that came up to his chin.

Someone had to sit with him and keep watch. André volunteered. Léonce returned to the Péricourt house to fetch a change of clothes and powder her nose.

There were now two beds in the room. In one, Paul lay, insensible, and in another, a few centimetres away, a heavily sedated Madeleine lay motionless, an occasional twitch the only sign of the nightmares that had her muttering in her sleep.

André sat in a chair and continued to brood. He was unsettled by the unnatural stillness of the two bodies, and terrified by the child in this vegetative state. Moreover, he felt inexplicably angry at the boy.

The reader can doubtless imagine what the prospect of chronicling the funeral of a national hero had represented to Delcourt and the terrible blow that this would not now be possible. All because of Paul. This boy who had had everything given to him. This child on whom he had unstintingly lavished an almost paternal attention.

True, he had been an exacting tutor, and Paul must sometimes have felt the yoke a little heavy, but such is the lot of all schoolboys. André himself had suffered a thousand times worse at Saint Eustache and he had survived. He had thrown himself enthusiastically into the task, not of educating a child, but of moulding him. Everything he knew, he was determined to pass on to the boy. A child, he would often say, is like a block of stone and the teacher is a sculptor. André had succeeded in producing results that rewarded his efforts. Although there was much still to be done about the stammer, Paul's speech was unquestionably better. Much the same was true of the boy's right hand, which, though not perfect, was showing tangible and encouraging improvement thanks to discipline and concentration. One taught, the other learned, it was not always easy, far from it, yet nonetheless – and it touched André's heart to think of it now – he and Paul had become friends.

André was angry with his pupil because he could not understand why he had done what he had done. That his grandfather's death had been a terrible blow was understandable, but why had he not come and talked to André? I would have found the right words, he thought.

It was ten o'clock. The only light was the pale, yellowish glow from the lamps set around the courtyard.

André was pondering his disappointment when it occurred to him that he might yet have a slender chance. Could he write the article even though he had not been present at the funeral?

It would be a challenge, certainly, but as he looked at Paul supine on the bed, he debated the possibility. Would it not be a proof of his loyalty, of his faith in the future, to write the article? When he regained consciousness, would young Paul not feel proud to see the name of his friend, André Delcourt, on the front page of *Soir de Paris*?

To ask the question was to answer it.

André Delcourt got to his feet, crossed the room and tiptoed over to the nurse on duty, a portly woman sleeping in a wicker chair who woke with a start, eh? what? paper? Seeing André's handsome smile, she tore ten pages from the hospital register, gave him two of the three pencils on her desk and dozed off again, dreaming of a handsome young man.

The first thing that he saw as he crept back into the room was Paul, his glittering eyes wide open and staring vacantly. André was greatly moved. He hesitated. Should he go over? Say something? He did not know what to do and, realising that he could not take another step, he sat down again.

Resting the sheaf of paper on his lap, he took out the notebook on which he had scribbled his notes and began. It was a tricky exercise, he had seen only the beginning of the funeral: what had happened after his departure? The journalists covering the ceremony would doubtless provide dramatic and telling details about the ceremony to which he had not been privy. So he settled on a very different approach: lyricism. He was writing for *Soir de Paris*, addressing a general readership who would be flattered by a self-consciously literary encomium.

Before long the pages, crumpled and filled with crossings-out and marginalia, were illegible and so, shortly before three o'clock in the morning, more excited than he had ever been, he tiptoed back to the nurse's station to ask for a few more sheets. This time the nurse, irritated at being woken, all but tossed them in his face. He paid her scant attention, he had what he needed to make a clean copy.

It was then that he noticed Paul's eyes, still wide and glistening, staring directly at him. He turned his chair so he did not have to look at the disconcertingly pale face of the child, bandaged from head to foot and stiff as a board.

4

Shortly before seven in the morning, when Léonce came to take over from him, André did not go home, but instead took a taxi to the head office of the newspaper.

Jules Guilloteaux arrived, as was his wont, at quarter to eight.

"What . . . what the devil are you doing here?"

André proffered the article to the editor-in-chief, who had trouble taking it since he already had his hands full with papers written in a broad, assertive hand.

"The thing is . . . I had to get someone to fill in for you!"

He was sorry, but also intrigued. How could Delcourt have written an account of the funeral when he had departed even before the cortège set off and had not been seen since? In the course of his career, Guilloteaux had seen many strange and bizarre situations, but this one would certainly find a place in the repertoire of anecdotes that made him a prized guest at urbane dinner parties, come now, Monsieur Guilloteaux, surely you have a new story for us, they would cajole him like some elderly courtesan, please, Jules, the mistress of the house would wheedle, and Guilloteaux would clear his throat, what I am about to tell you is absolutely confidential, the dinner guests would close their eyes, already thrilled at the prospect of peddling the story that they were about to hear, well, it was the morning after the funeral of poor Marcel Péricourt . . .

"Very well," he said to André, pushing open the door. "Come in."

Without troubling to remove his overcoat, Guilloteaux sat at his desk and set down the article he had been carrying next to the one written by André, who, to mask his nervousness, was surveying the furnishings with the disinterested air of someone who is not really there and is preoccupied by other matters.

The editor read the texts, one after the other.

Then he reread them more slowly. André's article bore the headline: STATELY FUNERAL OF MARCEL PÉRICOURT OVERSHADOWED BY TRAGEDY and the subheadline: GRANDSON OF THE DECEASED FALLS FROM SECOND FLOOR OF ANCESTRAL HOME AS CORTÈGE DEPARTS.

The article began with a grandiloquent description of the funeral rite ("The President of the Republic, respectfully taking up a position in the solicitous shadow of the peerless financial paragon that was Marcel Péricourt . . .") and moved on to the sudden tragedy, skilfully preserving the element of surprise ("The assembled mourners were spellbound by the sight of the plummeting child, whose white shirt, fluttering open, accentuated his youth and innocence . . ."), then abruptly shifted to family drama ("This heart-wrenching calamity that plunged a mother into despair, a family into shock and all present into the most profound compassion . . .").

Breaking with the traditional style of such accounts, André delivered a three-act tragedy filled with emotion, surprise and catharsis. As he described it, there was nothing more thrillingly alive than this funeral. The young man was blessed, according to the credo of Jules Guilloteaux, with the two qualities indispensable to the art of journalism: the ability to write about a subject about which one knows nothing, and the facility to describe an event that one has not witnessed.

He looked up at André, set down his spectacles and clicked his tongue. He was on the horns of a dilemma.

"Yours is better, my friend! Much better! More forceful, more poignant . . . Honestly, I would have been proud to publish it, but . . ."

André felt crushed. Although he did not know it, Guilloteaux was famous for his unrivalled tight-fistedness.

"The thing is, I put another journalist on the job. You have to understand, son, you had disappeared and I needed an article! And, obviously, I have to pay him. So . . ."

He folded his glasses and handed the article back to André. The situation was clear.

"*Soir de Paris* can have it for free," André said. "Publish it, it's yours." The editor, nothing if not amenable, accepted. Well, in that case, I'd be happy to.

André Delcourt had just entered the world of journalism.

The moment she woke, Madeleine saw Paul lying in the hospital bed and rushed over to him.

So relieved was she to see him that she longed to take him in her arms, but was dissuaded by the sight of the full-body cast, and especially by the expression on his face. The child was not lying in the bed, he was laid out, his eyes wide, it was impossible to tell whether he was aware of what was going on around him. Léonce gestured helplessly. He had been like this ever since she arrived, he had not moved a muscle.

Madeleine began talking to Paul with a feverishness that was almost exultant.

It was in this state of mingled elation and terror that Professor

Fournier found her. He took a deep breath and tried to catch her eye, but it was fruitless, Madeleine clung desperately to the pale hand that emerged from the stiff binding.

Fournier carefully unlaced Madeleine's fingers and forced her to turn and face him.

"The X-ray . . ." he began, speaking very slowly, as though addressing a deaf mute, a comparison that seemed apt. "The X-ray shows clearly that Paul's spine is broken."

"He's alive!" Madeleine interrupted.

It was distressing for the doctor; the news he had to break was difficult.

"The spinal cord has been severely damaged."

Madeleine frowned, staring at Professor Fournier as though trying to work out the answer to a riddle. Suddenly, it came to her:

"You're going to operate and . . . oh . . . I need to prepare myself for a long and difficult operation, is that it?"

Madeleine nodded, I understand, obviously it will be a long time before Paul recovers.

"We are not going to operate, Madeleine. There is nothing to be done. The damage is irreversible."

Madeleine's lips formed a word that would not come. Fournier took a step back.

"Paul is paraplegic."

The word did not have the anticipated effect. Madeleine went on staring, waiting for him to continue: and . . .?

The word paraplegic was an abstract concept. Very well, thought Fournier, if I must.

"Madeleine . . . Paul is paralysed. He will never walk again."

5

In Paris, the bitter cold briefly relented. The city was overcast, shrouded by a mantle of milk white cloud whose intent was impossible to gauge until the icy, driving rain returned.

In the gloomy legal chambers of Maître Lecerf, gas lamps were lit, coats shaken out and hung on the hatstand, and the assembled company took their seats.

Hortense had insisted on being present, and was seated next to her husband. This woman, deficient as she was in breasts, in buttocks and in wits, considered Charles to be a man of genius. Although there was scant evidence to corroborate her exalted opinion of her husband, she continued to feel for him a boundless admiration that was only amplified by the fact that she had despised her brother-in-law, Marcel, who, she believed, had sought to destroy his younger brother out of sheer jealousy. If Charles had made a success of his life, it was not thanks to his brother, but in spite of him. The reading of the will, more so even than the funeral rites, marked the death of that old swine Marcel Péricourt; it was an event she would not have missed for all the world.

Charles and Hortense were seated in the front row next to Gustave Joubert, who, ordinarily, should have sat at the back, but was here as a representative of Madeleine, who had refused to leave the hospital.

The news of little Paul was not good. He had emerged from his coma, but Gustave, who had briefly visited the boy's bedside, had thought him deathly pale; the situation was far from encouraging. Representing Madeleine at such a crucial moment was clear proof that his role as spouse had not been usurped.

At the other end of the row, Léonce Picard, more ravishing than ever behind a lilac veil, had her hands clasped in her lap. She was here to represent Paul. God, but the woman was beautiful. With the exception of Joubert, who was a pure spirit, everyone in the chambers was either captivated or, like Hortense, discomfited.

Maître Lecerf's preamble, a mixture of legal points and personal reminiscences, went on for more than twenty minutes. From experience, he knew that no-one dares interrupt a solicitor in such circumstances, his listeners, fearing an ill-judged word will bring ill luck, are loath to tempt fate. Each stoically endured the delay while thinking about other things.

Hortense was thinking about her ovaries, which had always caused her a dull ache, the shooting pains she felt whenever the doctor examined her, she had heard all manner of stories on the subject that made her tremble from head to foot; she despised her womb, it had brought her nothing but grief.

Charles, for his part, was picturing the weaselly face of the junior civil servant at the Ministry of Public Works saying: "What you are asking of me is rather complicated, monsieur le député . . ." He had nodded to the office next door. "The minister is, well, he is greedy. You can't imagine. He's insatiable." I'll be glad when this is all over, Charles thought, tapping his foot.

Léonce was idly wondering what doubtless astronomical sums were about to be discussed. She was very fond of Madeleine, but she had to admit that it was difficult to live with people who were so outrageously rich.

Lastly, Joubert was steeling himself, expecting to be passed over yet again.

"And the dear departed Marcel Péricourt sent for me in order to set down his last will and testament."

End of preamble; it was almost eleven o'clock.

Marcel Péricourt's fortune was estimated at ten million francs in shares in the Bank and the Commercial Credit Union he had founded, to which was added two and a half million, being the value of the house on the rue de Prony. Charles was pleasantly surprised by these figures, which he had underestimated.

Marcel Péricourt's will listed the beneficiaries in order of importance. Since the death of his son, Édouard, Madeleine was his sole heir. She inherited a little more than six million francs and the family home. Joubert, representing her, merely blinked by way of acknowledgment. What Madeleine had gained was precisely what he had lost.

Unsurprisingly, Paul, being the last to bear the Péricourt name, was to receive three million in government bonds, which would not generate a great profit, but whose value would not decrease over time. This was to be held in trust by his legal guardian, Madeleine Péricourt, until his twenty-first birthday.

Joubert, who could tally figures better than anyone, held his breath, curious to discover how his employer had allotted the remainder, because, if one discounted the hôtel particulier, he had already dispensed ninety per cent of his assets in two bequests.

Charles bowed his head meekly. Logically, his turn had arrived; something that proved both true and false, since the next bequest concerned his daughters. Each was to receive fifty thousand francs, enough to handsomely augment the dowry their parents could afford.

Joubert was already smiling to himself. He no longer needed to calculate, but what came next was even worse than he had imagined. Charles Péricourt was allotted the sum of two hundred thousand francs. A pittance. A mere two per cent of his brother's fortune. It was not an inheritance; it was a kick in the teeth. Dumbfounded, Charles' face flushed crimson, his eyes staring vacantly as a dead bird's.

Gustave Joubert was not surprised by this. "I have done more than enough for him," Marcel Péricourt had told him privately. "He never manages to do anything for himself, except to court disaster. If he were rich, he would be bankrupt within the year and he would drag his family down with him."

The rest of his fortune was parcelled out in endowments of fifty thousand francs to various institutions, including the Jockey Club, the Automobile Club de l'Ouest, the Racing Club de France (Marcel had loved his clubs, though he never set foot in them).

The coup de grâce came in the form of a bequest of two hundred thousand francs to the association of war veterans, a symbolic gesture to his dead son, Édouard Péricourt. Charles Péricourt had merited no more than this symbolic gesture!

Maître Lecerf came to the concluding paragraphs:

"To Gustave Joubert, the devoted and honest colleague who has worked alongside me for so many years, one hundred thousand francs. And to the staff of the Péricourt household, fifteen thousand francs, to be paid out by my daughter as and when she sees fit."

Joubert, who had all the poise and self-control that Charles entirely lacked, considered his bequest bitterly. This was not even a kick in the teeth, it was charity. He had ranked last, just before the maids, the chauffeur and the gardeners.

Charles glanced around as though waiting for someone else to intervene. But the reading was concluded, Maître Lecerf closed his file.

"Um . . . excuse me, Monsieur . . ."

"Maître," the solicitor corrected.

"Of course, whatever you say . . . Is all this above board?"

The lawyer raised an eyebrow. To challenge a document he had drawn up was to challenge his rectitude, and this was something he did not like.

"What exactly do you mean by 'above board', Monsieur Péricourt?"

"Well, I don't know, exactly. But I mean to say—"

"Explain yourself, Monsieur!"

Charles did not know what there was to explain. But then a thought occurred to him, luminous, self-evident:

"What I mean to say, Maître, is it above board to give three million francs to a sickly child who'll probably be dead by tomorrow? Here you are giving him this colossal sum of money while he's lying like a vegetable in a hospital bed in La Pitié and will probably be sharing the family vault with his grandfather within the week! So, let me ask you again, is all this legal?"

The lawyer slowly got to his feet. His professional experience dictated prudence, but also firmness.

"Mesdames, messieurs, the reading of the will of Marcel Péricourt is at an end. It goes without saying that anyone who wishes to contest its legitimacy may apply to the courts tomorrow."

But Charles had not said his piece, he was like a dog with no sense of danger, capable of eating chocolate or drinking sump oil until it died.

"Wait, wait," he shrieked as Hortense tugged at his sleeve. "What if he's already dead, the kid, what if at this very minute he's dead? Eh? Is it still legal, this will of yours? Are you planning to send his inheritance to the graveyard?"

He made a theatrical gesture, calling as witnesses an assembled company that included only Léonce, since Joubert had deliberately turned his back and was putting on his coat.

"Well, I mean, it's true, what I'm saying! Are you telling me millions can be handed out to corpses, and no-one bats an eyelid? Well, bravo, that's all I can say!"

At this, he swept out of the chambers with Hortense on his arm.

The lawyer, lips pursed, shook hands with Léonce as she too took her leave.

"Monsieur Joubert . . ."

He gestured to Joubert, if you have a moment, and the two men went back into the office.

"If he so wishes, Monsieur Charles Péricourt may contest the will, but in the interests of the family, I should say—"

Joubert interrupted him.

"He'll do nothing of the sort! Charles is foolhardy, but he is also a realist. And if he should have any such impulse, I shall make it my business to dissuade him."

The lawyer nodded sagely.

"Ah, yes," he said, as though he had belatedly remembered something.

He slid open the desk drawer and, without having to look for it, took out a large, flat key.

"The late Monsieur Péricourt gave me this. The key to the library safe. For Mademoiselle Madeleine. But since you are her representative . . ."

Joubert took the key and stuffed it into his pocket. Neither man had any desire to prolong this conversation. Both knew that, under the circumstances, this was an action Charles might have every reason to contest, something that would not suit either of them.

Charles was still brooding and blustering. Hortense tried to lay a hand on his arm, but he brusquely pushed it way, I don't need you bothering me. She gave a little smile; she loved moments like these. Whenever her man was overcome by doubt or by rage, it was a sign that he would bounce back. Such is the way with wild beasts; it is when wounded that they show the best of themselves. The more defeated he seemed, the more victorious she felt. On the way home from the reading of the will, she felt positively euphoric: time would prove her right.

The car drove through the grey streets of Paris, whose appearance mirrored Charles' state of mind. A long period of changeable weather lay ahead. He made his calculations. On the scale of public service enticements, ten thousand francs was "greedy", twenty-five thousand was considered "voracious" and fifty thousand "insatiable". To this, it was necessary to add the numerous minor bureaucrats required to rubber-stamp the process, let us say another twenty thousand francs, plus ten thousand more for unforeseen incidentals . . .

Perhaps I am dead too, Charles thought.

Suddenly, he felt like an orphan. He was overcome by an urge to weep, but it was hardly dignified. He had no idea how to extricate himself from this situation. He missed his brother terribly.

The driver had turned on the wipers and was rubbing condensation from the inside of the windscreen with the back of his hand.

*

Joubert stood for a while watching the rain turn to sleet before climbing into his car. No matter the circumstances, he always drove himself.

He was not alone in feeling grieved by this coda to the great man's life.

He had only to step into the hospital room where little Paul lay and see Madeleine, dozing, her feet propped up on a chair, to realise that what Marcel Péricourt had left was of little importance, since nothing would survive him for long, all too soon everything would be swept away . . . It was distressing.

"Ah, you're back, Gustave?"

Madeleine got to her feet.

"Did everything go well?"

"Yes, absolutely, don't worry."

Madeleine had clearly never doubted the fact, and did not ask for any details. She merely nodded, good, good, that's fine . . . They stood for a few minutes looking down at Paul, each engrossed in thought.

"Maître Lecerf gave me this to give you. It's the key to your father's strongbox."

Had he been speaking about the problems of farming in China it could not have had less effect on Madeleine. And so, as she unthinkingly moved to take the key, Joubert grasped her shoulders to get her attention.

"Madeleine . . . whatever you find in the safe is not mentioned in the will, do you understand? Should the taxman . . . Be careful."

She nodded again, but it was difficult to know whether she understood the gravity of what he was saying. She began to cry. Instinctively, he opened his arms and she pressed herself against him, sobbing. The situation was highly embarrassing. Come now, come now, he muttered, but the dam had burst, Madeleine sank into his arms, saying, oh, Gustave, Gustave, not that she was really addressing him, but in his shoes, what was he supposed to think?

The moment lasted for some time.

Finally, she stepped back and snuffled, he hurriedly gave her a handkerchief and, gracelessly, noisily, she blew her nose.

"Please forgive me, Gustave . . . I'm making a spectacle of myself . . ."

She stared at him intently.

"Thank you for being here, Gustave . . . thank you for everything."

He swallowed hard, then realised that he was still holding the key. He proffered it again.

"No, you keep it, we'll deal with that later, if you don't mind."

Then she stepped towards him, creating a troubling frisson. She kissed Joubert on the cheek, leaving him stunned. He should have said something, but she had already turned and was gently tucking in Paul's sheets.

Joubert took his leave, went out into the street and got into his car. The windscreen wipers flickered feverishly, the gust of the car heater caught in his throat. He sat, overcome by some nameless emotion. Little accustomed to analysing her moods, he struggled to decipher exactly what it was that Madeleine had been trying to express. Perhaps she did not know herself.

Arriving at the Péricourt house, he handed his overcoat to the parlourmaid and, as he had done so often, he immediately took the stairs that led up to the library.

The room was little changed since the last time he had been there with his employer; small, distressing details remained, like the spectacles lying on the desk, the pipes that he smoked only in the evening.

Without waiting, he took out the key, knelt down in front of the safe and opened it.

He found a number of family documents, personal notes and a bag of royal blue cloth tied with a green cord that contained more than two hundred thousand francs in French notes and almost double that in foreign currencies.

6

Marcel Péricourt had been buried for nearly two months. The house was still shrouded in an uncomfortable silence, that leaden atmosphere that hangs over a family meal when there has been a quarrel.

Although no order had been given, in the minutes before the car arrived, all the servants silently made their way to the ground floor. One idly ran a feather duster over the banister, another rummaged in the study while a third bustled about looking for a broom she had mislaid.

This feverish whirl of activity doubtless owed something to the presence in the hall of a wheelchair that Mademoiselle Léonce had bought some days earlier: glimpsed between the slats of the crate in which it was contained, it looked like a caged animal whose ferocity was as yet unknown.

When it was announced that Monsieur Paul was coming home, the gardener, Raymond, had opened the crate with a crowbar and, after an initial moment of panic, a maid had stepped forward to clean it. She had burnished the metal as she did the copper pans and had polished the woodwork; the wheelchair shimmered and sparkled so brightly it almost made one long to be paralysed.

The servants had seen Madame only in passing, she would come to change her clothes, respond to any questions distractedly by saying "ask Léonce". She spent so much of her time at the Hôpital de la Pitié, one could not but wonder whether she planned to take up residence there, to become one of those invalids who retreat to a sanatorium and refuse to leave.

In the early morning, Léonce arrived and undertook some last-minute checks. André was there, wearing his sempiternal dark grey topcoat, his shabby shoes polished with an attentiveness born of despair. Joubert, to demonstrate that he was at home here, went and poured himself a drop of port, wondered how much influence

Madeleine would wish to have over business affairs, but broadly felt at ease.

During Paul's time in hospital, she had signed papers without troubling to read them, thank you, Gustave. She kissed him on the cheek when he arrived as though they were old friends. Had she been dressed to the nines and wearing make-up, Joubert would have accepted the greeting as of no importance. But from a woman with tousled hair, wearing a dressing gown and slippers with pom-poms brought from home, such behaviour was more unsettling, almost domestic, as though they were married, as though she had just emerged from her boudoir and kissed him before going down to breakfast. To say nothing of the fact that, to kiss him, she had to stand on tiptoe since he was considerably taller, clutching his arm to keep her balance, and pressing herself against him, well . . . Was she perhaps reconsidering the earlier proposal that had been abandoned for purely circumstantial reasons?

Perhaps their renewed closeness stemmed from her desire to be protected by someone, now that she found herself committed to the care of a gravely handicapped child?

It was almost half past ten in the morning when a car pulled up outside. It was Charles. Burning with impatience, he immediately made for the bar, poured himself a shot of cherry brandy and gulped it down. The man's ruddy complexion and the sweat glistening at the roots of his hair confirmed the rumours Joubert had had from his sources. Charles Péricourt's situation was dire. His situation was parlous, one source confided; the matter was quickly coming to a head, another claimed. If Charles were to summon the courage to ask him for help, Joubert did not know what he would do. Technically, coming to Charles' rescue afforded as many advantages as letting him founder. Or indeed pushing him under.

"Aha!" Charles suddenly roared. "Here he comes!"

A car pulled up.

Behind the window sat Paul, his close-cropped hair making

him look even frailer than usual. He was staring at the people lined up on the steps. Joubert and Charles were standing in the front row, André was behind with the servants. Finally, Léonce appeared and pushed her way through the crowd, went down to the car and opened the door.

She knelt down and smiled.

"Well, well, my little prince, you're home!"

Paul did not respond, his eyes were fixed on the top step where someone had placed the wheelchair.

There was a little drool at the corner of his mouth. Léonce regretted not bringing a handkerchief.

Madeleine, who had emerged from the other side, came around the back of the car. She had lost a great deal of weight. What was most striking about this homecoming was the gauntness of Madame and of Monsieur Paul.

"We're home again, my pet," Madeleine said, but there was a quivering in her throat, she sounded as though she might burst into tears. She turned to the assembled company. No-one moved.

They suddenly realised that the wheelchair should have been placed at the foot of the steps so that the child could be placed in it.

Raymond, the gardener, seized the armrests so hastily that hardly had he taken the first step when people called for him to be careful, sensing the scale of the impending disaster. Raymond arched himself backwards but was dragged down by the weight, almost fell and had to let go, the chair rattled down the steps, hurtling ever faster, Madeleine and Léonce barely had time to step aside. Staring straight ahead, Paul watched the unfolding catastrophe without flinching. In a shriek of metal, the wheelchair crashed into the side of the car then fell onto its side.

Raymond, having quickly scrabbled to his feet, mumbled an apology that no-one heard. He wiped his hands on his new overalls. The accident left everyone stunned. The sight of the wheelchair lying on its side, one wheel spinning uselessly, left everyone with a sense of failure, one exacerbated by the stony expression of the little boy with the cropped hair, his eyes, staring eerily, focused on nothing and no-one.

Charles stood, open-mouthed and dumbstruck. A dead fish, he thought. His heart bled at the sight of this senseless, unresponsive boy, whose futile existence was about to bring about his ruin and that of his perfectly healthy daughters who had their whole life ahead of them, this prepubescent living corpse was about to destroy everything he had created.

Babbling confusedly, Raymond crouched down next to the dented car door.

He took hold of the little boy and straightened up and it was thus, legs dangling uselessly, eyes staring vacantly, carried by the gardener, that Monsieur Paul made his homecoming.

7

There was a step change in Madeleine's life. She no longer wept, but since Paul was plagued by terrifying nightmares that had him waking, bolt-upright, howling in terror ("He thinks he's falling again, I'm sure of it," Madeleine said, wringing her hands), she would rush over and howl with him. She often slept next to his bed, and it was difficult to know who was comforting whom. She was constantly exhausted.

Her former genius for running the house, her organisational skills and her resourcefulness melted away. Although she was still constantly on the go, forever pacing the corridors with her familiar worried expression, she was incapable of making the necessary decisions, and her rushing around served only to displace the air. Take Paul's wheelchair, for example. One of the wheels had been buckled by the fall, the seat had split, it was unusable. When Léonce mentioned sending it away to be repaired, Madeleine had agreed, yes, of course, of course, but two days later it was still standing in the main hall like a relic in an attic. Léonce took it upon herself to have it mended.

The same applied to Paul's bedroom on the second floor, which was no longer suited to his predicament. Another room had to be chosen that could be adapted to his needs. Madeleine pondered a solution, but constantly changed her mind: perhaps this one, then someone would point out that it was too far from the lavatory, oh yes, you're right, perhaps this room, but it's north-facing, Paul would be terribly cold, and besides, there's very little daylight. Madeleine would bite her nails, survey the house, yes, that's true, then, overwhelmed, she would change the subject. She spent hours dealing with secondary details as though moving deckchairs on the *Titanic*.

Eventually, Léonce suggested that the best place for Paul was in Monsieur Péricourt's old room, there was a lavatory next door, and the room was bright and spacious. Exactly, said Madeleine, in the same tone she might have used if she had thought of the idea herself. Where is Monsieur Raymond, she asked. We'll put Paul's bed next to the window . . .

Léonce, ever patient, closed her eye for a moment.

"Madeleine . . . I think perhaps we need to make a few adjustments first. We can't simply move him into the room in its current state."

By this she meant, move him into a room that had not been touched since the day Marcel Péricourt had died there. Madeleine agreed. She nodded and went back to her son.

Léonce set to work. Change the rugs, the curtains, clean and disinfect the room, remove the antiquated furniture, buy something more modern, something more suited to a boy of seven who could not walk. For this, she needed money.

"Of course, could you ask Gustave to deal with it?" Madeleine said.

By rights Léonce should have been promoted to steward, and her meagre salary increased accordingly, but this, obviously, did not occur to Madeleine. But money mattered to Léonce. She was often heard to say laughingly, "I don't know where the money goes, it trickles through my fingers." And this was true; rare were the months when she did not have to request an advance.

Joubert, for his part, perfectly understood that all this additional, time-consuming work was not part of Léonce's duties as a dame de compagnie, but being a seasoned employer, he left the matter in abeyance: they were not about to increase the salary of an employee who did not dare complain.

André Delcourt did not resume his post as tutor to Paul, who, in his quasi-vegetative state, was incapable of studying. He nonetheless continued to be paid. Not knowing what to do with himself, he prowled the corridors of the house with a worried air, a book under one arm, praying that no-one would ask him to account for his time. The Madeleine Péricourt he had known, who had so often laughed as she pushed him back onto the bed, was a different person from the nervous, harried and anxious woman he encountered in the corridors who would say, André, could you go and fetch some magazines for Paul, I'm going to try and get him to read a little, something not too taxing, only to call him back a moment later, no, André, perhaps an adventure novel. I don't know, do what you think best, could you go right now? But by the time he returned, she had already moved on to something else, could you go and fetch Monsieur Raymond, we need to bring Paul downstairs, the boy needs some fresh air.

The prospect of having to look for another post was all the more infuriating because André Delcourt felt that he was on the threshold of something. His magnificent account of the funeral in February, though it had not earned him a sou, meant that his name was mentioned in various circles. Once, he had even been invited by the Comtesse de Marsantes, who held an open house once a week in her apartment on the boulevard Saint-Germain, and considered him an actual writer, despite the fact that he had not yet published anything. To put on a good show, he had invested the last of his savings in a suit – not tailored, obviously, but a second-hand suit that seemed to him striking enough to look the part; the back seam of the jacket had burst the next day and he had had to entrust it to a tailor's workshop in Sentier, the repair was not obvious, he thought, since he did not notice any condescending looks from the servants when they stepped aside as he strode into a salon.

For Madeleine, there was nothing, now, but Paul. She made it a point of honour to do everything herself. Since there was no working wheelchair, he had to be carried, something Madeleine would not allow anyone else to do. The child was painfully thin, he weighed barely fifteen kilos, very little for a boy of seven, but even so . . . "Let me do that, madame!" Monsieur Raymond would say. A dozen times she almost fell, but still she remained adamant. Paul would say, "L-le-let him d-d-do it, Ma-maman!" His stutter had never been so bad.

Everyone watched Madeleine bustle about him wondering just how far she was prepared to go.

Calls of nature were particularly demanding. Three or four times a day, Paul had to be picked up, laid on the bed and undressed, then carried to the lavatory, changed like a newborn, his useless legs lifted up, his body twisted and turned before being dressed again. It was heartbreaking. His eyes were fixed, vacant, he never complained. When she gave Paul sulphur baths, or massaged him with the opium preparation Professor Fournier had prescribed, Madeleine could be heard whispering into the boy's ear like a madwoman, he had become her purgatory.

She was haunted by his defenestration. She could not help but be reminded of her brother Édouard. Both of them had hurled themselves into the void. One, beneath the wheels of his father's car, the other onto his grandfather's casket. Marcel Péricourt was the rock against which the family had dashed itself.

Madeleine decided to conduct an investigation.

She began with Paul himself. She sat him on a chair, facing her, Maman wants to talk to you, Paul, Maman needs to understand . . . you get the idea. Paul blushed, fidgeted, turning his head this way and that, Madeleine insisted, Paul stuttered, n-n-no . . . n-n-no. Yes, Paul, yes, Maman needs to know, to understand. Paul began to cry quietly, Madeleine raised her voice, paced anxiously up and down, tore at her hair, it's driving me mad, she shrieked. Paul by now was sobbing uncontrollably, Madeleine was screaming at the top of her lungs, Léonce was out shopping, it was Monsieur Raymond who, alerted by the cries, took the stairs four at a time, threw open the door, come now, madame, you'll do yourself a mischief. By the time he had caught Madeleine by the shoulder to stop her running around the room like a headless chicken, little Paul had slumped down in his chair, about to fall, without the strength to pull himself up, clinging by his fingertips to the armrests. Monsieur Raymond did not know what to do, he let go of Madeleine and rushed to help her son just as the cook arrived and took Madeleine in her arms. This was the scene that greeted Léonce: Monsieur Raymond cradling Paul in his arms, the boy's legs limp, his face turned to the ceiling, and the cook, sitting on the edge of bed with her mistress' head in her lap.

Hardly had she recovered from this incident than Madeleine began to torment herself with questions.

A conviction formed in her mind. Someone in the household had to know something about what had happened; there was no other possibility.

Perhaps someone had been with him. The notion that someone in her household staff might be to blame at first seemed possible, then incontrovertible, it would explain everything.

She summoned her staff, there were six of them, not counting Léonce and André. Lining them all up together was the worst possible approach, it was ridiculous, as though someone had been stealing the silverware. Rubbing her hands together nervously, Madeleine demanded the truth. Who had seen Paul on the day of the accident? Who had been with him? No-one knew what to say, they all wondered what was about to happen.

"You, for example," she said, pointing an accusing finger at the cook, "I've been told that you were upstairs!"

The poor woman flushed, wringing her apron between her hands.

"It's just . . . I had things to do upstairs—"

"Aha!" Madeleine cried, triumphantly. "You see, you were there!"

"Madeleine," Léonce pleaded in a gentle voice. "Please, I'm begging you . . ."

No-one said another word. They all stared at the floor or at the wall opposite. This silence served simply to fuel Madeleine's rage. She suspected a conspiracy, she pointed at each of them in turn, what about you?

"Madeleine . . ." Léonce said again.

But Madeleine was not listening.

"Which of you pushed Paul?" she screamed. "Who threw my little boy out the window?"

Everyone stared, wide-eyed. No-one would leave here until Madeleine got to the truth, she would go to the police, the préfet himself, and if no-one was prepared to confess, she would have them all locked up, every single one of them . . .

"I demand the truth!"

She fell silent. She stared at the little group as though seeing them for the first time, then fell to her knees, sobbing.

The sight of this woman, prostrate and whimpering hoarsely, was enough to move the hardest heart, but no-one came to her aid. One by one, the servants left the room. That evening, a number of them gave notice. Madeleine spent two days in bed, getting up only when she had to change Paul.

From that day, the house was plunged into a curious state of torpor, the servants said nothing or spoke in low whispers, they felt sorry for Madame, but each was looking for another position, one where they would not be accused of attempted murder. Above all, they felt sorry for Paul, poor little mite, it broke your heart just to look at him . . .

Having exhausted all her theories, Madeleine began to imagine that the answer to this terrible question might come from heaven and went back to the church that she had abandoned on the death of her brother Édouard.

The priest at Saint-François-de-Sales gave her the only counsel he could: be patient and trust in the will of God. Under the circumstances, it was scant comfort. From Catholicism to divination is only a matter of degrees, and Madeleine soon began to frequent astrologers, psychics and mediums. She did not want to be alone. Léonce went with her.

They consulted card readers, crystal ball gazers, telepathists, numerologists and even a Senegalese marabout who rummaged in the entrails of a Bresse chicken and insisted that Paul had been trying to throw himself into the arms of the mother here present, that he had done so from a second-floor window did nothing to shake his conviction: the chicken was categorical. In all of these various methodologies, one thing remained constant: the question could not be resolved in a single visit; they would have to come back several times.

Madeleine brought photographs, locks of hair, a baby tooth that Paul had lost a year earlier. Tearfully, she listened to the explanations, which were all rather vague. An astrologer saw Paul's fall in the alignment of the planets, it had been written, and so they were back to God, the wheel had come full circle. With increasing panic, Léonce watched as money was handed over. Madeleine had spent more than six thousand francs.

Madeleine was not gullible enough to believe whatever she was told. In her profoundly wretched state, she did not know what to think, who to believe, so she fretted and cast about her, trying this or that without rhyme or reason. And, with depressing regularity, her endeavours failed.

Finally, the wheelchair came back from the workshop.

Paul was no better and no worse off, but at least Madeleine could move him around the first floor, could take him to the lavatory without straining her back. There was a small tray in front of him on which she could place a book, a toy, but Paul never read and never played, he spent most of his time staring out the window.

Eventually, his new room was ready. What had been Marcel Péricourt's bedroom was unrecognisable. For Léonce had chosen bright, cheerful colours and sheer translucent drapes. Paul said, th-th-thank you, Ma-ma-maman. It was Léonce who did all this, darling. Th-th-thank y-you, Lé-Lé-Léonce . . .

"Don't mention it, poppet," Léonce said. "All that matters is that you like it."

When Léonce suggested hiring a nurse attendant, Madeleine dismissed the idea out of hand.

"I shall look after Paul."

The two hundred thousand francs Charles had inherited was swallowed up by his property problems and he had only just put his head above the parapet again when a weasel-faced little reporter with red hair and beady eyes arrived to "investigate the building site on the rue des Colonies".

"What interests me is not the building work per se, but the fact that work stopped. Three days' stoppage and, suddenly, it's all go again . . ."

"Well, what can I say?" Charles bellowed. "If work has started up again, then everything is fine!"

"That is not exactly the opinion of the builder I met at La Salpêtrière . . . In a terrible state, he was. Four kids, a wife with no employment, a boss who remembers his name only to accuse him of negligence, but then slips him a little brown envelope – and not a particularly well-stuffed one, either: just enough to buy a pair of crutches."

Charles stared at him: what was the man getting at?

"It gave me an idea for an article. One week working on a building site and suddenly a labourer falls through the floor and finds himself in hospital with a badly broken leg, the human cost, I'm sure you get the picture . . ."

Charles could immediately picture the catastrophe that would ensue.

"I considered writing it, but I would much rather be paid to do nothing, you understand."

Charles, who also preferred to be paid to do nothing, could understand, but coming from a salaried employee the notion seemed to him immoral. The journalist, for his part, was philosophical:

"You know, a piece of information loses most of its value the moment it is published. Unpublished, it is worth considerably more. It's what you might call a creativity bonus . . ."

"You're nothing but a . . ."

Charles groped for the word.

"A journalist, Monsieur Péricourt. A journalist is someone who knows the value of information. In that matter, I am something of an expert: yours is worth ten thousand francs."

Charles had almost choked.

Now he was pacing up and down the waiting room, and it was Charles' glowering face that greeted Jules Guilloteaux when he arrived at his office at *Soir de Paris*.

A scandal at the rue des Colonies site, defective materials, a red-haired reporter (a little runt who loitered outside police stations and hospitals), ten thousand francs.

"My dear Charles," Guilloteaux boomed. "You are absolutely right! I shall summon him now and put a stop to all this immediately."

Charles was satisfied and relieved. As they bid each other farewell, Guilloteaux said:

"Oh, Charles . . . This property company you just mentioned, Bosquet & Frères . . . Does it by chance advertise in the press?"

"Absolutely not! Clients approach them! Advertising would be a terrible waste of money."

"Such a shame! Well, never mind, Charles. See you soon. As for this young reporter, I hope he'll prove accommodating . . ."

Having seen them come, not single spies but in battalions, Charles had developed a sixth sense for spotting troubles.

"What do you mean you 'hope' . . . ? You're not sure?"

"My dear friend, there is such a thing as deontology! A newspaper editor cannot simply impose his wishes on whomever he pleases, it would be utterly at odds with the principles of the profession."

The reasoning was grotesque. *Soir de Paris* was not a real newspaper, it employed no journalists, only hacks.

"Of course I can try, but if he should refuse . . ."

"Then kick him out!"

"I simply cannot do without such writers, Charles! They work for a pittance! They're indispensable to keeping the paper running . . . now, if we had more advertising . . . With forty thousand francs' worth of advertising, I would feel much more confident about your situation . . . I would be in a position to compel his silence."

Charles was stunned. Forty thousand francs . . .

"Very well," he stammered. "I'll see, I'll see."

As he opened the office door, Guilloteaux laid a hand on his arm.

"What about Sables et Ciments de Paris? Do they buy advertising?"

Charles had just agreed to seventy-five thousand francs' worth of advertisements that would never appear.

He would have to resign himself to taking a step that, however degrading, was now inevitable.

*

Gustave Joubert had allowed the notice period to pass unremarked, but it was now May and he did not see how he could wait much longer.

He sat Madeleine down in order to explain the situation, but the young woman simply stared at him as though he were speaking a foreign language. He took her hands in his and spoke as to a child:

"You are president of the board of the bank, Madeleine, and a president is expected to take the chair . . ."

"Chair the annual general meeting?"

She was panicked.

"A token appearance. I can write a little speech to reassure every-one that the bank is still in safe hands. No-one will ask any difficult questions."

The board of directors met in a vast room on the top floor of the bank's head office. A conference table capable of seating sixty people had been crafted especially.

Madeleine entered to a tremulous silence.

All the men stood up as she entered, this ghostly figure in a fashionable outfit, clutching a sheaf of papers that she instantly dropped. As someone rushed to help her arrange the documents into the correct order, the faces around the table were utterly perplexed.

As Joubert had advised, she gave a little nod, inviting everyone to take their seats. More than sixty men stared at her in silence, waiting to be convinced.

Her address was disastrous. Between hesitations, slips of the tongue and endless amendments, the speech was unintelligible, often inaudible, in short, pathetic. There was a risk that the directors would make a discreet exit, leaving Madeleine to finish her oration in front of three or four anxious shareholders sitting fifteen metres apart.

This did not happen.

When she finally looked up, there was a long silence. Joubert rose to his feet and, turning towards her, he began to applaud and was quickly joined by the entirety of the board. An unequivocal success.

Every one of them was utterly sincere.

Their greatest fear had been that this woman, confident of her rights, would seek to control the bank; they were entirely reassured. They were applauding because, in financial matters, she knew nothing, but she would know her place.

In organising this meeting and in writing a speech that was unnecessarily technical, Gustave Joubert was responding to a wish Marcel Péricourt had expressed some months earlier: "Madeleine will be my sole heir, Gustave, that goes without saying, but . . . advise her against becoming involved in the business, she would only feel out of place. And if she should express such a desire, find some means to dissuade her."

Without uttering another word, Madeleine sat through the remainder of the interminable meeting. When she took her leave, she was surrounded by directors and shareholders desirous of saying a few words, conscious that they were unlikely to have the opportunity to do so for another year.

Circling her bedroom, Madeleine stared at the wall, at the window; it reminded her of those long-ago nights when she would have to wait before joining André "upstairs". This was the expression they had used at the time: "See you tonight . . . upstairs." She felt ashamed, as though the memory that she had ever been happy was an affront to her son and his plight.

Almost midnight.

It took her more than an hour to decide, to open the door, to creep along the corridor to the back stairs and go up.

When she came to André's room, she pressed her ear to the door and, hearing nothing, she turned the handle.

André gave a start.

"Madeleine . . .!"

Surprise, embarrassment, panic – it was impossible to tell what emotions that single word contained. André was holding some paper and a pencil. Madeleine, Madeleine, his voice quavered as he quickly set what he had been writing on the nightstand and stood, dumbfounded, staring as though he did not recognise her, like an archaeologist before an unexpected discovery.

Madeleine immediately stretched out her arms, she wanted to say, "Don't be afraid," she was already regretting her decision to come. She glanced at the bed where . . . Once more, she felt a wave of shame and blushed, tempted to make the sign of the cross. She burst into tears.

"Sit down, Madame Madeleine . . ." André whispered, as though there was a chance that they might be discovered.

On the bed? No, she could not bring herself to. This left only the chair, which André pushed towards her. He had called her Madame, as he used to do when there were others present.

"Please excuse me, André . . ."

He gave her a handkerchief. She composed herself and looked around, as though seeing the room for the first time; she had not remembered it being so small.

"André . . . I wanted your opinion. Why do you think that . . . that Paul . . ."

Once again, she began to sob. Come on, Madeleine, come on. At length, she managed to formulate her question, which took on a self-incriminating tone.

"Don't torture yourself so," André said. "It serves no purpose to blame yourself, I assure you."

"I acted wrongly, didn't I?"

Madeleine was thinking about divine punishment, but, spoken aloud in this room, her words seemed to blame their relationship for what had happened. André was not prepared to accept this.

"Did it make you a bad mother?"

"I was probably more distracted . . ."

"Paul was hardly abandoned – he had you, me, his grandfather! Everyone loved him . . ."

His vehement tone was a balm to Madeleine. She did not notice that already he was talking about Paul in the past tense. She stood up and gestured to the papers on the nightstand.

"I'm disturbing you, you were working . . . Are they poems?"

She looked at him as though he were a boy on the eve of his first communion.

"I'm happy for you, André."

She went to the door and remembered she had to give it a sharp jerk to prevent the hinges from squeaking.

André felt unsettled.

This unexpected visit merely confirmed his precarious position within the household. He would have to leave. But how would he live without his tutor's salary? He dismissed the few solutions that occurred to him. His professional references qualified him only to take up a position tutoring Latin or French. He would first have to find a post, then spend endless hours with obstreperous pupils to earn a derisory salary with which to feed and clothe and house himself – my God! – with barely forty francs to his name, and rents constantly rising.

On the threshold, Madeleine turned.

"I just wanted to say, André . . ."

She spoke in a whisper, like a woman talking in church.

"You were so good with Paul. It's true. You are welcome to stay here as long as you like. I hope that one day Paul . . . Don't hesitate to . . ."

André would never know what he should not hesitate to do, since Madeleine abruptly fell silent, went out and closed the door.

André went on living at the Péricourt house, affecting to believe he was compelled to do so by what he condescendingly referred to as "the exigencies of existence". In fact, he had rather less pride than he believed. On Madeleine's orders, a chambermaid visited his room once a week, his linens were changed, his room was heated and his salary continued to be paid on the first Monday of every fortnight.

Whenever Madeleine encountered him, she stopped: Oh, André, how are you? She would look at him the way she had looked at Paul when he was little, that mixture of gentleness, generosity and solicitousness for her own feelings you find in certain mothers.

8

Having shuttled between the bank and the hospital, Gustave Joubert now found himself shuttling between the bank and the Péricourt mansion. He personally drove his Star Model M while he waited for the release of the new Studebaker Big Six, and was invariably accompanied by an accountant, Monsieur Brochet.

It was an established ritual. As they arrived, Joubert would apologise to Monsieur Brochet. He was consciously deferential to staff, as Monsieur Péricourt had been before him. The more respectful you are to subordinates, the more they fear you, Péricourt used to say, they are intimidated, they feel almost threatened by your politeness, it is a rule of psychology.

Monsieur Brochet would sit on a chair in the hallway, a voluminous folder of documents to be signed in his lap. Joubert would go into the library where, depending on the hour, a parlourmaid would bring him tea or a small glass of port. In passing, she would offer a drink to Monsieur Brochet, who would raise a hand, no, nothing, thank you. In such proximity to his boss, he would not dare drink so much as a glass of water.

Madeleine would appear promptly, hello, Gustave, hand on his forearm, standing on tiptoe, a fleeting kiss on the check, and would leave Paul's door ajar "in case he should need anything . . ." Joubert would open his folder and launch into a list of current matters, offering a detailed explanation of each.

When this was done, they would summon Monsieur Brochet, who would lay his folder in front of Madeleine, and Joubert would go through the documents, as he had done in Marcel Péricourt's time. Madeleine would sign whatever was put before her. Monsieur Brochet would go back and sit in the hallway, no thank you, he would say, raising his hand to the parlourmaid suggesting he have something to drink.

Securing Madeleine's consent was an easy task, but, deep down, Joubert did not enjoy it. He had a banker's moral code: one could not simply ignore money, it was almost immoral. Coming from a woman, it was less surprising, but it was disappointing nevertheless.

The ritual required that Joubert not leave the house as soon as the signing was over. He was not an underling to be dismissed the moment a task was completed. Usually, Madeleine would say, have a seat, Gustave, I'm sure you have a minute to spare for an old friend . . . She would beckon a maid, and more tea or port would be served on the low table next to the grand piano (out in the hallway, Monsieur Brochet would raise his hand, no thank you), and Joubert would broach the only subject that truly interested Madeleine: her son.

She would recount the minor incidents of the day, Paul had taken a little soup. She had tried to read to him, but he had fallen asleep, the poor child was exhausted. According to the events described, Joubert would nod or shake his head, then he would get to his feet: I really must excuse myself, Madeleine. Of course, here I am taking up your time when you have so much work, run along, Gustave, hand on his forearm, up on tiptoe, kiss on the cheek, see you on Thursday. Wednesday! Of course, I'm sorry, Gustave, Wednesday.

Today, Madeleine immediately noticed a deviation from the ritual.

"What is the matter, Gustave?"

"It's your uncle Charles, Madeleine. He is . . . that is to say he has encountered certain difficulties. He requires money."

Madeleine folded her arms – Tell me all.

"He should be the one to explain his predicament. Then you can decide . . . We have the means to help him, it would not be . . ."

Madeleine nodded, tell him to come and see me. Satisfied, Joubert checked his pocket watch, made an apologetic gesture and got to his feet. Madeleine showed him to the door, as always.

She reached up and planted a kiss on his cheek, thank you, Gustave.

He had analysed the situation at length and, of all possible hypotheses, this, he decided, was the most auspicious moment . . . And he had missed it, had been too hasty.

It was a shame, but nevertheless, slightly behind his planned schedule, he took the plunge, reached out his hand and, finding Madeline's waist, he pulled her to him.

She was rooted to the spot.

She stared at him without blinking, then gently lowered her eyes.

He was very tall and, in this position, she had to crane her neck.

"Madeleine . . ." Joubert whispered.

Her neck began to ache, she lowered her head, what was going on? She saw Joubert's hand resting on her hip. Did he have something else he needed to ask? The hand moved to her shoulder, it was gentle and brotherly.

She had lowered her eyes, a sign of acquiescence, he towered over her – very well, perhaps his opening had been inauspicious, but he had landed on his feet.

She looked up at him again.

"We are friends, are we not, Madeleine?"

Well, yes, they were friends . . . Madeleine gave a cautious half-smile to indicate that she was waiting for him to finish.

Joubert had rehearsed his lines:

"We had a plan, once, a plan that did not come to fruition. But

70

time has passed, and now everything conspires to bring us together: the death of your father, Paul's accident, the responsibilities of the business . . . Do you not think that, perhaps, it might be wise to look at things afresh? To place your trust in your old friend?"

His hand was still resting on Madeleine's shoulder.

She studied Joubert's face, the words he had just spoken went round and round inside her head without finding an exit. A thought suddenly occurred to her. Could it be that Joubert was . . . asking for her hand in marriage? She could not be certain.

"What are you asking, Gustave?"

Surely we understand each other, he thought. By dint of circumstance, he had been forced to defer his gambit slightly, but, that aside, he had recited his speech without mistakes, in the correct order, he could not understand the confusion.

Madeleine knitted her brows, pressing him for an answer.

Joubert had considered numerous outcomes, but at no point had he imagined that he might not be understood. He had not prepared a speech in order to dispel this, and was thus compelled to extemporise. If she had not backed away, it meant she was waiting for his confirmation, so he exchanged words with actions. He took her hand and pressed it to his lips.

Now, the message was clear. He kissed her fingers and, for good measure, murmured, "Madeleine . . ."

There, that would surely suffice.

"Gustave . . ." she responded.

He could not be certain, but he thought he had discerned a question mark in her voice. What he found most infuriating about women was that everything had to be said, spelled out, they are so unsure of themselves that at the least ambiguity they are overcome by doubt, they vacillate, with women one had to be forthright, firm, clear. Official. It was tiresome.

He was not about to make her a declaration, that would be ridiculous. He struggled to find the words, and remembered the first time he had met his ex-wife. The memory surfaced like a bubble of air, taking him by surprise. Like Madeleine, she had looked at him with the same hesitant, irresolute air. He had bent down. He had kissed her. That was what she had wanted. There had been no need to say anything more. Such is the way with women, either you talk on and on because they need words and more words, or you replace the whole hullabaloo with a kiss or something equivalent (although, for women, nothing is ever equal to a kiss) that performs the same function.

Joubert weighed the pros and cons. She was standing next to him, an encouraging smile on her lips. He would have to take his courage in both hands.

As she watched him, Madeleine was beginning to feel relieved. She had jumped to an unfortunate conclusion, but it had clearly been a misunderstanding. Did he perhaps have personal difficulties? The idea frightened her. If this were the case, would it prevent him from continuing in his role at the bank? Worse, was he considering taking a position elsewhere? What would she do? It was high time that she showed him her appreciation. He stepped a little closer.

"Gustave . . ."

This was the sign he had been waiting for. He took a deep breath, then bent down and pressed his lips to hers.

It was instantaneous, she stepped back and slapped him across the face.

Joubert straightened up and took measure of the situation.

He realised that Madeleine was about to dismiss him.

She feared he was about to resign, to abandon her.

She wrung her hands nervously.

"Gustave . . ."

But already, he had gone. My God, Madeleine thought, what have I done?

*

Gustave Joubert was plunged into a state of turmoil. How could he have been so mistaken? Too shaken to consider the situation objectively, he could not help but brood.

In the past, his pride had often been wounded. Monsieur Péricourt had not been an easy man to work with, but what Joubert had endured from his employer a thousand times, he was not prepared to tolerate from a woman, even if she were Madeleine Péricourt.

Was this the end of his career? There was a plethora of young bankers who would sell their souls to serve Madeleine, especially as she had already demonstrated that she was not averse to young men.

And he would have to find another position. Oh, I have only to consult my contacts, he thought, and this was true, but it was unthinkable that, after a broken engagement to his employer's daughter, he should be dismissed for reasons that made him blush.

And so, some hours later, he decided to take matters into his own hands in order to keep up appearances.

He composed his letter of resignation.

He opted for a simple formulation announcing his impending departure and stipulating that, in the meantime, he was at the disposal of the board of directors and its chairman.

As he waited for the messenger to arrive, he paced his office. This man who kept at bay any emotions that might influence his judgment felt an immense sadness. How could he work anywhere but here, where he had spent his whole life? The very thought was traumatic.

The messenger was a young man of about twenty-five, the age he had been when he first joined the bank. All that time and effort he had devoted to this establishment . . .

He handed his letter to the courier, who gave him an envelope bearing Madeleine's name.

She had forestalled him.

Dear Gustave,

I am sorry for what just happened. It was a misunderstanding. Let us not speak of it again, shall we?

You have my complete confidence.

Your friend,

Madeleine

Joubert returned to his role at the bank, driven by a smouldering anger. Instead of being pragmatic, realistic, Madeleine had behaved in a manner that was illogical, idealistic and, in a word, sentimental.

The decision to remain in his post was, unquestionably, an admission of weakness, to which Madeleine was witness, and also its architect and principal beneficiary . . .

And yet, paradoxically, even at his lowest ebb, Gustave Joubert wondered whether this latest humiliation did not herald a new era in his life.

9

Three months the boy had been home from hospital and still he did nothing but stare out the window. In a desperate attempt to engage his attention, Madeleine decided that some more cerebral activity might do him some good. And this came within André's purview.

Thinking of Paul, slumped in his wheelchair, paralysed and incontinent, André could not imagine by what miracle he would be able to teach him.

"Very well," he ventured nonetheless. "We can try."

In his mind, he was not about to go back to working with his former pupil, he was merely trying to safeguard the meagre salary on which his existence depended. Teaching Paul Latin was preposterous, arithmetic seemed beyond the capability of a boy who was barely able to wipe away his own drool, history was a little too theoretical, so André settled on ethics.

Nevertheless, as he stepped into his former pupil's room, he harboured no illusions, indeed he felt overcome by an uncontrollable dread. He had not seen the boy for several weeks. The room was murky, rain streamed down the windowpanes, Paul, with his sallow complexion and his emaciated face, looked like a dead leaf. Madeleine gave André a sign of encouragement, then discreetly slipped away with a feigned insouciance, you're all boys together, I shall leave you to it . . .

André cleared his throat.

"My dear Paul . . ."

He thumbed through his book, looking for a phrase appropriate to the circumstances, but they all rang hollow, the situation thwarted even the best of intentions.

He settled on: "No difficulty is insurmountable to he who is prepared to fight with courage and determination." He felt the maxim was pertinent: in his present ordeal, Paul needed to marshal his courage and, regardless of the difficulties, he . . . Yes, it was a good start. He took a step and repeated, "No difficulty is insurmountable to he who is prepared to fight," and, after a deep breath, he looked pointedly at his pupil.

The boy had dozed off.

Inexplicably, André understood the ruse at once. Paul was pretending to be asleep. Although his face was expressionless, the child was clearly feigning.

André was piqued. After all the time and effort that he had expended educating the boy, was this how he was repaid? Neither the shrunken figure in the wheelchair nor the thread of spittle hanging from the child's lips was sufficient to appease the cold rage André sometimes felt when faced with an injustice.

"I will not have it, Paul!" he said in a loud voice. "Don't think you can take me in with such a crude trick."

And, when the boy did not move:

"I'll thank you not to take me for a fool, Paul!"

This time, he had shouted much more loudly than he intended. Paul's eyes flickered open. Startled by his tutor's bellowing, he grabbed the little golden bell and waved it.

André turned back to the door. Madeleine was already there.

"What on earth . . .?"

She rushed over to Paul, gathering her son in her arms, what is it my angel? Over his mother's shoulder, Paul stared coldly at André. It was a look of . . . defiance. Yes, that was it. André was taken aback. He clenched his fists, no, he would not stand for this, he could not.

"Are you alright, my darling?" Madeleine said feverishly.

"It's n-n-nothing, Ma-maman," the boy said piteously. "I'm t-t-tired . . ."

André bit his lip and said nothing. Madeleine, worried and attentive, pulled the blanket over Paul's legs and drew the curtains.

"Come, André. Let's leave him to rest. The poor child is exhausted . . ."

The step that Charles was about to take was painful, but he hoped that at least it would be the last, that he would not be forced to appeal to Gustave Joubert, one of his brother's hired hands, it was unthinkable!

His ordeal seemed never-ending. He had to extricate himself at all costs.

He found the Péricourt house much changed. The place was shrouded in sepulchral silence, broken only by the rare appearance of one of the servants – of whom there were now only four. At the foot of the sweeping staircase there was now a steel platform which, by means of a handle and a system of pulleys, made it possible to hoist Paul's wheelchair up and down. It looked like a medieval instrument of torture.

The parlourmaid said, "Madame is waiting for Monsieur upstairs." Charles arrived out of breath. In the shadowy half-light, it took a moment before he made out Madeleine, sitting bolt upright next to the wheelchair, slowly stroking the withered hand of Paul, who seemed unmoved by the situation.

"Please, take a seat, Uncle," Madeleine said, her bell-like voice at odds with the melancholy atmosphere of the room. "To what do we owe the pleasure?"

Charles was seized by a sudden doubt. That determined, almost wilful tone filled him with a curious sense of foreboding.

He took the plunge.

Since it was common knowledge that women understand nothing about politics or business, he stressed the emotional aspect, which is their forte. He was the victim of malice. Worse, of manipulation. People had misused the authority he had delegated . . .

"What can I do for you, Uncle?"

Charles hesitated for a moment.

"The thing is . . . I need money. Not a great deal. Three hundred thousand francs."

Two weeks earlier, he would have had a more conciliatory reception. Madeleine had been advised by Joubert to help her uncle and, after the unfortunate misunderstanding, had been so panicked at the thought that he might leave the bank that she would have gladly done as he suggested, and Charles would have departed with a cheque without having had to open his mouth. Since then, everything had been settled. Joubert had come to the house. He had thanked her. He had taken the letter in which Madeleine reaffirmed her confidence in him and tossed it onto the fire, in a faintly melodramatic gesture. Madeleine's fears had been allayed and, when he left, she felt free to decide as she saw fit.

"Three hundred thousand francs?" she said. "Surely that is approximately the value of your shares in the bank? Why do you not sell them?"

Charles had never imagined that Madeleine might take an interest in such matters.

"The shares are our only assets," he explained patiently. "They are to provide dowries for our daughters. If I were to sell the shares . . . well . . ." he gave a little laugh to emphasise the grotesqueness of the situation, "I would be penniless!"

"Oh . . . Are things so bad?"

"Absolutely. If I am appealing to you, it is only because I have exhausted every other avenue, believe me."

Suddenly, Madeleine was disconcerted.

"Surely you are not saying that you are on the verge of ruin, Uncle?"

"Indeed I am. Within a week I could be bankrupt."

Madeleine nodded her head sympathetically.

"I would have willingly helped you, Uncle, but you must understand that what you have just said makes me wary."

"How so? What do you mean?"

Madeleine folded her hands in her lap.

"You are, you have just told me, on the verge of bankruptcy. But Uncle, as you well know, one does not lend money to a man . . ."

She let out a short, hard laugh.

"Were I not afraid of seeming vulgar, I would put it more bluntly: one does not lavish money on a corpse."

She turned away for a moment, took a kerchief and wiped the trickle of drool from her son's chin.

"Indeed, I cannot help but wonder whether it would be quite above board to give money to a condemned man?"

The baseness of it! Charles wailed:

"The name of Péricourt will be dragged through the mud, is that what you wish? Is that what your father would have wished?"

Madeleine gave her uncle a sad smile. She felt sorry for him.

"My father spent his whole life helping you, Uncle. Don't you think that he has earned a little peace in death?"

Charles jumped to his feet so abruptly that he knocked over his chair. He was on the brink of apoplexy.

Yet Madeleine would have been mistaken if she had imagined she was victorious, for Charles, having spent his life in unending political battles, had developed reflexes that ensured he never emerged from a confrontation seeming foolish.

"I wonder just exactly what kind of woman you are . . ."

The question was posed with the keen inquisitiveness of a man faced with an enigma or unexpected intricacy.

"Or, rather," he said, turning his gaze to Paul, "what kind of mother you are."

The word quivered in the air.

"What . . . what do you mean by that, Uncle?"

"What kind of mother leaves her child to fall from a second-floor window?"

Madeleine rose to her feet, thunderstruck. It was an accident!

"What kind of mother are you when your son, a boy of seven, feels so miserable that he decides to throw himself out a window?"

This attack left Madeleine shaken. She faltered, looked about her for support. Charles stalked out of the room and, without turning, added:

"Sooner or later, we all face our day of reckoning, Madeleine."

10

Last stop before bankruptcy. Charles was appalled to discover just how out of step he was with the world in his view of things.

Seeing Charles stride into the dining room of the Jockey Club, Joubert folded his copy of *L'Auto*, set down his napkin, got to his feet and held out his hand. He gestured to his table and said, regretfully:

"Pardon me, Charles, for taking you out of your way, but a soufflé waits for no man."

Charles was mollified, he had received an apology.

Joubert handled his cutlery with a daintiness that was rather feminine, but did not look down at his plate. He fixed his piercing blue gaze on Charles as he chewed with exasperating slowness. Well? he seemed to say. Charles, who had always cordially disliked the man, began to loathe him. Joubert, he knew, was perfectly aware of his situation. He found it infuriating, all these people who wished to see him forced to drain his cup to the lees. He felt an urge to overturn the table in a fit of rage but was dissuaded by the prospect of his impending ruin.

"My quandary has not resolved itself."

Joubert took a moment to put on his spectacles and study the crumpled document Charles pushed across the table, then gave a low, admiring whistle.

It was not so much the amount that concerned Joubert, but the fact that the name of Péricourt was at risk of being sullied. Madeleine had refused to help her uncle, her womanly instinct once more prevailing over more strategic considerations.

Joubert dabbed his lips and set down his napkin.

"Are you certain that with such a sum you will be able to extricate yourself from this affair?"

"Unquestionably!" Charles blustered. "I have made my calculations!"

Gustave Joubert smiled and rose from his chair. He crossed the room to the private strongbox reserved for him and, from a bag of royal blue cloth tied with a green cord, took two hundred thousand francs, which he slipped into an envelope emblazoned with the crest of the Jockey Club. On his return, he simply placed the envelope on the edge of the table.

Charles mumbled something unintelligible by way of thanks.

"Good evening, Charles. Give my regards to Hortense."

"Thank you, Joubert."

A reflex. He had addressed the banking executive by his surname rather than his Christian name. He was, after all, merely an underling.

Madeleine was no fool. However much André hugged the walls and tried to make himself inconspicuous, his indolence was about to become a problem. To those who toil from morning to night, the presence in the household of a strapping young man who is drawing a salary simply for sitting in his room scribbling verse seems shocking and unjust. An indignation that was understandable even to the rich.

Oh dear, Madeleine thought as she gazed at her powdered face in the glass, perhaps it would be best if I wore a veil . . .

Jules Guilloteaux was expecting her, my dear Madeleine, he took her arm and led her into his office as though she were a convalescent.

Later, at one of his society dinners, Guilloteaux would need only the slightest persuasion to recount the scene, come now, Jules, very well, truth be told, anyone who once knew Madeleine Péricourt would be hard pressed to recognise her today; he would explain that she had worn a little veil, describe her face ravaged by grief, her drawn features, it would be impossible to put an age to her, but he would hesitate before broaching the highlight of his star turn, come, come, Jules, don't keep us in suspense, if you insist, then, although as I said, she looked as though she were at death's door, she came to see me about her lover. *No!* Oh, yes indeed! Everyone revelled in this moment in the tale.

"But, my dear child," he had called her this since birth, having been a close friend of her father, "what do you expect me to give him to do?"

Had he been pleased with the account of Marcel Péricourt's funeral? The editor in chief acknowledged that, yes, the article had won many plaudits, he has a way with words, your friend, I mean your protégé.

"Perhaps he could write, I don't know, a column . . ."

"Such things are the preserve of experienced journalists, Madeleine! What would people at the newspaper say if I took on someone whom they don't know from Adam to write a regular column?"

Madeleine was a banker's daughter; she knew that all things begin or end with the subject of money and that Jules Guilloteaux's protestations were merely a question of figures.

"I'm asking you to employ him, not to pay him."

Guilloteaux bowed his head, pensive. Was Madeleine prepared to personally pay for him to employ her young friend? A last vestige of scruples gave him pause.

"It is all very well wanting to please Madeleine," he told André the following morning, "but I'm running a newspaper, not a charity, what sort of work can I possibly give you?"

The young man wiped his sweaty hands on his trousers.

"A little column called 'Sketches', I thought," he murmured. "Character sketches, things glimpsed here and there, but with a particular slant."

From his pocket, André took a sheaf of paper and unfolded it: an article concerning . . .

"Apothecaries? Why apothecaries?"

Guilloteaux clicked his tongue as he skimmed through the article. A handful of Parisian pharmacists had just been imprisoned for opening their shops on a Sunday.

"Meaning that it is easier to get drunk in the café on the corner than it is to buy something to nurse a child who, granted, had the temerity to fall ill on the Lord's day."

In an ironic tone, André reeled off a list of the professions that, according to this logic, the law should also sanction: firemen, midwives, doctors, *et cetera*, and concluded with a brief but passionate plea in favour of the freedom of practising one's profession. "Let members of parliament continue to parley pointlessly, as is their wont, but let them not meddle with those who, for the common good, are prepared to rise with the lark, at which hour the members of the Assemblée and the Senate are still sleeping the sleep of the just."

It was a good article. Jules Guilloteaux looked a little stunned.

"I have to admit, it has a certain brio . . ."

Fifteen minutes later, André was engaged as a journalist with *Soir de Paris*, with his own column, signed A.D. Forty lines. Page three, Wednesdays and Fridays.

"Those are the best days, they will allow you to make a name for yourself. It will be a trial period. Of course, I can't possibly pay you, as I've already discussed with Madeleine Péricourt, you understand."

When he told this story at society dinners, he glossed over the matter of payment, allowing his audience to believe that he had taken on the young man out of the goodness of his heart, and that he paid André Delcourt just as he did any other journalist.

11

In the months between summer and Christmas, Paul grew two centimetres and lost three kilos. His sleep problems continued, and he was constantly woken by nightmares. Then there was the matter of diet; he ate almost nothing. Professor Fournier complained, Paul needs to put on weight, it's vital. The word terrified Madeleine. Three or four times a day she would sit next to the boy's wheelchair, plate in hand, trying to find some new subterfuge, a song, a nursery rhyme, a fairy tale, a tantrum. Paul was good-natured and agreeable, but:

"I c-c-can't k-k-keep it down, M-m-maman," he would say.

Madeleine would send the plate back to the kitchen with

instructions for the next meal, she had tried everything, messengers were dispatched to the far side of Paris on the day she decided that broccoli purée would work miracles.

A year after the "accident", it was still she who changed Paul's napkins, who carried him, but, being increasingly exhausted, on February 3, 1928, she fell while she was carrying him to the bathroom. The boy brutally bumped his head against the foot of the bath, Madeleine felt guilty and Léonce, who had been advocating that they engage a nurse since the summer, was finally proven right. Thus began an endless parade of nurse attendants.

This one was too rough, that one too flighty, too young, or too old, the next seemed suspicious, and there was no counting those who seemed grubby or sour-tempered, dissolute or cretinous: no-one who suited Madeleine, because Madeleine wanted no-one.

Léonce did her best to explain that it would be difficult to find a nurse utterly devoid of flaws, but it fell on deaf ears until the arrival of a young woman of about thirty who had the look of a farm girl: broad hips, broad shoulders, voluminous breasts, a cheery appearance with red cheeks, small sunken eyes, hair so blonde it was almost white, lips permanently parted to reveal a dazzling smile of sturdy white teeth; she was very outgoing.

She stood in front of Madeleine and rattled off something that proved completely incomprehensible, since she was Polish and did not speak a word of French. She handed over a sheaf of foreign references on which she commented, one by one, in Polish. Léonce began to laugh, Madeleine managed to retain her composure, though, like her friend, she found the situation totally absurd. Even if the young woman's references could be checked, Madeleine would never have agreed to become the talk of the neighbourhood, "the one who hired the Polack". She listened patiently until the young woman had finished speaking, carefully folded the references and announced that she could not employ "a nurse who is Pol . . . I mean . . . a nurse who cannot communicate".

The young woman, misunderstanding what had been said, gave a broad smile, seeming unsurprised that she had triumphantly passed the initial interview, and she nodded to the bedroom door, opening her eyes wide to indicate that she was eager to meet the child.

"Moze teraz do niego pójdziemy?"

Madeleine patiently repeated what she had said but hardly had she begun to speak than the young woman had burst into the room and was striding over to Paul's wheelchair. Madeleine and Léonce hurried after her.

The nurse was garrulous by nature. No-one understood a word that she said, but they could read her every thought on her face, like an actress on the silent screen. And she visibly did not like the current arrangement. She pushed back the wheelchair, looked around for a cloth and, grumbling to herself, began to wipe down the table on which Paul had drooled. She laid a blanket over his legs, picked up his glass, went to rinse it, turned Paul's wheelchair so that it faced the light, then drew the curtains slightly so that he was not dazzled and, having done this, she put away the night table he was not using, stacked the books he never read, and all the while she talked and talked, punctuating her chatter with sudden laughs as though engaged in a private question-and-answer session in which the questions were amusing and the answers positively hilarious. Everyone was dumbfounded. Even Paul, as he watched her buzzing about the room, tilted his head and screwed up his eyes, trying to penetrate the mystery, then finally gave a half-smile, and I can honestly say that never since his return from hospital had he seemed more engaged.

Then, suddenly, everything changed.

The young woman stood, frozen, flaring her nostrils like a hunting dog, she glared at Paul, knitted her eyebrows and spoke sternly, it was obvious that she was angry. She picked up the child like a sack of laundry and carried him to the bed, laid him down and, still grumbling to herself, began to undress and change him.

As she performed this intimate toilette, she continued to chatter. It was impossible to tell whether she was speaking to Paul or to herself, probably both, her tone at once cheerful, stern, reproachful and amused, a combination that brought a faint smile from Paul. The second in less than fifteen minutes. Suddenly, she burst out laughing and, holding the napkin at arm's length and pinching her nose, she staggered to the laundry basket as though about to pass out from the stench, then she set about dressing Paul, who, for the first time, tried to make his presence known:

"Y-y-you f-for-forgot the . . ."

"Ba, ba, ba, ba!" she said without pausing in her work.

When she had finished, everyone present knew that Paul would never wear a napkin again.

Because Vladi wished it so.

Wlładysława Ambroziewicz. Vladi, she would say, raising both forefingers.

There was something simple and childlike about her, something bracing and filled with *joie de vivre*.

Léonce saw Madeleine's impassive expression, she had folded her arms as though determined not to be won over. Léonce tugged at her sleeve.

"It's going well," she whispered. 'Don't you think?"

Madeleine was horrified.

How could anyone think such a thing! The Péricourt family was not about to employ a foreigner to take care of Paul. And a Pole at that!

But at that moment, the attention of the two women was distracted by the sound of voices. The nurse was sitting in front of Paul, holding his hand and reciting what was clearly a Polish nursery rhyme. She was rolling her eyes like an ogre in a pantomime, and at the end of each verse, she gently pinched the boy's cheek.

Paul was staring at her, his eyes shining, a faint smile playing on his lips.

That same day, Vladi was moved into a room on the third floor next to André.

At least she's a Catholic, thought Madeleine.

André's excitement as he arrived at the offices of *Soir de Paris* to deliver the copy for his column was unlike anything he had ever felt. He had woken that morning with a phrase running around his mind: "Even the darkest night will end and the sun will rise . . .", a phrase that expressed both the weight of his hopes and his penchant for hyperbole and grandiloquence.

His article, entitled "Hurrah! A Scandal!", was a satirical celebration of the series of dramas that had shaken the country. While such outrages had once been exceptional, now "they have happily become the primary subject matter of journalists, thrilling even the most demanding readers with the dazzling diversity of their range and scope. Thus, the man of independent means can revel in banking scandals, the statesman can delight in political scandals, the moralist in scandals of morality or sanitation and the man of letters can be affronted by artistic or judicial scandals. The Third Republic caters to every taste. And does so every day. In this domain, our esteemed members of parliament have demonstrated an imagination they have thus far failed to evince in matters of taxation or immigration. The voter cannot but hope that his elected representative might channel some of their creativity into employment. Or, rather, unemployment, since in France the two words are now almost synonyms."

On his way to deliver the piece to the features editor, he had the intoxicating feeling that he was finally entering the world of letters.

He felt a pride tinged with unease at the prospect of meeting his colleagues. He could not dismiss the thought that his status as a columnist imposed by the owner of the newspaper might ruffle feathers initially, but such things are quickly forgotten and, surely, journalistic solidarity is shaped by the demands of a profession in which esprit de corps gives short shrift to minor personal issues.

"My name is—" André began.

"I know who you are," the features editor said, turning towards him.

"I've brought—"

"I know what you've brought."

In the vast room, there reigned a silence that was . . . reproachful. This was the word that came to André.

"Leave it there."

The editor gestured to a tray as he might have to a wastepaper basket. By the time André had thought of an apposite response, he found himself alone. So began a long, agonising torment: had he got off on the wrong foot? What fault had he committed? Would the features editor even deign to read his article? If he did not like it, would he ask André to revise it, or simply discard it? Worse still, might he revise it himself?

His column was indeed published, at the foot of page three, uncut, just as he had delivered it, and signed with his initials.

What André had initially interpreted as reproach was quickly revealed to be unalloyed hostility. No-one greeted him when he arrived at the offices, conversations fell silent whenever he appeared, more than once a cup of coffee was spilled in his lap, he found his bowler hat in the toilet bowl, it was extremely irksome.

This terrible ordeal, begun in September, was still raging in April of the following year.

Eight months of humiliations and setbacks in which offence vied with derision.

A typist who had taken a shine to André told him:

"People here don't take kindly to someone who works for nothing."

Before long, he was venturing into the newspaper offices only at the last minute to place his article in the tray whose sole function, he realised, was to be a quarantine, a place in which a pariah could deposit something that no-one wanted to touch. If he had had a little more money, he would have paid a messenger to go in his stead.

He broached the subject with Jules Guilloteaux.

"It will pass, don't worry!" said the old man, who exulted in dissent between members of his staff.

It would pass if I were paid a salary, André wanted to say, but did not dare.

The rejection he suffered within the offices of the newspaper was inversely proportional to the esteem that his columns earned him in the outside world. The waiters at Bouillon Racine invariably congratulated him, as they had, early in the year, on a much discussed article on Charlie Chaplin.

THE LITTLE JEWISH TRAMP

It cannot be said too often: Charlie Chaplin is, without doubt, the greatest artist in world cinema. Proof, if it were needed, comes in the form of his most recent film, "The Circus": here, in the space of seventy minutes, there is more humour, more humanity, more imagination than in all the American films of the year combined.

More profundity, too. Since the character of the Little Tramp is best seen as the archetype of the Jew.

Hounded from everywhere as a result of his incessant faults, pitiful, devious, the character, who does not hesitate to steal food from a child, is a congenital ne'er-do-well, ever on the lookout for some ploy, a cunning plan that will allow him to do as little as possible while taking advantage of others and of the circumstances in which he finds himself. When he succeeds, he smugly and blissfully lounges in comfort. Until a fresh kick in the a*** once more firmly puts him in his place.

Hence, as we laugh uproariously, at least we can be sure that this, at least, is something he did not steal.

*

A few weeks after taking up her position, Vladi brought Paul a book entitled *Król Macius Pierwszy*, which she read to him.

She was a "lively" reader. She acted out the characters and accompanied each scene with mimes and sound effects intended to heighten the narrative effect of a story that Paul, obviously, could not possibly understand, since it was written in Polish.

Léonce, who happened to walk into the room at such a moment, watched several minutes of this rousing performance. When Vladi paused, sensing Léonce's puzzled gaze, Paul flapped his hands, keep reading, keep reading, there could be no doubt that he was enjoying every minute.

Vladi read him the story a dozen times; he never tired of it.

Another initiative, from Madeleine this time: a Victrola Portable Phonograph, deluxe model, costing 875 francs, together with some twenty discs of French songs, jazz music and operatic arias. Paul greeted the machine with a grateful smile, "T-t-th-thank y-y-you, Ma-ma-maman." Although he was not a churlish child, he did not even lift the cover. Léonce would come by and put on a 78 by Maurice Chevalier, humming along to "Valentine". Madeleine, when she visited, would play music by Duke Ellington and his Cotton Club Orchestra, and Paul would smile sweetly. Then the gramophone would fall silent, Paul would slip back into his torpor and the record sleeves would gather dust.

Vladi loved music, she often sang while she was working, quite out of tune, no jazz or chansons, her tastes tended towards opera. So when, while cleaning the room, she discovered a recording of arias from Bellini's "Norma" among Paul's collection of records, she bounded about like a little goat.

Paul, who often found Vladi's ruses entertaining, wearily agreed to her request to play "Casta Diva". This time, Vladi did not sing along with the music, instead, during the introduction, she slowed her every movement as though, at any second, she expected something astonishing and terrible would happen, then, as the room filled with the voice of Solange Gallinato, Vladi hugged her feather duster to her heart. She closed her eyes to the fluttering trills of *queste sacre*, begun almost in a whisper and ending with a clear yet intimate note, as though confiding a secret. The breath taken by the diva in the first bar, the effortless unfurling to the fateful semitone, the A-sharp of *antiche piante*, which came like a confession. Vladi returned to her chores, but slowly, pausing for a moment to acknowledge the slow fall of *a noi volgi il bel sembiante*, which Gallinato, in her inimitable manner, dared to conclude with a slight crack in her voice that was heartbreaking. The coloratura notes, so often heard, so vulgar in commonplace performances, here took on a freshness that seemed almost ethereal as Gallinato strung them together like pearls.

Overcome by emotion, Vladi stopped in a corner of the room. Ah, the unexpected power of that climactic high C, shattering, devastating, it could cleave your heart.

Vladi turned back to the window and smiled, in spite of herself. Paul seemed to have fallen asleep, his head was tilted to one side. Carefully, she tiptoed over to switch off the gramophone.

Instantly, Paul's hand reached out in an authoritative, commanding gesture. He was listening.

His eyes, still closed, were bathed in tears.

12

Tradition dictated that a different restaurant be chosen each year. And so, after Drouant, Maxim's and Le Grand Véfour, this year the alumni of the École Centrale class of 1899 – dubbed "the Gustave Eiffel class" – were to meet at La Coupole.

As always, there were about fifteen former students, and the seating plan offered a keen evaluation of the little group. So-and-so was not seated next to his tablemate of the previous year since, in the interim, he had slept with the man's wife, another had risen in stature thanks to a number of successful business deals and had thus been moved closer to the head of the table.

Gustave Joubert found himself sitting between Sacchetti, who worked at the Ministère de Commerce Extérieur, and Lobgeois, who managed the Compagnie des Mines de Dourges. The latter, who was merely assistant director of drilling operations, was none-theless still gilded with a semblance of authority, since in 1899 he had been first in his class, narrowly pipping Joubert to the post. It was curious, neither time nor professional failure (nor Joubert's resentment) had tarnished the reputation conferred by that dazzling bygone achievement.

The conversation followed its usual course: first politics, followed by the economy, business and, lastly, women. The factor common to all of these subjects was money. Politics determined whether it was possible to earn money; the economy, how much one might earn; industry, the manner of earning it; and women, the manner of spending it. The annual gathering was both a dinner between brothers-in-arms and a contest between peacocks. Every-one came to strut and preen.

"So, the second round of the elections," Sacchetti said. "I'd say it's in the bag, wouldn't you?"

Since no-one knew which "bag" was meant, everyone could interpret it according to his lights.

"The Red menace will not infect this country," said Joubert. "With God's help, we will be able to kick the communists out of France."

"And pay our debts," Sacchetti agreed.

There was no more common ground than the matter of debt. Regardless of their positions on the franc, they all shared the conviction that the state, teeming as it was with civil servants, was inefficient, profligate, inimical to private enterprise, imposing monstrous taxes

92

that were crushing precisely those businesses and prosperous individuals who were *creating* wealth in a country crippled by debt from the war effort. They were convinced that the French government had become a variant of the Bolshevik system. What was needed was more freedom, less bureaucracy, and the debt to be repaid . . . This happy consensus fuelled the conversation during the ris de veau au sauternes.

Joubert made the most of a lull in the conversation to grasp Sacchetti's wrist.

"If you have a moment, my old friend, I'd welcome your opinion of Romanian petroleum . . ."

Within the Ministère de l'Industrie, Sacchetti was responsible for energy, steam, hydraulic, coal and so forth.

"You'd do better to look towards Mesopotamia," he said. "Perhaps, the oilfields in Kirkuk. A province in Mandatory Iraq. Much more promising, I assure you."

Joubert was surprised. On the Stock Exchange, Romanian oil had been performing exceptionally well and share prices had continued to soar, indeed, Joubert feared that his interest might have come too late.

"I can't tell you where I came by the information," Sacchetti went on, "I'm sure you understand," Joubert gave an almost imperceptible blink of assent, "but you can take my word for it, there's something not quite right about Romanian oil. It's a bad business."

"But their most recent loan—"

"—will be used to mop up their losses. Since everyone is duped, shares will continue to rise. But when it comes, the collapse will wipe out many people. Trust me, my friend, oil is still very much the future. But not oil from Romania. From the Middle East, from Iraq."

Joubert was cautious.

"But how can you be certain? The geological survey has not even been completed . . ."

"Well, then, pray heaven it is not concluded before you have time to secure a stake. Because, by the time the results are announced, every smart investor will have got in before you and there won't be a drop of oil left to slake your thirst."

Dessert was announced.

"Obviously, I never said a thing."

Although the exchange bordered on insider trading, Sacchetti said this only for the sake of form. The Third Republic was built on such arrangements; influence peddling had never been more lucrative.

A sigh of relief, the subject was finally about to move on to women. Gustave gave a knowing smile, which others attributed to his supposed prudishness. He had little to say on the subject of women; oil, on the other hand, was such stuff as his dreams were made on.

At least a dozen times, Paul insisted on listening to the phonograph record on which Solange Gallinato had recorded a number of the most famous arias in her repertoire: "Una voce poco fa", "Oh! Quante volte, oh, quante!".

Léonce was immediately dispatched to scour the music shops. The baffled salesman at Melodia asked the age of the music lover, eight years old, I see, and what does he like, we don't know yet, he listens to one record over and over, arias from opera, I see, but what sort of opera does he like? Léonce did not know.

"Opera buffa . . ." suggested the clerk. "Comic opera?"

Léonce instantly agreed. Comic was precisely what Paul needed.

"Something light and lively!"

Melodia had something even funnier than opera buffa: they had operettas.

Léonce made her choice and returned with a collection of the titles she found most entertaining, ranging from "The Merry Widow" to "The Land of Smiles" by way of "Gaîté Parisienne", all of which sounded terribly amusing. She was very proud of herself.

94

Paul excitedly accepted the gifts, eager to listen to the discs. Madeleine discreetly set a plate of food on his table, and while she and Léonce subtly beat time, and Vladi tapped her foot to her own rhythm, Paul ate and listened to these new acquisitions.

He sat, unmoved, through "Here come the waltzers, here comes the ritournelle", stared intently at his fingernails during "Overhead the moon is beaming, white as blossoms on the bough", sighed audibly during "At first, monsieur, you did embrace me . . ." but the first bars of "Giddyap, my pretty bronco! Come along, there's room for two" proved too much: Ma-ma-ma-maman . . . The phonograph was stopped, everyone crowded around the wheelchair, leaned in close, desperate to understand. It took fully fifteen minutes. Paul asked that he be taken to the shop to choose some music himself.

"Don't you like these ones, my darling?"

Madeleine was in despair. Paul was an impeccably polite boy, not the kind ever to say anything disagreeable. He insisted that everything was fine, th-th-they're v-v-very n-n-nice, but everyone realised that things were far from fine. He bit into an apple in order to appease his mother. Madeleine gave her assent.

And so, one fine April morning in 1928, Paul entered the hallowed halls of Paris-Phono. I say "entered", but that is a little premature. The wheelchair would not fit through the door and had to be left outside. Vladi picked the boy up, carried him under one arm, as she often did, and planted him like a bookend on the counter, all the while giving detailed explanations that left the staff entirely nonplussed, since not one among them understood Polish.

The salesman spent the afternoon playing Paul what he considered the finest recordings. Vladi spent the time stuffing herself with cream cakes in the company of the chauffeur, who had long been suggesting that he might pay her a friendly visit in her garret room.

Amelita Galli-Curci, Ninon Vallin, Maria Jeritza, Mireille Berton . . . "Madame Butterfly", "Carmen", "La Sonnambula", "Roméo et

Juliette", "Faust" . . . Paul picked out a few, but he proved exceptionally demanding. As he listened to one, he would jerk his head back, the sales clerk nodded dolefully, the coloratura *was* a little too daring; to another, Paul squeezed his eyes shut and hunched his shoulders as though fearing something was about to fall on him, the clerk agreed that the higher register was a quarter-tone off key. Paul purchased four box sets. There had as yet been no mention of Solange Gallinato. At the cost of some considerable effort, Paul managed to articulate the name. The sales clerk closed his eyes in rapture. Several more records were added to the pile, almost the complete discography of the Italian soprano.

Just as Paul was leaving, the young sales clerk ducked under the counter. As he reappeared, he hummed the opening bars of "Rachel, quand du seigneur . . ." and gave the boy a printed postcard of Solange Gallinato in the role of "La Juive".

Paul also took with him the complete catalogues of His Master's Voice, Odéon, Columbia and Pathé.

That evening, he ate heartily.

Later, when the chauffeur stealthily climbed the stairs to pay his (long awaited) social call on Vladi, it was almost one o'clock in the morning, but he had no fear of being heard, the whole house echoed with the voice of Gallinato.

Ella verrà . . . per amor del suo Mario!

13

In July, Paul asked for a second gramophone. There was no doubt that his health was improving.

His days were filled with activity. He personally changed the styli on the phonographs, catalogued his records, took notes, updated index cards, ticked off titles in the catalogues of record companies.

He insisted on being taken to the library, where, while Vladi rummaged in the stacks with assistant librarians, he spent his afternoons copying out encyclopaedia entries, reading endless press cuttings about major concerts in Europe, and researching the careers of opera singers and the premieres of new operas all over the world. He had an entire notebook devoted to Solange Gallinato, who, he had decided when he first heard her voice, was the consummate diva.

Asking his mother to help with his spelling, he wrote a letter to the diva:

> *Dear Solange Gallinato,*
> *My name is Paul, I live in Paris and I am a big fan of yours.*
> *My favourite operas are "Fidelio", "Tosca" and "Lucia di Lammermoor", but I also like "Die Entführung aus dem Serail". I am eight years old. I live in a wheelchair. I have almost all your records; I am still missing a few because they are difficult to get, like the 1921 "Barber of Seville" at La Scala, but I will find them. I would be really happy if you could send me a signed photograph.*
> *Paul*
> *I admire you very much.*

It was assumed the letter had been lost in the post but, in July, a signed photograph arrived of the diva in the role of Medea, with the dedication "For Paul, affectionately, Solange Gallinato". There was also a short, handwritten note that concluded: "I was very touched by your laiter."

The photograph was duly framed and hung above the gramophone.

The reader can imagine Madeleine's relief. Paul was beginning to build up his strength once more and, though he was still often engrossed in his thoughts, it was while listening to Mozart or Scarlatti; he was eating well, his colour had improved and he divided much of his time between the library and the record shop. Madeleine had not lost all hope that she might finally have a serious conversation with him and penetrate the mystery that tormented him.

"You should leave him be," Léonce would say. "You know what Professor Fournier always says . . ."

"Give the boy a bit of bloody peace!" was what the doctor actually said.

Madeleine tried to quell her impatience and sent out for Moorish sweetmeats of almond paste.

André was becoming concerned by the situation. Obviously, he was happy for Paul, but now that the boy was better, was he expected to return to his duties as tutor? The memories of their last encounter terrified him.

For the time being, Madeleine made no mention of it. André spent his days putting the finishing touches to his unpaid articles for *Soir de Paris*. Women in sports, public readings, men's fashions, the feast of Saint Catherine . . . In his column he had addressed a wide range of topics in the hope that Jules Guilloteaux might offer him a genuine position at the newspaper, or, rather, the same position, but with a salary.

Although the owner of *Soir de Paris* never broached the subject, he rarely missed an opportunity to congratulate André: "Very good, that column of yours yesterday. We might make a writer of you yet, if the bogeyman doesn't get you." He was pleased with André's work. Not enough to pay him, but pleased nonetheless.

At first, André had decided to wait until the end of the year before demanding that he be remunerated, but Christmas had come and gone, January had arrived ("Priceless, that column of yours about Epiphany!" Guilloteaux acknowledged), and all too soon it was April ("Excellent, that article about the Ideal Home Exhibition, hit the nail on the head! Ha, ha!"), summer was looming, and André realised that, in a few weeks, he would have been there a whole year. Twelve months of twice-weekly columns without so much as a gesture from management.

Nor had things improved at the newspaper, where he was still forced to endure the hostility and vindictiveness of his colleagues.

Then, one day in late July, a union representative a little more fired up than the others grabbed André by the collar, dragged him down to the basement and delivered a series of upper-cuts that left him on his knees, panting for breath and vomiting, feeling as though his chest might explode. On his hands and knees, he crawled to the exit, watched by a group of sniggering unskilled labourers, the youngest of whom spat at him, the spittle landing on his lapel.

This was the last straw.

Back at the Péricourt mansion, he was shaken by an all-consuming rage he struggled to define. Exploited. This was how he felt. It was a word he associated with communists, though God knew he wanted nothing to do with such people; what, a year ago, had seemed like the beginnings of a journalistic career, now seemed like a swindle.

André paced up and down his room, kicking the walls. The weather had turned very warm and the small dormer window let in very little air, he spent his nights tossing and sweating, the room seemed somehow smaller, the furniture shabbier, and though the Polish girl at the end of the corridor was perfectly accommodating when he visited her twice a week, she spent every evening singing out of tune, dear God, he could no longer endure this state of affairs, and so he fastidiously composed a letter of resignation. Did he even need to, given that he was not paid a salary?

He grabbed his coat, strode angrily to the newspaper offices and burst into Guilloteaux's office.

"Just the man I was hoping to see! So, a weekly column . . . what do you say, would you be tempted?"

André was dumbfounded.

"Only a single column, but tastefully boxed, and on the front page!"

"What sort of column?"

Guilloteaux looked wary.

"Well, Marcy does economics, Garbin does politics, Frandidier does what the hell he likes. But there's no-one dealing with the man in the street, d'you see? The folks who buy *Soir de Paris* want some-one to write about them. Why else do you think they're so fascinated by human-interest stories, in local tragedies and freak accidents? Because this is the sort of thing that could happen to any one of them."

André gave a helpless shrug.

"But local news stories are—"

"I know! And that's not what I had in mind. I'm thinking of a column that would say out loud what people say only in whispers."

"A humorous column?"

"If you like, but it would have to be gallows humour, because everyone knows that there is nothing people like better than to complain! It needs to have a certain erudition, that's why I thought of you."

"A certain erudition . . ."

"Absolutely! One of the things that readers love is the idea that intelligent people think as they do, it flatters them. But, if they're to read it, it also needs a certain simplicity. It's all a question of balance."

Still reeling, André tried to spot the catch.

"Would it be paid?" he asked.

"Well . . . not very handsomely. The economic crisis . . ."

André understood the economic crisis, and had long since learned not to confuse the fortunes of the newspaper with that of the proprietor. He would believe in the economic crisis the day Guilloteaux was forced to fire his Indochinese servants.

"But it would be paid?"

André was proud of his audacity. Guilloteaux immediately winced, as though someone was trying tried to pull one of his teeth, then finally grunted:

"Yes, it would be paid."

"How much?" asked André, feeling in particularly fine fettle.

"Thirty francs per column."

"Forty."

"Thirty-two."

"Thirty-seven."

"Oh, very well then, thirty-three. But just you mind, I want a column that provokes . . . controversy."

Guilloteaux turned away, deliberately hunching his shoulders to signal his displeasure, an unmistakable sign that he was happy with the deal.

"Oh, and you'll have to come up with a name!"

"What the . . . I already have a name!"

"No-one cares a fig about that. One way or another, you have to make a name for yourself."

Guilloteaux leaned forward and whispered confidentially.

"Choose a nom de plume. Everyone will assume that the pseudonym is a shield for an eminent thinker or famous writer. Oh, and remember that most readers like horoscopes, so choose a name that conjures up superior wisdom."

And so, in early August, on the front page of *Soir de Paris*, there appeared the first column penned by "Kairos":

A MAN WORTHY OF THE NAME

Fourteen years ago, the country was called upon to mobilise. As one, the people of France rose to the challenge, channelling their courage and their strength into a war without precedent and steeling themselves against a period that would be strewn with personal tragedies. Forty months later, having suffered untold sacrifices, exultation began to give way to disarray, and a bell of doubt and disquiet began to toll. In this fateful moment, it was to the hands of a man of seventy-six that the Nation entrusted its destiny. A man who had always been in error, who could scarcely agree even with himself, ever quick to take offence, often brutish, tyrannical and with a temperament tending towards the dictatorial. It sometimes happens that a man of few ideas becomes a great man by force of circumstance. Monsieur Clemenceau had only one policy, and only one thought: "Domestic policy, I wage war; foreign policy, I wage war. I do nothing but wage war [. . .]. When Russia betrays us, I continue to wage war [. . .] and I will carry on doing so to the last quarter-hour."

It was simple, and it was precisely what the valiant people of France needed to hear.

In a few days, Monsieur Clemenceau will celebrate his eighty-eighth birthday. A recent photograph of him taken in Saint-Vincent-sur-Jard in Vendée shows a man still hale and hearty, walking with determined tread.

When we look up at the great and the good who govern us today, by contrast, they seem colourless, bloodless, vacillating and inconsistent. And we feel tempted, like Diogenes of Sinope, to take up our lamp and ask: "Is there no man left in France of the stature of Clemenceau?"

Kairos

Ever since the dreadful misunderstanding between them, Madeleine had never again managed to feel entirely at ease around Gustave Joubert. She had chosen not to change anything about their routine to stress that nothing about their relationship had changed but, a year later, she still felt embarrassed as she rose on tiptoe to peck him on the cheek and said, good morning, Gustave.

The man was an enigma, Madeleine never knew what he was thinking. He would give an account of the businesses, sip his coffee and stare at her with those terrifyingly blue eyes . . . While Paul was engrossed in the *History of Italian Opera* at the far end of the room, Joubert entertained Madeleine with current affairs:

"Monsieur Raoul-Simon finds himself in something of a difficult position. I propose to help him out. It is never a bad idea to have a member of the Counsel in one's debt . . ."

Madeleine would smile with him, feigning a complicity whose extent she did not truly understand. She signed the documents he put before her. Sometimes, Joubert would insist on explaining them, he did not want to be reproached at some later date for failing in his duty to keep her informed. He would launch into something like:

"I don't wish to burden you with details, Madeleine, but it is high time that you consider restructuring your assets."

Madeleine would nod and wave, yes, of course. Of course.

"Government securities are no longer producing a profit, and that situation is unlikely to change in the near future. Restructuring would entail selling failing securities in favour of more profitable shares."

"Very good, yes, that sounds an excellent idea."

"It is a wise decision, believe me. But one that you should take only in full possession of the facts."

She understood.

"It is a vital bulwark against the future. To my mind, it is some-thing you should do, but I need an assurance that you understand exactly what it signifies."

She understood, she signed.

Distractedly, she asked:

"By the way, what was in Papa's strongbox?"

"Nothing compromising, I assure you. Some old bonds and securities . . ." Joubert had said and she had moved on to something else without even asking him for the key.

And yet – who knew how? – with the infallible instinct of

incompetent managers, she would sometimes home in on a particular sum with unerring accuracy.

In fact, it happened only once, in August, but it made a significant impression on Madeleine precisely because it had never happened before.

"What is this?" Madeleine said as she was about to sign an order in the name of Ferret-Delage.

Joubert stared at it.

"A loss. In the banking world, they're all too common. If we always made a profit, everyone would be a banker!"

Joubert's answer had been too quick, too glib, his impulsiveness was tantamount to a confession. Madeleine set down her pen and instinctively adopted the bearing she had seen in her father in such situations. She did not say a word, but simply waited for the answer to come.

The Péricourt Bank had made a poor investment on the stock market. A net loss of almost three hundred thousand francs.

Madeleine realised that, until now, she had believed Joubert to be gifted with an expertise verging on omniscience, and that she had been mistaken. Knowing that silence would be more unsettling than any reproach, that her power lay in the unknowability of her thoughts, she silently signed the order and moved on to the next document.

Although it was past time for him to leave, Joubert went on sitting, sipping his coffee, looking worried. Or stern, Madeleine could not tell. As though he was angry with her about something and about to reprimand her.

"Will you permit me, dearest Madeleine, to ask Mademoiselle Picard and Monsieur Brochet to join us for a moment?"

Madeleine was surprised: Yes, of course, but why? Joubert raised his palm: Wait a moment.

Monsieur Brochet stepped into the room and greeted Madeleine with a deferential bow. Léonce arrived a moment later, pirouetting and pert, you sent for me?

"Mademoiselle Picard," Joubert turned to Léonce, "Monsieur Brochet here is an accountant and . . ."

He trailed off, startled to see the ordinarily ruddy face of his colleague now flush crimson, purple, as though about to explode. He was staring at Léonce like a rabbit caught in headlights. True, she was pretty. She was wearing a jersey wool ensemble and a cloche hat. She had folded her hands in her lap and turned to Monsieur Brochet, tilting her head slightly, lips half-open in an unspoken question, and this was all it had taken to send the accountant's blood pressure soaring.

Joubert cleared his throat.

". . . and I have tasked Monsieur Brochet here present with verifying the outgoings of the Péricourt household."

Léonce grew pale and her eyelids fluttered at the shock. Madeleine started.

"Gustave, I have placed my complete trust in Léonce and—"

"That is the problem, my dear Madeleine, I fear your trust may be misplaced."

At this point, Monsieur Brochet was to have produced a list of his accounting grievances, but his dossier fell to the floor, scattering invoices and receipts everywhere. As he scrabbled on all fours at the young woman's feet, gathering up his papers, Léonce stared at Madeleine, Joubert stared at Léonce, and there reigned a heavy, awkward silence.

"Very good," Monsieur Brochet said at length. "The accounts, yes, well, there are advances and there are invoices—"

"Get to the point, Brochet, we don't have all day!"

The accountant began to read in a miserable, barely audible monotone.

At Madeleine's insistence, Léonce regularly asked Joubert for an advance in order to cover expenses and, in return, supplied receipts that Joubert distractedly stuffed into his pocket. The tally was always correct, to the last centime. He had no quarrel on that score.

It was only that that some of these receipts did not relate to a genuine purchase, and, on those that did, the seller had supplied a receipt that markedly inflated the actual price. Joubert had receipts dating back to February of the precious year: eighteen months of accumulated peculation.

Monsieur Brochet shook his head regretfully, such a shame, if only Mademoiselle had entrusted him with fiddling the figures, they would have been decidedly more convincing.

"Gustave," Madeleine ventured. "Please . . . this is all very embarrassing . . ."

Joubert was steadfast.

"Profits on curtains, rugs, wallpaper, paint, furniture, lamps, flooring, on the goods lift, on Monsieur Paul's wheelchair . . . After a while these things begin to add up, Mademoiselle Picard!"

Suddenly, Léonce made a volte-face.

"Do you know how much I am paid?" she demanded.

As she said it, she looked at Madeleine, who immediately realised that she had never troubled to think about such things. She was the one in the wrong, but she did not have time to interrupt.

"Thieves are all the same," Joubert was saying. "If they steal, they claim it is because they are not paid enough."

The word "thief", even from the lips of a banker, tolled like a death knell, encompassing as it did a succession of dire consequences: accusation, investigation, court proceedings, judgment, dishonour, gaol . . .

The fact that Léonce had made a profit on the price of Paul's wheelchair, and on the alterations to the room for her disabled son, should have shocked Madeleine, but she felt too guilty. Léonce had been more than a companion, she had been a friend who had stood by Madeleine though her divorce, and since Paul's accident she had been a confidante, she had managed the household when Madeleine herself had been unable. She had toiled for months without anyone taking a moment to think about her position or her salary. What was happening now was the result of Madeleine's self-absorption.

"It is called 'breach of trust', Mademoiselle Picard, and it is punishable by law," Joubert went on. "What is the total, Monsieur Brochet?"

"Sixteen thousand, four hundred and forty-five francs, monsieur, and seventy-three centimes."

Léonce began to cry quietly. The accountant was on the point of taking out his handkerchief, but remembered it was not clean.

"Thank you, Monsieur Brochet," Joubert said.

The accountant's tread could not have been heavier had he himself been the accused, that such a fine young woman should prove such an inept thief, what a waste.

Joubert let pass the long minute that he accorded to debtors before administering the coup de grâce; it was his way of remaining human in matters of money.

"What will you choose, Mademoiselle Picard: court proceedings or reimbursement?"

"No, Gustave, no, you have gone too far!"

Madeleine was on her feet, struggling to find the right words. Joubert did not give her time.

"Mademoiselle Picard did not misappropriate funds accidentally, Madeleine! She did so almost every day for months."

"But it's my fault! I kept asking her to take on more responsibility, I should have realised . . ."

"Are you saying that this somehow justifies her actions?"

Léonce continued to sob silently.

"Yes, no, what I mean is . . . The first thing we must do is raise her salary. Substantially. We will double her salary."

Léonce stopped crying and gave a surprised "Oh!" Joubert greeted the comment with a raised eyebrow that eloquently expressed his disdain for such rash, impulsive, profligate decisions.

He turned back to Léonce.

"Very well, we will double your emoluments beginning next

month. Practically speaking, however, they will remain the same, since the difference will be used to offset your debt. We will also retain fifteen per cent of your current salary so that the debt will be more quickly repaid. As to the interest generated by the misappropriated funds, Monsieur Brochet will make the necessary calculations and the sum will be added to the monies you owe."

In this, Madeleine could find no reason to argue. Indeed, Joubert did not wait, he was already on his feet, had closed his briefcase, the matter was settled.

After she had walked Joubert to the door, Madeleine came back into the room, she did not know what to do with her hands. She sat opposite the sobbing Léonce.

"I'm so sorry," Léonce said after a moment.

She looked up, her eyes filled with tears. Madeleine held out her hands but Léonce threw herself at Madeleine's feet and pressed her face into her lap, like the heroine in a melodrama. Madeleine stroked her hair, murmuring, it's alright, Léonce, I'm not angry with you, she could feel the young woman's body racked by sobs, smell her delicate perfume, she longed to tell Léonce just how much she loved her; Léonce, she said again, consider the matter closed, let's not talk about it again, now get up.

Léonce gazed up at her, her lips parted. Madeleine watched, breathless, as Léonce reached towards her.

Léonce took Madeleine's hands and placed them around her throat such that she could have strangled her. My God . . . Madeleine recoiled. Léonce kept her head bowed, her demeanour evoked contrition, penitence, self-abnegation. And passive offering.

Madeleine stretched out her arms to fend off these embarrassing protestations, but Léonce immediately clutched her hand and pressed it to her lips, squeezing her eyes shut. The she leaned forward and clasped Madeleine to her, her perfume . . .

After Léonce had left, Madeleine sat for a long time, petrified, rubbing her hands together. My God . . .

For the first time, she returned to the church of Saint-François-de-Sales. On the subject of the Lord's mysterious ways, the priest did not seem particularly at ease, but on matters of guilt, shame, sin and dubious pleasures he was entirely in his element.

14

Written on his slate: "Can we change the date of the September appointment with Professor Fournier, please?"

Madeleine's response was instantaneous:

"It's out of the question, Paul."

"But I won't be available on September 12, Maman!" the boy wrote. He was smiling. Madeleine turned to Léonce, who did not know how to interpret this message.

"Maman doesn't understand, my darling . . ." Madeleine said, kneeling next to the wheelchair.

"I can't go on the twelfth, I'm going to the opera!" Paul handed his mother a press cutting.

SOLANGE GALLINATO IN PARIS!
The Italian diva in concert at the Opéra Garnier
A limited engagement of 8 exclusive evenings
beginning September 12

Of all the bombshells Paul visited on Léonce and his mother, his sudden peal of laughter was by far the most surprising.

The bad news arrived two days later: there were no tickets available, neither for the premiere, nor for any of the other concerts.

"I'm so sorry, my darling . . ."

Paul was not sorry. "Can I see Monsieur Joubert, please, Maman?"

Thus, the routine weekly visit by the banker concluded with a request from Madeleine:

"Paul would like a word with you, Gustave. He has something he wants to ask. I fear it may be outside your remit, but if you could just explain to him . . ."

"G-g-goo-good d-d-day, M-M-Mon-Monsi- . . ."

Joubert began to wonder whether the greeting alone might not take all day. Paul's lips quivered like butterflies, his eyelids flickered wildly, like an epileptic in the throes of a seizure. A panicked Madeleine intervened:

"It's alright, my love, it's alright! I'll explain everything to Gustave, don't get yourself in such a state."

"N–n-no!"

Paul's eyes grew wide. "A damned soul" was the phrase that came to Joubert.

Madeleine handed Paul his slate.

"In that case, why don't you write what you have to say, dear?"

No, Paul did not want to write, he wanted to speak. Well, after a fashion. For the reader, we can do something that Joubert could not: we can abridge. Because, without a word of a lie, almost half an hour was required for a conversation that comprised barely half a dozen sentences. These were: "I need three seats in the stalls at the Opéra Garnier for September 12." Madeleine explained that Paul wanted to attend, but the concert was sold out.

Paul: "Could you intercede, please . . ."

Ah, that "p-p-please", what an ordeal! At the first syllable, everyone understood, but Paul was absolutely insistent on getting the word out.

"But there's nothing I can do, Paul," Joubert said. "I realise you're young but the bank and the opera house are two very different establishments."

Paul was visibly unhappy with this response, his stammer became even more pronounced, no-one knew how to deal with the furious child. What shook Joubert was Paul's next suggestion. "Ask Monsieur Raoul-Simon to intercede, if you please."

Joubert suppressed a flicker of irritation, if the boy would at least dispense with polite formalities . . . Besides, he did not see how Raoul-Simon could possibly help, the man was deaf as a post and hardly likely to buy tickets for the opera. Paul briefly squeezed his eyes shut, it was tiresome to have to explain every minor detail. "He is also one of the trustees of the Opéra Garnier!" Joubert was taken aback.

"Well, perhaps he is, but that's no reason . . ."

"He owes you a debt. The Chemins de Fer de l'Ouest debacle."

"That's . . . that's true!" Madeleine exclaimed, suddenly remembering.

The boy looked calmly into Joubert's eyes.

That old affair, the boy had overheard, he had understood, he had remembered . . . And here he was bringing it up again.

"You're perfectly right, Paul," Joubert said at length, slowly enunciating the words as though weighing each phoneme.

The boy, he realised, had a calm determination he found impressive.

"I shall ask Monsieur Raoul-Simon . . ."

As soon as Joubert had left, Madeleine rushed over to her son.

"I don't understand, Paul, why didn't you simply write down what you had to say? It's very difficult for other people, you know."

Paul smiled and wrote: "I know. I think this way Monsieur Joubert will do everything he can to avoid having another conversation with me."

The three tickets arrived by special courier two days later in an envelope embossed with "Opéra de Paris".

Lowering the wheelchair to the ground floor using the goods lift, getting Paul into the car, these were as nothing compared to the difficulties they faced when they reached the foot of the steps leading up to the Palais Garnier.

"I'll go and ask," Léonce said. "Wait here."

And while women in evening dresses, men in smoking jackets and the countless reporters covering the event pushed past Paul and jostled Madeleine, Léonce trotted up the steps and disappeared for some time. The crowd was beginning to thin and Paul to show signs of concern when Léonce eventually reappeared accompanied by two young men in overalls, Lord knows where she had found them, one had only to set Léonce down somewhere for young men to come running, and these two, given the circumstances, had simply taken a little longer than their predecessors. They nervously tipped their caps in greeting and picked up Paul's wheelchair.

"Hang on tight, young man, this is going to get bumpy!"

They were not wrong, because there was a phenomenal number of steps to be negotiated, constantly slaloming between tight-knit groups since the crowd parted only reluctantly and, even then, cursing the inconvenience, a wheelchair at the Opéra, it simply was not done!

When they reached the concert hall, the difficulties became almost insurmountable. The audience in the stalls was already seated and it was clear that the wheelchair was too wide to navigate the central aisle.

The two boys looked to Léonce for instructions.

The shrill jangle of the bell announcing the beginning of the concert set everyone's teeth on edge.

"The young gentleman will have to stay here."

Madeleine turned. The speaker was a tall, supercilious man in uniform. He had spoken coldly, like an undertaker giving orders. They were far, very far, from the stage, Paul would scarcely see a thing. His mother knelt to explain the situation. The boy began to cry quietly.

And a situation that Madeleine had been prepared to accept a second earlier now seemed utterly intolerable. Slowly, she got to her feet.

"We have seats in the front row, monsieur, and it is from the front row that we intend to watch the concert."

"Madame, I am—"

"You are going to do whatever is necessary to get us there, otherwise we shall stay here and prevent the doors from closing so that the recital cannot begin. You will be forced to call the police in order to forcibly eject a boy in a wheelchair before the crowd of journalists and photographers we will summon to witness your actions, and that, I fear, will be the real performance."

People turned in their seats, what's going on over there, the wheelchair is too wide, it won't fit, the recital will be delayed, it really is too tedious.

"I am very sorry, madame," said the man in uniform, "but I can see no practical solution . . ."

"Really?" Madeleine said, astonished.

They looked down the aisle towards the stage. Here and there a cry went up, from the gods to the stalls, all eyes were now trained on the little group, is this concert going to start or not?

"All you need do," Madeleine said, "is ask those seated closest to the aisle to stand for a moment. That hardly seems impossible."

Léonce stepped forward and bestowed her most ravishing smile on the young men in overalls.

"I believe we have here two young men who are . . . muscular enough to carry the load, do we not?"

Had they been injected with testosterone, the two boys would not have grasped the wheelchair with more determination.

The little group began its difficult passage down the central aisle, apologising profusely, if I could just ask you to stand for a moment, thank you, monsieur, thank you, madame, it won't take a moment, just long enough to get the boy's wheelchair through, thank you, yes, I know, that's very kind of you . . .

Carried above the heads of the crowd like an indolent king upon a palanquin, Paul beamed. The young men set him down three metres from the orchestra pit.

Hardly had Madeleine and Léonce taken their seats than the hall was plunged into darkness and the curtain rose.

Solange Gallinato had not performed in Paris for eight years. She had been sulking ever since the press had almost unanimously derided her in young Maurice Grandet's "Gloria Mundi", an opera that began at the end of the story and, via a sequence of flashbacks devoid of any chronology, told a story of Romans and slaves that was rather difficult to follow. The satirists had had a field day and the public had come only to boo and hiss. After the third performance, Solange had left Paris, swearing that she would never again set foot in the city.

Hers had been a meteoric career, unscathed by this single fiasco. She had sung "Fidelio" in London, "Medea" in Milan, "Orpheus and Eurydice" in Melbourne, the international press was captivated by the dizzying spectacle of three millionaires who vied with each other for her hand in marriage, showering her with the most eccentric gifts, none of which prevented her, two years later, from wedding Maurice Grandet, eight years her junior. The whole world had thrilled to this extravagant love story, the couple had been spotted in Switzerland, in Italy, in England, where the dashing young Maurice, with his flowing curls, his feline manner, his brooding eyes, had broken the hearts of thousands of women by his unswerving passion for Solange, a love that never wavered despite the countless opportunities he was offered, and was cut short, three months after their marriage, when he died at the wheel of his Rolls-Royce on the Côte d'Azur.

Solange abandoned her career overnight.

One of the millionaires, a graceful loser, paid the enormous penalties for the five-year calendar of engagements to which she was already committed.

Solange Gallinato retreated into a life of seclusion on June 11, 1923. Not until the spring of 1928 did rumours of a comeback begin to circulate. No-one doubted that the diva would want to shine once more in "La Traviata", which had been her greatest success. Two successive repudiations were met with stupefaction. Gallinato would return not with an opera, but with a recital, and it would take place in Paris. A recital was a demanding choice, one that compelled the artist to shift emotional register and indeed her whole voice with each piece, and the programme could only be ambitious, comprising a succession of the most technically difficult arias. As for Paris, this was the city that had derided her only a few years earlier. It was a deliberate provocation.

Solange was forty-six years old. Recent photographs depicted her as a woman who had gained a lot of weight (she had never been svelte, but no-one imagined she would ever look like this). Sporting metaphors abounded. Opera was compared to tennis, to swimming, disciplines that require rigorous training and frequent competitions. True to the base impulses that attract large crowds to public executions, the concert hall contained a handful of fervent fans of Solange Gallinato, crippled with anxiety, and hordes of denigrators, stirred up for weeks by the newspapers, prepared to howl their contempt.

Solange did not walk onto the stage, she was there when the curtain rose, wearing a long blue tulle dress adorned with a startling number of ribbons, and a diadem in her hair. The audience applauded wildly, but the diva did not move, did not smile, did not make the slightest gesture. A strange silence settled over the proceedings. Gallinato looked like a schoolmistress about to scold a class of unruly students.

The first aria, which fully half the audience was prepared to boo, was the opening of "Gloria Mundi", of cursed memory, an opera that was unique – and this had been one of the reasons for its failure – in that it was accompanied only by the piano. This time, there was not even a piano, La Gallinato sang a cappella. It was unheard of. But what was stranger still was that, from the first notes, the whole audience was held spellbound by Solange's tragic voice as it poured out passion, regret and loneliness. Anyone who had ever been passionately in love, anyone who had ever felt jealous or abandoned, could not help but be heartbroken by this voice.

As though there was some secret pact between audience and artist, no applause greeted the end of this first aria, which was considered the repayment of a debt on the part of the audience, and the end of a grudge on the part of the diva.

Solange Gallinato did not move as the orchestra filed in to contemplative silence.

Then, from who knows where, Solange conjured a red rose, which she tucked into her hair, and this vast woman launched into "L'amour est un oiseau rebelle" with a sensuality, a *joie de vivre*, an exultation that left the audience stunned. Equal to every challenge, her voice proved sinuous and graceful, there was no strain, everything was effortless, and her concluding "Si je t'aime, prends garde à toi!" left the audience speechless. The astonished silence was broken by the shrill, reedy voice of Paul Péricourt shouting "Brava!" and this set off a thunderous ovation, everyone in the audience was on their feet, not because Gallinato was more talented than she had once been, but because she had managed to kindle in each of them that almost biological need to create heroes.

Pieces by Schubert, Puccini, Verdi, Borodin, Tchaikovsky . . . the recital was a triumph, the crowd demanded encores and more encores, their hands ached, they were overwhelmed and exhausted and when Solange Gallinato stepped out in front of the curtain, everyone fell silent. She waited for several seconds before simply whispering "Merci"; the audience went wild.

Getting out was a challenge, the wheelchair blocked the front rows and there was much grumbling. The great hall was deserted by the time those in charge permitted them to leave. One by one, the lights flickered out. The wheelchair was hoisted to shoulder height

116

and Paul was carried up the aisle and set down in the lobby. What happened next was a whirl of fabric, perfume, laughter, Italian phrases, make-up, hair, a rush of air, a presence that filled the whole space as she strode forward, wagging her finger at Paul.

"I saw you, my little Pinocchio! I saw you in the stalls, oh là là, ti ho visto!"

Solange knelt down, she had not even acknowledged anyone else. A dazed Paul was beaming.

"What is your name?"

"P-P-Paul P-Pér . . ."

"Ah, little Paul! You wrote to me! So, you are Paul!"

She pressed her fists to her enormous bosom, she looked as though she might melt.

Madeleine thought she looked old rather than fat.

They would see each other again, they would write, Solange offered seats in the stalls for the other performances, if your mamma agrees, of course . . . Madeleine simply closed her eyes, we will see. Oh là là, Paul, my little Paul. Solange was wearing a sort of boa of long orange feathers and she wound it around the boy's neck and kissed him on both cheeks, il mio piccolino, fulsome and effusive, Léonce did her best not to laugh, finally Madeleine interrupted the embraces, it is late, we must get home, oh là là, so soon . . .?

Solange insisted that Paul take one of the bouquets given to her at the end of the recital.

The car was brought round.

Paris was wonderfully balmy, quiet, poignant, Madeleine had the flowers put in the boot of the car.

As they drove home, she nodded at the orange boa.

"Paul, could you move that away? The perfume is terribly cloying . . ."

15

The journalists at *Soir de Paris* who had snubbed André for a whole year now made a point of greeting him. He was no longer the four-teenth guest, reluctantly invited to ward off bad luck, he was now among the first to be invited by those who wanted a lively evening, not one of those dull dinner parties to be avoided like the plague.

Being young and handsome, he did not lack for romantic offers but he continued, out of prudence, to visit Vladi on those nights when neither the chauffeur, nor Monsieur Raymond, nor the cook's husband, nor his son were there. The Polish nanny was attractive, charming and, regardless of his performance, left him with the illusion that she was grateful.

André dipped his pen into a broad range of subjects, with a predilection for those that dealt with ethical matters that were sufficiently simple and populist to be shared by the majority of his readers. For example: was it necessary to stabilise the French franc by bankrupting small investors who had put their faith in the coun-try's financial institutions? Was it acceptable that, in 1928, the rents paid by ordinary families, which had been frozen since 1914, were suddenly being increased by multiples of six or seven? Simple issues for simple people, immediately understandable and seemingly self-evident. He was sitting pretty.

Given his new-found success, André began to wonder whether the moment had come to work for a newspaper whose reputation was not sullied by that of its proprietor.

Alongside *Soir de Paris*, there existed quality newspapers and journalists with greater talent and greater freedom than those employed by Guilloteaux. But André was an "in-house journalist", just as there are "in-house mechanics"; there was no guarantee that his talents would be recognised elsewhere. Yet still he continued to dream of earning a little more, and he kept an eye out for his chance. At the first opportunity, he would renegotiate his salary.

He began to be offered all sorts of gifts.

It began with a bronze mantelpiece sculpted to represent a hunting scene. Since his garret room was much too cramped for such a thing, he declined. For want of space, he was assumed to be incorruptible.

André Delcourt was in the process of discovering his individual style.

Madeleine was feeling much better, though still shaken by her ordeal. Proof of this, if it were needed, came one afternoon when she encountered Monsieur Dupré.

Dupré, Dupré . . . Of course, you remember, a heavyset, bull-necked man, protruding ears and eyes that always seemed to well with tears, he had served during the Great War as sergent-chef under Lieutenant Pradelle. In 1919, Pradelle had hired him to organise and oversee exhumations in the military cemeteries. Later, he had been called as a witness in the "d'Aulnay-Pradelle case". He and Madeleine had regularly passed each other in the courthouse, bonjour madame, bonjour Monsieur Dupré. On the witness stand, he had made a stoical, dignified impression and had proved himself loyal to a man who had done little to deserve it.

He and Madeleine bumped into each other by accident. Discomfiture, surprise and embarrassment made them pause for a moment; it was a fatal error, they should just have chatted briefly, exchanged polite platitudes. Monsieur Dupré was working as foreman in an ironworks on the rue du Châteaudun. The conversation quickly trailed off. Seeing Madeleine smile uncomfortably, Dupré took the initiative to free her from an awkward situation. "These are hard times . . ." he said as he walked away. Perhaps, from the newspapers, he had learned of Monsieur Péricourt's death, Paul's accident, or perhaps he was referring to the fact that Madeleine's former husband was still languishing in prison, but she attributed his remark to how much she had changed physically, and was very upset.

She consoled herself with the fact that the household was once again running smoothly, or as smoothly as any house could with a crippled boy, a nurse who did not speak a word of French, a journalist who was paid to do nothing, a lady's companion who had stolen more than fifteen thousand francs and the heiress to a family bank who had not the first idea of what is meant by a stock's "transfer threshold" or "par value".

Just before Christmas 1928, André, who now had a small salary, announced that he was leaving the Péricourt house. He had "found a place" and did not say where.

"I am very happy for you, André, the chauffeur will transfer your belongings."

He had thanked Madeleine with a palpable embarrassment, almost a resentment; we are always a little resentful towards those who have been kind to us.

Evenings in the Péricourt household no longer had the same emotional or indeed anguished atmosphere that they had had the previous year. Madeleine continued to brood over Paul's reasons for doing what he had done, but, now that he had improved, was eating almost normally and was putting on a little weight, she was open to other subjects. She waited until the last minute before interrupting Paul, the staff need to sleep, my darling, I'm afraid you have to turn off the music. Silently, the records were put away, the door was closed and, once Vladi had gone up to her room, Madeleine would begin their evening, they would read a book or leaf through a magazine, Madeleine loved the "word-cross puzzles" that had just arrived in France. "I couldn't possibly . . ." Léonce protested, horrified.

Madeleine would raise an eyebrow when she heard Vladi's steps on the back stairs heading up to her room. The young woman was more exuberant than ever, she chattered like a jackdaw; in a year, she had not learned a single word of French.

Every Sunday, she dutifully attended mass at the Polish church. In her mind, the service seemed to begin the moment she left the house, because she wore a little veil when she went; she was a completely different woman. On Monday, she went back to flirting with the greengrocer on the rue de Chazelles, the pharmacist on the rue de Logelbach or the apprentice plumber on place de Vigny.

"You're not worried that that girl might be . . . a danger to Paul?" Madeleine asked Léonce.

"What, you mean . . .? No, no, he's a child."

Madeleine was sceptical but, with the exception of Léonce, this was her attitude to any woman who was overly familiar with Paul. Take Solange Gallinato. After their encounter on the night of the grande premiere, the diva invited Paul to three more concerts, at which his mother insisted on being present. Later, after Solange had left Paris to embark on a triumphant European tour, she had written Paul enthusiastic letters, she sent him signed programmes, menus from an ambassadorial dinner on which she had scrawled amusing comments that Madeleine found ridiculous, photographs, press cuttings and all manner of things that Madeleine often forgot to give to Paul, oh yes, something came for you yesterday or the day before, now where did I put it . . . ? Paul would smile and wave his finger: M-m-ma-maman . . .

"Does this woman have no-one except Paul in her life?" Madeleine complained to Léonce.

"Come now, Madeleine, don't be jealous."

"Me, jealous of that old hag? Are you joking?"

Léonce was reading the newspaper.

"Well, well," she said admiringly. "Romanian oil has been performing spectacularly well."

She pointed to an article in *Le Gaulois*.

"What are you talking about?"

"Stock prices for Romanian oil on the Bourse. They've risen twelve per cent annually for the past four years, and profits are set to increase for at least the next four to five years, it's scarcely believable . . ."

Ever since Joubert had caught her red-handed, anything that related to money, however obliquely, created an awkward silence between Léonce and Madeleine. This time it was too much, Madeleine refused to let it pass.

"Léonce," she said, setting down her pen, "I am aware that the situation you have been put in by Gustave Joubert is . . . a delicate one. I understand. But I beg of you, please don't try speculating on the stock market to try and repay the debt more quickly."

"But it is a guaranteed profit. It's here in *Le Gaulois*! And I read the same thing in *Le Figaro* too, a few weeks ago."

Together with boxing and bicycling, dabbling on the stock market had become one of the fashionable hobbies since the end of the Great War. Everyone was doing it, men, women, the rich grew richer, the poor were more patient, skill was beginning to rival effort.

It was a question Madeleine had been dying to ask for weeks:

"How much have you paid back to Gustave? I mean, how much do you still owe?"

Fourteen thousand francs.

To repay the debt would take years. Now that the subject had been broached, Madeleine felt relieved. In fact, she found the amount liberating. She went over to her escritoire, took out some papers, bent over them and returned with a cheque for fifteen thousand francs.

"No, no, no!" Léonce cried, pushing away Madeleine's hand.

"Please, Léonce. Please take it."

Her face drained of colour, Léonce also got to her feet.

"I can't accept it, Madeleine, you know that."

"Put it in your account, just don't pay Joubert back too quickly or he will suspect something. Tell him you made a killing on the stock market."

Madeleine attempted a smile.

"At least that way your Romanian oil will have been useful for something."

They stood for a moment, face to face, the cheque quivering between them in Madeleine's outstretched hand.

Until, eventually, Léonce took it.

She threw her arms around Madeleine.

The gesture was so swift and Léonce held her so tightly that Madeleine feared that she might faint. Léonce kissed her cheek, thank you, thank you, I feel so ashamed, you know that, Madeleine, don't you, you know how ashamed I feel, of course, of course, Madeleine said, feeling that she might suffocate or explode, she did not know where to put her hands, Léonce was pressed against her, she fell silent, and now it was simply her hands, here, on Madeleine's shoulders, on the back of her neck, thank you.

From the hallway, Madeleine thought she heard the voice of the parish priest from Saint-François-de-Sales.

The two women parted, Léonce was by the hat stand, pulling on her jacket, she came back, grasped Madeleine by the shoulders again, once more gave her a peck on the cheek, keeping her lips pressed there for a long time as though waiting for something, perhaps a kiss in return? Then, suddenly, she left the room.

Usually she said, "See you tomorrow," this time she said nothing, neither of them could speak.

While Léonce's delicate perfume still hung in the air, Madeleine could not move, she stood, thinking, my God, what if . . .

My God . . .

16

With André's departure from the Péricourt house, so ended perhaps the happiest period in Madeleine's life, the one that followed was more troubling: the strange connection that Paul had with women, be it Vladi or Solange Gallinato, the ambiguity of her relationship with Léonce (the Christmas holidays had been difficult, they had embraced beneath the mistletoe, cheeks pressed together, kissing the empty air) . . . Madeleine was therefore already in a state of confusion when, in January 1929, her uncle Charles added to the chaos by paying her a visit; his expression was forbidding, his brows were knitted, it did not bode well.

He had not requested a meeting, but had burst in panting and sweating and collapsed into an armchair.

"I've come to talk about money," he began.

This was hardly a surprise.

"Yours, for the most part."

This was more surprising.

"My money is doing very well, Uncle, thank you."

"Excellent. Well, in that case . . ."

Charles slapped his thighs, pushed himself to his feet and, with a muffled roar, headed towards the door.

"We shall talk again next year. When you are ruined."

Charles knew what he was doing. This was a word that had haunted Madeleine all her life; in her father's opinion, there was no more terrible word, except, perhaps, "bankruptcy".

"And what the devil makes you think I shall be ruined? Come, Uncle, come and sit down and explain."

Charles, who wanted nothing better, came back and slumped into the armchair.

"Things are bad, Madeleine, very bad."

At this, Madeleine could not suppress a smile.

"Really?"

Irked, Charles turned and stared out the window. Women!

"What do you know about the American economy, Madeleine?"

"I know that it is booming."

"Yes, that is how it appears. But I am talking about the reality."

"Very well, then. What is it about the reality that I should know?"

"That in every possible sector America is overproducing. Growth has been too swift, the bubble is bound to burst."

"The devil it is!"

"And if America collapses, no-one is safe."

"But I had the impression that—"

"Bankers in this country swear only by land and property, they are a century behind the times! They are convinced that they can survive a crash, the fools!"

"A crash, what crash?"

"The one that is looming right now! It is inevitable. There will be an economic tidal wave. And you are aboard a vessel destined for shipwreck."

Charles was very partial to metaphors, nautical, hunting, floral, it hardly mattered. His intelligence, being purely pragmatic, was incapable of invention and expressed itself only in terms of things he understood. Such rhetoric, typical of Charles, was as wearisome as another's illness, it triggered an impatience one had to be careful to suppress. Madeleine took a long, deep breath.

"What does Joubert advise?" Charles asked.

He folded his arms and waited. Madeleine was less surprised at the prospect of an American crash than at the fact that Joubert had never broached the subject. This realisation encouraged her to defy her uncle.

"I must say I am very surprised, Uncle. Surely, if the situation is so grave, the crisis so inevitable, the newspapers would talk about little else!"

"They are not paid to talk about such things, that's why! Pay them, and they talk. Pay them again, and they hold their tongues. Newspapers do not exist in order to inform, surely even you do not believe that?"

This cut-and-dried assessment was far from being true, but it reflected the world as Charles could conceive of it.

"So, you alone are both honourable and well informed?"

"I'm a member of parliament, my girl, I have served on the Finance Committee for years. We are not paid to spread panic, but we are sufficiently well informed to see the world as it is! I've talked about all this with Joubert, but it was a waste of breath. What do you expect? The man has spent his whole career in the same goldfish bowl, he knows only what he has seen before. And what is coming will be unlike anything he has ever experienced. Joubert is short-sighted, he's completely blind, take my word on it! The crash is coming, it is only a matter of time. And when it reaches France, the banks will bear the brunt."

"The government will save the banks, it can hardly do otherwise."

This was what she had always been told.

"The largest bank, certainly, the others will be left to croak."

It had never occurred to Madeleine that she might one day have to worry about her personal situation. True, now and then she had heard talk of this economic crisis, but she had never felt directly implicated.

Madeleine was beginning to stagger under the blows.

"What I fail to grasp in all this, Uncle, is your interest in the matter. You are not in the habit of according such favours."

"I am thinking about myself, and the favour I am doing for myself! I have no desire for you to drag the name of Péricourt through the mud. I have to work, I am no heiress! To be saddled with the name of a bankrupt family might cost me the election next year, and that I cannot endure. I simply do not have the means."

Charles leaned towards her. He seemed genuinely sympathetic.

"And nor can you. What would become of your son if you were ruined?"

He sat up, settled himself in the armchair, convinced that he had found the one thing that might tip the conversation in his favour. He was not wrong, though it proved a disappointingly easy victory.

"Banking is a precarious business. You need to have some investments that are less exposed."

"Wh . . . what did you have in mind, Uncle?"

He rolled his eyes heavenward; how should he know?

"That is Joubert's responsibility, for God's sake! What the devil does the idiot do with his time?"

Madeleine was shaken. The prospect of an economic crisis was difficult to conceive for a woman who had always lived in a world where there was so much money that one never thought about it.

She began to read the financial papers. There was much talk, albeit vague, about the risks of the American market, but most commentators agreed: thanks to Poincaré, France was not at risk, it had the most stable monetary system in the world, a wealth of regional and family businesses meant that it was safe from stock market fluctuations.

"Léonce, do you believe there will be a crash?"

"What kind of crash?"

"An economic crash."

"I've no idea . . . what does Monsieur Joubert say?"

"I haven't discussed it with him, yet."

"In your position, I would. Though there's no love lost between us, the man knows what he is talking about, you can surely ask him for advice . . . If you can't trust the man who administers your fortune, then we're all doomed."

Joubert frowned.

"Charles came here and told you this nonsense? He would do better to worry about his constituents."

"Parliament is hardly ill-informed when it comes to economic matters, Gustave!"

"Parliament is one thing. Charles is something very different."

As he listened to Madeleine recount her uncle's reasoning, Joubert stared at the floor and nodded; it was rare to see him so vexed. He wanted to talk about the French budget surplus, about the Banque de France gold reserves, but he elected to take a short cut.

"Are you trying to teach me my profession, Madeleine?"

"No, it's not that—"

"Oh, but it is! That is exactly what you are doing. Are you going to give me lessons in banking and economics?"

He was shocked.

He got to his feet and stalked out of the room. As far as he was concerned, the subject was closed.

However, if one pored over the news in search of a crisis, it was easy to find something disquieting; this was what Madeleine discovered every day, from the moment she began to worry about her future, and more importantly, that of Paul.

The relationship between Paul and Solange Gallinato had developed into a regular correspondence, two letters a week, sometimes three. In the limited words at his disposal, he commented on the new interpretations he had discovered. "I can't help but wonder whether, in the scherzo, the orchestra has not been replaced by a brass band." Or "She sings so perfectly that it is tedious." His whole bedroom was devoted to his sole passion, a number of phonographs and an impressive collection of records and boxed sets, to which had been added shelves of scores and sheet music bought by mail order from the four corners of Europe.

It was at this point that Solange first mentioned the trip to Milan.

Oh, there was much talk in the Péricourt household about this proposed trip. It was the subject of heated discussion, believe me.

Solange: *My little Pinocchio, a thousand thanks for your letter. Your kind thinkings are comfort when I am weary. This new tour is very tired. So, I have to myself a little idea. What do you think to a small visit in Italy this summer? I give at La Scala a recital on July 11,*

we could have nice dinner, visit a little Lombardia, you would be
to house for the Bastille Day. First your mamma must agree and
perhaps she comes with you if she wishes, but it would be charming,
no? Please to give her my affectionate regards. Your Solange.

To Léonce, Italy, La Scala, dinner on a terrace in Lombardy, was
like a romantic dream.

"What a delightful prospect . . ."

"Come, come, Léonce, she is writing to Paul as though he were
twenty years old and she wanted to take him as a lover! It is not
only ludicrous, it is unwholesome."

"Think of Paul."

"I am! It is far too long a journey for a child in his condition.
And besides, these letters filled with errors, she was wise to become
an opera singer, because as a schoolmistress . . . 'You would be to
house for the Bastille Day' – I ask you! It sounds as though she
expects Paul to parade in his wheelchair, it's almost insulting."

"Madeleine . . ."

A silence fell.

"What does Paul say?"

"What do you expect the poor child to say? Someone offers the
possibility of a trip to Italy, just like that?"

If Madeleine did not answer the question honestly, it was because
Paul, electrified at the prospect, had simply written on his slate: "I
have never travelled, you want me to do things that make me happy.
I would like to go very much."

Léonce, whose support Paul had discreetly petitioned, proved as
diplomatic and persuasive as always.

One evening, about to head home, as she was kissing her mistress
on the cheek, see you tomorrow, she grasped her shoulders and
leaned in very close, as though Madeleine had a speck of dust in
her eye.

"Everyone has a right to their pleasures, don't you think,
Madeleine?"

She tilted her head, lips parted, and, for a long moment, she held Madeleine against her breast.

"You would not deprive our little Paul of his trip?"

Madeleine, who bought Léonce's perfume for her, and had chosen Pour Troubler by Guerlain because it was quite expensive, was overcome by it. She could also smell the delicate lime-blossom scent of Léonce's breath.

Just you try and think soberly in such circumstances!

Madeleine was beginning to be haunted by the spectre of poverty.

There were nights when she was ruined, Paul was sobbing in his wheelchair, they had no servants, and she was forced to cook in a garret room out of the novels of Émile Zola.

The financial papers, on the other hand, were doggedly optimistic.

"That's the way of things," Léonce would say, increasingly concerned. "Catastrophes are all the worse because no-one expects them to happen."

Madeleine no longer knew what to believe, nor which way to turn.

She made another attempt.

Reluctantly, as though explaining something to a child for the hundredth time, Joubert launched into a detailed explanation of the French economy, using long, complicated phrases. Following her own train of thought, Madeleine was barely listening when she interrupted him.

"I was thinking about Romanian oil."

She handed him an article from Le Gaulois: ". . . the Romanian petroleum industry, rising by a further 1.71 per cent, confirms its status as one of the leading investment opportunities in Europe."

"Le Gaulois is not a financial newspaper," Joubert cut her short. "I have no idea who the journalist, this Thierry Andrieux, is, but I would not entrust him with my savings."

His blue eyes glinted with ill-concealed anger; his hands were trembling.

"You're not telling me that you're considering selling shares in your father's bank in order to acquire an investment portfolio in crude oil?"

She had never seen him so incensed. He swallowed hard.

"It is out of the question, Madeleine. And if you attempt to compel me, then you shall have my resignation."

It was rather strange, but the more Joubert remonstrated, the more credence Madeleine gave to her uncle's criticisms. She remembered Charles' words: "Our bankers are a century behind the times."

In late January, *Soir de Paris* devoted a whole article to the subject of Romanian petroleum. There was even a straightforward graph – something rare in *Le Soir* – detailing recent profits. This article came at a moment when Madeleine's imagination was plagued with nightmares about ruin and a fall in status.

What she found exhausting about Joubert was the resistance she encountered from him, when what she needed was help and support.

"I have had the worst possible reports of this business," he assured her, "from a very well-informed source. Romanian petroleum is a flash in the pan! If you truly want to invest in petroleum, you should look to Mesopotamia."

Madeleine sighed. Joubert had never seemed to her so old. So out of date.

She remembered the monies lost in the unfortunate Ferret-Delage affair. Three hundred thousand francs was hardly a trifle! Suddenly, she felt convinced that Joubert was no longer the right man for the job. He was managing the family bank as though they were still living in the nineteenth century, like a shopkeeper. Recommending Iraqi oil, when everyone agreed the future was in Romania. What sort of world did he live in?

"I shall give it some thought, Gustave. But I will require a detailed report, do you understand? The rumours of a crash are troubling, I need more information. Make it simple, for once. Make it clear. I would also like you to provide me with figures on the petroleum industry. A comprehensive overview of Romania. Feel free to include information on Iraq if you think it important."

Although Charles did his best to arrive as late as could be deemed acceptable, it was a wasted effort.

"No need to apologise, Charles, I have only just arrived myself."

If Charles was treated as a member of the club, Joubert was considered an habitué. Charles was asked what he desired, but there was no need to ask Joubert: the bottle of Crozes-Hermitage and the fish knife were already set out. It was galling. Even in conversation, he had to defer to Joubert, who chose the topics, careful to avoid the one subject that was of interest to Charles, which served only to exacerbate his anxiety.

The crayfish was followed by the sea bass, then, as they waited for the caramelised peaches, Charles could no longer contain himself.

"Any news of my niece, perhaps?"

Joubert allowed a few seconds of silence to tick away, enhancing what little information he possessed.

"She has been toying with the notion of Romanian oil . . ."

What exactly did he mean?

"She is torn. It is a serious decision that she has to make."

"But what the deuce are you doing?"

"I am rowing against the current. But since the Ferret-Delage affair, my professional standing with Mademoiselle Péricourt has been in serious decline. Which is excellent news, since I would not wish to have deliberately lost three hundred thousand francs for nothing."

The idea that Joubert could have deliberately lost such a sum was beyond Charles.

"All is well, Charles, do not fret. Thanks to that, I am almost entirely discredited. The more I oppose Romanian oil, the more she perseveres; the more I deny the economic crisis, the more she believes in it. Her doubts concerning me will tip her over the edge. We shall prevail."

Charles took a breath. Now that he had broached the subject, Joubert visibly relished recounting the positive effects of his strategy.

"I am strenuously attempting to dissuade Madeleine from an investment that I know will be ruinous, but what can I do? She no longer trusts my judgment. It is very foolish, very feminine, but there is nothing to be done. I have threatened to resign."

Charles stared, open-mouthed. Joubert leaned back a little to leave space for the approaching waiter. He smiled.

"What would you have me do? She has lost confidence in me."

The whole plan made Charles feel slightly queasy.

"Meanwhile," Joubert went on, "Iraqi oil is performing splendidly. Share prices have plummeted. They are now selling at less than a hundred francs."

The strategy was a simple one: if one investor bought a massive stake in Romanian petroleum, everyone would lose interest in Iraqi oil.

"And we can pick them up at fifty francs a share. Indeed, I have not given up hope that they may fall to thirty."

"That is when we should buy . . ." Charles ventured.

Silence. He had carefully rehearsed his line.

"By the way, I have the two hundred thousand francs you lent me . . ."

Joubert did not allow him to finish. Charles had played his role with Madeleine to perfection: employing the arguments Joubert had given him, he had rocked the Péricourt citadel. Thanks to him, Madeleine no longer had any confidence in Joubert and was preparing to do something that would prove disastrous for her but would enrich the two men far beyond their expectations.

In return, Joubert now raised a magnanimous hand and blithely dismissed this offer of repayment. He stared intently at Charles. Yes?

"Tell me what I should do . . ." Charles said. "I mean, how I should go about it . . ."

Joubert took a sip of his wine. A long, slow sip.

"An idea occurred to me," he said at length. "The two hundred thousand francs you owe, why not use them to purchase Iraqi oil shares? Within a few months, they will be worth a million."

Charles almost knocked over the table. In return for his betrayal, Joubert was not even proposing to discharge the debt. He had sold his niece to Joubert for nothing! A last vestige of civility forbade him from making a scene. Gritting his teeth, he managed to create an approximate smile. Joubert looked at him calmly. And . . . he was smiling! At least, Charles supposed that the thin-lipped rictus was a smile.

"You might even invest more than that," Joubert continued. "I think you might go as far as five hundred thousand."

Charles let out a sigh, he could still feel the violent palpitations that, a moment earlier, had threatened to choke him. But this was better. Five hundred thousand. This was the price Joubert was offering, on condition that he invested it in Iraqi oil. For his betrayal of Madeleine, he would receive more than thirty pieces of silver.

"I had thought of investing . . . seven hundred thousand," he muttered.

Joubert stared at the tablecloth.

"I would not advise it, Charles. In your position, I would not suggest investing more than six hundred."

Six hundred thousand francs. Which, within a few months, would be worth almost two million. Charles was satisfied and relieved.

"Perhaps you're right," he said. "Six hundred thousand should do nicely."

"It is Paul you should think about above all else, Madeleine," Léonce was saying. "He inherited certain rights and responsibilities from his grandfather, but cannot exercise them until he is of age. If the family fortune were to suffer an economic crisis before then, as you say is likely, how would you raise him?"

The figures had finally arrived. The economic crisis was a distant planet visible only to pessimists – even if, without wishing to be a doom-monger, optimists are rarely right for very long. As for Romanian petroleum, it was performing well while its Iraqi equivalent was in limbo. Its shares continued to fall.

Joubert seemed less well groomed than usual. In him, a collar that was slightly askew was tantamount to chaos. More than ever, he behaved like a condemned man eking out his last days. Whatever Madeleine decided, he was a beaten man.

"I have come to a decision . . ." Madeleine began.

Was she about to risk her livelihood on a roll of the dice? "Sooner or later, there comes a moment," her father used to say, "when, having carefully considered and carefully weighed the evidence, one must act. Otherwise, it is futile to gather information. For good or ill, one must trust one's instincts." His instincts had never failed him, he would add, which was something of an exaggeration. But Madeleine had to admit that she only fully understood his maxim at this very moment.

The Ferret-Delage affair still haunted her, three hundred thousand francs lost, the result of Joubert's instinct. When it came to major decisions, Joubert's instincts were no more valuable than those of Monsieur Brochet, or indeed her own.

"I have come to a decision."

"Yes . . .?" Joubert prompted her.

Since, according to everyone, Romanian petroleum represented the most profitable investment, what risk was she actually running? She was not taking a leap into the unknown, she had the figures in front of her, after all.

She acted. Silence.

"Very well," Joubert said, with the tight-lipped air of a man who has just been told he has halitosis. "We will do as you see best. But no more than half your holdings in this . . . 'Romanian petroleum'." (From his lips, it sounded like a swear word.) "Half of it in oil shares. As for the remainder, it stands to reason, you should diversify. Logic would suggest you invest the remainder in coordinated securities. Coherence, Madeleine, that is the most important thing."

He returned the following day and, without a word of comment, set a bulging folder on the table.

Madeleine spent almost two hours signing documents.

Joubert, his expression impenetrable, his lips pursed, merely pointed to the places where she was to initial and sign, here, here and here . . . From time to time, he gave a curt explanation: signing here would stipulate that . . . a signature here would entail . . . When Madeleine did not even pause to listen, he fell silent and merely turned the pages.

At close of business on March 10, 1929, while Paul's share of the inheritance remained in government bonds, Madeleine had invested the greater part of her share in a portfolio of shares of Romanian petroleum and related industries, and held only 0.97 per cent of the capital of her father's bank.

As she watched Joubert leave, Madeleine felt he did so with a heavy tread.

By contrast, Monsieur Brochet, who was waiting in the hallway, glimpsed the discreet smile of victory.

17

Time went on. And the news was good.

The sale of Madeline's stocks was a success: the Péricourt Bank was a trusted institution and her shares readily found buyers. As for the large share issued by the Romanian consortium, propelled by

Madeleine's colossal investment, it attracted the attention of many other investors and was an undisputed success. *Soir de Paris* dubbed it the "Formidable Romanian Powerhouse". As the weeks passed, Romanian shares continued their slow, prosperous ascent.

Joubert, tasked with conveying his signature book to other majority shareholders, now called around only occasionally. He was no longer calling on the owner of the bank (at the next Annual General Meeting, Madeleine would not be ridiculed), but on one of the largest fortunes administered by the Banque Péricourt.

As for the invitation to Milan extended to Paul, after much discussion Madeleine was finally forced to relent.

Weeks were required to draw up a very precise protocol that stipulated, among other things, that Madeleine would accompany her son. It goes without saying! I have no intention of leaving Paul alone with that madwoman!

Solange, excited by the prospect of Paul's visit (*and I am very contented that your adorable mamma will join you*), was now writing to her twice a day. The moment something occurred to her, she sent another letter. The two women corresponded over the details of the journey and of their stay but, alas, often struggled to agree; the whole business was filled with disagreeable surprises. Madeleine had been unable to get tickets for the train Solange had suggested so that she could meet them; Solange, for her part, was desolate that she had been unable to reserve the restaurant Madeleine had picked out in the guidebook; Madeleine requested that someone collect their bags from Milan station the moment they arrived but Solange, sadly, had no-one available until the following morning. As for Madeleine (*I am truly sorry, my dear Solange . . .*), she had been unable to buy the eau de toilette the diva could find only in Paris, while Solange was hopeful of finding a guide to tour the cathedral on Friday afternoon, as Madeleine wished, but, *disgracefully, nothing is certain, the Italians, as your know, i mia più cara, Madeleine, are molto inaffidabili . . .*", and so on. In the end, Solange had

had to threaten, albeit obliquely, to cancel the entire trip to get Madeleine to agree to allow the singer to spend one dinner alone with her *piccolo Pinocchio*.

"A candlelit dinner for two!" Madeleine wailed. "Really, Léonce, I ask you!"

"Make the most of it and go out . . . If I were you . . ."

Unlike Léonce, who clearly had some inkling, Madeleine had absolutely no idea how a woman like herself might spend an evening alone in Milan.

"And calling him Pinocchio, I find that very disagreeable, Paul is not a puppet! She'll have to change her ways, let me tell you!"

Paul watched this rivalry with a certain delight, as if it were a fight between two girls in a sandpit. "It d-d-do-doesn't m-m-matter," he said to Léonce, who found the whole thing infuriating.

They were to depart in the evening of July 9, on the 18.43 train. Their suitcases had been packed two days earlier, the trunks of clothes had been sent on ahead, four days before. Almost hourly, Madeleine checked that she had their tickets, their passports, pestering the household staff with endless details that betrayed her inexperience in matters of travel. The furthest she had ever been was Aurillac, to the home of a cousin by marriage, when she was nine years old.

But on July 9, the day of their departure, the news broke like a clap of thunder. The front-page headline in *Le Matin* read: SERIOUS THREAT TO ROMANIAN PETROLEUM.

Madeleine had been sitting at an occasional table eating breakfast while she waited for Léonce to arrive. Her teacup fell to the floor, she suddenly felt light-headed and grasped the edge of the table, which instantly toppled over, so that she found herself on her hands and knees with everything strewn across the floor. With the certainty of the unquiet mind, she knew that this news heralded more.

It took her several minutes to steady her trembling and eventually read the article.

The Romanian Petrochemical consortium responsible for drilling and exploiting the oilfields of the Pannonian Basin has announced that it is experiencing "serious difficulties" and, faced with the looming threat of bankruptcy, is urgently appealing to the Romanian government for help.

The French government, through the intermediary of a Senior Trade Adviser in Bucharest, has demanded an explanation from the Romanian authorities, since the recent share issue was largely acquired by investors in France, who now have every reason to fear the worst. The last hope for the shareholders is the Romanian government . . .

Madeleine paced the room, feverishly crumpling the newspaper, overcome by a panic that made it impossible to think, to consider, and now Léonce was late . . .

She rang the bell and gave orders for the chauffeur to go and fetch Mademoiselle Léonce immediately, it was urgent.

Suddenly she had a doubt. How reliable was the article in *Le Matin*?

She rushed to read *Le Temps* and *Le Figaro*. Both recounted the same information, varying only in their assessment of the gravity of the situation, which ranged from "extremely worrying" to "seriously alarming".

Charles? Gustave? André? Léonce? To whom should she turn?

She asked the parlourmaid to call Joubert.

"No, call Monsieur Charles Péricourt instead."

The parlourmaid looked down at the rug, the upturned tray, the toast, the jam, the teapot.

"No, call . . ."

Joubert? What good would his advice be now? Charles?

"Yes, actually, put in a call to Monsieur Péricourt."

There was no answer from Charles' office. Call Monsieur Joubert. But Monsieur Joubert was busy.

As though struck by a sudden inspiration, Madeleine smoothed out the newspaper articles and reread them. Breathe, she told herself, it surely cannot be such a catastrophe. There it was! The consortium was "urgently appealing" for help from the Romanian government. Nothing was settled yet. The worst was not a certainty. And besides . . . She rushed over to her escritoire, pulled out the drawers and, kneeling on the floor, she went through the folders Joubert had left with her.

There it was! Phew. She was breathless and her heart was pounding alarmingly. She made an effort to regain some semblance of calm. It was exactly as Joubert had said: "No more than half your holdings in this . . . 'Romanian petroleum'." Half of her personal fortune. And Paul's inheritance was untouched, invested in government bonds. Well, she thought, it should be possible to live on half the fortune of Madeleine Péricourt, though she had no concrete idea of what effect this might have on her life.

"It stands to reason, you should diversify," Joubert had insisted. "You need to build a portfolio of coordinated securities." She leafed through the bulging folder in search of . . . There! Joubert had insisted she buy shares in companies in Britain (Somerset Engineering Company), Italy (Gruppo Pozzo), America (Forster, Templeton & Grave) . . .

Now that she was certain she had not lost all, but only half, her fortune, the prospect of the disaster filled her with anger, with a bitterness from which she herself was excluded. Everyone was to blame: Charles, for alerting her to some hypothetical crisis, Joubert, for not finding the right words to discourage her, the newspapers, for failing to mention that they had been the first to champion a company whose collapse they were now announcing, Léonce, who had been the first to mention . . . Where was Léonce? If ever there was a day when she needed her friend by her side, it was . . . My God, it was ten o'clock, they were leaving on the evening train and she had not yet gone up to see Paul to tell him.

When he saw his mother's distraught expression, Paul wanted to ask a question, but when he was overcome by a powerful emotion, he found it impossible even to form the first syllables. He picked up his slate: "What is it, Maman?"

Madeleine burst into tears. Kneeling next to her son's wheelchair, she sobbed and stammered, it's nothing, my darling, just a little problem, I promise, but Paul found it difficult to believe that whatever had left his mother in such a state could be "nothing".

"Is Léonce not with you?" he wrote. This question, at least, cut short Madeleine's sobbing and she struggled to her feet.

"It's alright, my darling, I'll be fine, it's nothing. But I'm afraid that our little trip, my angel, won't be possible."

Paul's scream left the whole household stunned.

Madeleine was chilled by the contorted expression on her son's face, by the howl that came from his throat, from his belly, from his soul, a howl so desperate that her first thought was that Paul might once again try to throw himself out the window. She pressed his face against her, it's alright, my love, we'll find a way, she sobbed, I promise you, there, there, Maman will find a way . . .

"I will have to stay here . . . on business. But Léonce can go with you!"

She was very happy with her sudden idea. She held Paul at arm's length and looked into his eyes.

"What do you say? Will you be alright if Léonce goes with you?"

Alright, he said, his face ashen, yes, alright, Léonce.

The parlourmaid appeared to say that Monsieur Joubert had arrived.

Madeleine was wearing a rumpled nightdress stained with tea and jam, her hair was dishevelled, her face lined with tears and worry. From the look in Joubert's eyes, she could tell how awful she looked. Before he could say a word, she had excused herself, murmuring, I shall be right back. When she returned, having combed her hair and slipped on a dressing gown, Joubert had not moved. It was unusual to see him arrive empty-handed, almost worrying.

"When I read the news, I thought it best to come in person," he said gravely.

He nodded at the newspapers scattered on the floor.

"I have checked. These . . . Romanians have been hiding the truth about the state of their accounts."

He was more curt, more peremptory than usual, clearly in the grip of an emotion he found difficult to control. Madeleine collapsed into an armchair. Abandoning any semblance of modesty, she once again began to weep.

"I warned you," said Joubert, "but you refused to listen to me."

There was something so brutal, so insulting about this reminder, that he felt compelled to add:

"Don't worry, the Romanian government are not going to allow the company to founder!"

"But . . . what if they refuse aid?"

"Unthinkable. Negotiations will have begun at the highest levels, this is not merely a financial scandal, it is political. Perhaps your uncle will know more."

But Charles could still not be reached. Madeleine left a dozen messages at the Assemblée, with his committee room, with Hortense, no-one could say where he might be. He was probably in a meeting; a stark rebuke had doubtless already been sent to Romanian government, as Joubert said, this was a political scandal, Charles was almost certainly overwhelmed.

Eleven o'clock.

She had promised Paul that Léonce would take him, she needed to go and fetch her, to get things ready. She dressed hurriedly and the chauffeur drove her to 4, rue de Provence. But there was no-one living there by the name of Picard, "Not for a long while now," said the concierge, a short, stout, cheery woman who wore her oversized headscarf like a turban.

"What do you mean, 'a long while'?"

"Oh, goes back a year or more, I'd say. Wait now," she pressed a finger to her lips and narrowed her eyes, "shouldn't be too hard to work out . . . Monsieur Bertrand, the old reprobate, I hope he's burning in hell, well, he died in the May of last year, I remember the date like it was my birthday, it's not every day you get such good news . . ."

"Last May, you say?"

"That's right. And Mademoiselle Picard, she left a week or two afterwards. So, thirteen months, near as makes no difference, I said a year, I wasn't far off."

She held out her hand, Madeleine gave her twenty francs.

In the car, she counted the months off on her fingers. May of last year would correspond with the period when Joubert discovered her "indiscretions". The levy he imposed on her salary must have been such that Léonce could no longer afford to stay at 4, rue de Provence, and had to find somewhere less expensive.

She had been forced to move, and, out of shame, had not mentioned the fact to anyone.

Once again, Madeleine lamented her own selfishness, she had not noticed anything, had not troubled to enquire. In what hovel was Léonce living now? Madeleine would not allow the situation to continue. She would demand to know the truth . . . no, not the truth, that would be humiliating, no, she would simply tell Léonce that she could come and live at the Péricourt house. That was it. With no change to her salary. Now that André had left, there was nothing to prevent Léonce from taking the little room, it would need to be repainted, brightened up a little, but that would not take long . . .

At this point, she realised that she was behaving as though life would carry on, that nothing untoward was going to happen, that the business of her investments had simply been a nightmare that could be easily dispelled by focusing on her everyday routine.

There was no record playing, Paul was waiting for her. It was a grave moment. Vladi, unexpectedly silent, was sitting on a chair by the wall, knees pressed together, hands in her lap, as though in a waiting room. Paul stared at his mother.

"I'm afraid it will be difficult for Léonce to go with you, my angel . . ."

Paul's mouth fell open. In that moment, his face had the deathly pallor Madeleine had seen at the Hôpital de la Pitié. Without thinking what she was saying, she pressed on:

"Vladi will go with you, won't you, Vladi?"

"Tak, oczywiście! Zgadzam się!"

"I shall deal with the necessary paperwork."

Going to the Italian embassy, getting the names changed on the train tickets, having two suitcases urgently dispatched to Vladi, drawing up a letter of authorisation permitting the nurse to take her son to Milan, these things took up her whole day. But by half past five they had arrived at the Gare de Lyon, Paul in the travel suit Léonce had recommended buying, Vladi wearing her Sunday best (although the dress looked as though she had made it from a pair of curtains), and Madeleine, anxious, but determined not to repeat her admonitions to Paul, who had heard them a dozen times already, or to Vladi, who understood nothing; the cavalier manner in which she had stuffed the thick wad of Italian lire Madeleine had given her into a battered purse did not inspire confidence.

There were porters waiting out on the forecourt, Vladi pushed Paul's wheelchair to the platform. Amid the constant whirl of cases and trunks, of harried travellers, excited families and couples trembling with emotion, the porters stowed the wheelchair in the baggage compartment at the end of the carriage and carried Paul to his window seat in a first-class carriage decked out with red velvet and pale wood. Personal effects were placed in the netting above the seats. Madeleine could not resist pointing out Paul and Vladi to the conductor, a man of about thirty with a barrel chest and stubby legs, whose face seemed savage on account of the bushy eyebrows that pointed heavenward like radio antennae.

Madeleine felt a lump in her throat at the sight of her little boy leaving, though he was beaming, unaware of what was going on in his mother's life. Unaware? Perhaps not entirely, since, as she left the carriage (the conductor was insistent, the train is about to leave, madame, I'm afraid you must disembark), Paul whispered in her ear:

"Ev-ev-everyth-thing w-w-will be f-f-fine, Ma-maman. I lo-lo-love you."

Madeleine was still standing on the platform several minutes after the train had pulled out of the station.

For the first time, Paul had gone away; it was a feeling of serene and strangely bracing sadness. Anything could happen to her, she was prepared to endure anything, as long as Paul was safe.

Paul, too, felt torn, weighed down with guilt at the thought of leaving his mother. From what he had heard, which was almost everything, there were troubled times ahead. But whatever happened, he would have the memories of this trip, he would have visited La Scala, he would have heard Solange perform there, his experience would be something no-one could ever take from him.

The train conductor, who believed himself to be on a mission ever since Madeleine had pressed fifty francs into his hand, was the son of a Polish immigrant. Although he himself was French, he spoke the language of his parents fluently and, once the train had set off and he had carried out the tasks allotted him, he and Vladi launched into a conversation whose nature and implications Paul could easily intuit from Vladi's laughter and giggles, which he recognised from her encounters with the son of the coal merchant on the rue de Miromesnil and the lift attendant who worked at the Eiffel Tower and lived on the rue de Tocqueville.

As night began to draw in and he lay on his couchette, curled up beneath sheets weighed down by tartan blankets, Paul allowed a pleasant drowsiness to wash over him, and, before long, he ceased to hear the voices of Vladi and the conductor, and some minutes later was being lulled by the panting of the nurse and the exhilarating pulse of the train tracks, which reminded him of the insistent rhythms of the "Boléro" which the salesman at Paris-Phono had played for him two weeks earlier. He sank into excited sleep.

Madeleine had not even tried to sleep, having spent the better part of the night rereading the documents relating to her ownership of English, American and Italian shares.

By six o'clock, she had washed and dressed, but there was a knot in her stomach and a lump in her throat. Curiously, hers was not the face of a woman consumed by worry. Pale, grave and rapt, it looked more like the face of someone under sentence of death who, weary of waiting, walks to the scaffold with calm determination. Léonce would not arrive before eight-thirty. She summoned the chauffeur and set off.

"Oh, it's you!"

Hortense was wearing a leaf-patterned dressing gown and fur-lined slippers. Her hair bristling with curlers, she was the terrifying incarnation of the wife that most men fear they will marry. She did not invite Madeleine inside, but folded her arms.

"I am looking for my uncle, I need to speak with him."

"Charles is very busy, as I'm sure you can imagine. He is an eminent parliamentarian, in case you had forgotten, he is in great demand, he scarcely has a minute to himself."

"Even for his niece?"

"Oh, he has a niece? That's the first I've heard of it!"

"I need to see him . . ."

Hortense burst into peals of laughter.

"Well, isn't that just typical of the Mar-cel-Pé-ri-court family! Always on their high horse. They command and everyone obeys!"

146

This sudden hostility contrasted sharply with Hortense's usual imbecility.

"I don't understand wh—"

"That's hardly surprising! Your father didn't understand either."

Hortense was speaking in a shrill voice and shaking her head so vigorously that the curlers quivered and gradually came undone, such that, before she knew it, her face was framed by a cascade of curlpapers, bouncing about her head as though mounted on springs.

"Everyone is expected to dance to your tune! Well, that's all over now. Oh, they are riding for a great fall, the Mar-cel-Pé-ri-court family."

Hortense stepped towards Madeleine and viciously jabbed a finger at her.

"First of all, Charles is not at the beck and call of Mademoiselle. Secondly, he who laughs last laughs longest. Thirdly . . ."

Unable to think what might come third, she concluded:

"That's knocked you off your perch, hasn't it?"

Without a word, Madeleine turned and left.

She had the chauffeur drive her to *Soir de Paris*.

The editorial conference, that is to say, the meeting at which the journalists took orders from management, had not yet finished, and Madeleine was ushered into a waiting room.

Guilloteaux appeared some forty minutes later, apologising profusely, my dear, this newspaper will be the death of me, I'm getting too old for this profession, he had been saying this for a decade to all his visitors, every one of whom knew he would die at his desk. Madeleine had not got to her feet, she was staring at him, waiting for him to finish with the trite formalities. Almost reluctantly, he came and sat next to her.

"I imagine that your situation must be somewhat . . . complicated."

"And whose fault is that?"

Guilloteaux was as struck by this response as by a thunderbolt. He laid a hand on his chest in an attitude of outraged dignity.

"Your newspaper," Madeleine continued, "has dedicated count-less column inches to extolling the benefits of this Romanian investment."

"Yes, yes, of course."

He was relieved. It was palpable.

"But that was not, strictly speaking, advice, merely news. A daily newspaper prints stories useful to those who are its lifeblood."

Madeleine was struggling to understand.

"You're saying . . . those articles . . . were *paid for*?"

"That is something of an exaggeration! A newspaper such as ours cannot exist without support, as you well know. When the state supports a share issue of this magnitude, it is because it considers it necessary to the country's economy! Surely you are not going to criticise us for being patriotic!"

"You knowingly publish false information?"

"Not 'false', you go too far. We simply present the facts in a par-ticular light, no more. Some of our colleagues at rival newspapers present the opposite viewpoint, so everything balances out. That is the definition of plurality of opinion. You can hardly criticise us for being republican!"

Appalled, and ashamed that she could have been so naive, Madeleine stalked out and slammed the door.

18

At break of day, Vladi was sitting by the window, and, drawing heavily on Polish superlatives, was extolling the landscape, which, in fact, offered no particularly spectacular vistas. Shortly afterwards, the train spent half an hour laboriously chugging across shunting points before entering a smoky, crowded station.

By telegram, Solange had learned that Paul would now be

accompanied, not by his "dear maman", but by a nanny. Immediately, she changed her plans and, instead of greeting them in the pomp and splendour of the great hall of the Hotel Principe di Savoia, she decided to go and personally meet her guests at the station.

The presence of La Gallinato in Italy had stirred much excitement in the press, especially since, in the great tradition of operatic divas, she was unstinting in her caprices and her declarations. When announcing that she planned to go to Milan railway station, she shrouded the identity of her guest in great mystery. The reporters and photographers thought this signalled a new affaire de cœur, though no-one truly believed it.

In the past two years, Solange had grown decidedly fat, and now moved at a stately pace. That her voice and her talent had been unaffected by this change was somewhat surprising, in fact her singing had grown better and better – maturity, some said – and she was at the summit of her art.

She had left the hotel thus surrounded by a swarm of journalists and stringers. The staff at the railway station bent over backwards to escort her through the throng. The train pulled in to find her standing on the platform, draped in torrents of white tulle, wearing an immense hat, swathed in whorls of bluish smoke, imposing, aloof, exposed, posing as the perfect paradigm of the hysterical woman, resulting in many stunning photographs. When Paul first appeared, in Vladi's arms, and was subsequently settled into his wheelchair, the press roared its approval. Flash powder crackled, Paul gave a broad smile, it is, I believe, the only surviving image of him so gloriously happy. Solange, on her knees, Solange walking slowly, clutching the hand of her little Pinocchio . . . Before midnight, the photographs were on the front page of every newspaper, the improvident public stormed the box office of La Scala, tickets changed hands on the black market for outrageous sums.

Paul had his own suite, and through the communicating door he could hear Vladi's squeals of delight. At the arrival of a sumptuous meal, accompanied by champagne, she swooned and offered the waiter a come-hither smile that, in less than an hour, was the talk of the establishment.

Some minutes later, a curious couple caused a sensation in the hotel restaurant, where, with a dispassionate wave, Solange rejected the table prepared for her in the centre of the room in favour of one by the wall, next to the vast mirrors, a small, discreet, more unobtrusive table, a location where the photographs would be all the more striking.

Though Solange ate with great refinement, she wolfed down vast quantities of food, meaning that luncheon went on so long that she only just had time to have a long post-prandial nap, as was her wont, before setting off, an hour and a half before the public were scheduled to arrive, for the concert hall where she was performing that evening.

This was the first time that they had been together, *en tête à tête*.

Paul stammered little; Solange smiled. They talked about opera, about travel. She reminisced about her childhood in Buenos Aires (though in fact she had been born to an Italian mother in Parma), about her father and his stud farm of Peruvian purebloods in the Lerma valley, about her modest beginnings at the age of thirteen in a small concert hall in Santa Rosa, where, before the evening was over, she had had four offers of marriage.

Paul listened dreamily to these confessions. Having spent so much time at the library leafing through old documents, he was among the few people who knew that Solange Gallinato, born Bernadette Traviers in Dole (in the Jura), was in fact the youngest daughter of an alcoholic road worker imprisoned in Besançon on the day that she was born, two months premature, as a result of conjugal violence.

Paul studied her gravely. From the very first glance, he had seen in her the deep well of loneliness he had always sensed in her recordings. Solange was an unhappy woman, a fact that made his heart bleed. What transpired during the course of this luncheon that left Solange so utterly changed, no-one would ever discover. Had the tragic destiny of the great operatic heroines she had played brutally resonated with her own life? Did the sight of this spellbound little boy remind her of the desolate emotional desert in which she had been stranded since the death of Maurice Grandet? Was she seized by a sense of fatalism, of injustice, at the sight of this boy condemned to a wheelchair? Who can say? All we do know is, that evening, during rehearsals, she could not marshal the strength to stand and had to sit down in order to sing. She never got up again.

Panicked, the director of La Scala rushed on stage to ask what could be done. Flowers, she said simply. A mountain of posies and baskets was brought and placed on column and pedestals.

When the curtain rose, the audience found her sitting stiffly in a chair, raised slightly in a manner hidden from them by a mantel of satin, framed by a lush decor of flowers and plants – she looked as though she were singing in a botanical garden.

She completely changed the order of the programme, never to change it again. She began, in a heart-rending voice, with the opening of "Gloria Mundi", singing a cappella as she had done in Paris:

> *My dearest love,*
> *Here we are, in the ruins of the palace*
> *Where first we glimpsed each other . . .*

As Paul was listening to the opening notes of Maurice Grandet's opera at La Scala, it was half past seven in the evening back in Paris and his mother had just seen the headline in *Le Soir*:

ROMANIAN GOVERNMENT REFUSES TO BAIL OUT
STRUGGLING PETROLEUM CONSORTIUM
URGENT APPEALS OF FRENCH OFFICIALS TO NO AVAIL

Madeleine pored over the article, but could not comprehend it, the words stubbornly eluded her understanding.

It took her more than fifteen minutes to penetrate the thick sludge of the article and realise that, contrary to what everyone had hoped and expected, a considerable part of her fortune had just evaporated.

Léonce, who had probably been ruined, had not yet reappeared. Madeleine could do nothing to stop her tears, what comfort could she offer her friend if, as seemed likely, she too had been affected?

Madeleine struggled to imagine the concrete ramifications this bankruptcy would have on her life. Fewer household staff? Yes, no doubt. As to the rest, what more could she give up? Her lifestyle was hardly extravagant! To lose a large percentage of her income with no consequences was impossible, there were doubtless steps to be taken, but what were they? All this was terribly confusing. Thinking of Paul helped her to summon her courage. She had to face reality. She telephoned Gustave Joubert. He had just left his office at the bank. Madeleine changed her clothes and summoned the chauffeur.

She took the copy of *Soir de Paris,* whose headline, in the half-light of the car, seemed twice as large and twice as ominous. While they were held up in traffic near the banks of the Seine, she reread the various articles, all of which cruelly evoked the feverish speculation the company had earlier generated on the stock exchange.

Suddenly, her eye fell on another headline:

OILFIELDS OF EXCEPTIONAL SIZE
DISCOVERED IN IRAQ

Stocks in the company plummeted by eighty per cent before being purchased by a French financial institution which now stands to make one of the greatest short-term capital gains in the history of the Paris Bourse.

So, Joubert had been right. Madeleine was devastated.

*

On stage at La Scala, the lights had imperceptibly dimmed and taken on a pale ochre glow. Solange held her clenched fists to her breast.

> *What wild jealousy had you in thrall?*
> *Can it be that these meagre ruins*
> *Are all that now remains*
> *Of us?*

Joubert came downstairs, composed, staid. He was wearing Moroccan slippers and a silk smoking jacket, like a husband.

Madeleine did not say "Good evening", the words caught in her throat. She had only to look at the imposing figure of Joubert, those pale blue, piercing eyes that showed neither hostility nor sympathy, to realise that something in their relationship had definitively changed.

"Is there nothing to be done?" she asked abruptly.

"I fear not, Madeleine."

She swallowed hard.

"The greater part of my fortune was invested there, was it not? But, not everything, surely? You created a sizeable portfolio of stocks and shares in other companies, did you not?"

"That is true, Madeleine, however . . ."

"However?"

"For the most part, these were companies within the same industry, subcontractors, suppliers, clients . . ."

"But I hold British, American, Italian stocks! To my knowledge, the Romanian government has no control over foreign companies!"

"All of these foreign companies are involved in the petroleum industry. They, too, will collapse in the coming days."

"How much have I lost, Gustave? What do I have left?"

"You have suffered considerable losses, Madeleine. What remains is precious little."

"Are you saying that I have lost everything? My whole fortune?"

"To all intents and purposes, yes. Drastic measures will have to be taken."

"Must I sell the house?"

Silence.

"Must I sell everything?"

"Almost everything, yes. I am sorry."

Madeleine seemed to shrink by several centimetres. She turned around, bewildered, stumbled unthinkingly towards the door, then stopped and turned back to Joubert, still clutching her copy of *Soir de Paris*, which she proffered to him.

"Tell me something, Gustave . . . This 'French financial institution' that ramped up the price of Romanian stocks so it could buy Iraqi shares cheaply, was that you?"

Joubert was a cold, hard man, but the stakes of such a confession were too high, his courage failed him. He evaded the question.

"I did my best to advise you, Madeleine, you refused to listen."

Madeleine felt terrifyingly lucid. Her anger mounted as she gradually pieced together the events of the preceding months.

First, Charles had come to tell her that she was threatened by a looming financial crisis, that Joubert was out of his depth . . .

Then the headlines in *Soir de Paris* about the dazzling success of Romanian petroleum . . .

Joubert himself had done everything in his power to seem like a man offering dubious advice that she should on no account follow.

Madeleine suddenly realised the scope and scale of the manipulations that had been practised on her.

She wanted to kill him, to crush him underfoot like a snake.

"We will meet again on this same path, Gustave. The bonds and securities left to Paul are in my control, and I shall use them to put our lives in order and—"

"Which bonds and securities do you speak of, Madeleine?"

"The ones that Paul inherited from his grandfather."

"But, Madeleine, you sold them off."

Her shock was such that she clutched the handle of the door for support. Sold off? How?

"I advised you, and you agreed, to restructure your assets. This was in August of last year, surely you remember? I brought charts, graphs, figures . . . I explained to you that government bonds offered little return, a situation that was unlikely to change in the near future. You agreed to sell the bonds held in your son's name, as I advised. I particularly drew your attention to your wise decision."

Yes, she vaguely remembered: "You would sell off failing securities," he had explained, "and thereby consolidate the family bank . . ."

Joubert spoke in that scholarly, faintly demeaning tone he adopted when he wanted to make her feel intellectually inferior.

"When we restructured your assets, you assured me that you understood the process."

"So, Paul's bonds were sold?"

"To be precise, you authorised the bank to . . ."

Madeleine's voice rose to a scream.

"Where is Paul's money?"

"You invested it, Madeleine, together with your own fortune, in Romanian petroleum. Against my better judgment, I might add. You cannot hold me responsible."

"Then I have lost everything?"

"Yes."

Joubert slipped his hands into his pockets.

"And Paul has lost everything?"

"Yes."

"Let me get this straight, Gustave. In order to bring down the price of the shares you wished to purchase, you needed a powerful stooge. And you used me, and my fortune, to achieve your ends, is that correct?"

"I wouldn't put it quite like that."

"How would you put it?"

"I would say that you declined to take my advice."

"You lied to me!"

"Never!"

This time it was Joubert who screamed.

"You took your decisions alone and without my counsel. I provided you with a wealth of explanations, but you would get bored, you would sigh . . . You have only yourself to blame."

"You are . . . you are a . . ."

The word came. But in a last vestige of decency, she did not say it.

Joubert had been manipulating her for months. He had been acting on a carefully calculated plan.

"So, my entire fortune is now in your hands."

"Not at all. You lost your entire fortune at the same moment that I made mine, that is a very different matter."

Madeleine staggered, a parlourmaid came to her aid but she pushed the girl away, stumbled down the front steps and climbed into her car.

Just as the chauffeur was about to close the door, Madeleine stopped him, staring up at a first-floor window.

Léonce was looking down at her.

Joubert briefly appeared behind her, then vanished.

The two women stared at each other for a long moment. Then, with a leisurely gesture, Léonce let the curtain fall.

The lights had dimmed until the stage was almost in darkness.

The mesmerised audience strained to make out the source of this plaintive voice as it sang:

> *I loved you so completely*
> *I could never bring myself to hate*
> *But look upon this ruin*
> *You have fashioned from my fate . . .*

19

The Péricourt family home was sold on October 30, 1929, for considerably less than its market value since Madeleine needed a quick sale.

An auctioneer placed discreet tags next to each piece of furniture, every object, painting, book, curtain, bed, plant, chandelier and mirror, with the exception of those few things Madeleine was allowed to take with her. Many of those who trooped through the house had been among those who, two years earlier, had attended the funeral of Marcel Péricourt.

Madeleine stood, petrified.

Hortense strolled around the living room, back arched, like a general surveying a battlefield after a great victory, a small notepad in hand, pausing before a chest of drawers or a tapestry, stepping back to picture how it would look in her home, before moving on to the next item or jotting down the lot number.

"Tell me, Madeleine," she said, without troubling to greet her niece, "two thousand francs for this pedestal table . . . don't you think that a little excessive?"

She stepped closer to the table, ran a finger over the surface, as she often did to alert her maidservants to dust.

"Oh, very well, if you say so!"

She noted the price on her pad and continued her perambulations.

To hold back her tears and check the urge to slap Hortense, Madeleine quickly went upstairs. Paul's bedroom was filled with open boxes, crates and straw.

"It must be difficult to choose, my darling," she said, her voice low and tremulous.

"N-n-no, Ma-maman. It's f-fine."

The two were silent for a moment.

"I'm so sorry, I . . ."

"It r-really d-d-doesn't m-m-matter, Ma-maman."

Try as he might to reassure her, Paul realised that the situation was grave. The sale of the Péricourt house had raised just enough to buy two apartments. The first, on the rue Duhesme, would have seen Madeleine, Paul and Vladi living comfortably, but since it represented the family's only real income, it would be rented out.

The second clearly showed the extent to which they had had to lower their ambitions: a living room, a dining room, two bedrooms, and, in the attic, a room for Vladi that was smaller and gloomier that her previous room, though she pronounced herself content.

The apartment was on the second floor of 96, rue La Fontaine. The lift was too narrow to accommodate Paul's wheelchair. When they went out, Vladi had to sit the boy on a folding chair in the lift and carry the wheelchair downstairs. They could afford to keep only a maid-of-all-work.

For Madeleine, depression vied with crippling guilt. Within a few short weeks, she had seen her standard of living reduced to that of a middle-class woman who, in order to maintain even this humble status, would need to constantly economise, frequently go without, and keep track of everything. She would weep for hours, unable to stop herself, but she accepted what had befallen her with a fatalism that stemmed from acute, obsessive self-reproach. Granted, she had been badly counselled, but she had followed that advice without due consideration and, in that, she was entirely to blame. She had inherited a fortune she had proved unable to keep, that was the truth of the matter. Gustave Joubert had been right to remind her that she had signed "with full knowledge of the facts", it had been her responsibility to take an interest in business.

She had been educated to be a lady. Although he loved her dearly, her father had raised her believing that she would never be capable of great things. Losing the fortune he had bequeathed her served merely to confirm his judgment.

The move to rue La Fontaine took place on December 1.

The banns for the marriage of Mademoiselle Léonce Picard to Monsieur Gustave Joubert had been read a few days earlier.

Thinking about the betrayal of this woman she had considered a friend, this woman who had used her charms and her considerable wiles until Madeleine began to doubt her most intimate proclivities . . . all this was most distressing.

Four days later, Madeleine visited her lawyer, Maître Lecerf, to sign documents. Reviewing the results of the auction, she saw that Hortense had indeed bought the pedestal table for precisely two thousand francs, no-one had outbid her. The large portrait of Marcel Péricourt had been purchased by the new owner of the house "in memory of the great man who conceived this magnificent mansion".

"Monsieur Joubert paid two thousand francs for it," the lawyer noted.

"I thought the painting had been bought by . . ."

Madeleine trailed off. The embarrassed lawyer merely coughed.

It was thus that Madeleine learned that Gustave Joubert was now the owner of the Péricourt house.

At the end of the year, Madeleine sent a card offering the compliments of the season to André, who replied with a timid letter expressing warm regards, in which she wanted to believe. She telephoned the offices of the newspaper.

"Surely you won't begrudge a little visit to a friend who has no-one left but you? And Paul would be so happy to see you."

André was extremely busy, it would not be easy . . .

"In your exalted circle, you no longer frequent humble folk, is that it?"

Madeleine was surprised to hear herself use this argument. She felt ashamed, and was about to apologise, but André pre-empted her.

"Of course not! I would be delighted to see you, it is simply that . . ."

Tuesday would not work, perhaps later in the week, or ideally next week, some afternoon, or an evening would be easier, what about Thursday . . . Nothing suited, there was always some obstacle.

"Listen, André, whatever day suits you will suit us. And if you cannot find the time, no matter, we will think of you fondly."

"Shall we say Friday of next week? Unfortunately, I cannot stay long, I shall need to get back to the office to put the issue to bed."

This was not something he had ever done; sending the paper to press did not require André's presence.

When he arrived at the apartment, he set a little package on the hall table. He cupped Madeleine's hands in an ambiguous gesture that could be interpreted as affection or respect, she nodded to Paul, who was sleeping soundly, I'm so sorry, she whispered. André understood, he gave a faint smile, took three steps towards the wheelchair, like an anxious father approaching a crib.

Paul woke, saw André, and it was like a storm breaking, violent, unpredictable, the howl he let out was boundless. Eyes bulging, Paul wrapped his arms around his head as though trying to protect himself from some deafening sound and his scream, dear God, from where had he summoned such a deathly wail? Vladi burst into the room (Co się stało, aniołku?), she rushed over to Paul who pushed her away, he was in a trance, his head jerked feverishly, his eyes rolled back, he clawed at his chest as though intent on ripping it open.

Madeleine tried to suggest that André leave the room, but Paul's howls were so piercing he could not make out what she was saying, he was terrified, signalled that he understood and hurtled down the stairs as if pursued by the devil himself.

Madeleine ran over to her son, cradled his head in her arms and murmured words of comfort.

Paul was weeping hot tears.

"Go, please, Vladi," Madeleine said, "I shall take care of him," and she sat in the half-light for a long time, rocking him gently.

When, finally, he was a little calmer, Madeleine lit the small lamp whose orange lampshade gave an oriental lustre to the room at night. She sat beside her son and stroked his hands, now still, despite his continued tears.

She knew that it had finally arrived, the moment for which she had been steeling herself, and which she knew would cause her such cataclysmic pain. She wiped her son's face, blew his nose and returned to her chair.

The boy was gazing out the window, as he used to do. Madeleine asked him no questions, content simply to hold his hands.

Two hours passed thus, then a third. One by one, the living room, the street and the whole city were engulfed in darkness. Paul asked for some water. His mother brought him a glass, then resumed her chair and took his hand.

Paul began to stammer in a deep, almost adult voice. He stuttered a lot. The tears once more began to well up, and, with them, the truth.

It was very slow, very long, Paul's lips tripped over every syllable, sometimes mangling words, Madeleine listened patiently, her heart in her throat, and saw her son's life play out, a life about which she knew nothing, the life of a boy who was hers but whom she did not know.

First came the long dictation lessons when André bound the boy's left hand behind his back to force him to use his right, the hours spent in a straitjacket trying to force his crippled body, his useless hand to obey . . . A whack from the steel ruler on his fingertips at the slightest mistake . . . Boys do not cry, Paul, insisted André. Even in dreams, the sight of his tutor left Paul bathed in sweat, tossing and turning, and jolting awake in his bed.

One evening André caught the boy with a novel by Jules Verne hidden beneath his sheets. "Did I authorise this reading matter, Paul?" he asked, his voice a hoarse growl.

It is eight o'clock, downstairs in the dining room people are at dinner, the click of cutlery and the smell of cigarette smoke drifts up the stairs. Blushing, Paul confesses his guilt, so a spanking, pyjamas lowered, over André's knees, dirty little boy. After this, Paul goes back to bed. André bends over him, sympathetically, he listens for a moment to the sounds and the snatches of conversation from the dining room and, reassured, turns back to his pupil, strokes the boy's red buttocks sadly, a long moment passes, then there comes the sound of rustling fabric near the bed, the thud of shoes on the parquet floor is drowned out by a burst of laughter, someone down-stairs has clearly just recounted an amusing anecdote, then there is a commotion, the men head towards the smoking room leaving the women alone to discuss child-rearing, *such* a responsibility . . . Paul closes his eyes, presses his face into the pillow, he feels André lie down next to him, hears his hushed breath, his whispered words . . . Feels his hands, his weight. And then the pain. There, there, it's all over, you see, it's all over, and the searing pain as though he is being ripped in two, you see, André whispers in a guttural voice, he groans, he explains how sad it makes him when Paul does not do his work properly, then he groans again. Little Paul will make a promise to his friend André, won't he? Otherwise, next time the punishment will not be a rap on the knuckles with the metal ruler.

Madeleine remembers that, during this period, she would visit Paul's room three or four times a night. It's alright, my darling, Maman is here, and she would stroke his forehead. He was skittish as a kitten. Then Léonce would appear, get some rest, Madeleine, I shall watch over him for a while before I head home.

For Paul woke every night, alert to the sound of footsteps on the back stairs, terrified that he would hear André pause, tiptoe into his bedroom and furtively undress. Sometimes, he did not wake up until he felt André's breath on the back of his neck, reeking of alcohol and cigar smoke, felt his hands wandering . . . "He doesn't want me to leave, the little poppet," Madeleine would say laugh-ingly, as Paul sobbed at the news that she was going out to a dinner party or some entertainment. Come, come, she would say, sitting on the edge of his bed in her evening gown, her coat sometimes draped over her shoulders, Maman will not be late home, while he clung to her arm like a little animal, you have to grow up, Paul, and besides, you need to get some sleep, I don't want to be cross with you, you know that, and Paul would nod, Madeleine assumed that he was scared of the dark, I shall leave the light on in the hall and I won't turn it out until I come home, I promise. Good evening, André, Paul would hear Madeleine say in a low voice, you'll keep an eye on Paul, won't you? You are an angel, followed by a soft sound Paul could not decipher, like a surreptitious kiss, sometimes even a laugh, *shhh!* I must go, Madeleine would say, her voice light and gay. Then would come the whisper of taffeta in the stairwell, the gathering dusk, the glow of the hall light, as she promised, until André's shadow fell across the doorway, Paul would turn to face the wall, his racing heart, the urge to vomit, the padding footsteps by the bed, the soft thud of shoes dropped on the rug.

The image of his grandfather appeared. This tall, stocky man who smelled of pipe tobacco. Paul would usually find him seated at his desk; he would look up when he heard the door open, ah, it's you, my little man, what's the matter, come here to me, he was never too busy to take care of the boy, not once, never. His study was pervaded by the aroma of black coffee. Grandfather himself smelled of eau de cologne and he had a bushy moustache that tickled your neck when he hugged you.

Madeleine was transfixed by this image of her father, sitting in his study, hugging his grandson to him.

One day, Monsieur Péricourt had casually ventured:

"Don't you think perhaps it might be better to send him away to school, so he can be with boys his own age?"

"Please don't interfere, Papa! He is my son, and I shall raise him as I see fit."

Monsieur Péricourt was not blind. Nor was he deaf. Like

everyone else in the household, he must have heard Madeleine's muffled steps at night as she went up or down the servants' stairs, but how to broach such a subject with his daughter? It was impossible! He had not pursued the matter, but Madeleine had often found Paul in his grandfather's study, sleeping in his arms.

Paul did not speak of what was happening to his grandfather, he did not have the words. But it was here, amid the smell of pipe tobacco, in the folds of his grandfather's thick woollen dressing gown, that he found shelter, sleep and solace. The study was his only refuge.

Then, Grandfather died.

And so came the day of the funeral.

Léonce sends André to fetch him, a furious André who has been distracted from his first great journalistic commission, an incensed André who takes the stairs two at a time, finds Paul hiding in his grandfather's library and orders him to come downstairs.

The boy dawdles, he stammers. André slaps him with all his might then goes back downstairs, exasperated.

Paul is in tears. He is alone. There is no-one to defend him now that his grandfather is dead.

Paul opens the window and climbs up onto the sill.

And as he sees André appear on the steps below, he throws himself into the void.

Now he is sleeping in his mother's arms. A pale blue glow heralds the day. Madeleine has been here for hours, stiff and aching from cradling the boy, her body is racked by cramps but she does not move. She breathes slowly. She is surprised to realise that she is doing exactly what her father used to do.

The first sounds of morning, Vladi appears, stops in the doorway and whispers:

"Wszystko w porządku?"

With unerring instinct, she does not wait for a response, but comes over, takes Paul in her arms and lays him on his bed.

Still Madeleine sits, staring blankly into space.

She longed to kill him. She would go to his house, knock at the door, and, when he opened, he would instantly realise, he would take a step back and she would empty a whole cartridge clip into his chest.

These murderous fantasies were violent eruptions in the roiling magma of memories and reproaches. This long period during which she had seen nothing, had failed to notice that Paul's terrible pain coincided with the period when she tiptoed up the back stairs to be with André.

She would have killed him, if she had rushed round to his apartment, if she had not stopped to think. She would have knocked, and, the moment he opened the door, she would have hurled herself at him. She would have violently pushed him back towards the open window and, when he felt the edge of the sill, he would have realised, he would have tumbled, howling, into the empty air. She would have leaned over to witness the fall, his body curled into a foetal position crashing against the bonnet of a car then bouncing off and landing with a thud in the road, there would be a screech of brakes but the second car would not be able to stop in time . . .

Yes, if she had gone directly to his house, then, perhaps . . .

But she had not done so, and not simply because she lacked the strength, or because she feared the consequences – in truth, she did not even consider them.

No: she did not go because she too was guilty.

Dear God, what had she done, what havoc had her actions wreaked . . .?

Paul recovered his composure. The revelations left him exhausted, but within two days, when he began to eat again, and listen to a little music, Madeleine had the impression that he was relieved.

She was not.

We shall go to the commissariat. On second thoughts: the

commissaire will come here in person, he will take a statement and begin the process of pressing charges.

Paul squirmed, shaking his head wildly, and screamed:

"N-n-n-noooo!"

Madeleine promised to respect his wishes, though on two further occasions she tried to change his mind, each time triggering a panic attack, Paul did not want to repeat what he had said to anyone, ever!

When he said he was sorry that he had ever told her, she threw herself at his feet and begged him to forgive her, though she no longer knew for what.

The one thing that became clear in an otherwise confused week was that Paul would never testify; he would be incapable of facing such an ordeal.

Madeleine promised never to raise the subject again, and Paul nodded that he understood, although his whole body betrayed the resentment he bore his mother, a bitterness that would take much time to fade.

To the list of her own faults, Madeleine added this attempt to persuade Paul to suffer again, to relive the events it had taken him so many years to reveal.

Many years that ended with a decision taken in a split second.

Madeleine went to her writing desk, opened it, and, without hesitations or corrections, she wrote:

Paris, January 9, 1930

Dear André,

I am so sorry for what transpired when you came to visit. Paul had had a ghastly nightmare, one that left us all perturbed. And one that, unfortunately, deprived us of your company.

Please, do not hold it against him, against us. You are always welcome here, as I hope you know.

We had a little gift we wished to give you for Christmas,
Paul was dying to present it to you in person.
Do not leave us to languish, come see us again soon.
Your affectionate friend,
Madeleine

1933

So that they may be royally entertained, the gods demand that the hero fall from a great height.
after Jean Cocteau

20

When Gustave Joubert arrived at La Tour d'Argent on January 7, Lobgeois was the last to get to his feet, which said much about his state of mind. Sacchetti discreetly clapped twice and, after a moment's hesitation, the assembled company applauded, briefly, but it was sufficient for Joubert to say, come, come, my friends. He flashed a broad smile as he was greeted warmly. As Lobgeois offered his hand, he looked away, Joubert apologised for his tardiness, such modesty, they would forgive him anything. In the past two weeks, he had proved himself the man of the moment.

A general commotion, and scraping of chairs, the clatter of cutlery, the pop of the first champagne cork, the waiters approached, everyone raised his glass. A voice from somewhere: Speech! Speech!

Joubert modestly refused.

"But the champagne is all for me!"

Everyone laughed. Not that Joubert was any funnier than he had been last year; but that was last year.

Lobgeois, in sheer despair, had taken the seat facing Joubert. The other guests were already rubbing their hands, aware that this presaged a heated quarrel. Hostilities would not be triggered before the canard aux navets was served, so in the meantime, the men chatted idly, beginning, as always, with politics. This year, there was no need for polemic, everyone was in agreement: the left-wing government returned to power was a catastrophe.

In the recent elections, the hopes that these elite former students of the École Centrale had placed in Tardieu had not been shared by the electorate. This was hardly surprising: as a moderniser he had singularly failed to modernise anything, his belief in a "politics of prosperity" had been little more than a belief in himself.

"All the same," said someone, "the country needs to realise that reform is crucial."

Although this encapsulated the thoughts of those seated around the table, as a political statement it sounded sanctimonious and, in this group as almost everywhere in the country, politics was getting bad press. In addition to the wave of scandals that had eroded the last vestiges of goodwill and shaken even the most solid convictions, it was widely felt that no-one had grasped the nettle and taken the necessary measures to deal with the cumbersome administration. With his consummate skill, Sacchetti summed up the prevailing opinion:

"It's time to let those who know what is necessary do what is necessary!"

The first course had only just finished, but already the great idea had been broached. Such was the general impatience to hear Joubert speak.

For the reader to understand this feverish atmosphere, it may perhaps be useful if we explain what had happened in the three years since, late in 1929, Gustave Joubert had made an outrageous fortune from Iraqi petroleum in circumstances already familiar to us.

His new-found wealth meant that, for the first time in his life, Joubert felt he could make his own decisions. He had a passion for industry that had increased even as his misgivings about the future of banking were borne out. The spectacular failure of the Banque Oustric, which, in turn, brought down the Banque Adam, had swallowed up more than a billion francs. Small- and medium-sized banks, like the one founded by Marcel Péricourt, were most at risk.

Joubert had taken an interest in the Société Éts Souchon, an engineering company still run by its founder, who had lost both his sons during the Great War. Six somewhat obsolete machine tools, some twenty employees whose average age was worrying, a customer base that was fast shrinking . . . It was the perfect candidate for a buyout, and, having no surviving heirs, Alfred Souchon accepted. Before long, Gustave Joubert was able to congratulate himself on his instincts. The collapse of the Creditanstalt Bank, which immediately preceded that of the German bank Danat, which in turn foreshadowed the collapse of the Banque Nationale de Crédit, confirmed that the great ship of finance was foundering.

Joubert took the plunge. He resigned his post at the Banque Péricourt and devoted himself entirely to his own business.

His departure triggered a crisis of confidence among the customers and administrators of the Banque Péricourt. A run on one of the provincial branches spread to the main Paris bank. There were insufficient funds to deal with the numerous customers attempting to withdraw their deposits. The authorities had more pressing matters to deal with and, in less than two weeks, the Banque Péricourt went down with all hands.

Charles Péricourt made a very dignified speech that allowed him to bury his brother for a second time.

No-one thought to speak to Madeleine since she no longer existed to anyone who mattered.

By now, the new owner of Mécanique Joubert had already negotiated the purchase of four state-of-the-art machine tools, replaced his ageing workforce with that of a younger generation, and landed a number of choice contracts through friends at the Jockey Club and alumni of the École Centrale. Shortly afterwards, an astute deal with Lefebvre-Strudal to supply engine parts for their fleet of aeroplanes ensured that Mécanique Joubert was safe from the financial squall for at least two years. Joubert, now a captain of industry, finally felt he had found his place in the world.

The reader should not think that this swift if somewhat commonplace success was the reason that Gustave Joubert was being lauded that day at La Tour d'Argent, no, the real cause for this outpouring of praise was . . . Renaissance Française, a new initiative of which Joubert was at once architect, evangelist, sage and marketer, in short, he *was* Renaissance Française. It was he who had set out the terms: the shockwave of the American financial crash has finally reached our shores, Germany is engaged in dangerous rearmament, Europe is fracturing, while the French political elite, steeped as it is in nepotism and influence peddling, has learned nothing. It is time, he explained, for the powers that be to reach out to those men of wisdom, experience, confidence, patriotism and, especially, competence. To engineers.

This, then, was Renaissance Française. A movement, a "laboratory of ideas" composed of experts who would revitalise France.

Parliament had paid lip service to the movement, since it could neither ignore nor explicitly condemn a group that, from electricity to automobiles, telephones to chemistry, metallurgy to pharmaceuticals, represented the flower of French industry.

"The men of politics have demonstrated their abilities," Joubert said, "and they are sorely lacking. It is high time that men who are apolitical and patriotic tell the people of France the truth!"

(For "apolitical" read "anti-communist".)

"I can't see how it is possible to be both apolitical and patriotic," muttered Lobgeois. "It's beyond me."

Joubert smiled.

"Apolitical, my dear Lobgeois, means that we are, first and foremost, disciples of pragmatism. Whether it comes from the right or the left, any measure that sets about righting the country is welcome. As to patriotism . . . We simply feel that we must be prepared for any eventuality."

"What eventuality did you have in mind?"

Joubert gave a self-satisfied laugh.

"Hitler won the elections by a landslide last July, Germany withdrew from the Disarmament Conference in September, and none of this troubles you?"

"It's nothing more than diplomatic gameplay! Personally, I find Hitler rather reassuring. At least he will bring order to the mess that Germany has become . . . Hitler is not the enemy, Joubert. Our enemy is the same as his: communism."

A murmur of approval.

"You say that only because you cannot read."

The reply was dangerously close to an insult, which was contrary to the tacit rules of the group: even if they disagreed, members remained on friendly terms. Hence, Joubert hastily added:

"I apologise, Lobgeois, I misspoke. What I meant is that you cannot read German."

"And what would I have learned if I could?"

"That Hitler, who has plans to take power, considers France to be a sworn enemy."

"Ah, yes, I've read something of the sort . . ."

"It does not seem to have made a marked impression on you. And yet, '. . . der Todfeind unseres Volkes, Frankreich . . .' I'm sorry, you don't speak German: 'the mortal enemy of our nation, France, now deprives us of life by holding us in her grip and pitilessly robbing us of our strength . . . No attempt to approach those Powers ought to appear too difficult for us, and no sacrifice should be considered too heavy, if the final outcome would be to make it possible for us to overthrow our bitterest enemy . . .' I don't know what more you need . . ."

"Was that in the newspapers?"

"No, it was in *Mein Kampf*, the memoirs of Herr Hitler and the bible of the Nazi party."

"It is simply politics, Gustave, nothing more! No-one wants another war. Hitler is raising the stakes so that he can become chancellor, he may rant and rave, but he will seek a peaceful solution. War is too expensive."

"Each man must decide for himself. And history will judge."

Gustave Joubert did not wish to pursue the point because, around the table, there were as many proponents as opponents of his argument; it was a divisive subject.

Emboldened by the silence, Lobgeois decided to press what he believed was his advantage:

"And besides, this business is all very abstract. Your Renaissance Française plans to publish studies, but who will read them? It will recommend a programme of reforms, but who will implement them?"

An attentive observer would note that at this point, as on the previous topic, the group imperceptibly divided into two camps. It was a sign of the times; every subject was fuel for division, dispute, disagreement.

"We shall not always be abstract, Lobgeois, I can promise you," Joubert said, unruffled. "We will meet again at the end of the month."

"What can happen in a month?"

Joubert merely smiled.

Sacchetti, who realised better than anyone that the verbal sparring had gone on long enough, said:

"So is our annual dinner to become a monthly occasion?"

The men laughed, relaxed, and once again the champagne corks began to pop. The moment had come to talk of wives. Joubert discreetly checked his pocket watch as he thought of his own wife . . .

. . . Léonce, who, at that very moment, was on all fours, panting and moaning to the vigorous thrusts of a young man named Robert.

Someone pounded on the wall, are you nearly done in there? A woman's voice, shrill, angry. Léonce dissolved into giggles and collapsed onto the bed, dear God, such intense pleasure, it hardly seems possible, she was bathed in sweat. Robert was on fine form. Two minutes, my love, she pleaded. She rolled onto her back. The room was small and poorly ventilated, the air was thick with the smell of sex, of tar, of perspiration, trickles of condensation rolled down the windowpanes, could you open the window a little? The cool air revived her. She fanned herself as sweat beaded on her belly, her breasts. Robert lit a cigarette and sat on the edge of the bed. Without thinking, Léonce reached out, took his penis and began to stroke it; to her, it was like fingering a rosary.

"I think perhaps I should go. What time is it?"

Robert pretended to check the time.

"Where is your watch?"

He blushed.

"Oh no, you haven't sold it already?"

A thousand-franc watch with multiple dials that Léonce had given him only a month earlier.

Angrily, she got up and disappeared behind the folding screen that hid the washbasin and the towels. It was impossible to imagine a more slender figure, more curvaceous hips, more delicate breasts, more generous buttocks, a more carefully plucked quim, even Robert, who was not given to emotion, found her breathtaking.

While she busied herself with a swift toilette, she popped her head around the partition. He was still sitting on the bed, looking contrite. Léonce smiled, she found him endearing.

He was a man of about thirty, with a long, straight nose and close-set eyes with low brows. His thick lips were almost always parted to reveal yellowish teeth; if someone asked how he came by the scar on his cheek or the deformed ear, he would say he had been in a hunting accident, which was true after a fashion. The consequences of the incident meant that people either found him uncouth or frankly intimidating. Some women feared him. Léonce, with her taste for young thugs, was immediately entranced.

In civilian life, he was an automobile mechanic. As least, this was how he had begun his career because he had large, clumsy hands and had no aptitude for schoolwork, he had passed no exams, even a primary school certificate was beyond his reach, so he had quickly been made an apprentice. He had done his time washing parts in petrol for mechanics who thought of themselves as managers because they had a single employee under their heel. Robert loved cars, less for the mechanics than for the pleasure of driving, of climbing behind the wheel; some girls found it titillating, and these were precisely the ones Robert found attractive. He had hardly been apprenticed for a year when he began to come by on Sundays if the weather was fine, roll up the shutters at the back of the garage and borrow some car that was waiting to be collected. Since he had no money, when he got back he had to siphon a little petrol from the other vehicles to fill the tank. The taste was a little unpleasant, but not enough to put him off.

By nineteen, he had already taken countless spins in luxurious automobiles that he would never be able to afford. His brother would find the girls, he would borrow the cars and, at the end of the evening, they returned the cars and kept the girls, what splendid times they had! These had come to an end one night, in a Farman A6B Super Sport on the stroke of one o'clock in the morning, when a young lady who was a little merry from too much bubbly had dipped her head under the steering wheel to demonstrate her gratitude to Robert, who was so distracted that the car careened off a Peugeot Bébé, a Fiat Type 3 and a Citroën 11 CV before coming to rest in the shop window of a florist. Curiously, his garage owner had not dismissed him. He had simply given him a new role.

Since that day, Robert had been repaying his debt by dismantling stolen car parts and tampering with others destined for the export market. It was a fruitful apprenticeship.

Robert was pure instinct. Capable of thinking, granted, but not for long. He had always found it difficult to project beyond a week. This inability to imagine consequences made him a pleasure-seeker. He was childlike in the sense that, to him, only the present existed. The slightest effort was a struggle, he preferred to take what was on offer – a girl, a car, a banknote – indeed it is not entirely clear that he could differentiate between the three. Robert was not much of a thinker, but he was gifted with a sort of intuitive intelligence, he sensed things, he was a past master at taking cover when he needed, taking advantage when he could, taking his pleasure when it was offered, and taking to his heels when in danger.

After two years of purgatory working at the coalface, Robert woke one morning and instinctively knew that his debt was paid. This was who he was, there were no shades of grey, it was yes or no, and right now, it was no.

In fact, as he walked towards that garage in Saint-Mandé, he became convinced that he had extravagantly overpaid the original debt, thus had credit, and therefore wanted to leave with an automobile, not necessarily a large or "deluxe" model, for, by his lights, a car perfectly symbolised his freedom. The garage owner saw things rather differently. He lashed out with a car jack and Robert spent two months at La Santé, where he made new friends.

When he was discharged, he was a different man. He was done with garages (although his passion for automobiles was undimmed) and with working for others. Robert decided to work for himself. Being good with his hands, knowledgeable about mechanics, and streetwise, he had all the necessary skills to become a burglar, except that he lacked a strategy. So began a long series of capers whose common thread was that they never panned out as expected. After two hours struggling with a lock, he would finally manage to gain entry to an apartment only to find it empty, since the tenant had moved out two days earlier, he happened on safes whose doors were already open, on jewellery so obviously fake that fences laughed in his face, he encountered police officers at garden gates, all in all, he found it difficult to eke out a living.

Never for a moment did Robert imagine that his approach lacked method. To him, these uncertainties came with the profession. He first felt a flicker of doubt when he was surprised on the ground floor of a shop by a woman who, without warning, fired a shotgun at him. He managed to duck just in time, but shards of shattered porcelain ripped his cheek and sliced off half his ear, and he escaped bleeding like a stuck pig. As he once more left the hospital, he began to query his chosen vocation.

It was at this point that he was swept up in the Great War.

Wounded in the shoulder in his first battle, he had got through the rest of the war without pain or glory, attempting to have himself transferred to a new hospital, a new post.

Once demobbed, he had done "this and that", as he euphemistically called the string of shady deals that, one day, forced him to flee France. It was in Casablanca that he had met Léonce.

Léonce heard a clock strike two, if I don't hurry, I'll be late. She just had time for a quick wash, no time to iron the clothes she kept hanging on the folding screen. She loathed this hotel. More prostitutes prowled the corridors than there were cars on the place de l'Opéra. But this was Robert's thing. If a place was sordid, he felt like a fish in water. And the hotel was in the ninth arrondissement, on rue Joubert. That was another reason he had chosen it.

"Rue Joubert! Comical, isn't it? I have to say, I love the guy . . ."

"You're not the one who has to sleep with him," Léonce almost said, but Robert was selective and impulsive in his jealousies, and could be a little too free with his hands, and while Léonce enjoyed a little spanking, Robert did not always stop at that.

She was slipping into her petticoat when Robert popped his head around the screen and stroked her breast: "See you tomorrow?" She barely had time to turn around before he vanished, running to check the results of the races he had missed.

As she finished her cursory toilette, Léonce thought about Joubert. She had never been able to stand him, she hated everything about him, his smell, his skin, his breath, his voice. She could not help but wonder what his late wife had done – when it came to sex, he was as ignorant as a choirboy. Not even that: when she was a choirgirl, she had been quite familiar with the beast with two backs. This was the problem with late bloomers, they wanted to make up for lost time, but deep down she was more bothered by his snoring than by his seminarian proclivities, he had little stamina, so staring at the ceiling for fifteen minutes was hardly a penance.

Léonce had done well out of this venture. She had money (Joubert was generous to a fault), and free time (he turned a blind eye). It had required only that she marry him.

She hurriedly left the hotel. Out on the boulevard, her legs still felt like jelly. She looked at herself in a shop window before hailing a taxi. She had less than half an hour to transform herself into the model of a young bourgeois lady, more time than she needed.

Joubert and his wife checked their watches at precisely the same moment.

He was a little worried. According to tradition, at these dinners women were talked about but never seen. And so when, following her husband's instructions, Léonce burst into the room and apologised, I'm so sorry, I thought the dinner would be over, and turned and made as if to leave, Joubert realised he had scored a direct hit on his fellows, all of whom were stunned by the beauty of Léonce, no, no, Madame Joubert, there's no need to apologise, their eyes fixed on her face, on her hips, those who could see her in profile stared at her pert buttocks. She was wearing a ravishing gown of ivory crêpe de Chine, her hair was pinned with a comb of black Galalith. Please stay, madame, take a seat! Joubert was lapping it up. Sacchetti, who found himself seated next to Léonce, noticed that, beneath the haze of Coty perfume, this devilish woman exuded a powerful sexual scent.

Monsieur Dupré stopped in his tracks, the other labourers leaving the workshop pushed past him. Madeleine Péricourt, who was standing on the opposite pavement, could not be there by chance, especially since she was staring at him. He crossed the road.

"Good day, Monsieur Dupré."

He touched the brim of his cap by way of greeting. Madeleine's presence left him ill at ease. They had met once by chance – when was that, last autumn? – and had found little to say to each other. It had been a painful encounter. He had told her he was a foreman in a welding and fitting shop on rue de Châteaudun, not difficult to find.

"Might we . . ."

She gestured down the street, she wished to speak to him, the pavement was not the place.

They walked as far as rue Saint-Georges, he stepped to one side and opened the door of Chez Germaine, where he sometimes came for lunch. He led her down to the back of the café. In the room next door, men playing billiards were shouting to one another, no-one would overhear them. She ordered a lemonade, he ordered Vichy water. Did he not drink beer or wine, like other men, she wondered. To play for time, she studied the place with exaggerated interest, as though he had brought her to a place he often talked about and she was only now discovering for herself. This bourgeois lady in her hat had piqued the curiosity of other patrons, but Monsieur Dupré was a stocky man, he radiated physical strength, and something about his ears and his bleary eyes discouraged people from prying into his business. The billiard players returned to their game.

"What can I do for you, Madame Péricourt?"

Madeleine sipped her lemonade, Dupré had not touched his glass, he sat stiffly, staring at her.

"I came . . . to ask your advice."

"My advice?"

Mistrust was written on his face. He glanced from his hands to the table and from there to the billiard room. She took the plunge:

"I am looking for someone, you see."

"For whom?"

"Oh, no-one in particular, no, it is not that, I am looking . . . for someone . . . for a job. There, for a job."

"What kind of job?"

Again, his eyes darted around the room; Madeleine nervously drummed her fingers on the table.

"An . . . an investigation, one might call it. Into some people."

He nodded, an investigation, very well. The situation was taking a curious turn, he sat in silence, encouraging her to continue, but Madeleine trailed off, she seemed to have said all she had to say. Dupré sipped his Vichy water. "Investigations into people" invariably involved couples, adultery. If Madame Péricourt wished to have a lover, a future husband or a rival investigated, what did it have to do with him?

"There are people who specialise in such work, Madame Péricourt, private inquiry agents. They watch and wait, they know the law . . . They know when to call in the police to, well, you know, to catch the couple in flagrante."

"Oh!" said Madeleine, realising his misunderstanding. "It is nothing of that kind, Monsieur Dupré!"

"What kind, then?"

"Well . . . to watch people, as you say, to find out certain things."

"Things that might harm them, is that it?"

"Yes, that's it!"

Madeleine felt relieved. She gave a satisfied smile.

"And how exactly does this concern me?"

"I simply wondered if, by chance . . ."

"I would be the sort of man to undertake such work?"

"Oh no, Monsieur Dupré, not at all! No, dear God, not you . . . But perhaps you might know someone . . ."

Monsieur Dupré folded his arms. He kneaded his muscles and collected his thoughts.

"You think I know men who might do such work?"

"Well, yes, I thought, perhaps . . ."

"You are looking for a crook, and since your husband is otherwise detained, you have come to me."

"No, I assure you, it is not that at all . . ."

"Oh, but that's exactly what you are doing. I don't really know what it is you want, but you clearly need a rogue, and you assume you can find them among the lower classes."

Anyone observing this conversation would never have guessed from Monsieur Dupré's outward calm that things had taken an ugly turn.

"To a banker's daughter, I suppose a labourer and a crook are much the same thing."

Madeleine tried to interrupt.

"More than that, you assume that the man who once worked as your husband's foreman must be no better than his boss. That he must know people who are prepared to do anything, it's quite logical."

It was a perfectly reasonable accusation. What saddened Madeleine more than the prospect of leaving empty-handed and having to reconsider the problem was that, essentially, the man was correct.

"You are right, Monsieur Dupré, I have behaved very badly towards you."

She got to her feet.

"And I apologise."

Her sincerity was obvious. Hardly had she taken two steps from the table when Monsieur Dupré called her back.

"You didn't answer. Why get in touch with me?"

"I know no-one now, Monsieur Dupré. And no-one deigns to know me. I could do nothing – nothing but wait and hope – and, I don't know why, I thought of you."

"'All human wisdom is contained in these two words – Wait and Hope,'" Dupré murmured almost to himself, then he looked into Madeleine's eyes. "And on whom would you have revenge, Madame Péricourt?"

Everything was simple now. There was no need to lie.

"A former banker, a member of parliament with the Alliance Démocratique, and a journalist at *Soir de Paris*."

She smiled broadly.

"As you see, they are all well-bred people. Oh, there is also a former employ— Well, a former friend . . . I mean . . ."

"Sit down, Madame Péricourt."

Madeleine hesitated and then took her seat.

"How much are you prepared to pay for this work?"

"That would have to be agreed . . . I have no experience."

"I earn one thousand and eighty francs a month."

The sum shocked Madeleine. She had been struggling to save for three years, and she was still a long way off that.

"It will be a long and difficult job, one that requires skill. I am a skilled labourer. I cannot work for less than that."

After a moment's thought, he added:

"Plus expenses, naturally."

"So, you would . . ."

Monsieur Dupré planted his elbows on the table, leaned closer to Madeleine and whispered:

"Madame Péricourt, I am not asking you why you want to bring these people down. You are looking for someone to do it, I know how to do it, that I can guarantee. My price is my current monthly salary, not one centime more or less. Think about it. You know where to find me."

They were already on their feet, it had all happened so fast, they were at the door. Madeleine quickly opened her handbag when she saw that Monsieur Dupré was about to pay. He raised a warning hand.

"You have already insulted me once today, do not try it a second time."

He paid the bill and, out in the street, nodded a goodbye and turned on his heel.

He lived four Métro stations away, but, rain or shine, he always made the journey on foot, it was a point of principle. Monsieur Dupré was a man of principle.

He brooded over the decision he had so impetuously made. The more he thought about it, the more he felt it had been the right decision. A senior banking executive, she had said, a member of the Alliance Démocratique, it sounded a lot like the Banque d'Escompte et de Crédit Industriel, generally known as the Banque Péricourt, which had collapsed some months earlier and cost hundreds of minor investors their savings, and the member of parliament who had conveniently avoided disaster. As for the journalist at *Soir de Paris*, a reactionary rag, it hardly mattered who it was, they were all as bad as each other.

The reader will doubtless be wondering, as Madeleine did, what reasons could have prompted a labourer like Dupré to accept such a proposition. It was simple: this was a man who had gone to war believing, as so many did, that this would be the war to end all wars. He had answered the call of his nation, and had kept his word, but the nation had not kept its promises. He had spent thirty months in a gruesome hell that had cost him both his brothers and everything he possessed (he had lived in northern France, where every village was razed), and now it seemed to him increasingly likely that the Great War would be followed by another. After he was demobbed, he had worked for Madeleine Péricourt's husband, Henri d'Aulnay-Pradelle, a penniless aristocrat and ruthless social climber who had exploited his workforce, Dupré first and foremost, in the same way that, as an officer, he had exploited his troops. He would have sent the former to their deaths just as calmly as he had the latter. The power of wealth, the cynicism of capitalists, the blatant social injustice, all these things told Dupré that the 1917 revolution had already faltered. His demobilisation, the difficulty of finding work in a France indifferent to its heroes, the depressing experience of working as foreman for d'Aulnay-Pradelle, all of these things had rekindled his erstwhile communist instincts. He had joined the Communist Party in 1920, only to leave it a year later. After four years of war, he found the hierarchy and the discipline too difficult to deal with. But he still nurtured a furious desire to change the system, he had developed a highly personal form of anarchy. Too rational to plant bombs indiscriminately, as people used to do (he did not believe in sacrificial victims), or to assassinate the Président de la République (he did not believe in symbolic gestures) and too individualistic to militate within an organisation (he did not believe in the collective), he lived alone and said little, because he rarely encountered people who shared his opinions. And individualism that bordered on egotism had made him a recluse. Society is very lucky that I didn't turn to violence, he often thought. Deep down, he was a libertarian, in the way that other people are Christian: for himself, feeling no need to demonstrate his faith. Nor had he been convinced by the prospect of a world without private property, governed by free association. Not because he did not subscribe to anarchist theories, but because, sapped by war and by post-war apathy, his instincts were purely negative.

He was frequently forced to change jobs because he took every opportunity that presented itself to support workers' demands, to argue in favour of strikes, to challenge the powers that be – it never ended well.

For Dupré, the thought of ruining a banker, of crushing a bourgeois parliamentarian, of bringing down a yellow journalist, was simply another way of helping to foster disorder and instability – a modest form of sabotage, certainly not heroic (he did not believe in heroes), precisely the sort of job that made him feel as though he was usefully contributing to the rising chaos.

It was a small room, but the principal problem was not the size, it was the noise. Not the noise from the neighbours, but the noise he was forbidden to make.

Once his room had been finished, and Paul had put the first record on the gramophone ("Turandot", Act II, Solange as the Princess: *In questa reggia, or son mill'anni e mille, un grido disperato risonò*),

Monsieur Clérambeau had pounded on the floor of his apartment with a broom handle. Two minutes later, he had rung the doorbell. Vladi, with a beaming smile, had opened the door as though expecting a wedding party.

"Witam!"

Monsieur Clérambeau had been horrified.

"W czym mogę pomóc?"

He had stomped back upstairs. "I'm hardly going to argue with a Polack!" he said to Madeleine the next time he came.

Every time Paul put on a record, Monsieur Clérambeau grabbed his broom. Madeleine was caught in a dilemma. Moving Paul's wheelchair around was difficult, though not impossible. Forbidding him from listening to music was unthinkable.

"It d-d-doesn't m-m-matter, Ma-ma-maman . . ." Paul would say.

Vladi and Madeleine stood for some time staring helplessly at the silent gramophone, at the posters and at the photographs on the wall.

"Chyba znalazłam rozwiązanie . . ." Vladi said, pointing towards the ceiling.

She disappeared for much of the afternoon. When Madeleine had to carry Paul to the toilet herself, she realised there was no doubt, he had put on weight.

At about six o'clock, Vladi reappeared, accompanied by a young labourer with pale skin and wide-set eyes who was wearing dusty overalls and nervously rubbing his hands. Vladi gazed at him affectionately and, with a jerk of her chin, gestured for him to explain himself. Instead, he simply opened the blue bag he had set on the floor and took out a cork tile as thick as his thumb.

"You stick it on the walls. And the ceiling."

Madeleine thought the idea sounded promising, but was worried about the cost, everything always came down to money. There could be no question of asking for a discount, but a considerable number of tiles would be needed. Not to mention the adhesive, and the labour . . .

The young labourer (his name was Jacques, they learned on the day before he dropped out of circulation) opened his mouth, Vladi took his hand, pressed it against her chest, she was half a head taller than he was, she smiled at him proudly, as though he were a son about to recite his party piece.

"It's all been arranged. With . . ."

He could not remember Vladi's first name, but it was all arranged. The work took two weeks.

The room looked as though it had shrunk by a square metre. Stepping inside, the muffled atmosphere was slightly unsettling, but its efficacy was indisputable. Paul placed "Turandot" back on the gramophone.

Had it not been made necessary by their intense correspondence, Paul might never have told Solange of his change of address. She asked questions: *Are you happy in your new home? I imagine you have a much bigger room, don't you?* She was surprised that he gave her no details.

They had not seen each other since the night in Milan, despite the fact that Solange had invited him to come to London, where she had appeared in October 1931, then to Vienna four months later. Paul always politely declined; due to problems that he never speci-fied, he could not travel. He never mentioned the invitations to his mother. Some months earlier, his father, Henri d'Aulnay-Pradelle, having been recently released from prison, had visited, ostensibly "to say goodbye to his son", but actually to ask for money, he was leaving for the colonies to try to "build a new life for himself". The sight of his wife's reduced circumstances had brought a smug, cruel smile to his face, as if he saw it as some higher judgment. Humili-ated, Madeleine had wept for hours. Since then, Paul had avoided raising the subject of money, and, hence, there were many other things that could not be discussed. Poverty was a real problem.

The growing malaise Solange felt was not based on anything tangible, the letters Paul wrote were increasingly interesting, he was growing up, maturing, and his knowledge of opera was impressive, but she could have sworn that he was buying fewer scores, he no longer asked Solange for concert posters, although he was always grateful when she sent them. Had he been disappointed by his trip to Italy? Had his mother taken it badly? Moreover, the reasons Paul had given for his mother's absence had been vague . . . If Solange did not realise that Paul was no longer buying records, it was only because he was still listening to them at Paris-Phono, where the salesman was amenable.

Meanwhile, Solange's career had taken a somewhat curious turn. Since her engagement in Milan, she sang sitting down, which was both a mystery and a challenge to the law of physiology. Technically, such a constricted airstream should not produce such sounds, it was impossible. And yet, her recitals went from strength to strength. Her voice was perhaps a little huskier, but that only added to its character, her breathing, somewhat shortened because of her weight, forced her to perform verbal gymnastics that gave a unique colour to her interpretations. Solange was as imposing as a cathedral, tragic, and *sui generis*. The broad face, the haunted eyes, the sagging jowls, the generous body enfolded by stately swathes of taffeta was as surprising as a Buddha singing countertenor.

The flowers with which she initially surrounded herself had given way to a set. Some weeks after her performance in Milan, she had engaged the services of Robert Mallet-Stevens, the celebrated designer, to create a backdrop for her. The result had been a huge success. This staging, through somewhat stilted, had become a part of her performance. When Solange appeared in London, she commissioned a set by Stephen Owenbury. For her Rome recitals, she commissioned Wassily Kandinsky to paint huge canvases; for a performance in Madrid, she asked Pablo Picasso. As the months passed, numerous artists provided paintings, from Raoul Dufy to

Mickaël Zeug, vast creations destined to accompany the recitals of the woman known as La Gallinato, which were invariably an event. In her choice of artists, she showed a preference for women. Sonia Delaunay created a sea of deep blue veils that rippled thanks to the bellows hidden in the wings. This was merely the start of a series of installations by Violetta Gomez, Laura Mackiewicz and Katia Noaraud, which reached a sort of apogee with the vast ensemble of Art Deco motifs created by Vanessa Newport that descended from the flies, one by one, during Solange's performance at the New York Met in March 1932.

It became tradition to make a great mystery of these artistic productions. Only the recital programme was released to the press; the name of the artist and the nature of the set were more closely guarded secrets than German rearmament. Until the curtain rose, no-one knew what it would be like. There were always those prepared to sell information to the local press, a veritable cottage industry of stolen images and information that worried theatre managers but delighted Solange, who loved indiscretions, as long as she was the star. Two days after a performance, pictures of the set and the performance were being sold as postcards, as leaflets, as supplements, copies of which Solange would send to Paul, accompanied by a note strewn with exclamation marks. Indeed, in early 1932, a public auction was held of works created by Fernand Léger for the May recital in Lisbon, with profits being donated to the victims of the Yellow River floods.

In September 1932, Solange appeared in Paris at the Salle Gaveau (sets by Roger Harth). Paul and his mother were gifted front-row seats, next to the ministers of state. Solange appeared, in a torrent of green and purple veils, as imposing as a statue of the Commendatore, and, as always, began the recital with an a cappella version of the overture from "Gloria Mundi", which was fast becoming a classic aria, some of her rivals had already attempted it. The recital was a triumph.

Solange, as we know, was solipsistic. She gave the impression that she thought only of herself, and while she now remained seated, even during her curtain calls, she was no less effusive. But she had a keen eye, and when she saw Paul and his mother, it did not take a second for her to realise that they had come down in the world. Madeleine was well dressed, impeccably groomed, but she had lost something of that insouciance possessed by women of wealth, her step was a little more hesitant, her expression a little more unsure, it was barely noticeable, but Solange noticed. She instantly abandoned her plans for a sumptuous dinner and, feigning tiredness, invited Paul and Madeleine for a "little collation" in her room at the Ritz. Even that, she felt, was too luxurious, but it was the best she could manage at such short notice . . .

None of this escaped Madeleine's notice. Though annoyed, she was grateful to the singer for her tact. For the first time, the two women could have a sincere conversation and realise how sad it was to forsake their earlier rivalry. Madeleine could sense the shadow that sometimes flickered in the eyes of this enormous woman with her ridiculous, extravagant gestures whose tragic voice could pierce the cruellest soul. Perhaps, without saying as much, both women found themselves face to face with a sister who had suffered greatly.

From the four corners of the earth, Solange began to send scores, photographs were replaced by records, posters by boxed sets.

Although his mother's life was difficult and stressful, Paul was not unhappy. For Madeleine, it was a revelation to discover that one could be happier with less money. Relieved of his painful secret, Paul was experiencing perhaps one of the most radiant periods of his life. The frequent nightmares had become sporadic. Vladi was a joyful, mischievous playmate. Paul would read voraciously, he spent whole afternoons at the library. Vladi would settle him in the reading room, surrounded by the newspapers and the books he had requested, then she would wink and say: "A teraz pójdę na zakupy . . ."

Paul would close his eyes, as though covering for the rash behaviour of a younger sister who was in his charge.

21

Women came before all other things. Being an anarchist does not make a man any less a man. And women had always been Dupré's weak spot. And when he saw the demoiselle, she only served to confirm his belief. It had been enough to see her face. Ravishing. As he shadowed her back to the taxi rank, he was keenly aware of the danger she represented to all those whose paths she crossed, he expected a pile-up at any moment. She exuded sex the way some men exude money. She did not walk, she swayed. In two hours on rue Saint-Honoré, she spent the salary of ten labourers. This was Dupré's scale of reference, a labourer's salary. It was not difficult to see what she was doing with her husband, the former senior executive of the Banque Péricourt, she was squandering his fortune. But there was doubtless more where that had come from. The hôtel particulier alone was worth a small fortune, and its contents would double that valuation, two automobiles, a phalanx of servants, a burgeoning business with gleaming new machine tools and mechanics paid the union minimum, the Joubert household was thriving, and this made Dupré eager to unearth something.

When he saw Léonce Joubert head towards rue de la Victoire at ten o'clock, he did not follow her, but went into a café and ordered a glass of beer. She was going to meet her "piece of rough", one Robert Ferrand, face of a small-time thug, cap tilted over one eye, and the look of a pimp. Dupré would have happily given the fool a beating, but that was not his job. Ferrand lost every penny he got from Léonce on the horses, and Dupré had gone to the racecourse to check – it was a tidy sum. In fact, it was sad. That the rich were rich was unjust, but logical. But a lad like Robert Ferrand, clearly born in the gutter, allowing himself to be kept by some rich man's whore – that was vulgar. Humanity had little to recommend it.

As he sipped his beer, he decided it was time to look at the matter from another angle. He could not simply report back to Madame Péricourt on the machinations of a thug and the fact that Madame Joubert was keeping a lover, it was not enough. And not what she expected of him.

He checked his watch, paid for his beer, and headed for the town hall in the thirteenth arrondissement.

André Delcourt had been loyal to the salon of the Comtesse de Marsantes, whom he addressed informally as Marie-Aynard, because she had welcomed him back when he had been a nobody. Now, he was a somebody (by the standards of the boulevard Saint-Germain, which are somewhat relative) and he had gone from being a protégé, to a mascot, to the crowning jewel of her little salon.

The columns he wrote for *Soir de Paris* were keenly awaited and eagerly devoured. He blossomed in the role of monastic intellectual, which he had adopted early in his career for want of funds. He took his leave from dinner parties early. Although rare, he opined, a man who worked late and rose early was a gentleman. He ate little, he did not drink. This frugality bordering on asceticism impressed many, and made it possible for him to accept every invitation, as many as six in a single week, to miss no encounter that might prove advantageous to his career, yet still retain the allure of an exceptional man. His address book was exhaustive, but no lawyer, no senator, no ministerial lackey could boast that they had helped André Delcourt's career. Being indebted to no-one, he was unassailable. He lived a tranquil life. He passed for a recluse, a pure spirit, and this was not far from the truth. He spent much of his time masturbating.

Jules Guilloteaux also frequented the salon of the Comtesse de

Marsantes. She adored the press, and journalists were her speciality. On such occasions, André behaved as though his boss was not there, responded to his witticisms in a roundabout fashion and demonstrated a bitterness that Guilloteaux pretended not to notice. As ever, it was a matter of money. Although André had become the star columnist of the most popular newspaper in the country, his salary had risen by only four francs since his first day.

That evening, André found himself at table with Adrien Montet-Bouxal, with whom he had travelled to Rome in 1930 for the celebrations in honour of Virgil and Mistral. The member of the Académie Française had made a brilliant speech. Although André had tried to join in conversations about the Italian Renaissance, the works of Michelangelo, the scabrous private life of Caravaggio, the trip had left a bitter taste, he had felt utterly mediocre. All the more so because, on his return, André had penned a series of sensational articles published as *New Italian Chronicles,* whose allusion to Stendhal hardly smacked of modesty.

Over supper, the elderly Academician had reminisced about the journey, but in this telling, what André had once considered a celebration of the intellect now sounded like a drab occasion filled with petty details.

"What can you expect? I was tasked with offering the encomium to Virgil, so naturally, the whole delegation was against me . . ."

For Montet-Bouxal, the whole journey was reduced to the comparative sizes of hotel rooms, the disadvantageous seating plan at the ambassador's dinner, the order of signatories in a visitor's book. The Comtesse de Marsantes was clearly aware that André took these remarks as a personal insult, since they belittled his trip and, by extension, his articles. At the first opportunity, she intervened.

"What about you, dear André, what do you think of Italy?"

The line was baited for a little speech that André liked to give:

"Western civilisation is the daughter of ancient Rome . . ."

Once embarked on the subject, he could be almost lyrical.

"The 'Latin block' of France and Italy: this is the greatest bulwark against the German menace."

Fiercely hostile both to communism and Nazism, and a member of the Comité France-Italie, André saw Italian fascism as the antidote to the errant ways of parliamentarianism, which, he believed, was consuming Europe and leading to decadence. Discussions about the virtues of fascism constantly rippled the waters of this little world; it was in the air.

"Any news of dear Madame Péricourt?" asked Jules Guilloteaux.

They were on the street, waiting for a taxi.

"Very little . . ."

She sent him a note from time to time, suggesting that they have tea somewhere. In André's life, Madeleine was little more than a memory. He would have liked her to stop sending him invitations altogether, but she was clearly still clinging to the memories of a former life filled with regrets, memories that she needed in order to survive. He had gone to her home only once. Thankfully, little Paul had been out, but the apartment had been bleak. The homes of the newly poor are just like those of the nouveau riche, everything is on display. Witnessing Madeleine's fall in status compared to his meteoric rise was painful for him because he remembered a time when he had needed her. This was the one thing he feared: that she might remind him of that fact. Worse still, that she might speak of it to others and the rumour would spread. He had not risen to his current rank without making numerous enemies who would be only too delighted to chuckle at his past as a "kept boy" during the months he had lived at the Péricourt home without working, a furtive lover hidden in the servants' quarters . . . How hard it would be to survive such a stigma. And so, as a precaution, he met with Madeleine occasionally, at her insistence, for as brief a time as possible. Madeleine never made the least reproach, the slightest demand, she simply wanted to see him, to talk to him for a while. She looked older now, she had put on weight, she would talk about Paul who – she said – was growing up. André would pretend to take an interest in her and her son, but, at the first opportunity, he would remember an appointment, an obligation, and would rush off, furious that he had allowed himself to be put in such a situation.

"Jules . . ."

"Yes?"

Guilloteaux was leaning into the street, as though watching an imaginary taxi.

"I have had a number of offers . . ." André ventured.

"What, again? You've had a glimpse of fame and suddenly my newspaper isn't good enough for you!"

"That is not it at all."

"Of course it is! Your column helps to sell newspapers and you feel that your earnings are too meagre. Do you have the slightest idea what our accounts look like?"

In his desk drawer, Guilloteaux invariably had a few columns of falsified figures that indisputably proved that, far from making money, *Soir de Paris* was costing money and, for months, had been on the brink of ruin, and that it was only because of the determination of its managing editor, to say nothing of his personal funds, that it continued to be published, and, if it were up to me, I would shut up shop, but what can you do, a hundred families depend on this newspaper. And I don't have the heart to see them thrown them out onto the street, *et cetera*.

"It is not simply a matter of money, it's a matter of principle."

"God's teeth! Since when did anyone in this business have principles?"

"I deserve more than I am earning."

"Well, then, go and look elsewhere, I don't have a sou to my name. What can you do? There is a financial crisis."

André gritted his teeth. His managing editor knew exactly what he was doing: although André might indeed be in demand, and might have received offers that were financially more rewarding, there was no other newspaper with the circulation of *Soir de Paris*. To move to any other newspaper, even for an increased salary, would be a demotion.

He was trapped. And he had begun to hate Jules Guilloteaux.

Past noon. Léonce was running late.

Every time she had to walk past the full-length portrait of Marcel Péricourt, she shivered, he eyed her scornfully, haughty and severe . . . Joubert had paid two thousand francs for this daub; she would not have paid a centime. It was the one thing that he had insisted on keeping.

When the subject had first been raised, the prospect of living in the house of her former friend (or former employer, depending on one's point of view) had tormented Léonce. Guilt still gnawed at her, she longed to explain herself to Madeleine, but there would be so much to say . . . Besides, a woman she had helped to ruin was hardly likely to listen to her reasons and find them acceptable.

Léonce was about to leave when she heard Gustave's voice downstairs. Good God, what kind of time was this for him to come home! She hid on the landing and waited for him to go into the library, then she hurried downstairs to the kitchen and rang for the maid.

"Can you tell the master that I had to go out before he got home?"

The maidservant fetched Léonce's coat, her hat and her gloves. Léonce slipped her a banknote and left by the servants' entrance. On the rue de Prony, she hailed a taxi, furious with herself, as she was every time that she solicited the collusion of the servants. She would never truly be the lady of the house. Gustave, who knew this only too well, often talked about engaging a housekeeper. Obviously, this was no more than a threat, a way of telling his wife that she needed to pay attention to how much she was stealing from him, a way of proving how accommodating he was, in this as in so many other things. It was also a veiled allusion to the comic little scene he had forced Léonce to play when she was still a lady's companion to Madeleine. Joubert had surprised Léonce dipping her hand in Madeleine's purse – Robert was constantly asking her for money – and she had not known which way to turn. It would have been futile to lie, Joubert had all the power. But with unerring instinct, Léonce had sensed that Joubert's stiff, austere persona masked an almost total lack of sexual experience. It had taken her less than an hour to make him pop like a champagne cork. Afterwards, following his directions, she had played her role for Madeleine, sobbing, feigning contrition and shame while Madeleine squirmed with embarrassment. This act of betrayal had allowed Léonce to up the ante. As a permanent fixture in Joubert's fantasies, she was now on the road to becoming a kept woman and Robert could go to the racecourse every day.

And then, disaster. Joubert did not see things in the same light. He insisted they marry. Léonce paled. She had done everything she could to be the perfect mistress, only to find herself relegated to being a wife. Using every feminine wile, she had had Joubert scraping himself off the ceiling to remind him of the things one can do with a mistress that one cannot do with a wife, but when he finally managed to catch his breath, he had not changed his mind, either she agreed to become Madame Gustave Joubert or she could get out right now. She had been careful to say nothing of this proposal of marriage to Robert, who would not have given her a moment's peace until she agreed. He also had instincts. Three days later, he had racked up a five thousand-franc debt. Léonce had gone to Joubert, accepted his proposal of marriage and asked him for an advance of six thousand francs on the costs of the wedding.

Oh, dear God, the wedding . . .! Lo and behold, Robert had wanted to attend the reception and pass himself off as a guest. He had appeared amid the bankers, the society ladies, shareholders and politicians wearing his checked suit, honest to God! He had drunk like a fish, been taken for an interloper and thrown out on his ear, giggling and winking lasciviously at the bride . . . Léonce could not help but laugh up her sleeve. Fortunately, Joubert had seen nothing, he had been at the far end of the garden.

One o'clock. Léonce let out a deep breath. She could be at rue Joubert in less than half an hour. Robert was probably already lying on the bed, smoking a cigarette.

From the drawing-room window, Joubert spotted Léonce in the taxi as it turned onto boulevard de Courcelles.

From the very beginning, he had had her followed, not to gather information on her indiscretions, which were an implicit part of their contract, but to ensure that she did not one day put him in a difficult position, at the centre of a scandal.

René Delgas, he discovered. Very well, René Delgas it would be, then. Joubert learned that he was a small-time crook and impecunious. Of all the possible lovers she could take, Delgas was the most suitable since the man was penniless. So much the better, he would not leave Léonce while he still needed money and Joubert needed a wife who was composed. There had been a time when Joubert could allow himself to be the subject of vague rumours, but he was a different man now.

A very different man . . . He almost surprised himself.

Take shoes, for example. Time was, he would not have given them a second thought. Now he loved shoes. Hand-crafted. Two thousand francs a pair, he even had a boot black, a little black boy who came by his office three times a week. Then there were the suits, and the shirts . . . He had not realised he could be elegant. Léonce had exquisite taste in such things. Without her, he could have built a fortune and squatted, in a three-piece suit bought a decade earlier, on a pile of gold that would make even Rothschild blench. When she had scampered into his bed with the skittishness of a cat and sent him soaring like a rocket, the fireworks had left him breathless.

With Léonce, he had truly hit the jackpot. He could boast that he had one of the most enchanting wives in Paris, dignified in company, discreet at city dinners, decorous on every occasion, and at home a peerless strumpet.

An instantaneous fortune, an enviable position, a magnificently decorative wife . . . Good God, he had even bought the Péricourt house. When he left his home, he always glanced at the portrait of Marcel Péricourt. What the man had achieved was as nothing compared to Joubert's plans.

Léonce had the taxi drop her off on the corner of rue Caumartin. As a precaution. Joubert had had a detective follow her before he published the banns, so he would know exactly what he was dealing with. As though she would not expect it. Joubert might be a great mind in matters of finance, but when it came to life experience, he was a neophyte.

Rather fat, with a nose like a turnip and a bushy black beard, the detective looked a little like Ribouldingue from the *Pied Nickelés*. She had led him through shops and through galleries (such a bore – art, honestly she could not see the point of it), she had to slacken her pace so that he did not lose sight of her. She had let him shadow her for a day or two, before leading him to a hotel on the rue du Bac, where she holed up in a room with René. René Delgas, a friend Robert had met "on his travels", as he referred to his spells in prison. Léonce had been extremely exacting as to the candidate, she did not want her future husband to think that she was prepared to take just anyone as her lover. Nor did she want him to find out about Robert.

René had proved suitable. A handsome young man who dabbled in various things. In fact, though it was a closely guarded secret, he was a forger, one of the finest in Paris. They had spent the afternoon in the hotel room smoking and talking, and afterwards, Léonce had crept out, hugging the walls like a sneak thief and glancing behind her to feign concern and to check that Ribouldingue was still following.

Joubert was suspicious by nature; he had had her followed for more than two weeks.

Then, once he was reassured, Ribouldingue had moved on to other couples, other hotels, other clients. It had come at just the right moment, since she was beginning to tire of the charade. René was charging a hundred francs to sleep through the afternoon, to say nothing of the cost of the hotel.

22

A great commotion reigned in the hangars of Pré-Saint-Gervais. Workers on ladders had just finished mounting a large sign:

RENAISSANCE FRANÇAISE
AERONAUTICS ATELIER

Inside, Joubert had rounded up all the journalists present, some twenty in all, who were staring up at the elevated platform that circled the vast hangar, which was lined with glass offices furnished with tables, chairs and blackboards.

From a large vehicle, labourers unloaded two gleaming new Lefebvre-Strudal machine tools.

"The French aviation industry," Joubert began, "comprises a hundred aeroplanes made by ten different manufacturers equipped with fifteen different types of engine. It is completely chaotic!"

The assembled company felt as though they had missed an episode. They had no idea what they were doing here.

"Well," Joubert continued, "this atelier has gathered together all the major aeronautical companies from France and Britain."

A question floated over the group of journalists like a cloud of unknowing: to what purpose?

Joubert gave a broad smile and explained.

"Huh? What?" someone yelled. "I didn't hear, can you say that again, give a man some space, could you please repeat that?"

Joubert glanced left and right, and noticed a wooden crate that was lying there seemingly by chance. He stepped onto it, the crowd fell silent and Joubert repeated what he had said in a measured tone that underscored the simplicity of his proposal:

"We are going to build the world's first jet-propelled aeroplane here. We are going to revolutionise the aeronautics industry."

No-one quite knew what the phrase "jet-propelled aeroplane" meant. They remembered only one thing: up until now, aeroplanes had been powered by propellers; a jet-propelled aeroplane not only had no propellers, it would fly much faster.

Three days later, this fact was on the lips of all those gathered around the huge dining table at La Closerie des Lilas.

The aperitifs were flowing freely, and the atmosphere was gay by the time Joubert arrived, escorted by his wife, who was admired precisely because she did not look like a wife.

Joubert greeted his guests warmly, especially Monsieur Lefebvre, proprietor and director of Lefebvre-Strudal, whose business accounted for sixty per cent of Mécanique Joubert . . .

Even André Delcourt had not been able to resist accepting the invitation. He had always cordially disliked Gustave Joubert, and the sentiment was entirely mutual. But he had watched the success of Renaissance Française from afar, and in his constant quest for reassurance he wanted to prove that he, too, had become someone.

"Delcourt! Come, dear boy! Come!"

Joubert was on his feet, his arms wide.

André humbly indicated that he would be happy with a seat at the far end of the table, no, no, no, Joubert gestured commandingly.

There was jostling, a scrape of chairs, a clatter of forks, a glass was overturned, Joubert ducked, sending a ripple of laughter around the table, a new place was set next to Joubert, who now found himself sitting opposite Sacchetti and Guilloteaux with Léonce to his right and André Delcourt to his left.

"So, my dear Joubert," Guilloteaux bellowed across the table, "you're planning to win the next war single-handed!"

The comment elicited chuckles and Joubert accepted the quip with good grace.

A journalist from *Le Figaro* interrupted:

"You think the French aviation industry isn't up to the job?"

Joubert set down his fork and laid his hands flat on either side of his plate, seeming to consider how best to explain.

"Two years ago, the French government bought some aeroplanes, the prototype for which has yet to make a successful flight. And do you know how many they bought? Fifty! Meanwhile, under Hitler, Germany is rearming. Her intentions are hostile. The French army will need aeroplanes that are lightning-fast."

This notion of speed resonated with all those present. Over the past fifteen years, speed had been steadily increasing – automobiles and trains moved faster, the world turned more quickly, there seemed little reason to think that the heavens would be exempt from this worldwide speed race. The idea of a war breaking out suddenly, of an army advancing like a galloping tide at Mont-Saint-Michel, was familiar to everyone.

"The ideal would be to come close to the speed of sound," Joubert went on. "But we have settled on seven to eight hundred kilometres per hour, that would be a good start."

This swaggering statement instantly divided opinions between those who thought Joubert was arrogant and those who thought he was insane.

"And you have the means to do that?" came the exasperated voice of the reporter for *L'Intransigeant*.

"We have a very solid British patent."

The patent was that of an English physicist who, lacking the five pounds necessary to renew it, had lost his rights. Joubert had picked it up for a song. And, as an elementary precaution, he had acquired it in his own name. Since Renaissance Française belonged to him and to him alone, the patent should too. It was logical. To manage the patent, he had set up a handsome company with the stentorian name La Nationale d'Aéronautique. The partners provide funding, the state provides subsidies, the clients place large orders with Mécanique Joubert, which rakes in the money, dispenses royalties to shareholders, while Joubert accepts the plaudits of the government and pockets the profits. It was time these people learned how a former banker could transform industry.

"What if the government does not support you?" said Guilloteaux.

Joubert slowly looked around the table.

"Then we shall get by without it. We are doing this for France. Governments come and go. France endures."

Scattered applause swelled to an ovation.

One of the diners got to his feet, others followed, Joubert gestured to the members of his association, who bowed their heads modestly.

"Tell me something, dear boy . . ."

Joubert had laid a hand on André's arm. It was half an hour later, the dinner was in full swing, the journalists had taken their glasses and had moved to sit among the industrialists in order to glean a little more information.

"I do hope you are planning to explicitly support our venture."

"I have no doubt that you will find many of my colleagues in the press are prepared to 'explicitly' support your venture," André replied.

Joubert nodded, very well, I see, he sighed a little wearily, stared straight ahead as though for a moment he had entirely forgotten his guests. Then he leaned towards André.

"Do you have any news of our dear Madeleine?"

"Very little. We see each other from time to time."

"Tell me, how long did you live in the Péricourt house?"

André swallowed hard.

"No, don't trouble yourself," Joubert said, once again laying a hand on the young man's arm. "It is of no importance, it was merely idle curiosity."

The following morning, on the front page of *Soir de Paris*, Madeleine read the thunderous declarations made by Joubert at La Closerie des Lilas.

She could not help but smile when she saw the photograph of Gustave Joubert, a picture of false modesty, seated between Léonce, more ravishing than ever, in a cloche hat and a triple-string pearl necklace, and André Delcourt, stone-faced, as though he had found himself there by accident and had no interest in the proceedings.

Madeleine was ecstatic. Although she had never smoked in her life, she felt an urge to light a cigarette.

She neatly folded the newspaper, summoned the waiter, paid for her coffee and left the café.

It was time to go and find dear Léonce.

23

They met each week. Monsieur Dupré was punctilious in making the reports that justified his salary. At first, they would meet in a café, but the clamour made things difficult and, besides, a lady, in a café, at night . . . Madeleine did not want the meetings to take place at her apartment, with Paul and Vladi nearby. Dupré had suggested they meet at his rooms. And so, every Wednesday, Vladi spent the evening with Paul while Madeleine visited the cramped third-floor rooms on rue de Championnet.

The bachelor apartment made Madeleine feel a little ill at ease, it was clean, tidy, impersonal, no photographs in frames, no reproductions on the walls, a faint smell of wax polish, little crockery, no books. It had that spartan anonymity one finds in hotel rooms.

The ritual was always the same. Dupré would greet Madeleine, she would remove her hat, he would take her coat and hang it on a peg, make some coffee, then they would sit on either side of the table. On the oilcloth, two cups, a sugar bowl and a coffee pot – all doubtless bought especially for these meetings – clashed with the decor. Monsieur Dupré would give his report as he sipped a coffee that he never finished. There was something flinty about him, it was impossible to imagine him falling ill, arguing with a neighbour, or finding any problem insoluble.

From time to time, they met elsewhere, as circumstances dictated. Madeleine had become so accustomed to seeing Dupré in his apartment that, in other settings, she felt something was amiss, as when one meets a shopkeeper one has only ever seen in his shop. So it had been today, at the tearoom on rue de Chazelles. Madeleine had watched him stride across the room, weaving between the tables set with white linen and the lamps with their guilloche shades: he was not the sort of person one expected to see there.

"The coast is clear," Dupré said, discreetly leaning towards her. "If you need me to stay . . ."

Madeleine was already on her feet.

"No, thank you, Monsieur Dupré. Everything will be fine."

Outside, they went their separate ways, Madeleine heading towards boulevard de Courcelles, Monsieur Dupré in the opposite direction.

She felt nothing when she saw the large, imposing gates of the hôtel particulier that people still referred to as "the Péricourt house", like those buildings razed by fire whose names survive, people still say "Doctor Leblanc's house", although three families have come and gone since, or "the Bernier crossroads", despite the fact that it was demolished twenty years earlier.

Inside, Madeleine found the new decor to be in excellent taste. The housemaid led her up to the library. As she entered, she heard a little cry and turned with a smile.

"Good morning, Léonce, I do hope I'm not disturbing you."

Léonce did not move. She too would have liked to adopt a relaxed, almost nonchalant air, but she could not. A thought occurred to her.

"Gustave will be home at any moment!"

It was intended as a threat. Madeleine beamed.

"No, no, have no fear, Gustave has just left, he will not be back until late this evening. There is a meeting of the board of governors at Renaissance Française, they are rarely over before eleven o'clock. And even then, he may well decide to take some friends to the Café de Paris, you know how much he loves oysters."

This response unsettled Léonce. Not simply because Madeleine looked so well, or because she was better informed than Léonce, but above all because it was phrased as though Madeleine was Joubert's husband and Léonce the visitor.

"Come and sit by me, Léonce, come . . ."

The housemaid reappeared. Was there anything Madame wanted?

"Yes, some tea . . ."

Léonce could not help but add, "What do you think, Madeleine?"

"Tea would be perfect."

Sitting next to each other, the two women surveyed the journey each had made in the past three years. It was Léonce, now, who was lavishly dressed and Madeleine who was wearing the unassuming clothes of a bourgeoise attentive to details. Gone were the jewels, gone the air of serenity Léonce had always despised, that conviction that their places in the world were fixed and immutable. Their positions were now reversed. Léonce stared at her manicured nails while she waited for the tea, surprised to find Madeleine looking her up and down, more out of curiosity than bitterness. What did she want?

In the silence that stirred old memories in both of them, Léonce thought of Paul.

"He is very well," Madeleine said. "Thank you for asking."

Léonce calculated how old he must be now. Why had she never thought to send him pocket money? She desperately wanted to know whether he was aware of her betrayal.

"I did not mention that I planned to pay you a visit, I am sure he would have been envious."

Tea was served. Léonce ventured:

"You do know, Madeleine—"

"Do not reproach yourself," Madeleine interrupted. "For one thing, it is too late and, besides, perhaps you had no choice in the matter. I mean to say . . ."

She reached for her handbag and opened it.

"Come now, let us not be sentimental."

On the low table, Madeleine placed an official document that Léonce immediately recognised, then poured herself some more tea.

Casablanca Registry Office. The marriage certificate of Mademoiselle Léonce Picard and Monsieur Robert Ferrand.

"I can understand that a woman may love men," said Madeleine, "but from there to marrying two at once . . ."

How had Madeleine come by the document?

"It was not difficult. Well, no more difficult than procuring a false document stating that one is a spinster in order to marry a second time. You are a bigamist, Léonce. A misdemeanour that the law tends to frown upon: one year's imprisonment and a fine of three hundred thousand francs . . ."

Léonce was devastated. This was her greatest fear. She had experienced poverty, she knew what it was like, but prison . . .

"And the same for Robert Ferrand."

Madeleine immediately saw that this argument fell flat. Léonce was clearly not about to risk her freedom for Robert. Léonce glanced at the door.

"You may want to think again. Running away would require a considerable sum of money. How much do you have? Perhaps you imagine you can filch a few thousand francs from Joubert in order to procure false papers, buy a ticket to some foreign country and live there for a few months before coming back? You would not get far, Léonce . . . No, I honestly would not advise it. Especially since you would be subject to an arrest warrant, you would have to find a country that had no extradition policy, you would have to hide, that would be expensive, you would never have a moment's peace. Only a hardened criminal could get away with such a plan. In fact, to ensure you do not do anything foolish, you are going to give me your passport."

Silence. Léonce got to her feet, left the library, went up to her bedroom. She tried to consider the situation. Joubert never gave her large sums of money, he preferred her to ask frequently instead, more banker than husband. She had less than a thousand francs and, even then, she would have to give Robert four hundred that he owed to someone or other, he always had some story, she never knew whether it was true. Madeleine would demand a lot of money, but she could not ask for more than Léonce could give without risking killing the goose that laid the golden eggs. Taking her handbag, she went back downstairs and gave her passport to Madeleine, who opened it.

"You are not particularly pretty in this photograph, it does not do you justice."

She looked satisfied.

"Would you be so good as to give me your handbag?"

Léonce obeyed. It was a beautiful suede bag from Lamarthe. Was Madeleine intending to steal it? She merely took out the purse and the visiting cards.

"A very stylish typeface, very sophisticated . . ."

Then she got to her feet.

"You will be my eyes and ears in this house, Léonce, I want you to tell me everything about Joubert the moment it happens. If you attempt to hide something from me, I will not telephone, I will not write, I will not come to see you, I will have you sent directly to the police station with your marriage licence. Am I clear?"

Léonce hesitated.

"Tell you . . . what, exactly?"

"Everything. I want to know the names of everyone with whom he speaks or dines or signs a contract, the gifts he gives his clients and those he gives to politicians, the newspapers where he has journalists in his pay, everything, you need not pick and choose, I shall do that. Listen to his conversations, read his diary, note down everything, copy out the addresses, the telephone numbers. Every week, we will meet for tea at Ladurée on rue Royale. If just once you do not come, I—"

"Yes, yes, I know, I get the picture!"

"There is no need to be angry, Léonce!"

Madeleine pulled her coat around her. She was going to leave without asking for money. Léonce scarcely dared believe it. Then, suddenly, she saw the situation in a very different light.

"You are not going to ruin him, are you?"

"These are complicated times, Léonce. You cannot keep your second husband, his money, your first husband and your freedom. Believe me when I tell you that your freedom is most precious."

Madeleine could read Léonce's mind.

"And you will have to discuss the matter with your first husband, Robert Ferrand. Because I shall need his help too."

Léonce's eyes grew wide. Madeleine smiled benevolently.

"Ah yes, I'm afraid that is marriage. For better, and for worse."

The two women stood, facing each other. Her head tilted to one side, Madeleine studied Léonce, then leaned forward and pressed her lips to hers. Fleetingly, yet long enough to taste the softness, the moist warmth, the delicate perfume. The gesture was not loving, it was done simply so that Madeleine no longer had to think about it, as one might pick up change. She took a step back and gazed at Léonce with a sort of maternal satisfaction. Then she walked to the door, turned and smiled.

"Please do not mistake this for full and final settlement."

Madeleine immediately knew that this was something she would not confess to the priest at Saint-François-de-Sales.

24

Charles sincerely believed that he was a prudent man because every outlay, every box of cigars, every dinner at Le Grand Véfour, every evening in a bordello, was, he reasoned, an exception and it had never occurred to him that the sum of these exceptions could ever exceed his means. In this, as in politics, he practised scapegoating: the fault always lay with someone else. His wife, Hortense, was a perfect target.

In Charles' mind, nothing more clearly illuminated his misfortune than his marriage to her. The unfortunate event, which he was persuaded he had never desired, weighed upon his life like fate. Hortense was exhausting. Happily, he had his daughters, although here, too, his pleasure was not unalloyed. The series of specialists he had brought in to correct the dental disasters of Rose and Jacinthe had concluded that the only solution was complete extraction. Days spent in a dental clinic, a fortune for each extracted tooth and two magnificent sets of dentures that, given their cost, might as well have been solid gold. The girls now boasted teeth of suspect symmetry and disturbing whiteness, like waxworks at the Musée Grévin. Having been forbidden to smile in their childhood, the girls were now making up for lost time. They spent their late adolescence flashing teeth that, alas, given their uneven gums, slipped, came unhooked and jutted disturbingly from their mouths. Keeping the dentures in place was a full-time occupation. At nineteen, the girls were scrawny, knock-kneed, with chalky complexions and their mother's high, pert breasts. Charles, who thought his daughters more beautiful than ever, could not understand why they had so few suitors, and not a single supplicant. He believed the problem was their dowries. Money, again, everything came down to money.

Hortense devoted all her energies to finding potential husbands. Tea dances, balls, soirées, at homes, outings, society parties, no stone was left unturned in an attempt to find eligible men for Rose and Jacinthe, but debacle followed disappointment. Charles, however, continued to believe that his "rare pearls" were possessed of every ladylike accomplishment. True, they could not dance, but their manners at table were acceptable, which had not always been the case. As to deportment, they had had tutors and no longer slouched as badly as they once did. For social graces, they had learned by heart volumes of *Conversations for Ladies*, their only difficulty now was placing the correct subject at the correct point in a discussion. Rose had recently launched into a long recitation of the page on Greece, when the subject was actually Greed, but there had been no lasting repercussions. This year, they were obsessed with macramé, the whole house was awash with doilies, screens and napkins, each more beautiful than the last. But in spite of this, there were no gentlemen callers. "I don't understand it," Charles would say, it was beyond his comprehension. Perhaps, Hortense suggested, since they were identical twins, men felt they had to take both . . .

Charles would close his eyes: the depth of his wife's idiocy was incredible.

When, in mid-February, Hortense told him that, by dint of machinations and intrigue whose finesse could readily be guessed, she had managed to capture the attention of Madame Crémand-Guéron, whose son, Alphonse, a boy of twenty-one, was matriculating at the Grandes Écoles, Charles thought he could see light at the end of the tunnel.

The meeting took place one evening. Charles did not hurry home and adopted the studied nonchalance of a prospective father-in-law who would be niggardly in granting his consent.

He was greeted by Hortense.

"He's here . . ." she whispered.

She was slightly stooped because of the stomach cramps she often suffered and attempted to hide because she knew how much they annoyed her husband, but her face was a mask of feverish, slightly alarming, joy.

Charles had given as much thought as he could to this meeting between the young people and, although he had never met Alphonse, he felt a certain indulgence, a genuine compassion towards the boy who now found himself forced to choose between identical twins, a choice he himself would find difficult to make.

Hortense, too, was aware of this obstacle and had persuaded Rose and Jacinthe, who had always refused to dress differently, at least to wear different-coloured ribbons in their hair. While this would not make the choice any less difficult, it would facilitate telling them apart. After endless negotiations, it was agreed that Rose would wear green and Jacinthe blue.

The former had swathed her chignon such that it all but disappeared beneath the folds of a ribbon as wide as a soup spoon, making her look like a cleaning woman in a psychiatric hospital. Jacinthe, for her part, had created an elaborate coiffure, pinned here and there with coiled strands of ribbon. Her hair piled on top of her head made her look as though she was permanently startled.

Charles entered.

Hardly had he set foot in the drawing room than he stopped, flabbergasted by a brutal revelation that caused his stomach to sink.

The young man was sitting in an armchair, his knees pressed together, his hands in his lap.

Opposite, on a small bench, Rose and Jacinthe were sitting side by side.

214

Charles glanced from the supposed suitor with the timid expression to his daughters in their Sunday best, from tall, slender Alphonse, with his dark curly hair, his pale eyes, his sensual mouth, to the twins wearing identical, low-cut tulle dresses.

He was staggered by what he saw.

Because the young man was as beautiful as a god.

Because he had never seen his daughters in a situation where they were so obviously eager to please.

He realised that they were hideous.

They smiled and bared their false teeth, their cheeks and their chests were sunken, their knees bony. Excited by the arrival of this swain, they bustled like young chickens, letting out strangled giggles that betrayed a sexual desire rendered all the more obscene by the astonishing similarity of their reduplicated ugliness.

How was it that Charles had never realised? Yesterday's blindness and today's sudden epiphany were easily explained: he loved his daughters, loved them desperately. He longed to chase away this young man, to hug his daughters to him. They looked ridiculous. He wished he could die.

The encounter was an ordeal.

Hortense suggested the girls play a duet on the piano, Alphonse smiled sweetly but did not utter a word. They massacred a melody that no-one could possibly have identified. The young man silently applauded, the girls gave a little bow, Rose almost tripped and went sprawling but caught herself in time, then they rushed back to the little bench, where they perched like chickens. Their coconut-scented perfume pervaded the room.

"Well?" said Hortense.

She beamed broadly, revealing teeth that were not particularly beautiful. The apple does not fall far from the tree, thought Charles.

Alphonse left.

"Thank you, monsieur," he said. "I have had a most agreeable evening."

Charles studied him more closely, not only was he handsome and elegant, he was also polite. Everything he could have wished for in a son-in-law.

"Come, come, boy," he said. "Off you go, this has gone on long enough."

The two men shook hands. Charles had a sudden flash of intuition, though he had no idea whence it came.

"Are you interested in politics, Alphonse?"

The young man's face lit up.

"Good," said Charles. "We shall see what we can do for you."

Hortense thought the evening had gone splendidly, she had high hopes. So much the better, thought Charles, it will keep you busy. Hortense followed him into his bedroom. He was getting undressed. He had not eaten, he had no appetite.

"A pity he's an only child, that Alphonse. Now, if he had a brother . . ."

"Go away, Hortense," Charles said as he slipped off his long johns. "Leave me in peace, I have work tomorrow."

Hortense raised her palm, I understand, I understand, and crept out.

What a glorious day she had had.

André Delcourt was much troubled by Joubert's demand that he explicitly support the aeronautics project. But Joubert's veiled allusion to his years at the Péricourt mansion led André to worry that wagging tongues might cast him as a young man being kept by a rich heiress, a rumour that could destroy André's burgeoning reputation.

It seemed less compromising to accede to his demand.

FRANCE DESERVES BETTER THAN ITS POLITICAL ELITE
Those who govern us would do well to listen to those who are the lifeblood of the nation.

Here we have a group of industrialists, motivated purely

by disinterested patriotism, who are prepared to study the issues most pressing to the nation and offer solutions – this, then, is an elite prepared to get things moving. We should salute them.

In the face of the perils that threaten our country, these men are developing the first jet-propelled aeroplane, one capable of daunting even our most bellicose enemies. It is an exhilarating, ambitious and patriotic venture, one that will require the support of the government, that is to say, the nation. Let us not imagine, even for a moment, what may befall if that support should be withheld.

There, André had done what he was asked.

Indeed, the following morning, André received a visiting card from Renaissance Française that expressed no gratitude, but merely congratulated him on his "excellent, impeccably unbiased article".

André had sided with Gustave Joubert. But he had done so only under duress.

At the first hurdle, Joubert could be certain that he would find André blocking his path.

25

Every time Paul embarked on a new book, opened a new notepad, Vladi would roll her eyes to heaven, oh, these intellectuals! She frequently looked over his shoulder when he was reading or writing, which always amused Paul.

This had led to a little clarification with his mother some months earlier, when she had got it into her head that Vladi could help with his education, which Madeleine now dealt with.

"She could, I don't know, she could help you revise your

recitations? She may not speak French, but she could make an effort, don't you think?"

"N-n-no, Ma-ma-maman, she c-c-couldn't."

Paul attempted to change the subject, but when his mother got an idea into her head . . .

"All she need do is read phonetically! Even if she does not under-stand, she could at least check that."

"N-n-no, Ma-ma-maman, she c-c-couldn't."

"I should like to know why!"

And so, reluctantly, Paul felt that he had to tell her.

"B-b-because Vladi c-c-cannot read."

This was a revelation to Madeleine, who had seen Vladi sit down with Paul, often at his request, with a copy of *Król Maciuś Pierwszy*, a story of King Matt the First. But Paul, who had a keener and more sophisticated ear, had noticed that, from one reading to another, the sounds she made on certain pages were not the same. Certain formu-las recurred, as they do in fairy tales, but, for the rest, Vladi was not following the story, she was reciting it from memory, arbitrarily turning the pages of a book she was incapable of reading.

Whenever he went to the library, Vladi would pick up between thumb and forefinger the books he had selected and wearily set them down as though she could not understand how anyone could be interested in such things.

Paul frequented several Paris libraries. I say "several" because Paul knew exactly what he wanted and regularly had to find a new establishment to satisfy his curiosity. None afforded easy access for his wheelchair; Vladi had to traipse up and down flights of steps car-rying him. Not content to scour the shelves dedicated to music and operas, his interests were many and varied. Whenever he happened upon a friendly librarian, he never missed an opportunity to ask if he could give him outdated newspapers, reviews and magazines, from which he clipped articles; Paul had become very industrious.

When she noticed this, Madeleine was both proud and happy.

Should he pursue his studies? Was it possible to attend university in a wheelchair?

"N-n-no, Ma-ma-maman, I'm f-f-fine."

This did not please Madeleine, it was the attitude of a dilettante. With the means now at their disposal, Paul could not expect to live off his mother indefinitely, and besides, she was not immortal. In fact, she had no idea what he was doing. She would survey the piles of borrowed books without seeing any logic. True, Paul was eclectic, but there was a feverishness to his curiosity, an urgency that she did not understand.

One afternoon, while he was at the Bibliothèque Sainte-Genevieve, Madeleine spent hours pacing the living room, steeling herself to do something she found shameful, yet could not resist.

She went into Paul's bedroom, sought out his notepads, discovered chemical formulae, but also a collection of advertisements clipped from newspapers and magazines. Madeleine was scandalised to discover advertisements for feminine products ("For beautiful teeth . . . think Dentol") which all featured scantily dressed young women ("The truly modern woman wears a Nylar slip"), who seemed uninhibited ("She lost weight thanks to Galton tablets!"). She froze when she came across an advertisement for a product called "Gyraldose . . . for a woman's intimate hygiene" that depicted a young woman in a negligee (whenever women had a message to convey, they began by taking off their clothes), and for Quintonine: "Does spring leave you listless, are you melancholy, lethargic . . .?" How sad she looked, the indifferent young woman who illustrated this situation! With her blonde hair, her snub nose, her eyes staring into space, who would not have wanted to console her, to bring her cheer? "Quintonine: a little girl becomes a woman . . ." Honestly.

Madeleine burst into tears.

It did not trouble her that Paul was fascinated with such things, her son was about to turn thirteen, surely this was typical of his age. No, what upset her was that he could not do as other boys . . .

Sooner or later, Madeleine would have to address Paul's sexuality, but she was not ready to do so now.

What to do? When nature asserted itself, a healthy boy would eventually meet a young girl as wild as himself or an older woman prepared to do a good deed, or he could break open his piggybank, but with Paul, in a wheelchair, what was there to do? Time was, there had been Léonce, who was always a wise counsellor in such matters, now there was only Vladi.

Vladi . . .

Madeleine shook her head, trying to dispel the dark thoughts closing in.

There was no point in continuing her prying, she decided to put away the notebooks, but she did not have time before Vladi suddenly appeared in the room. Madeleine was still clutching the drawing of a beautiful woman with a low-cut décolleté who seemed to be troubled by acne and was being offered a remedy. Without a word, she handed it to Vladi. The nurse was clearly aware and not remotely alarmed by the advertisement.

"But," Madeleine said, "you don't think that . . . that I . . ."

Vladi did not hesitate for a second.

"Nie, nie, to jeszcze nie ta chwila!"

She seemed very sure of herself. Standing in front of Paul's bed, an indignant Madeleine tried to brush her away, but too late! Vladi pulled back the eiderdown and the blankets and pointed to the spotless sheet beneath.

"Sama pani widzi!"

Madeleine blushed to the roots of her hair, as though it was her own sexuality that was at issue. Vladi shook her head vehemently as she made up the bed again, muttering to herself.

"Nie, nie teraz! Jeszcze nie!"

Madeleine did not share her calm confidence. Perhaps in Poland boys of thirteen thought of other things. But Paul was not collecting advertisements for lingerie out of idle curiosity.

This was the first time that she missed her former husband. At least in such matters she could have counted on him.

This was one more reason, if another were needed, not to allow Paul to go travelling, as she had briefly considered. Solange had invited him to Berlin. She had boasted (the boast was doubtless true, but why did she have to make everything about herself?) of her friendship with Richard Strauss, no less. Apparently, the composer was a "ferrrvent admirrrer" of La Gallinato. Madeleine wondered whether, in German, the diva also rolled her *rs*. Strauss had heard her perform his "Salomé", and the poor man had been shaken to his core. In short, having accepted an invitation to go to Germany in February to participate in the celebrations for the fiftieth anniversary of Wagner's death, Solange had been forced to withdraw: *I am prostrate and confined to bed.* It was impossible to know whether this was true, she lied as easily as she breathed. The Germans, apparently, had been bitterly disappointed. To judge from Solange's letters, it was surprising that they had marshalled the courage to carry on in her absence. Strauss was not one to bear grudges and had immediately issued a new invitation, and Solange, magnanimous to a fault, had consented to go there in September *for a celebration of German music. Just imagine, my little Pinocchio: a programme of Bach, Beethoven, Schumann, Brahms, Wagner! Surely you will not disappoint your old friend on such an occasion!*

The concert was to take place on September 9, at the Berlin Staatsoper on Unter den Linden.

Paul had not accepted any of Solange's invitations to travel abroad since his visit to La Scala in 1927. This time he had dared to ask, and Madeleine had been on the brink of agreeing, but she could not allow Paul to travel on his own, given his roiling sexuality. They would need two train tickets, several nights in a hotel, to say nothing of food. Madeleine felt guilty, because she had the means at her disposal, but she did not intend to spend the money on a trip, even for Paul; she needed to pay Monsieur Dupré.

She refused. "I . . . un-un-understand, Ma-ma-maman."

There was much comment in the press about Solange's plans to give a number of recitals in Berlin in the autumn. The diva loudly proclaimed her joy at the prospect of "being among the German people, whose very soul is music". The new government of the Reich (it is February 1933, and Herr Hitler has been chancellor for only a month) was delighted that the great artiste was coming to pay homage to the glories of German music. Although criticised for its harsh measures against the Jews and against whatever it considered decadent culture, the Reich was overjoyed to have found an admirer in Solange Gallinato; the red carpet would be rolled out, the Chancellor himself would be attending the premiere. Solange declared that she was thrilled and flattered by this gesture.

It is true that, in the course of her life, Madeleine had had few dealings with the working classes, but this man was not at all what she expected. The elegant scarf around his throat, the pleated trousers, the patent leather shoes. Léonce sensed her confusion.

"Robert does not really work these days, now that he has . . . private means. But he served his apprenticeship."

Madeleine folded her arms. Do tell.

"With Dumont," Robert explained. "In Vincennes."

Sitting opposite, Monsieur Dupré set down his beer, and studied the forged identity card made out in the name of Roger Delbecq. He tossed it over to Robert.

"You were given six hundred francs for an identity card. How much did you pocket for yourself before coming up with this rubbish?"

Robert pouted. It was true that he had rather overcharged. René Delgas had done the work for thirty francs. Léonce came to his rescue.

"I agree, the result is not very good, but only because we had so little time . . . Obviously, it was rushed. But we will have it done again, won't we, poppet?"

Poppet agreed, but that meant very little, he always agreed to everything. If Léonce had had a passport and the means to flee France, she would have considered Robert as just another piece of baggage.

Madeleine, for her part, was thinking about dates. Interviews for the post were set to begin in two or three days. Things had got off to a bad start.

"Tell me, Monsieur Ferrand, what exactly did you do when you worked for Dumont in Vincennes?"

Robert pulled a face.

"A bit of everything, you know how it is . . ."

Madeleine did not know how it was. Monsieur Dupré took a deep breath. For a second, it seemed as though he might slap the young man across the face. Léonce intervened:

"Darling, Madame Péricourt is asking what kind of work you did."

"Oh . . . Well, we swapped out engines, used acid to obliterate the serial numbers, we repainted the cars, stuff like that."

"And when exactly was this?"

Embarrassed, Robert stroked his chin, let me see . . .

"Must be about twenty years ago . . . Yeah, that's right, I came back from my travels in 1913, I went to war in '14, you can work it out yourself."

Madeleine looked at Léonce, then at Monsieur Dupré, then turned back to Robert.

"Could we have a moment, Monsieur Ferrand?"

"No problem," Robert said, folding his arms.

"Poppet," Léonce said, patiently, "Madame Péricourt is asking if we could be alone for a minute."

"Oh, right."

Robert got to his feet and hesitated. The bar? The billiard room? He opted for the latter.

"Yes, I know . . ." Léonce said. "He has been out of the business for some time."

She realised that it would be difficult to justify Robert's application for the post. His only skills were confined to the bedroom. They were invaluable, but even she had to admit that they had little to do with engineering.

Monsieur Dupré said nothing, he was once again leafing through the file that Léonce had copied out in an elegant hand the previous night. A document filched from Joubert's briefcase while he was asleep. An incomplete list of the questions that would be asked of candidates during the interviews.

Madeleine had hoped to get Robert Ferrand employed at the Aeronautics Atelier of Renaissance Française, but she did not rate his chances against candidates with genuine skills, whose experience did not predate the war.

The whole group was despondent. From the billiard room, they heard a loud guffaw and Robert shouting:

"Ha! See that! Cannon off two cushions! Not bad, eh?"

Monsieur Dupré looked at Léonce.

"I don't want to be rude, Mademoiselle Picard, but what do you expect us to do with your boyfriend? We are talking about an elite group of engineers recruiting for specialised, highly experienced employees. Now, if we were to ask him the angle of a trick shot in billiards, he might be capable. But if he has not seen a machine tool in more than twenty years, they will laugh in his face."

Indeed, that is exactly what happened.

The first engineer, an Italian, stifled a laugh, but this only served to set off his two colleagues. Even Joubert could not suppress a smile.

"Come, come, gentlemen," he said. "Show a little compassion."

Was the man a complete idiot, Joubert wondered. He had presented a curriculum vitae larded with unverifiable references and had been unable to give an answer, however vague, to seven out of eight questions. Was it really fair to set him in front of a machine tool only to humiliate him further? They had eight candidates still to interview. Joubert closed the file and made a helpless gesture.

"You have to understand, for a job such as this . . ."

Robert puckered his lips and shrugged, well, yes, obviously . . .

Joubert was having a good day. A good day that had now lasted for several weeks. Never in his life had he been so happy; everything he touched turn to gold.

He could already picture the reaction engine that would be produced by his factory.

Two months earlier, on February 10, 1933, he had had a moment of glory when the Minister for Industry and the Minister for Aeronautics had visited the Atelier, accompanied by journalists and reporters. One by one, Joubert had introduced his team: the aerodynamics specialist, the combustion expert, the ignition authority, the wind tunnel whizz, the streamlining engineer, the alchemist of alloys, it was a tedious litany, but one Joubert enjoyed reciting. Two days later, the government had announced that it would "actively participate" in the project, as though it could avoid it . . . Subsidies would flow into the coffers. And, over the months, Joubert had every intention of siphoning off a large part of the state budget. He was euphoric.

With his team of experts in place, it was now time to find engineers capable of making the parts they had designed.

Joubert got to his feet, the interview was over, on to the next candidate. Robert shook hands with the panel, still smiling, there were no hard feelings, he could hardly have expected any other outcome.

Joubert, in ebullient mood, walked him to the door.

"Well . . . At least we know you love your automobiles."

"Oh, yes, indeed."

"That is something we share. Tell me, if you had the opportunity, what would be your dream car?"

"Well, you know, I've driven the Blue Train Special, so, once you've done that . . ."

Joubert was speechless for a moment.

"You . . . but how? When?"

"Back in '29. I have a friend who does bodywork. He was doing a paint job and needed someone to drive the car back to Mantes-la-Jolie, so I got behind the wheel."

Joubert was astounded. In 1928, Bentley had released the Speed Six. It was in this that Woolf Barnato had raced the Cannes to Calais train. At the end of an incredible journey, it arrived in Calais four minutes before the locomotive. To commemorate the event, the Bentley had produced a model that Barnato nicknamed the Blue Train. Only one had ever been made. No-one really knew where it was. With a 6.5 litre engine capable of 180 horsepower, it was the stuff of legend.

The Italian engineer approached.

"We need to move on to the next candidate, Monsieur Joubert, time is short."

Joubert, almost feverish, could not help but turn back to Robert.

"So, the Blue Train Bentley . . . what was it like?"

Robert opened his mouth, struggled to find the words.

"You cannot possibly imagine, monsieur."

So it was that Robert failed to get a position as a specialist engineer at Renaissance Française's Aeronautics Atelier, but was offered a job as a caretaker.

For more than two months, Madeleine had been meeting with Monsieur Dupré at his rooms to get updates on his investigation. He omitted no detail about the people he had seen, those he had questioned, the places he had been, the hours he had spent waiting, the monies he had spent. Madeleine was becoming impatient, but she did not feel entitled to interrupt the labourer as once she would have interrupted the senior executive of her family bank, and so the evenings dragged on interminably as the coffee in the two cups grew cold.

While Monsieur Dupré had produced excellent information

about Léonce, he was also keenly aware of the movements and machinations of Charles Péricourt. He had bribed the concierge of Charles' building and the secretary to his dentist's secretary, and a parliamentary usher had proved particularly loquacious after the third Cinzano. Monsieur Dupré gave Madeleine a detailed account of the disastrous meeting with Alphonse Crémant-Guérin. Dupré had exerted considerable effort in attempting to extract information about André Delcourt, but in vain. Delcourt went to the newspaper offices, attended dinners in the city, he had no leisure pursuits. When at home, he wrote late into the night.

"Is there nothing to be done?" said Madeleine.

Although Dupré did not like to admit it, he suspected that it would be difficult to find a chink in Delcourt's armour.

"Nor do I think he can be bribed," he said, as though Madeleine had the means to do such a thing. "He does not visit bawdy houses. He does not have an eye for women."

"Perhaps you should be looking in an altogether different direction."

Madeleine blushed at her audacious remark. Monsieur Dupré was careful and meticulous enough to have carried out a thorough investigation. Doubtless, he knew that Madeleine had once been Delcourt's mistress, which made her comment sound more like a confession.

Monsieur Dupré shrugged. Madeleine's heart skipped a beat.

"Listen, Monsieur Dupré, I can tell you—"

"He flagellates himself."

"Excuse me?"

Monsieur Dupré had been in Delcourt's apartment.

"How did you get in?"

"I am a locksmith by profession."

"I see. And you say that—"

"He has a whip in his apartment. An exotic, colonial device. Well used."

Madeleine was surprised but not shocked. It seemed in keeping with André's temperament. And if he found it an effective means of suppressing his urges, he would be difficult to catch.

Nonetheless, Madeleine was calm. The only thing that concerned her was money. What little she had managed to save was fast trickling away. Assuming there were no disagreeable surprises, she could survive until December. After that . . .

Monsieur Dupré gave his usual, long, detailed report on the subject of Léonce. When he had finished, Madeleine rose, Dupré fetched her coat and held it out, she slipped it on, then she turned back and they kissed, he carried her to the bed where, calmly and meticulously, he made love to her.

26

Paul could understand his mother's position. They were in straitened circumstances, she had to count every sou, a trip to Berlin was unthinkable. And yet he longed to hear Solange give another recital, since these had become increasingly rare. *Your friend is molto stanca, very tired, my little man, I refuse many dates, others I cancel, your Solange is foolish old babushka.*

She liked to elicit sympathy, and Paul was happy to oblige. *You are wise to rest. If you are tired, it is only because you have given pleasure to so many people, you have performed all over the world. From time to time, it is no bad thing to refuse.*

This last sentence, written unthinkingly, lingered in his mind. Something was stirring within him, something he did not understand.

He had his first inkling when he read in the newspapers that a Dutch union leader named Marinus van der Lubbe had set fire to the Reichstag in Berlin on February 27, the eve of the elections.

Paul saw photographs of the blazing building and read the vengeful statements of Minister Hermann Göring about the putsch being planned by communists.

Paul did not entirely understand what was happening in Germany, but it was clear that the situation was troubling. Some days before the elections, emergency powers were issued banning all social-democratic publications and suspending the civil liberties of German citizens, some two hundred people were arrested, while thirty thousand swastika-wearing volunteers were tasked with maintaining order. Every morning, they were issued with a truncheon and a loaded pistol, every evening they were paid three marks. Thirty thousand people gathered at the Berlin Sportpalast to hear Chancellor Hitler talk about his racial policies. Clearly things were happening in Germany.

Curiously, what most struck Paul were two minor incidents. A theatrical comedy and a masked ball organised by a Dutch association in Berlin had been banned. Paul found it difficult to reconcile this information with the enthusiasm of Solange, writing to him from a rest cure in Lucerne: *I am taking the waters, I spend all day to bathe. But still I work. It is not too much late to come to my great recital in Berlin. Your dear maman will not let you come? I hope it is not question of money. You would not hide such secret from your old friend, I know. I prepare my programme for Berlin of everything most German with many unexpected things that people do not hear every day. But I must work quickly. And commission the set!*

With her letter, she had included a number of clippings from French and foreign newspapers trumpeting her autumn recital in Germany: LA GALLINATO TO SING FOR HITLER and SOLANGE GALLINATO TO CELEBRATE GERMAN MUSIC IN BERLIN.

Paul's doubts grew deeper in mid-March when the Reich issued a decree disbanding a number of musical associations that did not seem to please the new regime. He could not understand how a

country so deeply rooted in music could prohibit recitals and concert hall performances.

And this was the same country where Solange seemed so excited
to perform.

Paul brooded. There was something he was missing. Ordinarily,
in such a situation, he would ask his mother, but, even ignoring the
fact that there was still a rivalry between the two women, he felt
strangely reticent to broach the subject . . . He feared that Solange's
forthcoming recital was a bad idea.

André trudged reluctantly to the home of Montet-Bouxal. Although
it would be a chore, it was the kind of invitation it was difficult to
refuse. Moreover, André found it galling to visit the vast apartment
with its immense library and its imposing display cases filled with
objets d'art, engravings, books and curios – the quintessence of
everything he wished he was, everything he longed to possess, all
the dreams that still seemed unattainable.

He perched on the corner of a sofa; he would leave as soon as
seemed decent.

"Ah, Italy . . ."

Montet-Bouxal launched into a long critique crammed with
allusions, San Vitale, Bernini, the "Tarquinia Madonna" . . . From
the mouth of this wizened little man, these encyclopaedic ramblings
sounded like clichés. André was in hell. What was he doing here?

It was early April, and the weather had been surprisingly clement.
With age, the arrival of spring, which once the elderly Academician
had scarcely noticed, now seemed like a minor event. From time to
time, he turned to the half-open window, screwed up his eyes like a
cat, sniffed the fresh air drifting into the room, then reluctantly
returned to his papers with a sigh.

". . . and so we thought of you."

Engrossed in his own thoughts, André had not heard the subject
of this sentence.

"Of me?"

"Indeed."

Had André heard correctly? A magazine?

"No, a daily newspaper! It has more heft, you understand. And that is what we need if we are to communicate our ideas, to persuade the public."

Influential members of the Comité France-Italie, together with a number of industrialists and some more enlightened wealthy families, had come together to finance a newspaper that would articulate the ideas that had once again made Italy a great nation.

Montet-Bouxal struggled to his feet, shuffled over to the sofa and sat down heavily. He patted the seat next to him, come, my boy.

"Fascism is a modern doctrine, on that, I assume, we agree?"

The elderly writer's hands were cold and gnarled, André longed to pull his own hands away but politely restrained the urge.

"In Paris, there are many talented writers who would be delighted to work on a political newspaper with a mission to persuade. To promote such a noble cause."

André's head was spinning. Editor of a Paris daily!

"We have offices on the avenue de Messine – who could ask for better?"

Montet-Bouxal gave a rather feminine giggle. To begin with, there would be only three or four journalists, but even so . . .

"We shall arrange for you to meet our generous patrons. We could begin publishing in September. Assuming you are interested, of course . . . We do not yet have a name, but we shall think of one."

"*The Lictor.*"

The name had come unbidden.

"Is that not perhaps a little . . . abstruse? Never mind, we shall see."

Montet-Bouxal got to his feet and pulled his smoking jacket around him. The interview was at an end.

André was elated.

Within a few weeks, he could be in the limelight of public affairs, as the editor-in-chief of a modest, granted, but prestigious newspaper . . .

Where he could not earn less than he did with Guilloteaux.

Robert's greeting was invariable: "Fuck, did you ever see weather like it?" It was a formula that worked regardless of the weather, even at night, and it required no response. This particular evening was no exception. Having made his greeting, Robert climbed into the car and stared vacantly at the road, chain-smoking as they drove. Dupré longed to push him out the passenger door.

They arrived at Châtillon at midnight.

As they left the town, Dupré switched of the headlights and drove slowly and carefully towards the factory. He planned to park some distance away.

Dupré had done everything in his power to get Robert to memorise the instructions. But to no avail. Robert invariably missed out something – oh yeah, he would say, that's right, I forgot that bit. To him nothing was important. In the dimly lit automobile, Dupré tried one last time.

"Oh, really?" Robert said as he listened to the instructions, as though hearing them for the first time. It was enough to make anyone scream.

And so Dupré was forced to do the one thing he had hoped to avoid. With a heavy heart, he took out a sheet of paper on which the instructions were written in block capitals. Leaving evidence of this kind in the hands of such a man was all but suicidal, but what else could he do?

Robert read it aloud as best he could. There was no way of knowing whether he understood the words he was reading.

"Alright, go," Dupré said. "Off you go."

He had considered reversing their roles, but that would mean leaving the car with Robert, who would doubtless drive off at the first hint of trouble, leaving Dupré in an awkward situation . . .

"Alright," said Robert.

He was perfectly calm. He got out and opened the boot.

"What the hell are you doing?" roared Dupré, scrambling out of the car.

"I'm just getting the—"

"For God's sake, what does it say in the instructions I gave you?"

Robert rummaged through his pockets.

"Where the devil did I put the piece of paper . . . Oh, there it is."

It was pitch dark. Robert took out a cigarette lighter, but Dupré managed to snatch it away in time.

"Do you want us to get caught?"

In despair, Dupré reminded him of the instructions. Robert nodded.

"Oh, yeah, that's right, I remember now . . ."

"Yeah, that's right, now get going, idiot."

He watched as Robert moved away, holding the crowbar aloft like a candlestick. If anything goes wrong, I'll leave the cretin here, Dupré thought, though he knew he would do nothing of the kind. Despite the frustration and disgust Robert Ferrand inspired in Dupré, somewhere in his mind there was still a flicker of working-class solidarity, which he realised was utterly misplaced when it came to a crook like Ferrand, but which he could not snuff out.

He stared straight ahead towards the dark outline of the factory in the distance.

Robert reached the building. To the right? To the left? He could not remember. It was probably in the instructions, but that would mean finding the piece of paper, and he could not remember which pocket it was in, and besides, trying to read it, here, with no light . . . He opted to go left.

After a moment he hesitated. He was just about to turn back when he saw the fence. Reassured that his instincts were sound, he kept walking, used the crowbar to make a hole in the fence, he was now in the yard. He found the buildings a little imposing.

Dupré was nervous. The plan in itself was not particularly complicated, but with a moron like Ferrand, nothing was certain. And so he was surprised when he heard footsteps and saw Robert reappear, all smiles.

"Is it done?" he asked, anxiously. "Did you see the nightwatchmen go past?"

"Yeah, course."

Dupré heaved a sigh.

"And you opened the stopcock of the tank a little?"

"Yeah, like you told me."

Dupré could scarcely believe it.

"Alright, then, let's go."

They unloaded the two jerrycans and set off. When they came to the fence, Robert slipped through and Dupré handed him the canisters, which he ran and placed in the workshop, which he had opened using a skeleton key. Dupré, who had spent three nights watching the factory, knew that the security guards would not reappear for at least an hour.

"Alright, so, you wait for me right here."

"Sure, boss."

"And don't smoke."

"Sure."

Dupré crept silently into the factory. It smelled of petrol. He headed towards the tank and found that the stopcock was indeed slightly open and fuel was trickling onto the concrete. Slowly, he poured the contents of the jerrycan around, the smell beginning to catch in his throat. Then he set the two cans next to the door, glanced around the yard, took a twisted length of paper from his pocket, lit it, and tossed it into a pool of petrol. He hurriedly relocked the door using the skeleton key and ran to the fence.

He was thirty metres from the car when the explosion came.

It was a modest affair, but the flames had clearly made their way along the petrol trails because, by the time they turned back towards Paris, the glow of the fire could be seen from the road.

27

Madeleine's reference to André's sexual preferences had been nagging at Dupré. Was this the reason she was intent on destroying him? Had he been looking at Delcourt through "the wrong lens"?

He resumed his surveillance, a task as tedious as Delcourt's life.

He followed him to and from the newspaper offices, to the places where he dined, to the rue Scribe, the Jardin du Luxembourg, Square Saint-Merry and the Bibliothèque Saint-Marcel where he sometimes worked. Then one morning, as he was stationed outside the library, it all fell into place.

Delcourt always arrived at Square Saint-Merry at four in the afternoon, and always sat on the same bench, from which, Dupré discovered, it was possible to watch the gates of Saint-Merry Boys' School, where classes let out half an hour later. In the Jardin du Luxembourg, he always sat near the pond where the boys played with their boats. On rue Scribe, his favourite spot directly faced the dance school; Delcourt clearly knew the timetable, he was never there when the girls came out of class.

A week later, Delcourt returned to the Bibliothèque Saint-Marcel and Dupré settled himself at a nearby desk, leafing through the first book that had come to hand, a volume on Chinese culture. Delcourt spent the whole afternoon with his legs crossed, one hand under the table, gazing at the young librarian.

"It does not get us very far," said Monsieur Dupré.

"True," said Madeleine. "I am beginning to think that we shall have to approach the problem in a different fashion."

At this point, Dupré could not resist saying:

"This ill will you bear him, does it have something to do with these . . . proclivities?"

At first Madeleine pretended that she had not heard, only to realise that her silence might be misinterpreted. Did Monsieur Dupré truly think that she was merely a scorned woman, angry that her former lover preferred the company of boys? A petty reason: Madeleine had her prejudices, but this was not among them.

At moments like these, Monsieur Dupré stared at his coffee spoon.

"It concerns Paul . . ." Madeleine said, and began to sob. Dupré got up and came to comfort her.

"Thank you, Monsieur Dupré," she said raising her palm, "but that is not necessary . . ."

She continued to weep, and then she explained the situation, and, in doing so, discovered that the wound was still raw. She was deeply upset, she blamed herself for everything, for being inattentive, indifferent.

"No," said Monsieur Dupré. "The man is a degenerate bastard, that's all there is to be said."

He was right. There was nothing else to say.

Madeleine took a breath. The vulgar word simply expressed a simple truth. As he escorted her home in a taxi, both were thinking of little Paul. If their thoughts were different, they were united by a similar rage.

As the reader will remember, Charles Péricourt had always been haunted by the thought of financial ruin. On many occasions, he had thwarted the terrible fate that, he believed, had been dogging him. And never had he come as close as he had this evening.

This was his day, this was his hour of glory – or it might have been an hour earlier: now the moment had passed, it was too late, if Charles had had a revolver, he would have blown his brains out.

He could hear his own breathing, hoarse and shallow, like the death rattle of a man about to expire.

"It could still come!" Berthomieu said. "There is no need to fret, Charles, these things will be resolved with time."

Charles had invited the parliamentarian to dinner in the hope of inside information, but Berthomieu had arrived with nothing more than a ravenous appetite, he had devoured enough for four.

"The government is planning to increase the tax on income by ten per cent," Berthomieu had commented as he attacked the Black Forest gateau. "It has to make some gesture to placate the ordinary taxpayer."

This was something Charles knew only too well.

Over the past four years, the national deficit had swelled to fourteen billion francs. The government needed to replenish the state coffers, to cut civil service salaries, to slash public services. Various options had been considered: an indirect tax on automobiles, on flint, on taxis, but in the end there had been no choice but to tax income, and, since every man believed he paid more than his neighbour, the government had pledged to reinforce tax inspections to raise an additional seven hundred and fifty million francs.

And it was this that had offered Charles a chance.

The government proposed to pass a law aimed at curbing tax evasion. A parliamentary commission was to be set up, to analyse, amend or add to the proposal. As the junior party in the coalition, the Alliance Démocratique had only one ministry and so, in choosing a president to head the commission, it was considered prudent to make some gesture to redress the imbalance. Charles Péricourt's name had been mentioned.

To understand Charles' euphoria, it must be remembered that, at the time, parliamentary commissions were powerful enough to dictate government policy. Ministers lived in fear of having to appear before them, and rarely emerged unscathed.

For Charles, this was momentous.

There would have to be a vote, but the opposition, as a matter of principle, would not participate. Over the past forty-eight hours, rumours had swelled that Charles would be the sole candidate for president of the commission; colleagues had already tried to congratulate him, but Charles turned away, fearful that they would bring him bad luck.

Although resolved to speak to no-one about the matter, Charles made one exception, for young Alphonse Crémant-Guérin, who, to the great surprise of Hortense and the bitter disappointment of the twins, had not paid a second visit.

The Crémant-Guérin family could boast two former members of parliament. Although Alphonse's mother had wanted her son to study at the École Polytechnique, the boy had been determined to attend Sciences Po. She wanted him to be a general; he wanted to be a minister. Or perhaps something greater still. "Ah, president," his mother had said, "now that is a very different matter." She had acceded to his desire to study at Sciences Po and immediately embarked on a hectic, hectoring, at times humiliating, round of visits to distant family relations she thought might be able to open doors for her only son and usher him into the corridors of power. Alphonse had been embarrassed to see his mother behave like Princess Trubetskoy, but when he had received an invitation from Hortense, he realised that, painful though it had been, her persistence had not been in vain. Excited at the prospect of being initiated into politics by a veteran parliamentarian like Charles Péricourt, Alphonse had often visited Charles' office at the Assemblée Nationale after his disastrous evening with the twins. And so, when the idea that he might be president of a parliamentary commission was floated, Charles had been unable to resist, he had dispatched a telegram to Alphonse: *Political matter – STOP – come see me – STOP – Charles Péricourt.*

Alphonse had immediately appeared.

"So, where exactly are you in your studies?"

Alphonse was "matriculating". Charles, being an autodidact,

whose sole qualification had been a brother who was a banker, did not know precisely what this meant.

"I am about to be offered the presidency of a commission." Alphonse was dumbstruck.

"This is completely confidential."

A flustered Alphonse threw up his hands, he was prepared to swear on his mother's life, on the constitution, on the Bible.

"If everything goes according to plan, I shall need a competent assistant, you understand."

Alphonse blenched. Now that the word had been said, Charles was in his element.

"My wife tells me that you have not been to visit my daughters in some time . . ."

Alphonse had left the office, reeling.

It was something that, in hindsight, Charles regretted. Not bribing the young man, but tempting fate.

It was now half past ten, Berthomieu was sipping his Armagnac and there was still no word from the minister despite the fact that Charles had twice informed him that he would be spending the evening at Le Sarrazin.

The waiters were politely lined up next to the entrance to underscore the fact that it was also the exit. It was time to leave. Berthomieu belched loudly, once again opined that the blanquette de veau had been a little too salty, then, taking a couple of fat cigars from the box and stuffing them into an inside pocket, he had rejoined Charles, though only after the latter had settled the bill.

"It will come, old man, it will come," said Berthomieu.

"At this time of night?"

Charles was in the depths of despair.

His first disappointment had been to discover that he was not the sole candidate. There had been talk of Brillard, Sénéchal, Mordreux, Filipetti . . . The election he had hoped to win easily now risked becoming an obstacle course against candidates with genuine talent.

Berthomieu, his belly sated, was eager to go home to bed. He patted his pockets, it's not the end of the world . . .

"Goodnight, Charles!"

He hailed a taxi and climbed in. Then, because he still retained a vestige of social nous, he decided to wind down the window as the car pulled away and bellow:

"Don't you worry about the other candidates! They are fools to a man, they cannot hold a candle to you! You will bury them all!"

It is true that Charles had a considerable advantage over his rivals: financial matters had been his chief political concern ever since he was first elected. Truth be told, he had railed against tax evaders only inasmuch as he had railed against taxation; denouncing what he called the "financial inquisition" was his stock in trade. If he were elected, presiding over a commission charged with rooting out tax evasion would involve a delicate repositioning, but this would not be the first time he had had a political change of heart. He liked to remind people that changing strategies had been crucial in the Napoleonic wars.

He retraced his steps, tapped on the window of Le Sarrazin. A waiter came to the door. Charles wanted to make sure that there had been no messages for him. No, nothing, the staff were eager to go home.

Charles was despondent. Alphonse had contacted his secretary to "respectfully" inquire whether there was any news. Charles did not care that he would have to break his promise to the young man, but the thought of further compromising his daughters' future was devastating.

"Ah, there you are!"

For no reason he could fathom, Hortense always kept a bowl of soup warming on the stove; perhaps her distant ancestors had been of peasant stock.

"What would you say to—"

"Don't start with the bloody soup!"

240

Charles hung up his hat, pushed away the wife who was "always under his feet", went into his bedroom and slammed the door. He tossed and turned all night, imagining that Brillard was elected and that he was not given so much as a seat on the commission, dreaming of surprise elections and seeing himself beaten, washed up, out on the street.

He woke at four in the morning, bathed in sweat, and spent the rest of the night staring at the ceiling. At seven o'clock, he crept out of his room. His daughters did not rise before eleven and it was forbidden to make any noise in the house.

In the drawing room, Hortense sat up when she saw her husband and gave him her broadest smile.

"Did you sleep well, my love?"

Charles did not bother to answer.

"Ah, I meant to say last night . . ."

Hortense held out a pneumatic telegram that had arrived the previous evening at eight o'clock.

"You were so exhausted, I did not want to trouble you with work matters."

It was in this manner that Charles Péricourt discovered that he had been elected president of the parliamentary commission into tax evasion.

28

Joubert arrived at the factory shortly after dawn. More to calm his nerves than because there was anything he could do. He spent a moment talking to the caretaker, and had him retell the story of his drive from Paris to Mantes in the Bentley Blue Train Special. A pity the man had a vocabulary of barely two hundred words: "amazing!", "bloody fast!", "what a ride!" and "so smooth!" If the cretin had travelled on the Orient Express, he would doubtless have said exactly the same.

The truth was that Robert had only ever seen the damned car once. And even that had been from a distance, as it passed him on the street. Whenever Joubert raised the subject, he had to rack his brains to think of something to say.

He enjoyed his work at the Aeronautics Atelier. The cleaning and maintenance work was done at night, which meant he was free to spend his mornings fucking Léonce and his afternoons at the racetrack. A girl cleaned the upstairs offices, while he dealt with the ground floor, the workshops and the storeroom. "Our work here is extremely precise," Joubert was at pains to emphasise. "I need the place shining like a newly minted sou." Robert did little more than pass a broom, sweeping the dust under the machines. After a quick dab with a mop, he would empty whole bottles of detergent over the floor so that the smell suffused everything, and when anyone walked in, it gave the impression that the place was spotless. As a result, Robert spent most of his time playing cards with the night-watchmen while he waited for the day shift to arrive so that he could go home.

To kill time, and to quell his anxiety, Joubert went up onto the gangway and surveyed the Atelier.

Industry was much more violent than the world of finance. When he was managing the Banque Péricourt, he had put just as much pressure on his employees, sacked them at will, refused pay rises and increased working hours, but it was all done in a quiet manner, there was no yelling in the corridors, no slamming of doors. If a typist was sacked, someone might hear her sobbing in the toilets, but it created no ripples in the bank and everyone quickly and easily moved on. The world of industry was very different, everything happened in the open air. The vicissitudes of the past few weeks had not remained secret, the teams of workers talked of little else, morale had been affected and things had begun to spiral downwards.

The blaze that had occurred at Lefebvre-Strudal had been a bitter blow to Joubert.

The police determined that it was arson, but the investigation had made little progress.

Lefebvre-Strudal, which accounted for half of Mécanique Joubert's turnover, had immediately laid off its workforce for the time being and cancelled all of its orders. There was nothing Joubert could do, it was a case of force majeure, his finances were beginning to founder.

The reaction engine was still resolutely on the ground while the budget had taken off, he had had to secure a bridging loan of two hundred thousand francs. Meanwhile, a series of technical problems had forced them to reschedule by a week, by a fortnight, the schedule and the budget were stretched to maximum.

Much as Robert hated his work, he loved sabotage. He justifiably took the credit for many of the disruptions that had occurred since the factory opened. He could count five, each of which had delayed progress by several days. The most recent involved him tossing three thimblefuls of dust into a water tank. All the dust had settled at the bottom of the tank like a moribund fish. When the cistern was refilled, the dust rose again, so that the results of the later tests were seriously askew. And four days' work had been lost.

"Sabotage?" suggested Joubert.

Now that the word had come to him, it haunted his every thought. In a period of suspicion and of international tensions, it was a word that terrified everyone. Joubert tallied the number of incidents. The problem was that the Atelier employed too many people to keep a watch on everyone. The fluids analyst was quick to reassure him.

"Sabotage? Oh no, Monsieur Joubert. There's nothing we can do, we filter and filter, but there are still impurities."

He did think that, on this occasion, there were more impurities than usual, but he did not mention the fact because he was personally responsible for the filtering systems and had no desire to go into detail.

As if these difficulties were not enough, there was a larger issue they had had to face: the decision to develop a radial compressor had been misguided.

Their studies showed that only an axial compressor had the power, and, even then, it would require a modification to the aerofoils. It did not send them back to square one, but it did delay the schedule by three months.

This news had exhausted the patience of Renaissance Française, whose members decided that there should be "an expert assessment", no less! A delegation of five people who would insist on poring over the books, the plans, the accounts, the suppliers, the personnel files, Joubert could not believe his ears, it was worse than a tax inspection. It was he who had created the company, he who was the beating heart of this movement, and now he was to be "assessed" like some suspect taxpayer.

Lobgeois took his role of investigator very seriously.

"This entry here for one hundred and twenty thousand francs, Gustave, where did it come from?"

"It was a transfer from my business account to the Aeronautics Atelier when it required a bridging loan."

"This business is a bottomless pit and you are trying to hide the fact!"

The tension was palpable.

Even Robert, who was pretending to clean the room next door, realised that things had turned sour for his boss. Robert had spent the night cutting slivers the size of nail parings from the radiator hoses. A sudden smell of burning rubber made everyone's head spin.

The roar of the turbine in the Atelier suddenly slowed, as though the engine was panting for breath. Joubert was already on his feet and racing towards the gangway.

Smoke rose in an oily black cloud, there was a muffled implosion.

A security guard raced over with buckets of sand, while designers and engineers appeared from their upstairs offices and stood on the walkway. From above, the reaction engine looked a sorry sight, like something in a scrapyard. Joubert took the steps four at a time.

The turbine had grown hotter and hotter . . .

"The radiator hoses couldn't stand the heat," said the Italian. "They completely disintegrated."

Slipping on a pair of gloves made from parachute silk, he began to unscrew the casing. Everyone gathered around, their faces anxious. All that could be said was that there was a great deal of melted rubber. Whether the melted radiator hoses were the cause or the consequence was impossible to determine. No voices were raised, everyone was aware of the schedule and the repercussions of this stumbling block. Eleven days lost.

The acrid stench pouring from the engine, a mixture of burnt rubber, petrol and overheated oil, left the five delegates who had followed Joubert flapping their hands as though shooing away flies. The smoke was very unpleasant.

"Is it serious?" someone asked.

"A minor setback," Joubert said evasively.

But his face was ashen. The men who made up the delegation were all engineers; there was no need to spell out the implications for them.

Joubert was reluctant to turn around, but he could sense Lobgeois behind him, his thin smile like a knife in his back.

André expended considerable energy seeking out people willing to contribute articles, columns, theatre and book reviews for the daily newspaper of fascist allegiance that he was to edit in the autumn. There were many, something André found reassuring: fascism was in the air, and intellectuals and the writers he contacted were enthusiastic, believing that it would be the best bulwark against the seemingly inexorable rise of Nazism.

André was in his element, persuasive, seductive.

The plans for the newspaper were still secret, but the money was already on the table. He needed to recruit three journalists, he would choose neophytes whom he could control. He did not want to pay them much. In the meantime, he would use *Soir de Paris* to disseminate the ideas that he would soon loudly trumpet.

CRIME

The shocking scourge of abortion is a double failing: both political and moral.

Political first. In a France whose population is ageing, can we abide women who attempt to take the lives of the children that our country so desperately needs? Our German neighbours take a different view: they are building a powerful nation thanks to a flourishing youth. When we cross them, will they find a weakened France whose children have been decimated?

But it is chiefly a moral failing, because the act itself is an attack on the most fundamental of rights: the right to life!

What sanction does society mete out to murderers found guilty of cruelty and premeditation? The death penalty. Why should we treat this crime differently? It is now imperative that such killers – the basest of the base – face the ultimate sanction, in the name of a higher power that none can gainsay: love.

Those criminals who practise abortion are guilty not only of a crime contrary to common law, they are guilty of a crime against love, the love that should prevail over all things, over fate, over destiny, over misfortune . . .

That love which is the sacred gift of all God's creatures.

29

This is my property! thought Madeleine, trying to steel herself. She swallowed hard and, as she made her way up to the fifth floor, she mentally rehearsed the arguments she had categorised in order of importance. This conversation had to be handled with calm determination. She pressed the doorbell.

Monsieur Guéneau personally opened the door.

"Maître Guéneau!" he corrected her.

He was a tall, broad-shouldered, heavyset man with thinning hair, a purplish complexion and dark, wrinkled bags under his eyes. He suffered from a severe squint. He was wearing a gaudily coloured dressing gown that had seen better days.

"May I come in for a moment?" Madeleine said.

"No, you may not."

From his firm tone, it was clear that Guéneau was spoiling for a fight. Keep things calm, Madeleine told herself, be conciliatory, avoid conflict.

"I have come about . . ."

By now, Madeleine was certain, ears were pressed to the other doors on the landing. The situation was a delicate one, but the prospect of coming away empty-handed urged her on.

"I have written to you on three separate occasions. You did not reply, so I have come to see you."

The man merely stared at her, determined to make this as difficult as possible. Madeleine mustered her courage.

"Your rent is two months in arrears, Maître Guéneau."

"Quite correct."

This was what she had feared. A tenant who is embarrassed feigns surprise, pretexts and accidents, makes promises, but faced with a tenant who did not contest the facts, what could she do?

"I came . . . I would like . . . What I mean . . . can we discuss the problem?"

"No."

She felt herself waver when she should have responded decisively. "The law is the law, and it is on my side." She had been to see the notary public who had drawn up the lease and he had been categorical.

"Very well," she said. "If you do not wish to discuss your arrears, you will have to move out. And pay your outstanding rent."

"That's impossible."

He did not move, but beneath his apparent calm, he was seething with rage, his face darkened, the bags beneath his eyes swelled. His taciturn responses were no more than a dam holding back a torrent of words.

"In which case, I will have no choice but to have you evicted from my property."

"I think you mean my property! I have a lease, Madame Péricourt, and that means that this is my home!"

"It is your home only if you pay the rent."

"Not at all. Failure to pay does not in itself void a lease."

Yes, the notary had tied himself in knots attempting to explain the point: a difference had to be made between the right to occupy the premises and the duty to pay, which were, apparently, unconnected.

'But . . . but you are obliged to pay your rent!"

"In theory, yes. But since I do not have the means to do so, you will have to accept the fact."

The rent was Madeleine's only income.

"I shall compel you to pay, monsieur!"

The man smiled. Madeleine instantly realised that this was where he had been trying to steer the conversation.

"To do so, you will have to file for an eviction. It is a long process. A moderately well-informed tenant – a retired lawyer, say – has a number of ways to delay the proceedings. You would not believe how long it takes. It can go on for years."

"That is impossible! I need that money to live!"

The man let go of the door and pulled his dressing gown around him.

"This is the situation we find ourselves in, Madame Péricourt. You have invested your money in an apartment that will not earn you another sou for a long time. I invested my money in a bank that collapsed last November."

Madeleine was dumbstruck.

"Indeed, it is an institution with which you are intimately familiar. The Banque d'Escompte et de Crédit Industriel."

"I have nothing to do with that bank!"

What she needed to say to defend herself was unsayable.

"Was it not informally referred to as the Banque Péricourt? Your family's ruin deprived me of everything I had. I consider my tenancy here to be legitimate compensation, and I will never leave. I will devote every ounce of energy that I possess to staying here, because, if I am forced to leave, I shall be out on the streets. Perhaps you are not directly to blame, but that is not my concern."

Madeleine opened her mouth, but the door had already closed.

The landing thrummed with a silence like the dull roar of an aeroplane. She felt her temples pulsing, she thought that she might faint.

For a moment, she considered pressing the doorbell, but she gave up since she did not know what else to say. The peephole was dark. Behind the door, Monsieur Guéneau was watching.

This was worse than anything she had imagined. It was mid-May. She could survive until December. If she factored in her expenses and the money she was paying Monsieur Dupré, it would only be September.

What would become of her, of Paul, if she could not find a solution?

Then, suddenly, the anger drained away. She realised that this was a sign of the times, an era that had become terribly brutal.

*

Every Tuesday, Monsieur Guéneau went to the market on rue du Poteau. As he crossed the courtyard where the rubbish bins were stored, he heard a noise behind him and turned.

"Monsieur . . . Jénot? Grénot?"

A man approached, his eyes were close-set, his lips were parted and he was looking down at a piece of paper. He did not seem very sure of himself.

"Guéneau! And it is not Monsieur, but Maître!"

Robert grinned broadly and stuffed the paper back in his pocket. He seemed so thrilled that, for a moment, Monsieur Guéneau thought he was about to leave, as though his mission had simply been to check the spelling of his name.

"May I?"

In a kindly gesture, Robert reached out and took the tartan shopping bag and carefully set it on the bottom step of the stairway. He was holding a thick cane with a pommel of knotted wood, the sort one sometimes saw at marches by far-right groups like Croix-de-Feu or Action Française.

The club struck the lawyer mid-femur with an ugly, muffled thud. Monsieur Guéneau opened his mouth, but the pain was so excruciating that no sound came. The young man immediately stepped closer and helped him sit down next to the shopping bag, whispering, there you go, you'll feel much better there.

Bathed in sweat, Monsieur Guéneau stared, mesmerised, at his leg and was about to reach down and grasp it when the second blow came, at precisely the same spot, with the precision of a clockmaker. Although the sound was not quite the same – softer, more muted – the force of the blow was greater. Indeed, now the femur was sticking out at a forty-five degree angle.

When, eventually, the pain signal reached his brain, Robert clapped a hand over his mouth to silence the agonised howl, whispering tsk, tsk, tsk.

"It's nothing. A plaster cast and it will heal up nicely, you'll see."

Eyes bulging, Monsieur Guéneau glanced from the grotesquely contorted limb to the broad grin of the man nodding at him.

"Obviously, if you continue not to pay rent, the next time will be very different. I'll break both your knees and you won't walk again for a long time. And if you go to the police, I'll shatter both elbows. You'll be able to fold up like a towel in bed."

Robert screwed up his eyes. He tried to remember whether there was anything he had forgotten. No, everything was in order. He got to his feet.

"So, try not to forget the rent. It's important."

He jerked his chin at the lawyer's broken leg.

"I've left you a little reminder."

As he crossed the courtyard, Monsieur Guéneau's howl filled the stairwell.

In the tearoom, the ladies were seated at a circular table.

"Did everything go to plan, poppet?" Léonce asked.

Whenever she spoke to Robert, she finished her sentences with the same encouraging smile Madeleine adopted when Paul was struggling to say something.

"Like clockwork."

Léonce turned to Madeleine, you see, I told you.

"Thank you, Monsieur Ferrand."

Robert touched the brim of his cap.

"At yer service. If you need me to go back . . . well, Monsieur Guéneau and me, we hit it off."

Monsieur Dupré's apartment smelled of wax polish; someone obviously came in to clean. The idea of a woman coming into this cold, monastic cell was so incongruous that Madeleine imagined Dupré, on his knees every Sunday, polishing the parquet floor.

"The man is a well-meaning cretin," Dupré had warned her. "Such people can be difficult to contain."

Ever since Robert Ferrand had secured a job at the Aeronautics Atelier, Madeleine's greatest fear had been that his passion for sabotage would unmask him. She issued strict instructions and never missed an opportunity to remind him that, if he disobeyed, she would carry out her threat to send him to prison: it was the only way to make him see sense.

Madeleine glanced at her watch. Half past nine. On certain evenings, Dupré's reports were more succinct. She had a little time to spare. She turned around.

"Monsieur Dupré, could you help me unlace this girdle, please?"

"Of course, Madeleine."

In his approach to sex, as in his other endeavours, Monsieur Dupré was efficient. This was nothing like her youthful fumblings with André, but, in a way, it was better. She discovered foreplay. Neither her husband, an impetuous man, nor André, a passive youth, had troubled to take time on such matters. There was an increasing list of sins that she did not confide to the priest at Saint-François-de-Sales. During lovemaking, they talked little, but when it was over, Madeleine never forgot to say:

"Thank you, Monsieur Dupré."

"A pleasure, Madeleine."

But that evening, when she had dressed after a quick wash behind the screen (Monsieur Dupré was in the other room, smoking by the window), she did not head for the door as usual.

"Perhaps you can advise me about something, Monsieur Dupré . . . at what age do boys . . . I mean, how old are boys when . . . ?"

"It depends on their character. Some are young men by the time they reach twelve, some are ignorant until as late as sixteen, it varies."

The answer did not suit Madeleine.

"The thing is . . . I am a little worried about Paul."

Monsieur Dupré frowned.

"In his case, the matter is indeed delicate."

He had no difficulty imagining Madeleine's dilemma. And he did not know what he would do if she were to ask him to. Could he take an underage boy in a wheelchair into the sort of establishment he himself had rarely visited? It seemed problematic.

Time passed. Madeleine was waiting for a gesture Monsieur Dupré was disinclined to make, for a word he was reluctant to pronounce.

"Do you not think that perhaps you are premature in your concerns?"

"It's possible . . ."

She resolved to talk to Paul.

My God, how to go about it, how to begin and besides, what could she do for him? Tomorrow, that was it, tomorrow she would discuss the matter with Paul, she would play it by ear, she would improvise.

When she arrived home, Paul was not asleep, he was listening to music. She slipped into the bathroom; she did not want to kiss him without first having a thorough wash.

Though she was alone, she blushed at this thought.

Once undressed, she stood in front of the full-length mirror. She was not fat, strictly speaking, just a little rounded, not all men were repelled by such things. But these were curves that fashion did not approve of, that was the problem. Madeleine did not feel unhappy, she felt outmoded. The current fashion was for women who were slender, even gaunt: look at the advertisements – women who were thin as a rake with buttocks and breasts that were small and pert, not at all like hers. She stuck out her tongue, then let out a shriek, and, although she was completely naked, she covered her breasts – Paul was there, in the doorway, looking at her. He laughed at his mother's reaction.

"It's al-al-alright, Ma-ma-maman."

Madeleine hastily pulled on her dressing gown, went over and crouched beside the wheelchair, as she always did.

"What are you doing there, darling?"

Paul picked up the slate and the chalk: "I heard you come in, I just came to say goodnight."

She looked at her son. He, too, had put on weight. His face was round and chubby. She would have to be vigilant about sugars and fats.

It was late, the apartment building was shrouded in a silence broken only by the occasional rumble of a stove, a footstep in the stairwell, a vehicle down in the street. It was an ideal moment for intimate conversation, Madeleine knew that this was the time to talk to her son, and realised that she did not have the courage.

She opted for evasion.

"I'm getting fat—"

"N-n-not at a-all!" Paul countered instantly.

"I am. I should go on a diet."

The boy smiled and picked up the slate again:

"You should try one of these slimming creams, they cost a fortune, but I can advise you."

Madeleine did not have time to ponder this response, Paul had already spun his chair around.

She felt uncomfortable as she watched Paul set his scrapbooks of advertisements, including one she had not seen, on the table and slowly thumb through them. Suddenly, he stopped.

"Ma-ma-maman?"

"What is it, darling?"

He picked up the slate:

"The man you meet at night, why is it a secret?"

Madeleine flushed, opened her mouth to answer, but Paul had already passed on to something else. He pointed to an advert:

"There!"

It was a picture of a portly woman with a sad expression. The slogan was reassuring: "Obesity is a ridiculous and dangerous

254

debility. It is the only one that elicits mocking laughter and unkind remarks." The choice was obvious: sink into depression or take a course of Mattel tablets.

Paul gave a broad smile. Madeleine, still shocked by the question he had just asked, felt her head spin. Finally, she managed to decipher the words: "Obesity is a ridiculous and dangerous debility." She was not sure she understood.

"You think I should buy this?"

"Or th-th-this . . ."

Paul turned the pages on which were pasted advertisements for Professor Portal's pills, Lophyral cream, Sainte-Odile salve, Verty lotion. Some of the women were slim and radiant, others were fat and despondent, depending on whether or not they had availed themselves of the advertised products.

"I ha-have l-lots of them."

Madeleine had found only a single scrapbook. In fact, there were three, which Paul now leafed through, his expression grave but pleased. Dentol, for healthy white teeth; Charbon de Belloc Activated Carbon, eat what you please; Chesebrough Vaseline, choose quality . . . And the star attraction: Thermogene, effective against coughs, rheumatism, influenza and lumbago.

"It's very interesting," said Madeleine.

This was what she used to say to Gustave Joubert when he talked about secured loans, or annual percentage rates.

They came to the scrapbook Madeleine had seen, but it no longer had the same devastating effect. She stole a glance at Paul's handsome profile, he looked thoughtful and – she groped for the word – contented.

"Tell me something, darling, why do you have all these advertisements?"

Paul wheeled himself as far as the wardrobe and returned with another book, a large, thick volume like a town hall register. It was filled with mathematical formulae.

"N-n-not ma-mathematical," he explained. "These are ch-ch-chemical fo-fo-formulae."

He picked up the slate again. "Products like these sell by the thousand, Maman."

"I know."

"But do you know what they are?"

"New products designed to—"

"No, Maman, there is nothing new in them. Most are ointments discovered long ago, you simply add some plant oils, some perfume, some colour, that's all."

"I'm afraid I don't quite follow you, my love."

Paul nodded to the large register.

"All of these products are simply formulae from the Codex that have been slightly modified."

"The Codex?"

"The *Codex Medicamentarius Gallicus*, the national pharmaco-poeia of approved formulae. It's a public reference book, anyone can use the formulae. And they do."

Madeleine finally understood. She was happy. Relieved that Paul's fascination with these products was purely scientific and encouraged that his intellectual interests went beyond the opera.

"Well, well, you have taught me something this evening."

Paul looked at her quizzically.

"Yes, it's all very interesting," Madeleine said. "Now, it's very late—"

"Do you know why these products sell?"

"We can talk about all this tomorrow, Paul, you need to get to bed."

"They sell because of the advertising, the products themselves are worthless, they are easy to manufacture, but people buy them because the advertisement is persuasive."

Madeleine smiled.

"Very clever, I admit."

"And they are expensive, Maman, because the people who buy them value their looks so much that the price hardly matters."

Madeleine gave a little laugh.

"I'm very happy that you've found a passion, a profession that interests you. Chemistry is an excellent idea."

"No, no, Maman, I'm not interested in chemistry!"

"Oh? So what is it that interests you . . . advertising?"

"No, Maman."

He nodded to the press cuttings.

"Th-th-these people do ad-ad-advertising. I wa-want to do pu-pu-publicity."

Charles Péricourt hired Alphonse Crémant-Guérin to be his assistant and introduced him to his colleagues.

"If you need anything at all, do not hesitate to ask him, he is very efficient."

Afterwards, Charles had taken the young man aside:

"We would be delighted if you were to visit us at home."

The following week, Alphonse took action.

"Monsieur le président, without wishing to be importunate, I would very much like to come and pay my respects to your lady wife and your charming daughters."

The invitation set Hortense all of a flutter. At which of the twins did Alphonse intend to set his cap? And, how would the twin who was not chosen react?

"Don't you perhaps need another assistant, Charles?"

Her husband did not answer.

Alphonse came to dine. He was not a fool, he knew what Charles Péricourt expected, but the two daughters were so ugly that his brain simply froze.

The twins, for their part, were eager to simplify his task. They realised that there was only one young man, and, while they had not excelled in mathematics, or indeed in any subject, they knew that he would have to choose. Rose assumed that her status as the elder twin gave her priority and Jacinthe, who had always been dominated by her sister, acquiesced, prepared to wait her turn.

It was Rose, therefore, who was tasked with bringing in the biscuits – an acrobatic feat that impressed all those present.

For Charles, it was excruciating. He suffered on two counts: he loved Rose, and he understood Alphonse.

As a diversion, they talked about politics.

There had been much talk about the new commission over which Charles was to preside. Not all of it positive.

Politicians had been so discredited in the eyes of the electorate that, even when they told the truth, no-one listened. And yet, on this occasion, the intention was not suspect. Parliamentarians were genuinely worried by the national debt. Many entertained the somewhat fanciful idea that France could again experience the healthy economy it had once enjoyed, they believed that this was merely a passing crisis, they could not conceive that this was the new world order and would endure.

The newspapers were filled with stories about "the Péricourt Commission".

"It's very encouraging," Alphonse opined.

Her elbows on the table, her head cradled in her hands, Rose gave an approving chuckle.

"You think so?" said Charles.

"It is a topic that is on everyone's minds. People are impatient. The government will find it extremely difficult to ignore the measures you propose. Your position is very strong."

Charles sighed. The comment was insightful. Ah, how he longed to have this young man as his son-in-law.

30

For several days, Léonce had been on tenterhooks. Robert could be free with his hands, but that was Robert, and there were certain things Léonce accepted in her first husband that she had no intention of tolerating in her second. Joubert was not violent, or at least not particularly, many a husband was less strict. But Joubert could be irritable, hot-tempered, sometimes he would grab Léonce and, while servicing her, would stare at her as though he hated her or as though he had asked a question and was seething as he waited for an answer. He would come off inside her without a flicker, without a moan. Léonce found it slightly frightening.

This was a man under pressure, one who would throw off his coat, his hat, march across the tiled floor without a word or a look at her, and shut himself away in his study.

Léonce would press her ear to the door, the servants passed, stared at her, bent double, with her eye glued to the keyhole, she did not care. She was beyond caring about such things.

Joubert would make telephone calls, send pneumatic telegrams summoning people. Madeleine would ask to whom these were addressed. The answer was simple: to everyone. They were to meet that evening. Urgently.

Between telephone calls and telegrams, Joubert had a lot of time to brood. From Clichy to Pré-Saint-Gervais, the clouds were gathering.

The results of the inspection had not been long in coming. Renaissance Française was cutting off funding, it insisted it needed "tangible results" before dipping its hand in its pocket again.

Joubert replaced the receiver, he had sent his last pneumatic telegram. He got to his feet, Léonce just had time to make as if she happened to be passing.

"Have a cold collation sent up to my room," he said, as though speaking to the cook. "Immediately. I shall need to leave shortly."

*

Meanwhile, Robert Ferrand squeezed his eyes shut as he set down his cards and once again heard the words "belote-rebelote, last trick, and game". It was tiresome.

"Let them win, we can't afford to antagonise them." This had been Madeleine's order as communicated by Léonce.

It was true that this was no time to rile anyone; the situation was very tense. Unsurprisingly. At first, Robert rarely encountered anyone at the factory, since he started his shift just as everyone else was leaving, but as the weeks passed, and the engineers worked longer and longer hours, he had to duck in and out as he mopped the floors and it was increasingly difficult to pretend that he was cleaning.

"Everybody scatter!" roared one of the security guards, who happened to have gone to the toilet between hands. A car had just pulled into the yard. The men hurriedly gathered up the cards and scrabbled to button their uniforms, Robert ducked into the storeroom. As Joubert stepped into the factory, Robert sloshed a bucket of water across the floor, forcing him to step over the puddle.

"Sorry, boss."

Joubert did not respond. He was less and less friendly these days, he prowled around the factory, angry and preoccupied, he barked curt orders. Robert did not blame him, in fact he sympathised, these constant setbacks . . .

By eleven o'clock that night, everyone was gathered around the table in the large meeting room.

As a direct result of the Renaissance Française inspection, only thirteen now remained of the original twenty-three employees. Each of the business partners had repatriated an engineer or a couple of technicians. But of course, Joubert said each time, we don't need them here, things are going very well, in fact we are running ahead of schedule. Like hell.

Following a number of insidious articles in the newspapers

hinting the Atelier was running short of funds, one of the suppliers was now insisting on payment before delivery. The government had suspended all subsidies. A crisis of confidence was looming. Joubert had spent enough years as a banker to know that he no longer had the equity to apply for a loan anywhere. He was on the brink of the abyss, and he was alone.

"The government's decision has placed us in a very difficult position," he said to what remained of his team.

Joubert was hardly what one might call an empath, but, as a boss, he knew that badly treated employees work badly.

"What has happened today is something that can happen in any ambitious venture. I have invited you all here this evening to reassure you that I have complete confidence in your work. It is only when tried in the fire that a man proves his mettle."

He was quite pleased with this aphorism. Those around the table sat up.

"But we will need results. A successful test run, something spectacular. Once that is done, we will be set."

The assembled company had expected the worst. Perhaps even an announcement that the Atelier would have to close. Instead of which, Joubert was offering them breathing space. With a tight-lipped smile, he added:

"A demonstration using a scale model of the turbojet engine would pave the way to a full-size prototype. Do you think this is something we could achieve by early September?"

Ten weeks.

"It's possible," someone muttered.

Joubert went around the table and the managers gave an account of their department. The new turbine blades would arrive in a month, the turbines would be in operation within six weeks, there were some adjustments still to be made – three weeks at most – while any issues about the fuel mix and the aerodynamics could be dealt with later.

Ten weeks. It was entirely feasible.

They would have to work hard, but they could soon begin testing the new alloys, the solution was within their grasp. It was reasonable to envisage a public demonstration of a scale model in the time allotted.

Good, thought Joubert. Tighten the screw without demoralising the staff.

André Delcourt was proving "difficult to snare", according to Monsieur Dupré, who regularly snuck into Delcourt's apartment, read his letters, flicked through his books, checked the bedsheets and the state of the bullwhip, and left with a few pages from a paper André had been reading or an old dressing gown he found in the dustbin (a new green quilted gown, equal to his pretensions and worthy of Voltaire himself, hung on a hook in the hallway), a fountain pen so dusty that it was clear Delcourt no longer used it, an empty ink bottle, the rough draft of a letter found crumpled in the wastepaper basket – all manner of trivial objects that Monsieur Dupré carefully picked up using a handkerchief, slipped into his pockets and later filed away in the small trunk under his bed.

"It is just a matter of time," Madeleine would say.

It was as though she were reassuring him. As though he were the injured party, not she.

They both read André's newspaper columns attentively in the hope of unearthing some nugget of information, some clue that might prove useful. It was a futile operation, for several weeks, André's columns sought only to please. This was an opportunity for Madeleine to leaf through the rest of the paper – she was more interested in the news than she once had been.

"'The Soviet ambassador, Monsieur Dovgalevski, has been discussing a range of political matters with the French government. This thaw in bilateral relations makes a rapprochement with the U.S.S.R. increasingly likely.' What will they think of next?"

"Would you rather France had a rapprochement with Nazi Germany?" said Monsieur Dupré.

"Of course not! But the idea that we would ally ourselves to those who betrayed us in 1917? No, thank you!"

"Fascism is the enemy, Madeleine, not communism."

"Well, I for one do not want to see the barbarians at the gates, Monsieur Dupré. And that is what they are: barbarians!"

Madeleine folded her arms.

"Do you really want the proletariat sowing the seeds of revolution here in France?"

"What could they take from you?"

"Excuse me?"

"I said, if the proletariat were to rise up, what could they take from you? Your money? You have no money now. Or perhaps you are worried about your pots and pans, your rugs?"

"But . . . but . . . Monsieur Dupré, I have no desire to see the Bolsheviks overrun our country, taking away our children."

"What you are talking about are Fascism and Nazism, that is a very different matter."

Madeleine was outraged.

"But these people are intent on fomenting chaos. If they had their way, there would be no morality, no God!"

"And you believe that God has been good to you?"

Monsieur Dupré returned to his reading. Madeleine did not respond.

Such conversations were not infrequent, and Monsieur Dupré's ideas, so unfamiliar to Madeleine, often left her pensive. It was clear that she was struggling to make sense of them.

"Monsieur Dupré, may I ask you a small favour?"

It was late, he had taken her home in a taxi. As usual, the car had stopped at the far end of the rue La Fontaine, because of the neighbours.

"Of course."

"Would you mind coming around some time to talk to Paul?"

There was an awkward silence.

"Talk to him about what?"

Madeleine almost laughed. Monsieur Dupré's hasty response made it clear he was unsettled. Madeleine could not resist teasing him.

"A personal matter, I believe. But if you would find it embarrassing . . ."

"Not at all, Madeleine, not at all."

But his tone was gruff. The tone he had when he was speaking to Robert Ferrand and it was clear that he longed to give the man a kick up the backside.

"Good night, Monsieur Dupré."

She smiled as she opened the door.

"Good night, Madeleine."

Monsieur Dupré had put on his suit. This was the first time he had been in the apartment.

Vladi instantly appeared, simpering as though she were the young lady of the house.

"Miło mi pana poznać!"

"Yes, yes, nice to meet you too," said Monsieur Dupré.

They turned into the living room, where Paul had just parked his wheelchair.

"Paul," said Madeleine, "this is Monsieur Dupré."

The boy held out his hand; Monsieur Dupré came over.

"Hello, Paul."

Everyone was clearly ill at ease. Madeleine broke the silence.

"Would you care for a cup of coffee, Monsieur Dupré?"

He did not want coffee. Ever since Madeleine had mentioned this favour, he had been anxious and restless. Although he usually slept soundly, he found himself woken by questions that should be of no concern to him. Now that he was here, he wanted it to be over.

He would not shirk his duty. He had carefully considered his plan. He had said nothing to Madeleine, a single mother must find help where she can, but, to his mind, her behaviour had been neither appropriate nor honest, so he felt a twinge of resentment.

Monsieur Dupré nodded at Paul.

"I've come to talk to this young man, I believe."

Vladi closed the door, Madeleine announced, "I shall go out to do some shopping," Monsieur Dupré did not cavil though he felt the reaction was somewhat cowardly.

He looked at Paul, who was not at all as he had imagined. The boy was almost fourteen, he was a little fatter than his mother had suggested, he had clearly been shaving his upper lip in an attempt to hasten the growth of a nascent moustache and had cut himself some days ago. The problem was the boy's legs. Pencil thin. The face was handsome, his father was a good-looking man. A vicious brute, but he was handsome, and always had a woman on his arm, though never his wife. The little room was crammed with books, folders, piles of records. The carpet had been worn away by the wheelchair.

"T-t-take a s-s-seat."

Mauricette. A girl on the rue Froidevaux. She claimed that she was eighteen but could not be more than sixteen. Pretty, really pretty. Her smile . . . It was the grace of her face that persuaded Monsieur Dupré. Obviously, that meant nothing, she could be a demon with the face of an angel, but you have to trust to something. Strictly speaking, she did not work the streets. She was erratic. And resourceful. She immediately hopped up on the bed and was taking off her stockings, chatting away sweetly, utterly unlike the others – not that he knew much about them. And she was clever too – when she saw that he was sitting down rather than taking off his clothes, she realised that this was a client who wanted something different.

"So, what did you come for?"

Seeing her standing at the end of the bed, determined not to be hoodwinked, he was saddened to think that she would experience

265

dozens of situations like this, not all of which would be so easily resolved.

Monsieur Dupré had simply taken out his money, paid for her time as though paying for the trick, and explained that he had not come for "that". She had argued every inch of the way, but, in the end, things had gone well.

"So, Paul, from what I've heard you need a little help . . ."

The boy blushed, and Dupré instantly regretted his choice of words, he had not wanted to be hurtful.

"Ma-ma-maman t-told you?"

"In rather vague terms. But I think I have grasped the essential."

Good. Paul was relieved.

"M-m-may I?" He nodded to his slate.

"Of course."

"I foresee three problems," Paul wrote. "Finding the right person, the right place, and then there is the matter of the money."

"Well put." Dupré smiled. The boy had a good head on his shoulders. With Mauricette, he would be on familiar ground.

"For the money, Maman has said that, if it is not too expensive, she can fund it."

"A wise decision, it is an issue that needs to be dealt with."

Paul nodded, this was the issue that had most concerned him, but his mother had insisted they would find the money. No matter how, they would find it. "As long as the price is reasonable!" she had added.

This was good news.

"As to the place," Paul wrote, "I'm not sure what sort of location would suit." He seemed confused, his writing becoming more fever-ish. "Actually, I'm not at all sure how it is done."

He looks at Monsieur Dupré and wrote:

"In practical terms, I mean."

He blushed at his own ignorance.

"Size isn't important, Paul. All that matters is that you feel comfortable there, that you feel safe. I think I have found exactly what you need."

Paul's face brightened.

"R-r-really?"

"I think so."

They both smiled. Everything was going well. The boy was adorable, it was a pleasure to help him out.

"Now, as to the right person, I was thinking of putting an advertisement in the newspaper," Paul wrote. "Something along the lines . . ."

He picked up a notepad.

"Oh, I don't think that will be necessary, Paul, I think I have found the person you need."

"R-r-really?"

Paul was dumbfounded. He burst out laughing. A laugh of sheer joy. Excitedly, he scrawled on his slate:

"If you've found a site for the laboratory and Maman has the money to get it going, and you know a qualified pharmacist, then things should be able to move quickly, shouldn't they?"

Now it was Monsieur Dupré's turn to laugh. On the other side of his face.

"Yes, well, probably . . . But I think maybe it would be best if you explained the whole project to me . . . I mean . . . in your own words."

Paul agreed, he was eager to explain his project in detail.

"Well, my idea is to set up a pharmaceutical laboratory . . ."

31

It was an hôtel particulier on the corner of the rue de la Tour and the rue de Passy, an affluent building indistinguishable from those around it, servants hurrying along the pavement. Paul had noticed the advertisement in *Le Temps*.

"Ma-maman . . ." He picked up his slate and wrote, "This is strange, don't you think?"

"What is strange, my darling?"

"This advertising slogan."

It was Paul's thing, he would put on his opera recordings and pore over advertisements, deconstructing the texts and parsing the promotional slogans.

"When you read it, you wonder what it is they're selling," he wrote on his slate. "What do you think?"

Madeleine ruffled her son's hair, what a clever boy you are.

There was no address given, only a telephone number. A woman's voice, with a faint accent.

"And may I ask to whom I am speaking . . . ?"

"Joubert, Léonce Joubert."

"Could you give me a number on which we can reach you?"

The woman would not answer questions, instead the company called your home, a subtle way of confirming your identity. Three days had passed when Léonce called Madeleine.

"They've given me a telephone number. I did exactly as you asked."

"Excellent."

"Monsieur Renault. Passy 27-43."

She had immediately been passed on to a gentleman with a warm, soothing, almost seductive voice, like an actor's.

"Renaud, with a *d*, not like the automobile company."

For the meeting, Madeleine had borrowed a corduroy suit from Léonce. It was something of a tight fit.

"N-n-no, Ma-maman, you l-look very pr-pr-pretty."

Paul was sweet, but he was not the one attempting to buckle the belt. All that really mattered was that she could pass for Madame Joubert.

Monsieur Renaud was fifteen years older than his voice intimated, and looked like a police officer. In a banker, this was disappointing. His bald pate shimmered like a billiard ball. He was charmed by his visitor, but he was in the business of being charmed to meet people.

Tea was served in his office, which was simply a drawing room with a sofa, two armchairs and a low table.

Monsieur Renaud completely understood that Monsieur Joubert could not come in person and so had sent his wife, who laid a richly embossed visiting card on the occasional table.

"What a sad end for the Banque Péricourt . . ."

He sounded genuinely upset. To a banker, the collapse of a credit institution is like a death in the family.

"But Renaissance Française, what a wonderful initiative. And the Aeronautics Atelier – what an ambitious enterprise!"

"But I fear these are hard times . . ."

Oh yes, Monsieur Renaud read the newspapers. That such a venture should find itself in difficulty felt like a cruel personal affront.

"In fact, Monsieur Renaud, this is the reason I have come to see you."

For a moment, the man closed his eyes in pain; he understood.

"If perchance things should change . . . to your husband's disadvantage, he would not want the state . . ." He tailed off, worried by his own boldness. "Far be it from me to criticise the government, you understand!"

Madeleine nodded, you have no need to apologise, we both know what we are dealing with.

The urbane pleasantries were at an end, they had weighed each other up and found that they understood one another. On the brink of financial collapse, Monsieur Joubert was attempting to hide his

269

assets before the taxman swooped in to take them. Monsieur Renaud was in the business of dealing with such inconveniences.

In its sole, understated advertisement, the Union Bank of Winterthur guaranteed potential clients that personal accounts would remain "absolutely discreet", nothing new under the sun, the secretive Swiss banker had by now acquired an almost worldwide reputation. The bank also assured its clients that a representative regularly visited Paris and other cities in France "to meet with clients" so that it could "work closely to address their concerns". It was this that had sparked Paul's curiosity.

In order to collect interest on any monies deposited with a Swiss bank, one had to go to Switzerland. And then return, with all the risks that this entailed. In recent years, a number of travellers had been stopped, compelled to open their briefcases and to give an account of their business dealings. It was all very disagreeable.

The Union Bank of Winterthur was a most accommodating institution. It relieved its clients of such onerous travails and brought the money directly to their home. This was the role of the "customer representative". You handed over your securities, the banking official collected any interest and brought it to you in coin of the realm. The taxman was none the wiser.

"We have a system . . . a completely new system. One of our own devising."

Monsieur Renaud was not a man plagued by self-doubt, but now his smug superiority reached new heights. Madeleine asked no questions, but merely waited patiently.

"The numbered account."

Madeleine gave a quizzical look to indicate that she did not quite grasp the idea. Monsieur Renaud leaned closer.

"When a client opens an account with, shall we say, a 'traditional' bank, the account bears his name. All of the transactions – deposits, withdrawals, *et cetera* – are linked to him. If anyone should wish to make trouble for him, it is a simple matter: they simply consult the ledgers and the client's whole life is there for all to see."

"But I would have thought that bank confidentiality . . .?"

"Of course, of course, madame! But such confidentiality is only relative. We, on the other hand, offer complete protection. Our approach is one that I like to call 'belt and braces'."

He had been unable to contain himself. The quip sank like a lead balloon. He loudly cleared his throat and continued in a grave voice:

"When we open an account, it is numbered. Even if our ledgers should be scrutinised, all that would be visible is a number that cannot be traced."

He picked up his teacup and sat back in his armchair.

"If I give you the number 120.537, you have no way of knowing to whom it relates. It is impossible."

Madeleine nodded.

"But, in order to carry out transactions," she ventured, "you need to know which number corresponds to which client."

"My notepad! It is the only document that establishes a link between a numbered account and a client's identity. I say the only one . . . in fact there is another, but that is kept locked in a safe in our parent company. Caution and prudence. As for my notepad, it is either in a strongbox, or I have it with me. The contents are absolutely secret, there are no typed copies, no carbon copies that might end up in a wastepaper basket. There are not three people in the whole world capable of connecting our account numbers to the corresponding clients."

He gave the wry laugh of a hotelier who trots out the same joke about their home-made jam three hundred times a year and still finds it amusing.

Madeleine was fulsome in her praise.

"My husband will be most impressed. His schedule is a little tight . . . He will need to make arrangements quickly. Just in case, you understand."

"Whenever and wherever suits him."

Madeleine gave a grateful smile. The question every banker finds most difficult to pose, though it is one he longs to ask, is unvarying: how much? Each banker has a formula. Monsieur Renaud broached the delicate question as though it were a mere detail:

"And we are talking about . . .?"

"Eight hundred thousand francs. In the first instance."

Monsieur Renaud nodded gravely, eight hundred thousand francs, good, good. He was smiling. God, how intoxicating is the smell of money as it passes from a client's pocket to one's own.

Phew. It was a relief to be able to unbuckle the belt and take off the suit. Madeleine carefully folded it and replaced it in its box with no regrets, too tight, she would need to lose a little weight.

In early April, photographs of German shops with windows daubed with slogans and doors guarded by soldiers appeared on the front pages of newspapers. This was the *Judenboykott* – "the great boycott of Jewish businesses".

According to *L'Excelsior*, "Overnight, skulls were painted on shop windows accompanied by warnings such as 'Danger! Jewish establishment!'" Paul was shocked.

A large sector of the French press denounced the violent actions of the Nazi militias. "Herr Hitler is trying to establish a ruthless, systematic suppression of the Jews that goes beyond these acts of violence."

Since April 4, passports issued to Germans wishing to leave the country had to bear the stamp "no restrictions", otherwise it was impossible to leave.

The headline in *Comœdia* the same day read: SOLANGE GALLINATO, NEW MUSE TO THE REICH.

If Solange had not mentioned the recital in Berlin and if she had not been so insistent that he attend, Paul would have taken little interest in Germany, but now that it had been brought to his attention, he saw that the country was the subject of deep concern and many articles discussed what was happening there.

Le Petit Parisien did not mince its words: "The Hitlerite is a fierce sectarian who despises everything that falls outside his opinions and is prepared to trample anyone who opposes his will or his ideas."

Could this really by the country in which Solange was so excited to perform? She sent Paul press clippings: "'The Reich will be proud to welcome Solange Gallinato to Berlin,' declares Joseph Goebbels"; "Reich Chancellor Hitler welcomes La Gallinato like a head of state".

My little Pinocchio, I am as happy as a sandboy, the programme for my recital is complete and I have sent it to Berlin. I am sure that they will be impressed! Are you going to come?

Paul felt he had little right to pass judgment on the dealings of grown-ups. Still, in one letter, he ventured: *Is it really a good idea to sing in Germany, Solange? Especially at the moment?*

Oh, my little darling, now is precisely the moment for me to go to Germany! This great nation of musicians needs artists to come and perform now more than ever!

This letter from Solange arrived in mid-May ("Solange Gallinato to pay homage to German culture"), only a few days after the newspapers published a photograph of a huge bonfire outside the Berlin Opera House in Opernplatz, with the caption: "Säuberung: 20,000 anti-German books burned last night!"

Everything Paul knew about bonfires he had learned in history books about Joan of Arc and Giordano Bruno, the precedents were not encouraging. "A vast crowd gathered around the bonfire," according to *L'Intransigeant*. "They sang patriotic anthems in the solemn tones of a church choir. Germany is the only country in the world where barbarism takes a mystical form, filling souls with pious joy."

Barbarism, bonfires, musicians banished, Jews persecuted . . . Paul could not have marshalled his thoughts into an argument, but he knew that what was happening was not good.

I do not wish to give you all details of my recital, because I hope you will be so intrigued that you will come to Berlin! It will be for my career a great moment, even perhaps the greatest, the Chancellor himself will be there, the ministers of the Great Reich and everybody who is anybody! I will say one more thing to tempt you: for the stage set, I have commissioned an artist you will adore – I will say not more than that. Everyone will be astonished, I assure you!

Paul was saddened by Solange's enthusiasm.

"If the Reich should ask, I shall sing all over Germany," she had declared, it could not simply be naive credulity. What he read in the papers anyone could read. Even Solange.

On June 10, eight hundred Jewish actors, musicians and singers were summarily "dismissed", among them Otto Klemperer, the former conductor of the Berlin State Opera.

By the end of the month, performances of works by Mendelssohn, Meyerbeer, Offenbach and Mahler were banned. Contemporary music was to be considered "degenerate", a warping of the tradition created by Bach, Beethoven, Schumann, Brahms, Wagner and Strauss – the very composers Solange Gallinato was so eager to sing in Berlin, to the glory of what she called "the Great Reich".

Paul began the letter many times, and he particularly hesitated over the conclusion.

Dear Solange,

Your decision to sing in Berlin has worried me greatly. From the newspapers, I have read that many people are unhappy there, many of them musicians. It is true that I do not know much about such matters, but people have been burning books and looting Jewish shops, I have seen the photographs. What pains me is not that you will be singing in Berlin, but that you seem so passionate in your support for the very people who are doing these things. I do not know how to say this to you. I have spent a long time weighing my words

*before taking up my pen. I am deeply indebted to you. When
I first heard your voice, it was as though I was reborn. If I am
still alive, it is thanks to you. But what you are doing now is
something that cannot be a part of my life. This is why I am
writing. To thank you from the bottom of my heart. But also
to say that I will no longer reply to your letters, because the
person who so admires these people with no thought for
anyone else is no longer the person I so loved.*

Paul

The wave of pessimism that had engulfed the Aeronautics Atelier
dissipated in a sudden reversal of the kind one sometimes sees in the
world of business. The horizon was cloudless once again, the skies
almost as radiant as they had been at first.

Instead of paralysing the team, the announcement of a test to be
conducted in September had galvanised their collective sense of
pride. Many spent half the night working at the Atelier and were
back again the following morning at first light. There were no Satur-
days and Sundays now. The growing demoralisation was turned on
its head because the solution seemed within reach. Fresh tests were
carried out on the fuel mixture, the wind tunnel, the heat resistance.
Joubert spent his days with the team, he was everywhere, immersed
in everything, with an energy that commanded their admiration.
He had a word of encouragement for everyone. Had he been capable, he would have told jokes.

And so began the virtuous circle.

The output of the turbines exceeded expectations, and, most
importantly, the new alloy was better than they could have hoped.
Ten days earlier, the first test had been attempted. When the reaction
engine roared into life, no-one dared believe it. The powerful thrust
elicited spontaneous applause. Joubert, who, as we know, was not
an emotional man, was on the brink of tears. He blew his nose to
hide his embarrassment, ordered two more tests, the first of which

took place four days later and was even more conclusive. Joubert was convinced that it would work.

And it needed to: time was getting short.

The company coffers were leaking like a sieve. Several times a week, Joubert had to answer to Renaissance Française. Graphs, progress reports, engineering plans, stock lists, expenses – he had to justify everything. Sacchetti would say, "What can you expect? These men don't have your ambition, they panic about nothing!" Joubert kept his nerve and protected his team. You deal with the most important task, I'll deal with the rest.

The last wind tunnel test was a complete success and it was decided that, early the following week, work could finally begin on making the fuselage, a schedule that factored in the possibility of setbacks.

The whole team waited impatiently for the new turbine blades. Crafted to within a quarter of a millimetre, and the result of weeks of studies and calculations, the manufacture had been outsourced to the most efficient, and hence the most expensive, company. Each blade cost more than two hundred thousand francs.

Robert, too, was impatient. Madeleine's instructions had been as clear as they were categorical:

"If you fail in this, Monsieur Ferrand, in the time it takes me to slip on a coat, I will be at the police station to hand over your marriage certificate."

Léonce was as worried as Madeleine because, outside the bedroom, she had rarely seen Robert successfully do three things in a row.

"You can do it, can't you, poppet?"

"Yeah, sure . . ."

He never had any doubts, which in itself was far from reassuring.

Except that he had a stroke of luck and, against all expectations, he seized it.

Robert had just finished his shift and was leaving the workshop when he noticed the delivery that had arrived that morning. There was a large package stamped "Compagnons Frères". Without stopping to think, not that he would have been able to, he tucked it under his arm and brought it home.

When he arrived at the Atelier the following morning, the place was in chaos.

No-one had been able to find the package. The security guard was categorical, he pointed to the spot where he had left it. The workshops had been turned upside down, the offices and the stores had been searched with a fine-tooth comb. A package could not simply go missing! Security at the Atelier was an obsession, a register was kept of all visitors, and anyone who was not a member of staff was allowed onto the site only with an escort, and so, two days after the announcement that the package had disappeared, the dread word was once again uttered: sabotage.

Members of the team began to eye each other suspiciously, there were engineers of five different nationalities, people began to whisper, rumours began to spread, all of which made Joubert very nervous.

This background noise, this anxiety, infected the atmosphere, work slowed to a crawl, some even mentioned "the Germans", everyone had read the articles about their aeronautical research – could there be a mole within the Atelier? Conversations abruptly trailed off whenever a stranger walked into the room, engineers talked only in hushed tones, everyone kept a watchful eye on everyone else.

Ten days later, Robert received orders from Madeleine to miraculously "find" the package, covered in dust, next to the little room where deliveries were made, pushed under the electrolytic cell – an area everyone believed had been searched several times.

Robert was hailed as a hero, but it was too late: by then, new turbine blades had already been ordered from Compagnons Frères.

*

Two young journalists had been sounded out. Three times a week, André dined with the families financing the project to present the mock-up of the newspaper (in the end, for want of a better title, shareholders had accepted *The Lictor*) and visited the home of Montet-Bouxal, the éminence grise behind the project.

The vast offices on the avenue de Messine, gifted by an aristocrat who had retired to Tuscany, were now furnished. André solicited quotations from a number of printworks. Money was always scarce, but André was more excited than ever.

The launch date had been postponed. The first edition was now scheduled to be published in mid-October. André was champing at the bit.

His column in *Soir de Paris* increasingly reflected the nature of his project and his convictions.

"Tell me something, old man," the ever-intuitive Guilloteaux said one day. "Don't you think you've been laying it on a little thick, recently? This column of yours has taken a curious turn."

DOES FRANCE NEED A DICTATOR?

It is the word that has been on everyone's lips now that Italy, guided by a strong leader, can once again claim to be driving the destiny of the Latin countries.

It is salutary to remember that dictatorship is a republican invention. Far from being the villainous caricature of popular opinion, the dictator is someone elected to the highest public office, who, in times of crisis, is granted untrammelled power for a limited period.

Faced with a political class that has lost all trust and a parliamentary system that has led only to chaos, the solution adopted by our neighbours presents a radical possibility, for there can be nothing ignominious in entrusting a man of valour with the means to implement a bold policy of recovery. Democracies depend upon the talents of exceptional men, men of staunch character such as France has had in the past.

If, tomorrow, such a man were to step forward, would it not behove us to learn from our own mistakes and from the dazzling spectacle of Italy's success?

Kairos

"But, Madeleine, we discussed this only three days ago . . ."

She invariably needed a pretext; she could not bring herself to broach the subject directly.

"I know, Monsieur Dupré, but even so, I need to review the situation."

Very well. Madeleine is the boss, she is paying the piper, she should call the tune. And so, they would sit in Dupré's cramped dining room and say nothing, since there was nothing new to add. Having pensively stirred her coffee, Madeleine would say:

"Well, I think that covers everything, don't you?"

"Yes, Madeleine, I think we have covered everything."

She would take off her blouse, staring intently at each button, unable to bring herself to look at Monsieur Dupré as she did so. He would calmly come over; he never allowed the situation to become awkward.

As to the conversation he had had with Paul, he did not go into detail because their little misunderstanding had not truly been a misunderstanding. Paul was fourteen years old, his complexion sallow, his face a little drawn, and the issue of puberty that Madeleine had hoped to ignore was real and present. Dupré saw Paul once or twice a week. A quick-witted, enterprising boy, very advanced for his age . . .

He had succeeded in finding a pharmacist, a Monsieur Alfred Brodsky, who seemed to have a head cold all year round, and had sought refuge in France a month earlier after his "Jewish establishment" was razed to the ground. When he left Breslau, he had managed to take only the means to clothe his family. It was all the more surprising, then, that some days later he received three large trunks that he had packed before leaving, filled with test tubes, flasks, phials, Bunsen burners, tubes and scales that had survived the disaster.

In matters of chemistry, Monsieur Brodsky was a believer. He had absolute faith in the powers of the pharmacopoeia. According to him, there was a drug for every ailment, even if that drug did not yet exist.

Paul explained his project to Brodsky, his plans to utilise the Codex, yes, yes, very ingenious, it is worth a try, a thousand francs, Dupré ventured, yes, yes, excellent. When Monsieur Brodsky left, no-one was sure whether they would ever see him again. He returned with a stoneware pot containing a greenish pomade made from beeswax which did not smell particularly pleasant and which, he admitted, would have absolutely no effect, "no more than lukewarm water", he explained, by way of analogy.

To Paul, this was ideal. Apart from the smell. It was a shame, he explained, because "we are almost there. Texture is important, colour is important, but the most important thing is the smell. You open a pot, it smells wonderful, you buy it." What they needed was "the same product, but designed for women".

"Very well, then, perfumed."

"No, Monsieur Brodsky," Paul wrote on his slate. "Absolutely not! A cream should never be perfumed, it should have a fragrance. Distinctly pharmaceutical, but pleasant."

Brodsky was racked by three or four sneezes (they came in salvoes), nodded his assent, then took his leave.

What worried Dupré was what would happen next. Madeleine was allowing her son to embark on a project that would cost more than fifty thousand francs, and Dupré did not see how it could work.

He felt trapped. He had embarked on the project to help a boy he found charming and extremely clever, now here he was setting up a business. Unless he did something drastic, he might end up being head of personnel in the family factory. The antithesis of his reasons for leaving the Communist Party.

He had succeeded in finding a pharmacist, all that remained was to find a site. It did not need to be a large space, at least in the first instance, but it was impossible to know how things would develop. Monsieur Brodsky calculated that the materials already at his disposal would be sufficient for a modest launch, but afterwards . . . Between spying on Delcourt, Joubert and Charles Péricourt, and now managing Paul's pharmaceutical business, Dupré found himself very busy. There were times when he did not know which way to turn.

"If all this is too much work, Monsieur Dupré, I completely understand."

But Madeleine would say such things as she slipped off her dress and turned to him, no, no, he would say instinctively, staring into space, and it pleased Madeleine that she could get things by using her feminine charms.

Unlike him, she felt very confident. Paul had had a good idea, Dupré was resourceful, granted there was the funding to be considered, but ever since her visit to the Union Bank of Winterthur, she had felt that she could turn the situation to her advantage. And now, seeing Dupré constantly occupied, Paul working on his project and Vladi bustling about all day, she could not help but ask:

"Monsieur Dupré, do you think that perhaps I should . . . how can I put this? . . . look for a job?"

The question came as a surprise. Even to Madeleine. But it had suddenly occurred to her that she was still living like a lady when in fact she no longer had the means to do so.

What she could not admit was that the idea had come to her while reading *Un mois chez les filles*, a book she would be ashamed to mention. A young journalist, Maryse Choisy, had spent a month posing as a prostitute in order to experience life in the brothels of

Paris at first hand. It was a delectably transgressive read. "Without qualm, I write shit, arse, cunt. These are plain, noble, honest words." Without going so far as to share her opinion, Madeleine thought that it was brave and opened her eyes to women at work. Obviously, she did not identify with scarlet women any more than she did with working women; her upbringing led her to think more in terms of female aviators, journalists, photographers . . . But she had had no real education. She had been raised to marry well.

"But I do not know how to do anything," she said.

It was difficult for Monsieur Dupré to focus on this rather delicate question, because, as she said the words, Madeleine removed the last of her clothes. Now she was standing, naked, her hands behind her back.

"Tell me, Monsieur Dupré, what would give you most pleasure?"

32

Charles had always considered the role of parliamentarian to be a caring profession: "We are like parish priests. We offer advice, we promise a radiant future to the meek; our problem is much the same as theirs, we need our parishioners to come to mass." Since the most important thing was to maintain a close relationship with the electorate, Charles' unit of work was the letter. And so he was somewhat panicked when he saw the thick folder Alphonse had set down in his desk. Good Lord, he thought, we would have been better off setting up a commission on waste!

What no-one expected – least of all Charles himself – was that he would find the subject he had been tasked to study interesting. This was uncharted territory. Granted, taxation by its very nature is unjust and inquisitorial, he reasoned, but given that it exists, it is a greater injustice that some pay while others do not. The former were patriots being portrayed as fools, while the latter were cynics getting off scot-free, it was shocking.

And he was sincere.

He asked for figures; there were none.

"What do you mean there are no figures?"

"The thing is . . . it is difficult to evaluate," said the secretary to the commission.

At the very least, fiscal fraud amounted to four billion francs, and more like six or seven billion. It was colossal.

Charles ordered a survey of existing legislation designed to regulate tax declarations and penalise evasion.

"It's like Swiss cheese," he concluded, after two weeks' research.

There were indeed many holes in the legislation; for anyone moderately well informed, it was not difficult to slip through the net. There was, it turned out, a relatively recent profession designed to help people evade tax, most often carried out by former civil servants from the Ministry of Finance.

"They are known as 'fiscal litigation agents'," explained the secretary.

"They are litigating against the state! Are they regulated, at least?"

There were no guidelines in place. Former civil servants were free to profit from their skills without scruple, since they did not have any. Clearly the commission had its work cut out for it.

Charles set about interviewing a variety of experts. What he needed to do was clear: he needed to crack down.

"Why was this not done before now?" Charles asked the General Inspector of Taxation, a tall, broad-shouldered man from the southwest who had failed in his career as a rugby player because he had the hands of a lacemaker, fingers designed for turning page after page, he had read everything, he remembered everything.

"Our inspections can extend to anything, monsieur le président, on condition, and I quote, that we 'do not violate the confidential relationship between banker and client'. And, since most tax evaders bank in Switzerland, we find ourselves helpless."

Charles looked to left and right. Like him, the other members of the commission were bewildered.

"But, but . . . what about the *bordereau de coupons* . . .?"

He was alluding to the system by which the names of taxpayers with outstanding liabilities were transmitted to the authorities.

"The system was abandoned in 1925. Bankers refused to comply. They argued that it was important to 'ensure that governments did not breach the confidentiality between bank and client'."

"So, if I understand rightly . . . we are doing nothing?"

"Quite so. Everyone believes that if we tax the rich, they will move their money elsewhere. And I quote: 'And when France is left with only the poor, then what shall we do?'"

"You are beginning to try my patience with your quotations!"

"The words are yours, monsieur le président, they were part of your 1928 electoral campaign."

Charles coughed.

The situation was all the more difficult because the 1933 Budget was the fourth in as many years to forecast a deficit, rising from six million to six billion and from six billion to forty-five billion. The national debt worried economists and panicked politicians, who in turn blamed the electorate. But when this torrent of blame and recrimination finally abated, the funds would still have to be found. The most readily accessible source continued to be the taxpayers' pockets, but anti-taxation associations were more virulent than ever, something that greatly worried Alphonse.

"There have always been protests against taxation," said Charles, who had personally encouraged more than a few.

It was Saturday. Blaming the onerous responsibilities of his work at the commission, Alphonse devoted only one afternoon a week to courting.

Saturday was "a day out with Alphonse". The two girls always went together, no-one could understand why.

In fact, the twins were gripped by a terrible dilemma. They could not decide which of them should marry Alphonse. Jacinthe had not disputed her sister Rose's claim by virtue of being older, but one night, in the bedroom, she had argued that the young man would one day be a minister, and perhaps something greater still, and that she had a better command of English than her sister, especially the present perfect. Rose agreed. How to tell their swain that they had reconsidered the matter? And what would happen if they were once again to change their minds? They decided that the decision was theirs alone and swapped places without informing anyone. Alphonse would go out with Jacinthe on his arm thinking she was Rose. To him, it made little difference, he had never been able to tell them apart, they were equally ugly. To say nothing of the fact that going for a stroll with both of them spared him the dangerous possibility that his intended might be seized by a passionate desire to flirt.

They went to the Louvre, where the sisters, who had revised for this occasion especially, mistook the Botticelli "Madonna and Child" for the one by Baldovinetti and jointly launched into a frenzied analysis that had nothing to do with the painting.

The following week, the girls had changed their minds. They decided it was better that Rose should marry Alphonse since, being an only child, he was likely to want only one child, whereas Jacinthe wanted lots – at least six (sometimes the total rose to nine).

Alphonse did not notice the difference.

In the matter of the missing package, Joubert had mixed feelings. The bad news was that it represented a loss of almost two hundred thousand francs. The good news was that the schedule had been delayed by only ten days. He congratulated himself on keeping his composure and not making the loss "official", when in fact he had simply lacked the courage to do so. Everything once again seemed possible. He did not wait for the results before announcing a public demonstration for early December, to which he invited Renaissance Française, the press and the government. He would show that everything had been perfectly modelled, that they were ready to begin manufacturing the first jet engine in history. In less than eight months, the first jet aircraft would be soaring in the skies of France.

He could see light at the end of the tunnel; it was about time.

Government ministers pleaded overwork and sent their juniors; Joubert did not turn a hair. When the first test proved successful, they would come crawling.

Those companies who had invested substantial funds and personnel in the project agreed to come, but could scarcely hide their scepticism. The newspapers, ever on the lookout for excitement and suspense, would turn out in force.

Joubert felt powerful. Had he ever truly doubted his success, he wondered, forgetting those moments of weakness that now seemed inconsequential.

The atmosphere in the Atelier was electric: they were coming to the end of a project that had started with a rush of confident euphoria and, though there had been difficult times, was bound for success.

The moment she received Paul's letter, Solange telephoned. From Madrid. The concierge had come upstairs to tell him, fuming ("The concierge's lodge is not a post office"). Paul had refused to take the call and she had trudged back downstairs, still seething ("A concierge is not a telephonist").

Over the next month, Solange inundated Paul with letters, gifts, scores, records and posters, to judge by the packaging. The packages themselves were never unwrapped. Every morning, as she dusted them, Vladi would say:

"Szkoda nie otworzyć tej przesyłki . . . W środku mogą być prezenty, naprawdę nie chcesz otworzyć?"

Paul would shake his head. He should have thrown them out, but he did not have the strength. Like a spurned lover, he wanted to walk away but found he could not. Photographs of Solange still adorned the walls, but he no longer listened to her records. Vladi, who realised that Paul needed some excuse, some pretext, continued to insist:

"Skoro nie chcesz otworzyć, uprzedzam cię, że sama to zrobię!"

In mid-August, Paul finally succumbed, alright, fine, he grabbed a large pink envelope that smelled of patchouli. It's such a terrible smell, Madeleine would say, I don't know how anyone can abide it . . . This was Solange's first response. Paul feared that she would defend the Reich. Worse, that she would say she was cancelling her Berlin recital, but for the wrong reasons. It mattered little to Paul whether or not she performed there if, deep down, she harboured Nazi sympathies.

Her handwriting was frantic, her phrases more grandiloquent than ever.

Oh, my darling, this is all my fault! I wanted to be mysterious so that you would be tempted to come, it was foolish, I allowed you to believe things that make me blush – and it takes a lot to make your old Solange blush! I called you on the telephone but you would not talk to me! You do not answer my letters! If you keep up this silence, I don't care, I shall come to Paris especially to see you, as soon as I have finished the recitals on my schedule, I will come and explain everything.

You know how much Richard Strauss adores me . . .

Solange was not merely flattering herself. On several occasions, Strauss had expressed his admiration for the "mystery that is La

Gallinato", a phrase that accurately described what it was like to see this enormous seated woman singing like a hummingbird, effortlessly eliciting tears with arias from "Tosca" or "Madame Butterfly". And so, Strauss, an intimate friend of Goebbels, had been the first to suggest that Solange's visit should be an exceptional occurrence and Goebbels had turned it into a political event. They had been encouraged by various statements from Solange herself: *I did not stint on flattery! When Herr Goebbels wrote to me personally to say that he would be proud to welcome me, I told everyone, and I always added a kind word about Herr Hitler, it made them very happy.*

The programme for the recital was exactly as the Reich expected: Bach, Wagner, Brahms, Beethoven, Schubert. By June, the German press were announcing that the performance was sold out.

Solange had waited until mid-July before telling Richard Strauss that she would also sing "Verlorenes Land" and "Meine Freiheit, meine Seele" by Lorenz Freudiger. *You cannot imagine the effect it had on them, my dear!*

Paul could easily imagine. Freudiger, the director of the Erfurt Conservatoire, had been an obscure composer until he was dismissed from his post in March for refusing to compose the Nazi anthem of Thuringia. The titles of the two works, "The Lost Country" and "My Freedom, My Soul", did not augur well for the Reich and would likely mar the event, something that Strauss attempted to communicate to Solange in diplomatic terms. "My dear friend," he wrote, "these two trifling pieces are unworthy of your talent. Moreover, they would cast a pall over an event that will be historic."

Historic, my little Pinocchio, can you imagine?

Paul began to smile.

"Mój Boże. . . ale. . . co to jest?" said Vladi, holding up the large package that had accompanied Solange's letter.

Paul said nothing, but carried on reading.

Strauss wrote to me twice. That done, the Reich – accustomed to giving orders that went unchallenged – simply struck the two pieces from the programme and considered the matter settled.

I wrote to Strauss to say that I completely understood the Reich's position and assumed that the recital was therefore cancelled.

There was much commotion in the higher echelons. Strauss, who did not lack courage, defended Solange's choices, but it was not his intervention that swayed the decision. The authorities had already done so much, Solange had already made so many statements, it would be more embarrassing to cancel the recital than to go ahead. Goebbels wondered whether, in his desire to hear La Gallinato sing for the Reich, he had not been reckless. To cancel the concert now would create a scandal throughout Europe and turn the spotlight onto Freudiger and others like him. In the end, they were two minor musical works, the Berlin authorities decided, they would pose no problem.

Their troubles are far from over. I have carried on making grand statements, praising the glories of the Reich. As for the set, I am sending you a copy of the project I commissioned.

"Mój Boże . . . ale . . . co to jest?" Vladi said again, proffering the package to Paul.

It took some minutes before Paul could express his thoughts:

"Wh-wh-what is it? It is a T-t-trojan horse!"

Having resolutely declined Solange's invitation to come to Berlin, Paul was now desperate that he could not be there.

Monsieur Brodsky had done much excellent work since July.

"What you are asking for is not particularly difficult, as it has no effect."

He would not budge, but he accepted a further five hundred francs; given his circumstances, it was a considerable sum.

By the end of August, the texture of the product had been refined, soft to the touch, slightly unctuous, it penetrated rapidly. The colour was a rich cream, almost like churned butter. As for the scent, after much consideration, Paul decided there were two possibilities: birch oil or tea tree oil.

"We need to start the testing phase," he wrote on his slate. He presented the little stoneware pots.

Léonce was outraged.

"Absolutely not, Madeleine, I am not a guinea pig! You cannot ask it of me."

"But it's harmless."

"Who told you that?"

"The pharmacist who made it."

"That German of yours? No, thank you! Besides, the man is a Jew."

"I do not see the connection."

"I don't trust him."

"Paul is the one who has asked. He has been massaging the product into his legs every day and he is not dead."

"Not yet, you mean."

"Oh . . ."

Léonce apologised. Alright, what exactly did she have to do? Madeleine could not decently tell her that the primary aim of the test was to determine whether regular use caused spots, pustules, abscesses or swelling.

"You simply massage the creams into your legs. One day the cream with the green lid, the next the one with the grey lid. And you tell me which you prefer."

"Very well."

Everyone was involved, Paul, Vladi, Brodsky, Dupré, Madeleine. But it was not a controlled test. Brodsky, convinced that the salve was as useful as applying balsam to a wooden leg, did not use it. Dupré regularly forgot, but, when asked, insisted that everything was going well. Madeleine did not use the cream because she feared the side effects, my skin is so delicate, so easily irritated. As for Léonce, she came up with a ruse typical of her temperament: she offered Robert a "sensual and stimulating" massage, assuming that it did not matter to which part of the body the cream was applied as long as it penetrated deeply. Tea tree oil won out over the birch by five votes to one, a crushing victory that was in fact somewhat relative since only Paul and Vladi were serious in conducting the test. Vladi was happy to daub herself with it from head to foot, and trailed the scent of tea tree oil in her wake (Ach, uwielbiam zapach tego kremu!), which made Madeleine laugh. Her relationship with Vladi had evolved considerably. She had hired the young woman because she had had little choice, but had never liked her. As a result, three weeks earlier, she had been more surprised than anyone by her reaction to the Crémerie Valet incident.

Fernand Valet, a dairyman on the rue Mignet, was a man of mediocre intelligence, but one who trumpeted his opinions because he liked the idea that he was a character. One morning, he decided he would no longer serve Vladi.

"We don't serve Polacks here no more! Go back to Warsaw and leave the jobs for decent French folk!"

Confused, Vladi had done her shopping elsewhere. When Madeleine noticed, she demanded an explanation. Vladi blushed, she felt guilty that she was Polish. Madeleine insisted.

"Nie mogę już tam chodzić. Nie chcą mnie obsługiwać."

Still the matter was not clear. Madeleine took Vladi by the arm, grabbed the shopping basket and showed up at the creamery where Fernand Valet was holding forth, as was his wont.

"No, madame," he roared angrily. "This is a French business! We only serve French people here!"

He looked to his customers, who were numerous given the time of day, to support his position. Everyone agreed. Valet folded his arms and looked Madeleine up and down.

Madeleine never knew where she got the idea, perhaps from the way Vladi had blushed. Or from the dairyman's macho posturing . . .

"So, it has nothing to do with the fact that this young woman refused to sleep with you?"

The assembled customers gave a scandalised "Oh!", but, since they were all women, mothers with children and parlourmaids, their shock was directed at the dairyman rather than Vladi, who stood, lips pursed, staring at the ground. Having heard, as many had, that Vladi was no shrinking violet, the dairyman had indeed been harassing her. But Vladi had her favourites. And Monsieur Valet, who was not among them, had taken umbrage . . .

With a series of pointed questions, Madeleine threatened to spread scandal throughout the neighbourhood: Was Madame Valet aware of his behaviour? Was sex a precondition for those who bought his cheese? Had droit de seigneur been restored to this particular Paris neighbourhood? Would Monsieur Valet have turned her away if she had been French? Would he have made the same lewd suggestions?

As she continued to fire questions, the other customers – spurred by female solidarity – left the shop. Monsieur Valet, furious but beaten, had no choice but to serve Madeleine a piece of gruyère, whose weight and price she carefully checked, and half a pound of butter.

33

The Atelier was filled to capacity. The guests today were not the enthusiastic supporters who had attended the January dinner at La Closerie des Lilas, they were sombre, austere figures who offered half-hearted greetings and peremptory handshakes. The junior civil servants, who had doubtless received clear instructions, declined the invitation to stay for lunch. The industrialists from Renaissance Française stared at the spread laid out by Potel and Chabot at the back of the Atelier, the white linen tablecloths, the champagne buckets, trying to gauge the price of the petits fours and the salary of the waiters. Even Sacchetti was distant, but diplomatic, that is to say, candid, convivial, Florentine. The press were having a wonderful time, every reporter and photographer in the city was present.

The whole team from the Atelier was in attendance, though it was now little more than a shadow of what it had been when the project was first launched. In fact, numbers were so reduced that the security staff and the cleaners had been invited too. Robert stood ramrod-straight next to the "upstairs girl", as he called the woman who cleaned the offices and whom he groped at every opportunity. He had already had a word with the waiters to ask for a couple of bottles of champagne, "for the staff", though he planned to take them back and drink them with Léonce. He had also filched a box of petits fours that he had hidden in his locker.

In a roped-off area that took up a third of the Atelier, a steel trolley mounted on rails was fitted with a scale model of the turbo-jet. Photographers were allowed to duck under the ropes to take close-up pictures. It was a spherical device encased in an alloy that was pale and gleaming as aluminium. It looked like a bottomless cauldron lying on its side.

Joubert was nervous, though no-one would have noticed. He said only a few words. Besides, no-one would have listened if he had made a long speech.

"Gentlemen, the engine you see before you is a scale model of one that, very soon, will enable fighter planes to fly at three times the speed they currently do. It is fitted with a . . ." he gave a terse laugh, "but I don't want to bore you with details. Let us just say that we are about to demonstrate the formidable power of jet propulsion. Later, the members of my team," he made a sweeping gesture, "will be happy to give you any details."

The photographers unleashed a broadside from their flashguns then stepped back over the rope to recharge their equipment. With a theatrical gesture, Joubert turned to the man in a white laboratory coat standing next to the engine with a blowtorch, which he now lit. The engine revved into life and a huge tongue of flame shot out of the back with the thunderous roar of a forest fire, it was impressive, indeed a little frightening, and those gathered round instinctively took a step back.

Joubert raised his arm.

The trolley took off at such speed that it brought an astonished gasp from the crowd. It hurtled along the track that had been laid and looked set to crash through the wall of the Atelier. Flashguns popped. The trolley was brought to a brutal halt by the attached chains, the engine was turned off, but the propulsion had been so powerful that it left a shockwave. Everyone stood frozen.

Everyone except Robert, who scratched his head. He often found himself confronted by things he did not understand, but this time he was dumbfounded, what had gone wrong?

The crowd, greatly impressed by the demonstration, erupted into deafening applause, smiles and handshakes, relief and congratulations.

Joubert humbly accepted the accolades, his arms spread wide, gesturing to the whole team.

Then he gracefully came forward, the applause grew louder, he stepped over the chain barrier and approached the jet engine. He turned to the photographers, shh, shh, Joubert waited, he had prepared a simple statement, couched in modest terms that would further underscore his ambition.

As the photographers raised their cameras, the engine emitted a high-pitched whine.

Joubert turned to look. The implosion was so violent that the blast sent him reeling and at length he found himself on his arse, hair and eyebrows singed, mouth hanging open, utterly flummoxed.

Robert smiled, oh well, this was much better. He could not understand how the contraption had held together for so long, given the quantity of mercury he had poured into the tank of aluminium . . . But everything had come good in the end; he felt pleased with himself.

Flashguns popped.

This photograph of Gustave Joubert sitting on his arse, gaping at the beautiful model jet engine reduced to a molten pool of metal, caused a great sensation in the newspapers.

Cartoonists depicted Joubert as a chimney sweep, left half-naked by the force of the blast, or soaring through the air on a rocket, like a film by Méliès.

In the grip of a depression such as he had never known, Gustav Joubert spent the whole morning holed up in his room.

No-one dared ask how he was.

What if he dies, thought Léonce. What would happen? Was she his heir? There was the house, of course, but if Joubert owed money, would she be expected to settle his debts?

All the servants began looking for new positions. Morale was low.

Joubert moved away from the window and stared at himself in the large mirror over the mantel, he stepped closer, and what he saw pained him. The untidy five o'clock shadow, the dark circles under the eyes, the deep creases at the corners of the mouth, this was a face he did not recognise, and it frightened him. He turned away.

Until this moment, Joubert had never known hardship. He had excelled at university, been successful in his career, become an industrialist, he had founded Renaissance Française to widespread acclaim, and his project to develop a jet engine had aroused enough jealousy and backbiting for him to realise that it was promising. As he shaved, he racked his brain for examples of historical figures who had risen from the ashes of a devastating failure. He could take heart from the aviator Louis Blériot! After his rift with Léon Levavasseur, Blériot had found himself in an unenviable position,

295

one that was made worse by his decision to work with Robert Esnault-Pelterie, but this had not stopped him successfully flying solo across the Channel in 1909. That said, Joubert could think of many more examples of people who, following a meteoric rise like his own, had fallen, never to get up again.

He did not need anyone to explain his situation. He was now the sort of man to whom, when he was a banker, he would not have lent a sou. He would merely have bought out the company for a token sum.

Late in the morning, he went downstairs but encountered no-one. Hearing his footstep on the stairs, Léonce pressed an ear to her bedroom door but did not open it.

Joubert decided to take a stroll, collect his thoughts. He was gloomy, but, deep down, he could feel something that stubbornly refused to surrender to depressive momentum. These twin forces clashed within him, leaving Joubert torn. It was a bright early-September day, the sky was cloudless and blue, the air warm. These are not the thoughts of a man about to throw himself into the Seine, Joubert thought.

Unsurprisingly, the entire staff of the Atelier had been informed by telegram on Sunday that on Monday morning they should return to the companies that had seconded them.

The following day, Sacchetti telephoned Joubert to explain that it would perhaps be wise for him to step down as president of Renaissance Française.

"It's only a temporary measure, Gustave, you do realise that. Time ripens all things, as Cervantes said. I'm sure you understand."

Renaissance Française has just appointed a new leader, Monsieur Sacchetti. It must be said that the previous incumbent, Monsieur Joubert, is not fit to be seen. As the former passed the baton to his successor, the two men inevitably mentioned the new world record (they are aviation buffs, after all . . .) set by the French aviators Codos and Rossi, who, last month, landed in Lebanon fifty-five hours after taking off from New York.

It is heartening to see that some aviators can succeed.

Kairos

Joubert spent two days holed up in his office. When he sent downstairs for coffee, Léonce felt duty-bound to bring it personally.

"Thank you, darling," he would say, without looking up from his accounts.

"Darling" was not part of his customary vocabulary.

"A number of things will have to change."

Léonce paused in the doorway. She would have liked to set down the tray. Holding it, she feared that she looked like a maid – which, as Joubert took pleasure in reminding her, was essentially what she was.

"Oh . . ." she said.

"A great many things."

Léonce already knew that this would involve money. Perhaps Madeleine had been right to suggest that Léonce find herself a new husband.

"I am going to wind down the company, sell off the machine tools, give up the lease on the Clichy property. We will have to sell this house. Together, that should raise one and a half million francs."

Despite the bald facts, this was not the voice of a broken man, Joubert spoke in the simple yet firm tone that, for years, he had used with his employees and the ladies of the typing pool. This time he was speaking to his wife, but that changed nothing. He was not soliciting her opinion, he was merely informing her.

"We can use half of the money we recoup to move to a decent neighbourhood. The other half I will use to fund my own work. The research on the jet engine is almost complete, all that needs to be solved is the issue with the alloy, I will hire specialists. After that, we only need to build the prototype."

Léonce said nothing. Joubert trailed off, perhaps expecting some word of encouragement.

"But . . ." she said.

It was all she could think to say. It was deeply wounding.

"I beg your pardon?"

These were the very words he had used when he slapped her. Léonce was relieved to be beyond arm's reach.

"But, well . . . it's the last chance."

There you have it, he thought. Even she saw him as desperate, perhaps condemned. Joubert had never thought of his wife as a companion, but, even so, she might show a little trust.

"What does it matter whether it is the first or the last, Léonce! The important thing is to seize an opportunity when the moment arises. And that moment is now."

This was not the time to get worked up.

"All things considered, this has been a very profitable venture. My partners have provided the funding for me to develop a proto-type from which I alone will profit, since the patents are in my name. A year from now, you will be wife to a multimillionaire."

"That's good . . ." murmured Léonce, without conviction. "That's good . . ."

Joubert drove to the Atelier. Outside the gate, he sounded his horn, but there was no-one there. The parking area was deserted, the huge sign emblazoned "Aeronautics Atelier" was still brand new; the venture had not lasted six months.

He opened the gates himself and parked next to the main office. When he went inside, he was surprised to find Robert Ferrand mopping the floor.

"What . . . what are you doing here?"

"To be honest, Monsieur Joubert, I have been wondering that myself, because I haven't seen a soul all morning."

"The Atelier is closed, didn't you know?"

Most of the material had already been taken away. Coils of copper wire, sheets of metal, pipes, compressors, torches, workbenches, tools – it was all gone. What a catastrophe.

"Really?"

"You must have noticed that the place is empty!"

"Well, yes, now you mention it, I wasn't really paying attention . . ."

"This place is closed. Permanently. You can go home, you will receive your final salary by post."

"Well, if that's how it is, I'll go."

Joubert went up to the deserted offices. Everything had been taken: the reams of paper, the office supplies, the drawing boards, the chairs, even the blinds.

He wandered around, gathered up the notebooks, the sketchpads, the drawings, everything that was lying around: it filled eight boxes. Then he opened the safe and took out the blueprints, the administrative records, the ledger, the patent certificates and carried them downstairs. Robert held the door for him.

As he left, Joubert turned back to the immense, deserted workshop.

"I never realised it was so big . . ."

Robert helped pack the paperwork into the boot of his car. Unusually, Joubert shook his hand, proof, if it were needed, that this really was the end.

"You go, M'sieur Joubert, I'll just fetch my things, I'll close the gates when I leave, don't worry."

"Very well, then . . . Good luck, my friend . . ."

"And to you, M'sieur Joubert."

"Beautiful car . . ." Robert added with a covetous look as he closed the gate.

That had been a narrow escape.

He waited until the hum of the engine faded before heading around to the back of the building to meet up with the three friends who had spent all night helping him load anything that could be sold into trucks.

The following morning, the staff members who came on behalf of their companies to recover the tools and the equipment loaned to the Atelier found the premises completely empty, but for a bucket and a mop that had been left in a corner by the back door.

34

The work of the commission was going smoothly. Charles felt confident. He never imagined that the situation would change at a place named La Coudrine, a tiny hamlet near Péronne in the Somme, of which neither he nor anyone else had ever heard, where there lived a farmer called Sauveur Piron who resolutely refused to pay taxes. He was reluctant, like many peasant farmers, to "fatten the fine gentlemen of Paris".

On Wednesday, August 16, 1933, a bailiff bearing numerous reminders, flanked by two gendarmes, pounded on his door intending to confiscate property to the value of the nine thousand francs Piron owed to the Treasury. The farmer's neighbours turned out to support him, insults were traded, and the gendarmes were forced to retreat. When, later, they returned with reinforcements, the farmers did so too. Under normal circumstances, this trivial story would not have gone beyond the four walls of the Treasury department, instead it proved to be a catalyst for a seething discontent that had been waiting for an outlet.

The time had come for a revolt against taxation.

Protest marches were organised. In late August, no fewer than forty-four marches were held in France, drawing members of patriotic youth movements and ex-servicemen, unionists, corporations and staunch anti-republican activists; the country teemed with malcontents and rebels who felt that they had been dispossessed, robbed blind. The biggest culprit was taxation. The great enemy was the state.

The government anxiously watched the glow of these far-off conflagrations as they gradually spread. Thousands of people attended rallies in Sedan, Épinal, Roubaix, Grenoble, Le Mans, Nevers, Châteauroux. All over the country, the forces of law and order were compelled to intervene. Cars and shops were set ablaze; fleets of ambulances were dispatched to deal with the casualties.

In Béziers, a collective decision was taken that echoed the general sentiment: "The undersigned taxpayers hereby call upon all citizens to act and, should it prove necessary, to default on their tax payments."

The dread word had been uttered. And not by the communists, but by shopkeepers, craftsmen, pharmacists, lawyers, doctors! Many taxpayers announced that they were prepared to send their unpaid tax declaration to their member of parliament.

The government found itself faced with a disastrous form of revolt: a general strike on taxation.

"So, he is planning to sell everything?" Madeleine said.

"Yes, everything, even our house . . . Oh, I'm sorry."

The house she was talking about had been Madeleine's childhood home, it had been built by her father. Madeleine gently raised her hand, no need to apologise. Léonce hesitated, then took the plunge:

"I thought that, now I've done everything you asked of me . . ."

"Yes?"

"I'd like my passport back."

"I'm afraid that will not be possible, I'm sorry."

Léonce was now desperate to leave France. She had already

decided where she would go, she had given the matter much thought. All she needed was the money. She had none. The only person from whom she could steal was Joubert, and he now had no money either. With Madeleine holding her in the jaws of a vice, and Robert squirming with pleasure every time he was asked to perform another dirty trick, Léonce could see no end to this story.

Speaking of dirty tricks.

Two days later.

The huge, ornate, cast-iron safe manufactured by Merklen & Dietlin had been installed before the war by Monsieur Péricourt. Joubert had always admired it for its deep patination and its filigree of graphite and brass. When he bought the house, he had not had the heart to replace it, though it was an antiquated model that any experienced burglar could easily crack.

Obviously, Robert, who had lost his touch – if indeed he had ever had it – did not qualify. He knelt in front of the safe, took out some picklocks and began to scratch at the escutcheon around the lock. Léonce warily watched him work; it was rare for him to succeed first time at even the simplest tasks.

"Sure that will be enough, poppet?"

"Just a little more."

He made a few more scratches and leaned back to admire his work; it pleased him.

Meanwhile, Léonce, having spied on Joubert countless times, opened up the globe where she knew he kept the large flat key to the safe. She opened the heavy door. They gathered up the blue-prints, the files, emptied out drawers all over the room as Madeleine had ordered. Robert was in his element, he looked like a child in a pillow fight. Making the most of his distraction, Léonce quietly pocketed an envelope that proved a huge disappointment when she opened it that night. She had hoped to find a small fortune, enough to buy a passport, a ticket for a boat or an aeroplane, and disappear, leaving Madeleine and her own problems behind. It contained only two thousand francs. She did not mention it to Robert, who would have squandered the lot at the racetrack before the week was out.

Having accomplished the trivial task entrusted to him, one that anyone could have done in his stead, Robert started running around the house whooping.

"Hey, get a look at this!" he shouted, as though Léonce did not know the house.

He had found the silverware and was pocketing fistfuls of cutlery.

"No, poppet, we cannot take that, it's too heavy!"

Robert thought for a moment. The weight of the cutlery made the decision for him, but as soon as Léonce had turned her back, he could not help but slip coffee spoons into his jacket pocket.

Léonce gathered up all the jewellery and the silver, going so far as to raid the petty cash purse that the maids used to pay for routine messages. Robert strutted around the house, as entranced as a prospective buyer, and collapsed on the large four-poster bed that had gone unused ever since Léonce had had her own bedroom and Joubert had had his, in other words, since their wedding day. Robert was spellbound by the cream canopy, these carved columns of plump cherubs, the fringed bedspread.

"It's completely . . ."

He was still searching for the word when Léonce joined him.

"What are you doing, poppet?"

She had not had time to close her mouth before he scooped her up and tossed her onto the bed.

"No, Robert, we can't!" she protested. "We don't have time."

As he dropped his jacket on the ground, there was a clatter of silver spoons, but Léonce scarcely had time to notice before Robert was on top of her.

"Not now, Robert!"

If Joubert should suddenly come home . . . Léonce whispered

no, no, but even as she did, she lifted herself up so that he could unbutton her skirt, my God, the effect this had on Robert every time, he fucked her until she was panting for breath. If Joubert had walked into the room, not only would she not have heard, but she would not have stopped rocking and thrusting. She let out long hoarse wails, her eyes bulged, then she fell back, drained, exhausted, and fell asleep.

"Shouldn't we get going?" said Robert.

How long had she been lying here? What time was it? She propped herself up on her elbow. My God, I can't take this anymore. She had been dozing for only a few minutes. Pass me my skirt, will you? She laughed, thank you . . . They grabbed their loot and headed downstairs.

"Robert!"

Léonce nodded to the French windows.

"Oh, yeah, shit!"

He had forgotten what he was supposed to do.

"What did she tell us to do?"

Madeleine had carefully explained everything. Robert smashed a pane of glass with his elbow and they crept out through the servants' entrance into the little yard that opened onto a back alley. Léonce's legs still felt like jelly.

They did not run into Joubert, who did not come home until almost seven o'clock that evening. Oh, monsieur, monsieur! The cook was in a state. She had only just returned. Monsieur, monsieur! Despite the lump in her throat, she tried her best to explain.

"Where is Madame?" Joubert asked.

The cook had not seen her mistress since morning ("It's dreadful, dreadful"). Joubert looked at the open French doors, saw the broken window, but not until he went into his office ("I didn't notice right off") did he comprehend the extent of the devastation. The safe stood open ("Gave me a terrible fright, it did, I can tell you"), the desk drawers were scattered on the ground . . . Such was his shock that he could not think straight ("So I called the police").

"What? You phoned whom?"

Though he would probably have done the same thing, he was taken aback. He needed a minute or two to think, but it was too late.

"Anyone home?"

A voice from downstairs. Joubert pushed past the cook, leaned over the banisters. At the foot of the grand sweeping staircase stood a plain-clothes detective and two officers in uniform.

"Commissaire Fichet. We were called about a burglary."

It took Joubert a moment to respond. The detective, an ageing, stooped, heavyset man in a beige overcoat, turned to the French doors and chewed the butt of a cigar as he stared at the broken window.

"Ah, yes, we've come to the right place."

The cook peered at the officer over the banister, her fist in her mouth, as though confronted by a rattlesnake.

"I suppose that upstairs is where the action is," said the commissaire.

He directed one of the uniformed officers to the living room, the other to the kitchen, while he slowly climbed the stairs.

Joubert was doing his best to appear calm and composed. Each passing second brought him closer to a situation that was new to him and whose implications were only just beginning to dawn.

Although the study was still in a terrible state of confusion, the huge safe loomed over everything. It looked as though it had been disembowelled.

"So there was no-one at home? In the middle of the day?"

He turned to Joubert and the cook.

"It's the domestics' day off," she explained.

"But you're here."

"Well, no, not really . . ."

Now that someone wanted her to explain, now that there was someone who would listen, she took the bull by the horns.

"I've been out all day doing the shopping. The Mistress, she gave me a list as long as your arm."

"Thank you," Joubert interrupted. "You can leave us now, Thérèse. I shall deal with this gentleman."

Since she deemed the police to be a higher authority than her employer, the cook waited for permission from the commissaire, but he was examining the door of the safe, studying it through round spectacles he held up like a lorgnette.

"Off you go, Thérèse," Joubert said impatiently.

"Was there much money in it?" asked the detective.

"Very little. A few thousand francs, I can work it out precisely."

"Valuables, then?"

"Yes . . . well, no . . . I mean, it depends on what you mean by valuables . . ."

"Anything that might be worth money."

"I shall have to check."

"You do that. We will need it to press charges. In the complaint . . . I suppose Madame Joubert has jewellery?"

"I shall have to ask her."

"So your wife is not here?"

It was obvious: giving the domestics a day off, sending the cook on errands – Léonce had made off with his money, or what was left of it.

"She is probably visiting a friend, she will be home soon."

The commissaire went out onto the landing, tried to get his bearings.

The other rooms had not been as thoroughly ransacked as the study, with the exception of a rather elegant bedroom ("Madame's boudoir, I take it"), where the chest of drawers stood open and the jewellery box was upended on the dressing table. The officer tramped back downstairs and went to study the French windows.

He had slipped his spectacles into his pocket and was scratching his head.

"That's curious. Usually, a burglar breaks in from outside. So, when he smashes a window, we find the fragments of glass inside. Our burglar seems to have gone the other way . . . very curious indeed."

Joubert took a step forward and feigned a look of surprise.

An officer appeared from the kitchen.

"The cook said they took the housekeeping money."

The commissaire gave Joubert a quizzical look.

"Petty cash set aside for everyday expenses. It is not very much, twenty or thirty francs at most."

The policeman paced the room, deep in thought, he stepped into the large dining room, where, once again, the drawers of the sideboard were open.

"Was the kitchen ransacked?"

"No, no, boss – in fact it was spick and span!"

"That's curious, isn't it?"

He shot a look at Joubert.

"It's as though the burglar knew exactly where to find things, he didn't have to look for the jewellery and the housekeeping money, he simply took them."

For both men, the pieces of the puzzle were beginning to fall into place.

"And then there are the scratches on the safe," he said to Joubert, indicating the floor upstairs.

Joubert gave a feeble shrug, I don't quite understand.

"When you crack a safe, the picklock might slip once, maybe twice. With a very clumsy burglar, you might even get four or five scratches, but ten or twenty, well, that's very rare. In my experience, anyone who can't master the tools would not be able to open a safe like that. Because that takes skill . . . It almost looks as though the scratches were intentional. To make it look like a burglary."

"Are you accusing me of—"

"No, monsieur! I am merely stating facts, trying to understand, nothing more. I am certainly not accusing you, monsieur, heaven forfend."

But it was written all over his face; that was exactly what he was thinking.

"But the thing is, when someone breaks into a house like this, when they find that everyone is unexpectedly out for the day, they show up with crates, they park a van nearby and they take anything of any value."

He stepped over to the sideboard.

"They don't take the housekeeping money from the kitchen and leave the silver behind."

The detective could see that Joubert was no longer really listening, his mind was clearly reeling.

"Well, we'll file a report. You draw up a list of everything that has been stolen and bring it to us at the commissariat. Soon as you like."

Joubert was still deep in thought when the officers left. With a snort, he raced around the house, throwing open doors – the man was right, nothing else had been touched. He went back to his study.

Léonce had come to steal his money and had found none. He plodded around the room, trampling the things scattered on the floor. But why had she taken the documents, the blueprints? It made no sense! They were of no value to her: she would never be able to sell them! Unless she was already in touch with one of his rivals, but that would be even worse, she would not get a thirtieth of what they were worth! Had her lover forced her to do this? Joubert shook his head, why worry about such details, he needed to focus on the essential.

The situation was fraught.

His wife had left him. He had been forced to shut down his business. His war chest had disappeared with his plans and patents.

He was left with the Péricourt house. It was not much.

How could everything have fallen apart like this? And so quickly?

He was concerned, too, by the fact that the scene had been staged. He could not make sense of it, could not understand the situation he was now in.

Madeleine set aside everything that was of no immediate interest. Everything she wanted was contained in two thick files. On the cover of the first, in large letters, Joubert had scrawled "ABANDONED CONCEPTS" (he must have been in a foul mood that day). This obviously contained the research that had been discontinued in May. The second was marked "CURRENT RESEARCH".

Madeleine carefully set them on the bench beside her, suppressed a smile of satisfaction, everything had worked out perfectly, but she was careful not to react in front of Léonce. Robert was standing, gaping. Seeing them together, one could not help but wonder how two such people had met, let alone married; there are some things in the lives of others that are impossible to fathom.

Madeleine simply smiled.

"You'll need to go into hiding, Léonce. Move to a different hotel."

"Why?"

There was rising panic in her voice. Madeleine had forced her to rob her own husband, now she was making her a fugitive.

"We live on the rue Joubert!" said Robert.

He never ceased to be amazed by this little detail.

"Be quiet, poppet," Léonce said, laying a pretty hand on his arm; she was utterly distraught.

She stared into Madeleine's eyes.

"How are we supposed to move, where are we supposed to find the money?"

"Oh, I agree, that is a problem. So tell me, Léonce, aside from the blueprints, did you find nothing else in your second husband's safe?"

"Nothing, honestly!"

Léonce all but screamed.

"How much nothing, roughly speaking?" Madeleine pressed her.

Robert was breathing on the window, misting the glass and drawing shapes with the tip of his nose.

"How much what?" he asked.

"Poppet! This is women's business!"

Robert threw up his hands, ah, women's business, now that was sacrosanct. He turned to the waiter and ordered another beer, had there been a billiard table, he would have tried his luck.

Madeleine looked at Léonce and smiled.

"Well?"

Léonce stared at her hands, then raised two fingers in reply.

"You are quite sure?"

"Absolutely!"

"Sure about what?"

This was Robert, returning to the fray. Léonce turned to him.

"Darling, could you leave us for a moment, please?"

They had women's matters to discuss, Robert, eager to prove that he was a gentleman, got to his feet.

"Without wishing to be in-indecorate . . . without wanting to be discourtly . . . if you don't mind, ladies, I shall go and smoke a cigarette."

"You do that," said Madeleine.

Then, when he was gone:

"Léonce, please, I beg you," she had taken Léonce's hands in hers, "how can you bear to spend your life with that madman?"

When it came to sex, Léonce had an easy retort, one she did not hesitate to use, but remembering the terrible things she had done to her friend, she tried not to be offensive. She simply prised away Madeleine's fingers, one by one, as though counting them.

"My dear Madeleine, you would not ask the question if you had found a man so skilled in, shall we say, intimate matters."

310

It was a cruel jibe and they both knew it. They withdrew their hands.

"I want my passport."

"I will return it to you in a day or two, but it will be worthless. Worse still, it could land you in prison."

Léonce turned pale. Was this the end? No passport meant no escape and hence no hope. Like a drowning woman, Léonce watched as her life flashed past, the life that had led from her childhood to this moment in this café: the hardships, her father, Casablanca, the sadness, the sex, the men, the escape, then Robert and Paris. Madeleine Péricourt and Joubert . . .

"When will you let me leave?"

"Soon. In a few days you will be free."

"Free! What about money?"

"Yes, I know, life is hard. Be content that I have not had you put in jail."

"What's to say that you won't do it when you don't need me anymore?"

Madeleine stared at her for a long moment.

"Nothing. As a matter of fact, I never promised as much. So, unless you want to tempt fate, I would advise you to be cooperative."

Madeleine went into Paul's bedroom.

"Tell me something, darling . . ."

It was a balmy night, all the windows were open, a warm breeze drifted in as though whispering in their ears.

"I have been thinking. Would you like to go and hear Solange perform in Berlin?"

"Ma-maman!" Paul yelled, wrapping his arms around his mother. She laughed.

"You're smothering me, let me breathe a little . . . my God."

Immediately serious again, Paul picked up his slate.

"What about the money? We have no money!"

"It is true that we do not have much. But since we moved in here,

I have forced you to make so many sacrifices. You don't buy music anymore, and, despite all the invitations, you have not been on any trips. So, anyway . . ."

She looked at him fondly.

"So? Berlin, yes or no?"

Paul gave a joyful shriek. Vladi raced into the room.

"Wszystko w porządku?"

"Yes, ev-ev-erything is f-f-fine," said Paul. "We're all g-going to B-B-Berlin!"

Suddenly seized by doubt, he grabbed his slate. "Maman, the recital is the day after tomorrow! You won't have time!"

Madeleine slipped a hand into her sleeve and pulled out three train tickets. First class. Paul knitted his brow. That his mother should relent and decide to make the trip at the last minute was plausible. That she should buy the most expensive seats was surprising. But that her ticket was made out in the name of Madame Léonce Joubert was inexplicable. Paul scratched his chin.

"Officially," she said, "I will not be travelling with you. You will go with Vladi."

"W porządku!"

"What did she say?" asked Madeleine.

"She says it's f-f-fine."

"But I need to explain something to you, because I am going to need your help."

35

The Gare de l'Est was thronged with people. Paul was very excited.

As Vladi lifted him up and hoisted him into the compartment, he was reminded of his trip to Milan. It seemed so long ago. Solange had met him on the platform, he could still picture the swarm of photographers and reporters, the swirl of veils as she emerged from the plume of smoke from the engine . . . He dreaded seeing her again.

In spite of the loss of social position, the poverty, the humble apartment, the difficult neighbours, the nightmares – rarer now, but no less intense – Paul had to confess: he was a happy child. His mother protected him, Vladi protected him, he had two women taking care of him, who else could claim as much?

Solange, for her part, had been alone for a long time. He reproached himself for having doubted her, for being angry, for thinking . . . My God, they were going to Berlin! The newspaper headlines came flooding back, it was deliciously unsettling, like an adventure novel. He turned and looked for his mother and saw Vladi, with that same beaming smile, he felt a lump in his throat as he realised how much he loved her.

Alerted to his arrival, Solange had responded immediately, the telegram had arrived a few hours before they set off. *So, you are coming!* (There were no spelling mistakes, since the text had been written by the telegraphist who, surely, had a basic education.) *I cannot tell you how happy I am! But your dear mother, alas, what a pity! I have insisted that you stay at my hotel with your nurse, the staff here are the most wonderful in the world.* (Solange dictated telegrams at four francs a word as though she were writing a letter – she did not count the cost.) *So much has been happening in Berlin I cannot wait to tell you, but you will see for yourself. It is a different world here, a very different world. Ah, my little Pinocchio, perhaps you have come to see your old Solange die, because she is weary, her voice is like a frog, you will be disappointed. But I shall be very happy to see you, I am waiting, I have so much to tell you. Come quickly!*

It was a sleeper train. A journey of fifteen hours.

Vladi once again fell in love with the velvet drapes, the carpeted carriages, the lampshades. And with a young conductor. He was not Polish, but a handsome lad nonetheless. Paul was asked to interpret – as though he spoke Polish!

"Vladi, may I in-in-introduce . . . F-François w-w-what?"

"Kessler."

Vladi giggled.

"Ich bin Polin," she said.

"Ich bin Elsässer!" said François.

"Na dann, ich denke wir können uns etwas näher austauschen . . ."

Madeleine did not appear until dinner was served. In the dining car, seeing Paul at his table, she sat at one nearby, they made subtle little signals, it was very funny.

Paul looked her in the eye as he smiled and asked the waiter:

"A g-g-glass of p-p-port, please."

He could read his mother's lips: You little beast!

The wine went straight to his head and left him with no appetite. Vladi wolfed down double helpings of soup, poularde aux oignons, cheese and baked Alaska. The young conductor came and went. Paul was beginning to nod off, Vladi carried him back to the compartment, but she could not let him sleep before they reached the border. To keep him awake, she talked to him and Paul listened half-heartedly, eager to go to bed.

Forbach, at last.

The wheelchair was lowered onto the platform bustling with travellers, police officers and railway porters. The passport officer had not often seen a boy like Paul, who seemed tall though with very short legs, perhaps as a result of his illness, or a wheelchair like his. Monsieur Paul Péricourt and Mademoiselle Włładysława Ambroziewicz. He stamped their passports. They reboarded the train, where customs officers were checking bags and suitcases. Paul was not asked to get out of his chair; if he had been, the officers would have found that he was sitting on two thick folders.

Madeleine too saw the passport officer. Madame Léonce Joubert.

The officer raised an eyebrow. The photograph was rather different from the woman in front of him, but this was not something he could say to a woman, especially when she was travelling first class and had a supreme air of self-assurance, so he bit his tongue. "There you go, madame, bon voyage."

The train rattled into life again. This time, Paul did not hear Vladi's stifled giggles, her sensual gasps, for there were none. She and the young conductor stood in the passageway for a long time, talking. Then Vladi announced:

"No, a teraz już pora iść spać. Dobranoc François."

"Gute Nacht dir auch."

This trip was truly exceptional.

Solange scarcely moved these days, it would have been impossible for her to go to the railway station in person. She sent a limousine to collect Paul and Vladi.

The chauffeur, wearing an armband emblazoned with a swastika, balked when he saw the wheelchair. He looked quizzically at this rather chubby boy who could not walk on two legs like everyone else. Vladi settled Paul into the back seat, picked up the chair and, without a word, folded it and put it into in the boot.

Through the car window, Paul saw his mother, as Madame Joubert, waiting at the taxi rank, and felt a pang of anguish.

The French press only ever wrote about Berlin or Germany to describe the most brutal episodes of Nazi propaganda. Paul, who had expected to see a war-torn city patrolled by militia, thought it looked rather provincial. There were people in the streets, but fewer soldiers than he had expected, and if he had not read the papers recently, he could easily have believed he was in any northern European city. Banners bearing the swastika hung from government buildings, the railway station, the university, the central post office, but had he not seen empty shops with shattered windows daubed with painted letters, he would not have realised he was in Berlin.

Solange was sitting like a monumental statue in the lobby of the Grand Hotel Esplanade.

When Paul appeared, she let out a cry that startled the staff and guests who turned to look. She enfolded him in her huge, flabby arms, kissed him as though she might devour him. Paul laughed, torn between the joy of seeing her again and the sadness that so much had changed. Close up, her face, larded with make-up and powder, looked like a grotesque, pathetic carnival mask. He felt afraid for her. Could she still sing? He remembered her telegram, *your old Solange now sings like a frog.*

"Are you alright, my baby?" Solange said. "You are not worried, are you?"

Paul felt reassured. Solange could sense things better than anyone he knew, this had always been the secret of her art.

They walked to the elevator. Solange shuffled slowly, the pommel of her walking stick engulfed by her chubby hand. She chattered on, her voice loud and crooning, rolling her *r*s even more than usual. Today she had a Spanish accent, on other days she was Italian or Argentinian – he never knew what to expect.

"Perhaps you would like to see the city? Ah, the Brandenburg Gate! You must see it, my little Pinocchio! I never go there now; I have seen it a hundred times!"

No sooner was the suggestion made than it was forgotten.

In Paul and Vladi's hotel suite, she collapsed on the deep sofa while Vladi unpacked the suitcases and trunks, put away the clothes, bustled around the bathroom whistling shrill tunes no-one could recognise.

"She's still the same . . ." said Solange.

"The s-s-same."

Solange began to recite a litany of "her misfortunes". She complained about everything, and although her natural inclination was to whine and moan, this time Paul had to admit she had good reason.

The concert scheduled for the following day would entail

last-minute negotiations since the Chancellor in person was to attend, and half the audience would be Nazi bigwigs, to say nothing of journalists, or, more accurately, propagandists. There was a tension in the air, Solange was being bombarded with requests, questions, it was crucial that everything go according to plan. Perhaps, now that she was in Berlin, Solange was finally aware that this project she had found so amusing over the past months was taking on a grave, political dimension, because these people were not natural comedians. Was she afraid? Paul felt that she was.

"Strauss is making my life hell. I can understand why, he is caught between a rock and a hard place, but I have told him what I plan to sing, and I will not change my mind."

Sometimes she dropped her voice as though the hotel room was bugged.

"I am more upset about the stage set . . ."

When he had seen the drawings for the project, Paul had laughed. She now handed him a photograph, the set was very different.

"Wh-wh-what is th-th-this?"

"It is a dust cover, my darling."

Solange could tell he was finding it difficult to understand.

"The problem is, it is impossible to keep the scenery a secret, there is always some photographer prepared to pay fifty dollars for someone to unlock the stage door."

The photograph Paul was holding depicted a wheat field against the sky, streaks of colour that, while not exactly ugly, had nothing to do with the design for the stage set Solange had previously sent.

"I shall let you in on a big secret, my dove. If the set had been shipped as it should look, someone would have said something and, given that there are already tensions about the fact that I plan to sing songs that they do not want to hear, it would have been destroyed and replaced by huge bouquets of flowers in Nazi colours."

It was a clever ruse.

Over the painted backcloth, the artist had pasted a second canvas

317

depicting a sheaf of ripe wheat. This could be peeled away minutes before the curtain rose to reveal the real set design.

"But that's the problem, my little sugar bunny, I'm not very steady on my legs, as you know, can you imagine me trying to peel off a canvas that is nearly three metres high?"

There were four large panels, the task would require energy, physical strength, a stepladder, and a head for heights.

"In short, my little Byzantine doll" (one could not help but wonder where she found these endearments), "it looks as though I will have to sing in front of this yellow daub – such a shame! Especially given how much work the young Spanish painter put into the set design, how will I find the words to tell him?"

Although the original design had made Paul laugh, it had been a laugh from the safety of Paris. Here in Berlin . . . One look at the grim face of the chauffeur who had picked him up at the station told him everything he needed to know. Suddenly, an idea occurred to him:

"P-p-perhaps Vladi c-c-could climb the s-s-stepladder?"

Solange turned to find Vladi standing on a chair. Rather than summoning a hotel porter, she had taken it upon herself to replace a curtain ring that had come loose.

The Reichsluftfahrtministerium occupied three floors of an imposing building near Wilhelmstrasse. The facade was draped with a Nazi flag and two soldiers, stiff as ramrods, glowered at the world through beady eyes. Madeleine had to summon every ounce of strength to seem confident and casual as she stepped inside.

There were problems from the moment she approached the reception desk. The official did not speak French, he had to go and find someone else.

"Ihr Pass, bitte!"

He pointed to a waiting room and Madeleine went and sat on a bench, resting the folders she had brought from Paris on her lap. A clock on the wall told her it was ten o'clock.

The recently established Ministry of Aviation was the bailiwick of Reichsmarschall Göring, an aviator decorated for his victories during the Great War and a close friend of Herr Hitler. From reading the newspapers, Madeleine had discovered that this was the ministry responsible for overseeing, designing and regulating the production of civil and military aircraft; she could find no better place.

"It is . . . for what reason?"

The new official, a young man of about twenty, spoke approximate French.

"I would like to see Field Marshal Erhard Milch."

Madeleine articulated slowly so that she would be understood. The young man stared at her intently. He was holding her passport, staring at the name, the photograph, but did not know what to say to a Frenchwoman who spoke no German and had shown up, unannounced, asking to speak to the Secretary of State.

"It is . . . for what reason?"

"I would like to see Field Marshal Erhard Milch."

The conversation was going round in circles. The young man walked away and spoke to his colleague at the reception desk.

"You sit," he said at length.

He headed up the sweeping staircase and Madeleine continued to wait.

The clock on the wall had almost struck noon by the time an officer of about fifty wearing a Nazi uniform appeared. He was now holding her passport.

"Apologies for the delay, Madame Joubert, but since you had no appointment . . ."

He clicked his heels.

"Sturmbannführer Günter Dietrich. What can I do for you?"

Madeleine could ill imagine launching into such a delicate conversation here in the lobby.

"It is a personal matter, Herr Dietrich."

"Of what nature?"

The Sturmbannführer was keenly aware of the awkwardness of the situation. And, when Madeleine simply gazed at him impassively, he added:

"Personal . . . Do you mean 'highly personal'? Does it concern your husband, Madame Joubert?"

The Sturmbannführer had won the first round. He knew about her, about Gustave, perhaps he knew more than she did about the reason for her visit. Paradoxically, finding herself in the weaker position was reassuring, since it left her no option. The firmer she was, the greater the chance that she would get through this.

"My husband sent me."

Dietrich turned and gave an order to the young man standing behind him. Then he said to Madeleine:

"If you would like to follow me."

He nodded to the stairs. They went up together.

"How was the weather in Paris yesterday, Madame Joubert?"

They knew when she had arrived, they probably knew where she was staying. Was there anything they did not already know about her?

"Very clement, Sturmbannführer."

A long broad corridor, and then another. From all around came the murmur of voices, the clatter of typewriters, the clack of nervous footsteps on the flagstone. The vast office had a seating area, he gestured to the sofa.

"I will not insult a French lady by offering her a ministerial tea or coffee – but perhaps a glass of water?"

Madeleine politely declined. Dietrich took the chair facing her, he was a head taller. He adopted a tone of feigned sympathy.

"So, Madame Joubert, are we talking about bankruptcy?"

"You might put it like that, Sturmbannführer. My husband held out for as long as he could, but . . ."

"Such a shame. It was a magnificent project!"

320

Madeleine conspicuously clasped her hands over the folder on her lap.

"Indeed. And so close to completion."

"Although the most recent tests were not entirely conclusive . . ."

His tone was deceptively light-hearted.

"As my husband says, the tests are intended to do just that: test. The various setbacks have made it possible to make breakthrough advances in the design of the jet engine. All that was required was for our sponsors to show a little patience and – dare I say it? – a little courage."

"And your husband is reluctant to see the fruits of his labours tossed aside. He would like to see his research continue."

"In the interests of the scientific community!"

Dietrich nodded, he accepted such noble intentions. He gestured to the dossier in Madeleine's lap.

"So, this is . . ."

"Yes, it is."

"I see, I see. And your husband will be, shall we say, a disinterested party in these negotiations . . ."

"Of course, Sturmbannführer!" Madeleine said, indignantly. "In France, intellectual property is not considered to be a vulgar commodity. We believe that creativity cannot be bought or sold!"

"That being the case, how does your husband envisage allowing the scientific community to profit from his research?"

"Free of charge, Sturmbannführer, free of charge! Aside from minor expenses, of course."

"Which would amount to . . . ?"

"My husband's estimate was six hundred thousand Swiss francs. I said to him, 'Gustave, that is unreasonable. Granted, you incurred considerable expenses, but people will think you are trying to profit from your work.' And I managed to persuade him, Sturmbannführer! He recalculated and I was right: the true figure is only five hundred thousand Swiss francs."

"These are significant expenses."

"I agree, Sturmbannführer, research these days is terribly expensive."

"What I mean, madame, is that the price is too high."

Madeleine nodded, I completely understand. She got to her feet.

"To be honest, Sturmbannführer, it was I who suggested coming to Berlin rather than crossing the Atlantic as my husband proposed, because sea voyages do not agree with me. Thank you for meeting with me, it was very kind."

She took three steps towards the door.

"It depends . . . how useful these documents prove."

Madeleine turned to Dietrich.

"Tell me, Sturmbannführer. How far advanced are you, I mean the glorious Ministry of Aviation, when it comes to jet engines?"

"Well . . . let us say that we are still in the early stages."

Madeleine patted her dossier.

"This contains everything you need to go from the 'early stages' to revolutionary research. Surely the Reich does not wish the world to think of its aviation industry as in the 'early stages'?"

"Indeed, indeed . . . But you must understand this is a delicate and difficult decision. Given the costs . . ."

Madeleine handed him the file.

"These are some excerpts. Blueprints, plans, the results of some of the tests, together with four annotated pages of the final report. To be perfectly honest, if you can spare me the boat trip to New York . . ."

She fanned herself as though already feeling seasick.

"I will have to have this reviewed by experts."

"Shall we say Monday, then?"

Madeleine paused. Dietrich smiled.

"At the same time? Oh, one more thing. Do not trouble to search my hotel room and do not imagine that you can intimidate me. The rest of the documents are in a very safe place."

The remainder of the documents were at the Grand Hotel Esplanade, in the suite shared by Paul and Vladi.

"Madame Joubert, such methods are utterly alien to the Third Reich! We are a civilised people."

"In that case, on Monday I will take the risk of accepting a cup of the ministerial tea."

36

The message was from Madeleine Péricourt. As the telegraphist dictated, André jotted it down in the margin of a piece of paper and stared at it for a long moment.

Dear André – STOP – informed by a friend – STOP – Léonce Joubert currently in Germany – STOP – most strange – STOP – affectionately Madeleine

At first, he thought it was a hoax. Not that Madeleine was likely to play such a joke, but the news was so startling . . . And if it were true, how had she found out? Who exactly was this friend? Madeleine had no friends these days.

André stopped short. He realised what was at stake. It was huge.

He thought about his newspaper, *The Lictor*, which was scheduled to launch a month from now. He could not wait. The news would be out of date. He had to strike while the iron was hot.

He rummaged through his contact books for a telephone number for Léonce Joubert. After all, she was the person most directly concerned. Either she was in Paris and the telegram was a hoax, or . . . While he waited to be connected, he imagined the consequences. Was he the only person with this information? Probably. He congratulated himself on having maintained a relationship with Madeleine, however distant. The telephone operator called back. There was no answer from the number.

André took the stairs four at a time, raced into the street, hailed a taxi, and headed to Madeleine's apartment.

"They went away the day before yesterday," the concierge said.

She was sorry not to be able to help this fine, upstanding young man. She was a widow.

"They've gone to take the waters," she said. "In Normandy somewhere, I can't say where exactly."

She could see that André was surprised.

"It's for the lad, doctor says the spa will do him good."

"When do they get back?"

"I'm not rightly sure. Madame said about a fortnight."

André hesitated for a moment on the pavement. He was deeply annoyed, but there was nothing he could do. Twenty minutes later, he was at the newspaper.

Jules Guilloteaux took the message between his pudgy fingers.

"Could she have gone to Berlin . . . on her husband's orders?"

"It hardly matters whether one or both of them is involved. If it's true, this is treason. For France, it would mean—"

"I don't give a damn what it means for France," said Guilloteaux. "For this newspaper, it's excellent!"

"We should call . . ."

"Tsk, tsk, tsk! We are not going to call anyone, my young friend, do you want the story to leak?"

They took a taxi together, each engrossed in his own thoughts. André was composing his column, and longing to tell Guilloteaux that, very soon, he would no longer be able to get this kind of scoop. Guilloteaux, for his part, was thinking of circulation figures.

"Are you absolutely sure?" said Vitrelle.

He was a tall, lean man, the scion of a family that boasted alumni of the École Polytechnique as far back as the Renaissance, and a panjandrum with the ear of the Minister for the Interior.

"My dear Vitrelle," said Guilloteaux. "If we were absolutely sure, we would not be here in this office and the story would already be splashed on the front page of *Soir de Paris*!"

"I say, that is going a little far! Here, let me call one of my colleagues."

From there, the news trickled out like meltwater in spring, swelling to a torrent as it cascaded from the higher echelons of the ministry to the dungeons of counterespionage.

"Do not print a word of this, Guilloteaux. In return, I guarantee that you will be the first to be informed."

"That was not quite what I had in mind."

Vitrelle's response was a silent question, a technique he had learned in the civil service.

"I don't want to be the first to be told, I want to be the only one. Otherwise, I'll publish the story right now!"

"Very well. You will be the first and the only person to be informed. Does that suit you?"

He laughed a little too loudly.

When he arrived home, André went back to working on his article, but his mind was elsewhere.

He had access to what promised to be a spectacular scandal. Better yet, an opportunity for revenge. Joubert had always treated him with contempt, and André was eager to make him pay.

It was decided that Paul would watch the recital from the wings. A boy in a wheelchair was not a shining example of humanity as conceived by the Reich, the formalities for the evening were already complicated enough, and, besides, Paul wanted to be close to Solange and to Vladi, who had eagerly accepted a mission whose importance she did not truly understand.

Twenty minutes before the concert began, Solange settled herself on the stage, clambering onto the dais, where she sat motionless while dressers and make-up artists bustled about. Her face a mask of marble, she gazed at the lowered curtain in a trance, one from which she would awaken only when it was all over, as though God himself clicked his fingers to bring her back to earth. Richard Strauss pleaded to be allowed to greet her, but was not allowed to come backstage.

At the appointed hour, the entire hall was filled to capacity, with the exception of the prestigious boxes, whose guests were fashionably late. Paul was sitting in his wheelchair between the curtains in the wings, and staring at Vladi as though she were the star who was about to take the stage.

From out in the concert hall there came a commotion; Paul peeked through a crack in the curtains. The Reich Chancellor had arrived with an entourage of uniformed officers and a few elegantly dressed women. Paul raised his hand and Vladi crept forward carrying a stepladder four times her size, which she placed in front of the canvas panels that made up the stage set.

Muffled cries, raucous shouts . . .

Realising that something unforeseen was about to happen, three stage managers rushed onto the stage, but Vladi was already standing on the seventh or eighth rung of the ladder. The three men looked up, then froze. Vladi had peeled away a corner of the canvas, which came away and fell slowly onto the stage, where it curled up like a piece of orange peel, revealing the real set. The three stage managers watched, mesmerised, unable to move. What was she wearing – or not wearing – under her skirts, to so petrify these men? This was what Paul was thinking as Vladi turned and gave him a mischievous wink that set off a fit of giggles.

Within seconds, she had peeled away half the canvas. She calmly climbed down the stepladder, moved it several metres and climbed up again to peel away the second half. None of the stage managers attempted to stop her. They stood like handymen at the foot of the ladder, staring up into the flies, as though at the door of heaven itself.

The second section of canvas glided to the floor, Vladi climbed down and gathered up the shreds of torn fabric.

The bell sounded for the recital to begin; the effect on the stage managers was like an electric shock, one of them grabbed the stepladder, and they disappeared into the wings without so much as a glance at the image that had been revealed and was now bathed in spotlights as the curtain rose to thunderous applause.

The concert hall was in darkness. In the centre of the brightly lit stage, in a cascade of tulle, silk and ribbons, sat Solange Gallinato, majestic, imperious.

The audience did not have time to react when the first note rang out, a cappella, the note they had all been waiting for, a note of legend that heralded three simple words that had been sung around the world:

My dearest love . . .

The audience in the vast Berlin Staatsoper were mesmerised by the diva, her powerful, modulated, broken voice pierced every heart, but they were equally mesmerised by the stage set, which was certainly not the triumphant harvest scene in a bland, reassuring palette of gold that had been announced and, they believed, approved.

Here we are, in the ruins of the palace
Where first we glimpsed each other . . .

The backdrop was a painted ruin, depicting a huge, dusty, decrepit cello with two broken strings that looked as though it had been found in a barn. Examined more closely, the instrument might have been a guitar, since it had a soundhole in the form of an open oyster.

What wild jealousy had you in thrall?
Can it be that these meagre ruins
Are all that now remains
Of us?

The twenty-nine-year-old Spanish painter had created a symbolic Solange that he had then duplicated, since, next to the cello, at the far end of the canvas, a huge turkey stood facing the audience, its tail spread like a peacock. It was a perfectly ordinary gallinaceous bird, a commonplace turkey, its eyes glassy, its beak open, but it possessed something that set it apart from other farmyard fowl (a number of smaller birds could be seen in the background): a huge fan of delicate, brightly coloured feathers.

Look upon the chaos
You have made of my life . . .

Chaos brooded over this opening aria. Solange had never sung the aria better, had never inhabited it so completely. Chaos hovered over the silence and the scattered, hesitant, uneasy applause. All eyes were turned to the box where the Reich Chancellor was sitting.

Faithful to the running order, the orchestra played the opening bars of "Mein Herz schwimmt im Blut", only to be drowned out by Solange's voice. The conductor looked up, confused, and saw Solange's right hand, palm raised to the orchestra pit, as she said commandingly, "Bitte! Bitte!"

The baffled musicians abandoned their score. For a moment, it sounded as though they were tuning up. Then there was silence. A hush fell over the concert hall. Solange closed her eyes and once again began to sing, a cappella, "Meine Freiheit, meine Seele" ("My Freedom, My Soul") by Lorenz Freudiger, a song the authorities had hoped to bury in the programme, but which she made the true opening of her recital.

Her eyes closed, Solange sang *Ich wurde mit dir geboren* (I was born with you).

A minute passed, then the Chancellor got to his feet, everyone stood up, still Solange continued to sing *Ich will mit dir sterben* (I will die with you).

In the wings, Paul was weeping, the Nazi officers left the boxes, and the whole hall erupted in a commotion.

Still Solange sang *Morgen werden wir zusammen sterben* (Tomorrow we die together).

The audience poured out of the concert hall, the musicians got to their feet in a clatter of instruments, Solange's voice was drowned out by jeers and boos . . .

Only thirty people were left scattered throughout the Staatsoper. Who they were, no-one ever knew. They were on their feet, applauding. The theatre was plunged into darkness and a huge laugh was heard, the laugh of Solange Gallinato, a laugh that was more music.

On the train home, Paul was reluctant to sleep for fear that everything he had witnessed would fade like a dream, he wanted to remember everything.

The Berlin Staatsoper in darkness, the loud protests of the few remaining listeners, Solange's laugh, harrowing and desperate. A minute or two had passed. From the wings, Paul could hear people groping for the exit, and then a light came on, Solange raised her head, a spotlight high above suddenly illuminated the tangle of tulle and hair that was Solange Gallinato.

Paul grabbed the wheels of his chair. Vladi suddenly appeared, it was she who had found a stage manager and turned on the spotlight.

A moment later, the three of them were alone on the vast stage, at the end of a recital that had not lasted twenty minutes yet had inspired them for a lifetime.

Vladi knelt in front of Solange, Paul wheeled himself closer. The three embraced for a long time.

"Come, Pinocchio, we need to leave!"

But instead of trying to get up, Solange took Vladi's face in her hands.

"You are a beautiful soul."

She bowed her head and softly, almost inaudibly, sang the opening bars of "Manon" – *Ah! le beau diamant . . .* – and kissed Vladi. Then she sighed.

"And now, the highlight of the evening: Solange Gallinato will stand up . . ."

Which she did.

Here they stand, our three characters, on the empty stage of the Berlin Staatsoper. On the right, Wlładysława Ambroziewicz, known as Vladi, who has experienced great hardship, but nothing has ever doused her faith in life, her desire to live, to be happy. She has paid no heed to what others think of her, she has loved men, sex, spontaneous hugs, earth-shattering orgasms, she is almost thirty, she has a strong constitution, a ravening mouth, the heart of a swallow, and, though she does not yet know it, something has ended.

On the left, in his wheelchair, Paul Péricourt. He too has known much hardship in his life, we have seen him plunge from a second-floor window onto his grandfather's bier. We have seen him mute, catatonic, on the point of death, we have heard him screaming on a night in December 1929 as he recalled the most heinous acts that can occur in any childhood, we have watched him wrap himself in music as in a cloak, besotted with the star whose voice has pierced his life.

Flanked by these two, with faltering steps, gripping a cane in each hand, Solange Gallinato leaves the stage after the most memorable recital of her career.

Three souls fit to burst.

This evening will change their lives.

A shadow appears from the wings, it is the conductor – though he scarcely conducted four bars all evening. What is he still doing here?

"Thank you," he says, his eyes filled with tears.

"Come, now," says Solange. "Why do you thank me?"

But she knows.

Behind her, on the stage, the three stage managers are praying that they will not be arrested tomorrow. They pull down the stage set by the Spanish artist, filling large bags with the shreds of a work of art that no-one will ever see again.

"Can we have a little light?" says Solange.

Most evenings, her dressing room is filled with people, admirers, bigwigs, critics, and Solange, a picture of false modesty, basks in their praises. Tonight, there is nothing and no-one. But Solange is happy, this is the most wonderful night of her life. She has often felt pleased with herself for trivial reasons, tonight she feels proud, which is very different.

"Did you see that, my little Pinocchio?"

Vladi hands her cotton wool and cleanser as she removes her make-up.

These are the images that Paul is picturing as the train hurtles back towards Paris. He wishes that his mother could have seen it.

"Come on," he says to Vladi. "You must be hungry."

"Oczywiście!"

The train rolls on.

Eventually, Paul falls asleep. He snores softly, a purring sound that Vladi adores. To her, it is a sign of blithe, carefree sleep, nothing like the young conductor, François . . . François . . . what was his name again? Ah, Kessler! That's it.

Out in the corridor, they speak German. He explains that he has swapped shifts with a colleague, he smiles. He does not say that he suggested swapping his shift so that he could see Vladi, because he did not have her address, he did not even know her name, all he knew was the date she was travelling back to Paris.

Solange Gallinato is on a train bound for Amsterdam, via Hanover. She was given no choice. During the night, German soldiers burst into her room, uniformed women packed her bags any old how. But they did nothing to upset her, they clearly had their orders, the crucial thing was that she leave Berlin that night, and Amsterdam would be her first stop. Very well, Solange thinks, she will travel back to Milan at the weekend, she does not truly live anywhere, certainly not here. She feels a little sorry for the Spanish painter, but he will laugh at what happened. She has met him only once, a handsome lad, cheerful, free-thinking.

As for Strauss, he did not come to say goodbye, he did not even send word; he is justifiably furious.

Solange thinks of her little Pinocchio. And the young Polish woman who clambered up the ladder.

Solange is weary.

Since she did not get to pack her bags herself, she has nothing to read, and so she falls asleep. Picture the scene. A first-class carriage on a night train, a whole carriage reserved for this celebrated woman who is so fat that she can barely stand without asking someone to help her. Usually, she is surrounded by people who fawn on her and entertain her; tonight, she is alone, she has been banished from Berlin, the scene of many former triumphs. If she is to believe his letters, Richard Strauss has never loved anyone but her. A conductor discreetly knocks – Yes? He opens the door to check her ticket and, startled, hurriedly apologises and closes the door again. Solange is a terrifying sight, a mass of wrinkles slumped on the Pullman seat, gasping like a beached whale.

In fact, she is a little girl.

She is seven years old, the same age as Paul when he threw himself out the window. Her father has just come home, he smells of cheap wine, she can hear chairs being knocked over in the kitchen, she gets out of bed, her mother is sprawled on the table, her father is on top of her, beating her, the little girl rushes forward, tugs at her father, but he is strong and gnarled as a vine, he works outdoors, his muscles are steel cables, she raises the only thing she can find, a cast iron skillet heavy as an anvil and brings it down on the back of his head, a blow that would fell an ox. Her father slumps to one side, there is blood everywhere, her mother goes to sleep with her children, leaving him to bleed, to die, and that is how life is all the time, her father is a caged animal. Every day brings with it its share of violence and fear, the children are covered in bruises, at school, no-one remarks, this is the countryside, they cannot keep track of every child with bruises . . .

What time is it, where is she? Solange struggles to remember, but she can feel a far-off pain, a primal pain, the rattle of the train pulses through her entrails, conjuring images. Amsterdam, she is there with Maurice Grandet, impossibly handsome, almost feminine, it is here that he composed "Gloria Mundi", rain falling on the city for a week. They are staying in a hotel overlooking a canal, they could be spending the week in bed making love, but Maurice is composing while Solange bends over him, breathing in his scent, soundlessly murmuring the notes that fill the stave as the hours pass, he tears up endless pages, still Solange waits, eventually Maurice comes to bed, collapses, exhausted, she pulls him to her and they sleep, but when she wakes, he is already back at the little desk overlooking a canal, working. When he finally finishes, they spend a whole afternoon in the hotel lobby, Maurice sitting at the old upright piano and Solange, score in hand, singing until the customers ask them to shut up, but then everyone laughs and asks for autographs. One day, in Melbourne, a man rushed up to Solange and showed her the hotel menu she signed for him, Maurice's signature must have been there too, Solange burst into tears.

Another window, this one overlooking the sea, on the French Riviera, Maurice is handsome, still just as beautiful, she has just bought him a Rolls-Royce, a moment of madness, the police arrive, they knock at the door, she is still in her nightdress, they turn away to give her time to slip on a bathrobe, they tell her that Maurice is dead.

Solange owes her talent completely to sadness and to grief, because this is her birth sign, from the beginning to the end, she has been a child of suffering, this is the end.

It is two o'clock in the morning, the train drones the quiet lullaby that brings sleep and dreams, Solange sleeps, she dreams, the train is about to pull into Amsterdam Central Station, a young conductor gently taps his ticket punch against the windows of each compartment, this is a first-class carriage, he is considerate with his guests. Madame? We shall be arriving in a few minutes.

Solange is still in Berlin, "Bitte, bitte!" she cries, she had not known she was capable of such violence, such courage. She is glad that she organised this recital for people she despises with every fibre of her being. It was futile, perhaps, but it was necessary.

She sings, her voice dropping to a low murmur:

Morgen werden wir . . .

The train pulls into Central Station.

. . . zusammen sterben.

Solange Gallinato, née Bernadette Traviers in Dole (Jura), has died.

37

"Are you not going to offer me tea, Herr Dietrich?"

Madeleine feigned insouciance, though she had not slept for two days.

She had dined at a restaurant on Leipziger Strasse, just as Solange was due to begin her recital. What was happening in the Staatsoper? What had that madwoman Solange come up with to make herself seem interesting? Afterwards, Madeleine had walked the streets of Berlin trying to compose herself, she glanced at her watch, ten o'clock, half past ten, it was time to go back to the hotel.

It would have been folly for Paul to telephone or to leave a message for her at reception. She could get news of what had happened, though it pained her.

She tossed and turned all night and by morning she was exhausted. There was still another long day of waiting. By now, Paul and Vladi would be on the train back to Paris, it was Sunday.

"I slept very well, thank you, Herr Dietrich. German hotels are the finest in the world."

"Did you have time on Sunday to see a little of the city?"

"I did. What a magnificent country you have."

She had not left her hotel. Down in the lobby and out on the pavement, a succession of men replaced each other, she could not have made a move without it being reported to Günter Dietrich, so she decided to stay in her room, she had her meals sent up, there were moments of fear and others of fury. In her imagination, she was travelling with Paul.

"I'm afraid my superiors have decided that the costs are too great, Madame Joubert, I am sorry."

Dietrich had poured the tea and told her an amusing story about the Sainte-Geneviève library, before suddenly launching into the heart of the matter:

"Our technicians did not find the documents you supplied of sufficient interest."

Madeleine gave an inaudible sigh of relief. They had not turned up any information about Léonce Joubert. Perhaps their spies in Paris had told them that Léonce had disappeared, as Madeleine had told her to do. As for the rest, they were each playing their role; if Dietrich had accepted her terms at that point in the negotiations, it would have been a very bad sign. His principled refusal corroborated the value of what she had for sale.

"I confess I am a little disappointed, Herr Dietrich, but I understand. And since we are here, I will let you in on a little secret: my husband always felt we should deal with the Italians."

"They have no money!"

"I have wasted my breath telling him as much! But, when my husband gets an idea into his head . . . 'No-one in Europe has any money,' he told me, 'but when it comes down to it they always manage to scrape together the funds to pay for what they want.'

335

According to him, Mussolini does not intend to play second fiddle to Herr Hitler. When Marshal Balbo had his squadron of seaplanes fly from Rome to Chicago in recent weeks, it was not simply for show, but because the fascist regime has military ambitions. I confess, Herr Dietrich, that such matters are beyond me. This is men's business."

Madeleine got to her feet.

Dietrich was embarrassed and it was palpable.

"Just one last question, if I may. In the event that my superiors were to change their minds," he lowered his voice to a confiding whisper, "you know how superiors are, they say one thing one day and the opposite the next . . . how would you want your husband's 'expenses' to be paid?"

Madeleine sat down again.

"This is a point on which we cannot agree, Herr Dietrich. He suggested a bank transfer, I would prefer cash, it is more . . . fluid, you understand. To preserve peace in the household, I think it would be best to keep everyone happy. Half and half."

She rummaged in her bag and took out a slip of paper.

"These are the bank details. If your superiors should reconsider, of course."

Dietrich took the paper. He felt a pang of doubt.

"The account is in your husband's name. Is this correct?"

"What can I say . . . Yes, this is a . . . a dormant account. Gustave is a man of great discretion. To guard against malicious people, they are everywhere."

Dietrich did not seem entirely convinced by this argument.

"Ideally," Madeleine went on, "if your superiors should change their minds, obviously, the source of the funds should also be . . . discreet, if you get my meaning. It could come from a foreign company, for example, and should appear as payment for an order."

"I understand . . . So, half of the funds to be credited to this account," he gingerly held the paper between his fingers, "and the other half to you, is that correct?"

336

"That is correct."

She got to her feet again.

"I shall be leaving Berlin tonight. Do you think that your superiors are likely to change their minds quickly?"

"It is entirely possible, Madame Joubert. Except for the cash. That would be a little more complicated in such a short space of time."

Madeleine gave a coquettish smile, as though teasing him.

"Surely you are not going to tell me that a highly organised state like the glorious Third Reich does not have a little piggy bank somewhere?"

By mid-afternoon, Madeleine was on tenterhooks, the minutes were ticking past, she had already packed her suitcase and was now watching from the window, checking the telephone was working. Just then the receptionist called to inform her that an officer was waiting for her in the lobby; she had not seen him arrive.

She went downstairs with the dossier, which the officer tucked under his arm, curtly gesturing to the street. He indicated the revolving door, as though ushering her outside. A black limousine pulled up, the young officer said something in an authoritative voice.

The concierge translated.

"This car is for you, madame."

"I don't understand . . ."

"He says not to worry, your bags will follow."

Madeleine took her coat and walked out of the hotel lobby to find another officer holding the door open, she climbed into the car. Through the window, she saw chambermaids bringing down her bags. On the seat next to her was a thick brown envelope containing a receipt for a bank transfer to the account she had indicated and a wad of cash as thick as her fist.

Knock knock, it was the receptionist, Madeleine looked for the handle to wind down the window. The young officer standing there said something in German. The receptionist leaned over to interpret.

"Sturmbannführer Dietrich wishes you a safe return to Paris."

*

Léonce had left him – good riddance, the girl was a liability – but Joubert was appalled by her shabby attempt at burglary. He had made requests for duplicate patent certificates, but the loss of the ledger was a substantial one, since it was here that he had meticulously noted the work being done by the designers each day, the test results, the recommendations, decisions of orientation. Léonce had doubtless taken the documents in her haste without knowing what they were, the little fool.

Based on the sale of the house and the business, Joubert devised a financial plan that would allow him to make a fresh start. The principal challenge was to re-establish the precise point at which the research had been abandoned so that it could begin again. He sat in his study for hours, opening the boxes he had brought back from Pré-Saint-Gervais, reading, sorting, taking notes, contrasting and comparing the results. It was a long, slow and often depressing process.

The great Péricourt mansion became a palace of winds. The staff had been dismissed on the day following the burglary, Joubert had kept only Thérèse, the cook, who brought a tray up twice a day to find him in his dressing gown, unshaven, surrounded by a sea of paperwork, careful Thérèse, go around the piles, step over the boxes, when she left, Joubert was still feverishly poring over documents, and it was not unusual for her to find the tray untouched when she brought up his next meal. Making his fortune had been exhausting, but nothing could be more draining than bankruptcy.

Joubert had given up the lease on the property in Clichy and put the house up for sale, he had sold the machine tools for cash for a third of their value, his financial circumstances were parlous. Nobody telephoned. Joubert had ceased to exist.

On September 11, five days after the disappearance of Léonce, police officers came to visit. He had not immediately come downstairs because he had been comparing the dates and the results of various

338

compression tests, but also because, in his mind, the burglary was now in the past. Suddenly he looked up. Perhaps they had found Léonce. Perhaps they had recovered the missing documents. In a single bound, he was on the landing.

It was not the same officer as last time. Joubert winced, the two men with him were in plain clothes, they had clearly not come from the local police station. He felt a twinge of unease.

"Commissaire Divisionnaire Marquet. Might we have a word, Monsieur Joubert?"

Instinctively, Joubert realised that something had happened. Something bad. He slowly descended the staircase, turning to glance at the portrait of Marcel Péricourt that towered over the hallway, and felt inexplicably guilty.

To compensate for his staggeringly banal features, the commissaire had thick, almost comical muttonchop whiskers. He handed Joubert a card that he did not read.

"I am sorry, but I am very busy . . ."

"Surely you can make a little time to talk about your wife, Monsieur Joubert?"

It has been confirmed that Madame Léonce Joubert, the wife of the former banker who recently filed for bankruptcy, is . . . in Berlin! In the capital of the Reich!

She even chose to stay at the Hotel Kaiserhof on Wilhelm-platz, an establishment much favoured by Nazi dignitaries, where Herr Hitler himself lived until he was appointed Reich Chancellor.

Surely a woman has the right to travel wherever she chooses? Unquestionably. But that would not explain why, on the afternoon of Saturday, September 9, Madame Léonce Joubert was seen entering the Reichsluftfahrtministerium, the German Ministry of Aviation.

"What do you mean, the Ministry of Aviation?"

"It is a simple fact, Monsieur Joubert, our counterespionage agents are categorical."

Having spent many years as a banker, Joubert was accustomed to all sorts of dirty tricks, but this was one he had not seen coming. Léonce had gone to sell his plans to the Germans? He could not believe it, but managed to recover his composure.

"I have not seen my wife since she disappeared on September 6, having robbed our home, taking her jewellery and the housekeeping money. In fact, I reported the incident at the time. I cannot be held responsible for her actions."

"Hmm . . ."

The commissaire stroked his whiskers, producing a disagreeable scratching noise that sounded like termites.

The more he considered the matter, the more unlikely it seemed to Joubert. Léonce was neither intelligent enough nor brave enough to take such a risk. Someone had set a trap for him. He did not plan to take the bait.

"Do you know anyone in the German Ministry of Aviation, Monsieur Joubert?"

"No-one."

"Does your wife?"

"How could you expect me to know that?"

"She is your wife."

Joubert took a deep breath.

"Monsieur le commissaire, my wife is a whore. I knew this before we married, but I turned a blind eye, clearly it is in her nature. I have recently experienced a number of . . . professional setbacks, as I am sure you are aware, and my wife, who was only ever interested in my money, decided that she had had enough. She staged a very clumsy burglary of our home, but I cannot imagine her going to Berlin with documents she would be completely unable to understand!"

"And yet she did go. To the Reichs-Luft-Fahrt-Ministerium . . .

to the Ministry of Aviation, on September 9. And she travelled back to Paris on the eleventh."

The police are baffled. A catastrophic financial failure that left the Joubert family penniless was quickly followed by a burglary at their home during which the plans were stolen for a jet propulsion engine that Germany would be only too happy to obtain. Lastly, Madame Joubert was twice seen in Berlin visiting the Ministry of Aviation.

Let us say the word: this smacks of treason. Has Gustave Joubert sold French industrial secrets that could compromise French national security to the Nazis?

"Are you accusing me of treason?"

The gravity of the accusation was terrifying. People had been executed for less.

"We have not come to that point, Monsieur Joubert, but you must admit that the evidence is troubling."

"It is for you to prove that I betrayed my country, not for me to prove that I am innocent!"

"The best thing for all concerned, Monsieur Joubert, would be to compare your statement with that of your wife."

"If my wife has fled the country, I do not see—"

"She is on her way back. Madame Joubert is currently aboard a train to Paris. Our agents saw her leave Berlin. If she leaves the train after it has passed the border, she will be immediately arrested."

Joubert did not know which way to turn. If Léonce was on her way back, that could only mean that she had been to Berlin. Was this preposterous story true? He panicked.

"Barring any accidents," said the officer, "she will arrive in Paris tomorrow. When she does, I take it you have no objection to seeing her?"

"I would like nothing better!" Joubert roared.

The clouds had parted, tomorrow he would see her face to face, he would make short work of the little bitch, his innocence would be proven beyond doubt.

"Yes, that would be fine, bring her to see me, I would like nothing better . . ."

The border.

The train stops, it is dark, people alight, customs officers climb aboard, they check suitcases. On the platform, other officers screen the alighting passengers.

Madeleine summons a porter to take her bags, steps up to the checkpoint and hands over her passport.

"Madame Péricourt, Madeleine."

They are expecting a Frenchwoman, a certain Léonce Joubert, but this is not her.

Madeleine smiles, the customs officer is satisfied, the photograph is clearly that of the woman standing before him, something that is not always the case. Next!

It is biting cold. Madeleine turns to see if the porter is following. Outside the railway station, people are jostling for the few waiting taxis.

A car flashes its headlights, a man gets out and comes to meet her.

"Good evening, Monsieur Dupré."

"Good evening, Madeleine."

He takes the suitcases and lifts them with an ease that Madeleine finds moving. He opens the car door. She climbs in.

"Did everything go well?" he asks. "You look exhausted."

"I am dead on my feet."

The car drives out of the city.

"Monsieur Dupré . . ."

She has lightly laid a hand on his leg.

"Monsieur Dupré, I realise that it is very late, but I desperately need to sleep . . . Might there be a hotel or an inn nearby, somewhere to . . . I mean, a room . . ."

"It is all arranged, Madeleine, we will be there in fifteen minutes, meanwhile you can rest."

The car has stopped, but she cannot rouse herself.

"Madeleine . . ." Dupré says. "We are here."

Madeleine opens her eyes, she does not know where she is. "Oh yes, thank you, excuse me, Monsieur Dupré, I must look a sight."

She steps out of the car, it is bitterly cold, they hurry to the door of the inn, Dupré has arranged everything, here is the key, the room is on the first floor. He takes her elbow, she is weak from exhaustion, you go to sleep.

Madeleine leans closer, do not leave the luggage unattended, there is a lot of money in there.

Dupré instantly turns around, Madeleine goes into the room. It is charming. Much more comfortable than she imagined. She undresses and has a quick wash.

Dupré has not come back, she glances out the window, he is standing in the courtyard, smoking a cigarette. A black cat rubs against his legs, he bends and strokes it, the animal arches its back, it is purring. Madeleine can understand.

She gets into bed and she waits. Monsieur Dupré timidly knocks and pops his head around the door. He comes in.

"You are not asleep."

Worriedly, he sits on the edge of the bed.

"Madeleine, I have something I need to say . . ."

She knows that he is going to leave her, her heart sinks.

"I have helped you. I have done everything you asked. But this . . ."

Madeleine wants to speak, but her throat is dry, and nothing comes.

"It is not as though I consider myself particularly patriotic, you understand, but to help the Nazis . . ."

"What are you talking about?"

"To give them research that might help them to . . ."

Madeleine sits up. She smiles.

"Come, Monsieur Dupré, I would never do such a thing! What do you take me for?"

He is surprised by Madeleine's vehemence.

"But . . . the blueprints . . ."

"True, I gave Sturmbannführer Dietrich four pages that would allow him to substantiate the quality of what I was selling. But, when I left, it was the folder formerly marked "ABANDONED CONCEPTS" that I gave him. It will take them a few days to realise that the research is worthless."

It is Dupré's turn to smile. For the first time since she has known him, thinks Madeleine.

"Now, Monsieur Dupré, would you care to join me in bed?"

As soon as he got back to Paris, Paul wrote a letter to Solange. Write to me in Milan, my little Pinocchio, promise? She had hugged him so hard he almost choked. What he wanted to say seemed paradoxical. The recital he would best remember was the one in which Solange had barely sung a note.

He began to write the letter, but he never had time to finish it.

On September 12, the Paris newspapers announced that Solange Gallinato had died on a train bound for Amsterdam.

Vladi held up the newspaper, staring at the front page as though hypnotised. She did not need to know how to read to realise that the headline beneath the photograph announced that the diva had died.

Paul did not cry, he was furious. He had Vladi take him down to the news-stand, where he bought a copy of every single newspaper. Back in the apartment, he read all the obituaries of Solange before tossing the papers across the room, devastated and distraught. What should he do? Since the diva had been found dead in her first-class carriage, all eyes turned to Berlin for answers. The Reich concocted a fiction that the press was only too eager to believe. After a magnificent recital, the singer had insisted on visiting Herr Hitler's box to meet him personally. During their meeting, she had reiterated her confidence, her hope and her complete support for the glorious Reich, and Chancellor Hitler had invited the diva to dinner. Unfortunately, ill health compelled her to decline the invitation. She complained that she was in a state of complete exhaustion. The authorities, alarmed by her condition, had suggested she cancel the later recitals and had organised for her to travel to Amsterdam the following day. As she took her leave, she had told Herr Goebbels and Herr Strauss that the Berlin recital "would forever be engraved on her memory and in her heart as the most important of her career". Given Solange's many dramatic statements of support for the Reich, no-one doubted that the story reported by the Ministry of Information was true.

Paul spent the day writing individual letters to each of the newspapers. That evening, utterly shattered, he wept.

He wept for a whole week.

He refused to allow Vladi to play records so that he could hear Solange's voice. It would be many months before he could listen to her again without grieving.

"A fervent Nazi supporter was interred today in Milan, at a funeral attended by the cream of Italian Fascism."

For Paul, this was the cruellest and most unbearable lie. He felt a rage and a bitterness much like that of his mother.

They were the same officers, they had asked that the meeting take place at the commissariat, which Joubert took as a good sign. The Berlin train had pulled into Paris in the late afternoon, it was now six o'clock, and Joubert was to confront Léonce, he despised her.

Ever since he had heard about her treachery (and her stupidity – what had the foolish woman expected?) he had spent his nights haranguing her, beating her, every morning he wished he could throw open her bedroom door, drag her from her bed by the hair, he would have thrown her out the window if he could.

If the blueprints were now in Germany, it meant that his project was finished, ruined, but he, at least, would walk away unscathed, while she would be thrown into prison, perhaps worse.

He slipped on his overcoat. The officers could tell that he was tense, ready to explode. They were just about to leave the house.

"Are you telling me that you have not arrested her?"

Joubert's hand was on the door handle.

"No, Monsieur Joubert. She managed to elude the officers stationed on the platform. Although no-one saw her leave the train, by the time it arrived in Paris, she was not aboard."

Flabbergasted by this news, Joubert stared at the two officers in turn. He took a step back.

"I must insist that you come with us, Monsieur Joubert."

Joubert was dazed. If Léonce had not been arrested, why did they want him to go with them? He got into the back of the car, behind the driver.

When they stopped at the first traffic light, he stared out the window.

At first, he could make no sense of what he saw. Was he dreaming? Had he just seen Madeleine Péricourt sitting in a car parked near the lights? It had been a fleeting glimpse, but so startling, so unexpected . . . "Violent", that was the word.

What could she be doing here? She did not live in the area. Could it simply be a coincidence?

He was utterly confused by the time he found himself in front of the commissaire with the extravagant sideburns, who was accompanied by an elegant man with a grave face who did not introduce himself but seemed to be his superior.

"We now believe that you were perfectly aware of your wife's trip to Berlin," said the officer.

"I knew nothing until you told me!"

346

"We further believe that she used false documents to alight from the train somewhere, and that she is now waiting for you to join her."

"You are joking!"

"Do we look like we are joking?"

It was the second officer who now spoke. He looked as though he worked for a ministry. The Ministry of Justice? He opened a manila folder.

"Are you familiar with a company called Manzel-Fraunhofer-Gesellschaft?"

"The name does not ring a bell."

"It is a Swiss company. Officially, an import–export company, but that is merely a cover. In fact, the company is owned by the German Reich, which uses it to make transactions with which it does not wish to be associated."

"I don't understand."

"This company has just transferred two hundred and fifty thousand Swiss francs into the account of the Aeronautics Atelier, which is wholly owned by you."

Joubert was frantic.

"I honestly do not understand."

And, for once, he was sincere.

"The French counterespionage service has provided irrefutable evidence that pages of your work have been seen in the offices of the German Ministry of Aviation."

"My wife may have . . ."

"We shall ask your wife to explain her actions, if and when we find her."

In that moment, though he did not know why, what came to his mind was the face of Madeleine Péricourt, whom he had briefly glimpsed an hour earlier.

He did not have time to think about this before the man from the ministry continued:

"Right now, Monsieur Joubert, all available evidence leads us to believe that, with your wife's complicity, you sold the results of your research to the German Reich, research that was contracted by the French government, which is high treason."

"Wait!"

"Monsieur Joubert Gustave, I must advise you that you are under arrest."

38

As a rule, Monsieur Renaud left the offices of the Winterthur Union Bank at approximately a quarter to nine every evening. In fact, inasmuch as possible, he tried to leave at *precisely* a quarter to nine, it was a question of aesthetics. To ensure that he was not late, his chauffeur parked on the rue Bellini at twenty minutes to nine and, when he saw the light in the portico come on, he would start the car, drive slowly, pull up, then get out and open the door as his employer stepped onto the pavement; it went like clockwork, like a Swiss watch, if you prefer.

But that evening, on the rue Eugène-Delacroix, although the driver stepped on the brakes, there was nothing he could do, the pedestrian crossing right in front took the full force of the bonnet of the Studebaker, was thrown into the air, for an instant driver and victim saw each other through the windscreen, and then the young man's body slipped off the bonnet, his lifeless hands not even attempting to hold on, and disappeared under the radiator grille. The driver scrabbled out, knelt beside the man and gently touched his shoulder, but the body was limp, lifeless – my God . . . Passers-by began to gather. One suggested they should call the police, or an ambulance, the chauffeur did not move, mesmerised by the pale face of his victim. "Is he dead?" someone asked. A woman screamed.

Coming down the steps, Monsieur Renaud was surprised not to see his car. It had happened twice in four years, so, although unusual, it was not impossible. He did as he had done on previous occasions, he walked up rue de la Tour towards the Trocadéro. He smiled softly. Some setbacks can offer welcome opportunities. If he had been in his car, he would not have been able to watch the elegant figure of this woman as she passed, trailing a subtle perfume that made him want to sniff the air, like a hunting dog. He watched as her jacket swayed to the rhythm of her hips, marvelled at her slender waistline, and intuited the curves of what he could only describe as a magnificent arse. He longed to walk past her, to see whether her face was as beautiful as her figure.

Suddenly she let out a shriek, "Ow!", and reached for the wall to stop herself from falling. Monsieur Renaud rushed over and offered his arm, just before she lost her balance. It was nothing serious, the heel of her shoe was broken, but the young woman, hopping on one foot, groped for support and found Monsieur Renaud's arm. Allow me, he said, aware of her warmth despite her gloves. She hobbled for a metre or two, leaning so heavily on his arm that he struggled to support her, was she going to drag him down with her? He glanced back at the street, his car would be here soon, dear God, what a situation, the young woman limped towards Villa Aimée, a cul-de-sac lined with handsome houses, steady on, he said, ow, she whimpered, still limping, he looked back at the street, it was the last thing he saw before he received a sharp swift blow to the back of his skull, one he would remember for some time.

It took Dupré less than a minute to rob him of everything he had, while Léonce took the spare pair of shoes from her bag, slipped them on and, without a word, crept out of the Villa Aimée and strode quickly down the rue de la Tour.

Dupré took everything: wallet, keys, kerchief, spectacles, book, purse, business cards, watch, wedding ring, signet ring, even Monsieur Renaud's belt, which had a fancy enamel buckle. "You were unlucky, monsieur," the police would later say. "It's very unusual for people to be robbed in this neighbourhood."

Dupré was elated, this was his first banker.

He snapped the duffel closed and headed down rue de la Tour in the opposite direction. He walked briskly, but without undue haste. Further off, a crowd had gathered, a car was stopped in the middle of the street, a body lay in front of the radiator grille. The driver, the bystanders, everybody was wailing . . . Dupré walked on, without slowing his pace or even turning to look. At that moment, there came the sound of male voices, two officers propped their bicycles against the car and walked over, "Police, stand aside, what happened here?" The response was not long in coming. At the word "police", the prostrate form bounded to his feet like a spring, he glanced briefly at the officers and then ran off down the street, swift as a hare, leaving everyone so stunned they did not have time to react.

Robert ran as fast as he was able, but, even so, the thought occurred to him: I shouldn't smoke so much.

Despite a blinding headache, Monsieur Renaud made a concerted effort to think clearly.

To the police, he said:

"I'm more shaken than hurt, he didn't get away with anything."

The commissaire was surprised.

"He probably didn't have time to rob me," Renaud ventured. "Maybe someone interrupted him, I don't know, he got scared . . ."

"So, nothing was stolen, you say?"

Monsieur Renaud patted his empty pockets and said, no, nothing. Well I never. No damage.

"Except for this." He gave a sad smile as he pointed to the bandage the nurse had wrapped around his head.

Naturally, the police officer did not believe a word. But people have their reasons, and this man probably did not want his wife to know where he had been – there was an obvious pale band where his missing wedding ring had been, and he was constantly hiking up his trousers since he no longer had a belt. What can you do, thought the officer, we can't force people to press charges, and if the gentleman is happy to let the thief get away with his loot, much good may it do him.

Monsieur Renaud immediately sent a pneumatic telegram to Winterthur. But, here, too, he did not explain the circumstances. He was haunted by a troubling question: what were the chances that his chauffeur would knock down a man who fled the moment the police arrived, just as he was being robbed in a nearby alleyway? He considered the two events, trying to connect them. It smacked of foul play, but, try as he might, he could not work out who might have done this, or what he could do about it. As a result, in the telegram, he made no mention of the business with his chauffeur, only the robbery he had suffered. Since he could not hide the fact that his notebook had been taken.

Everyone at the Winterthur Union Bank was in agreement. It was difficult to imagine what anyone could do with a notepad that contained only columns of numbers and names that had no obvious connection. They were reassured by the fact that the thief had robbed Monsieur Renaud of everything he had, since this proved he was only interested in money. And Monsieur Renaud had had the discretion not to make a statement or file a complaint; as far as their clients were concerned the matter was closed, like a Swiss vault.

Even so, Monsieur Renaud found his sleep was troubled. At night, young women came and stabbed him through the heart with their stilettos, cars ran him down, he found himself drowning in narrow wells whose sheer walls were like columns of numbers and names.

Faced with the scale of the popular protest against taxation, which was fast becoming an open revolt against the government, Charles had brooded for a long time. On the one hand, what protesters were demanding was what he himself had advocated for two decades, in order to win re-election. On the other hand, he was now president of a parliamentary commission tasked with ensuring that tax was actually brought into the state coffers.

The clashes had concluded in late summer with a tour of France that had ended with proposals for a general strike on tax. A large meeting was scheduled to take place at the Salle Wagram on September 19 to decide the matter.

This call for revolution was what ultimately decided Charles. "When all is said and done," he declared before the commission, "a refusal to pay tax amounts to evasion since it is intended to 'deprive the public purse of legitimate tax revenue'." Therefore, he concluded, it was entirely within the purview of the commission to propose government legislation to protect state resources.

While thousands of protesters were preparing to support speakers who intended to denounce the "tax inquisition", "decadent parliamentarianism" and "Republican mismanagement", Charles was laying out his proposals to the commission.

As the "Wagram watchword" announced that the people were prepared "to abolish parliament", the commission approved the project.

At the September 19 rally, amid chaotic scenes, it was decided that a unanimous statement should be delivered at the Élysée Palace denouncing "the larcenous, incompetent government". A sea of protesters clashed with police on the Champs-Élysées and the Place de la Concorde. Utterly determined and appropriately armed militant royalists, joined by young men from Action Française, skirmished with the forces of law and order whom they later accused of provocation. Faced with a barrage of rifle butts, they smashed through the police roadblocks only to be charged by mounted guards; calm was not restored until nightfall, by which time there were almost forty casualties.

After an all-night session of difficult debate, the following morning the commission sent a draft bill to the government intended to criminalise "anyone who by violent action, threats or concerted manoeuvres, organises or attempts to organise collective tax evasion".

Charles was exhausted but satisfied.

With the whole country gripped by unrest, the government has decided that its best tactic is to swiftly pass a bill intended to punish protesters that has been drafted by Monsieur Charles Péricourt, an unlikely knight in shining armour on the subject of tax and taxation.

Our elected members of parliament, usually so proud of the French Revolution, are in no position to condemn the citizens fighting for their freedom, since "When the government violates the rights of the people, insurrection is for the people and for each portion of the people the most sacred of rights and the most indispensable of duties." That is Article 35 of the Declaration of the Rights of Man and of the Citizen.

Kairos

Paul wanted to organise a sort of general meeting, a solemn moment at which the name of his product, the promotional campaign and the slogan would be revealed.

Aside from the inner circle that comprised his mother, Monsieur Dupré, Vladi and Monsieur Brodsky, he asked that Léonce be invited. "With her first husband," he added.

As they waited for the couple to arrive, and while Monsieur Brodsky continued with his mysterious calculations, Paul pored over his documents, and Madeleine and Monsieur Dupré leafed through the newspapers, as they often did when they found themselves together. "We are bound to unearth something eventually," Dupré said, thinking of André Delcourt, though nothing had yet come to light to confirm this hope.

Dupré was reading the political pages, while Madeleine was engrossed in reading about court cases, the trial of Violette Nozière, the twists in the case of the Papin sisters, so Dupré was surprised to hear her suddenly say:

"I don't know about you, but I do not trust this man Alejandro Lerroux."

Madeleine's mention of the newly elected Spanish prime minister was utterly unexpected.

"Lord knows, I had little time for his predecessor, a rabid anti-clerical bigot! But this man seems to be steering Spain towards a fascist regime, what do you think, Monsieur Dupré?"

Dupré was about to answer when Léonce arrived with Robert on her arm. Madeleine was already on her feet, come in, come in, Léonce. Paul, are you not going to kiss Léonce?

Léonce and Paul had not seen each other in the four years since July 1929.

Her arrival had a profound effect on Paul, reminding him as it did of the years of affection, hugs and kisses, but also of the betrayal that had ruined his mother.

This painful impression was mitigated by the fact that Paul had just finished reading *Manon Lescaut*. Although he had often listened to Solange sing arias from Puccini's "Manon", until this moment he had not realised that, in his imagination, the Abbé Prévost's young heroine was the image of Léonce. Perhaps when he saw that the years had not yet taken their toll on her beauty, Paul, now in the full flush of desire, felt something unbearable or painful. He began to sob. Since the death of Solange two weeks earlier, Paul had had his fill of grief, he struggled to contain his emotions, and it was in this moment that Léonce realised how much he had grown up.

Léonce went over and knelt by the boy, she clasped him to her arms, and gently, wordlessly rocked him for a long time. Neither of them spoke. In her perfumed embrace, Paul did not rediscover the calm serenity he had so often sought as a child; he now associated Léonce's perfume with something very different.

Léonce, for her part, felt sad as she considered what it meant to be an adolescent boy in a wheelchair. To her, it was heartbreaking.

Paul had no wish to be pitied. Very gently he pushed her away and, without stuttering, said, "I'm fine."

Madeleine pointed out that the "meeting" looked much like a family photograph. A curious family.

The little group squeezed into the small living room, the ladies sitting in the front row: Madeleine, Léonce and Vladi, their arms crossed, women who never doubted anything. Standing behind Madeleine, Monsieur Dupré carefully laid his hands on the back of her chair. Standing behind Léonce, Robert casually fingered his wife's necklace as though wondering why he had not sold it yet. Lastly, Monsieur Brodsky, standing behind Vladi (they constantly whispered to each other in German, no-one could think what they had to say to one another).

So that he would stammer as little as possible, Paul had learned his little speech by heart.

As though unveiling a monument to the glories of contemporary commerce, he revealed a sketch of a willowy young woman in three-quarter profile, her back half turned to the viewer, one leg out-stretched as though to see whether she had lost a heel.

"Gosh!" she said, absolutely astounded.

Seeing the graceful curve of her buttock, the viewer could only agree with this exclamation.

Above the drawing, in sober type:

DOCTOR MOREAU'S CALYPSO BALM

"Balm," Paul explained, meant that the ointment did not sound too medical. Moreover, it echoed the word "balmy", which customers would subliminally register.

"Calypso" sounded sophisticated, romantic, amorous, related to Greek mythology, emphasising that the product was intended to enhance a woman's seductiveness.

"Doctor" provided the necessary scientific backing for the balm. Which left only the enigmatic Doctor Moreau.

"Who is he?" Léonce asked.

"No-no-nobody. It is im-important that the product is not a-a-anonymous. It h-has to have been in-invented by someone in p-particular. S-someone who inspires c-confidence. Moreau s-sounds very French. Women will l-l-like it."

With a smile, he added:

"It s-s-sounds better than D-D-Doctor Brodsky."

On this, everyone agreed, even Monsieur Brodsky.

The selling proposition was specific:

Troubled by your weight?
Worried by your figure?
Use

Doctor Moreau's Calypso Balm

A simple, revolutionary remedy,
approved by the Faculté,
and acclaimed by the most
beautiful women in Paris

"Approved by the Faculté", intended to corroborate its scientific value, was acceptable since it was a product listed in the national pharmacopoeia that had simply been coloured and perfumed.

The charm of the little stoneware pot containing the balm was due mostly to the word "Gosh!" written on the lid, as though it were a perfume.

"I recognise that smell!" Robert said, opening the jar and taking a sniff.

"Of course you do, poppet," said Léonce, blushing.

They uncorked a bottle of champagne. Monsieur Brodsky chattered to Vladi in German. Léonce congratulated Paul, women will love it, and Paul heard: "Women will love you."

They no longer encountered each other, they no longer belonged to the same world, so when Guilloteaux was told that Madeleine Péricourt wished to see him, he assumed that she wanted something from him and said that he was busy.

"Tell him not to worry, I shall wait."

She settled herself in the lobby, patient and serene. By half past eleven, the situation was fast beginning to look ridiculous, so Guilloteaux changed his mind. If what she wanted seemed excessive, he would simply refuse, it would be no more difficult than refusing a pay increase.

Madeleine had changed. How long had it been since he last saw her? He racked his brain.

"More than four years, my dear Jules."

He had expected to see a pauper, instead he found himself faced with a smiling, well-dressed, middle-class woman and, reassured, he mentally expunged the debt he felt he owed her.

"How are you, my dear Madeleine? And how is little Louis?"

"His name is Paul. And he is very well, thank you."

Jules Guilloteaux had always made it a point of principle never to apologise or express gratitude. He simply shook his head as though he now remembered perfectly, ah yes, Paul, yes, of course, of course.

"And you, my dear Jules, how are you?"

"Oh, business is tougher than ever. You know the financial difficulties faced by the press these days."

"I mostly know about your financial difficulties. They have nothing to do with the press in general."

"Excuse me?"

"I do not wish to waste your time, my dear Jules, I know how valuable it is."

She opened her handbag, and nervously rummaged inside as though fearful that she had forgotten something important. Then

357

she gave a little sigh of relief, ah, there it was, a slip of paper inscribed with numbers.

Guilloteaux put on his spectacles and read. It was not a date or a telephone number, he looked at her quizzically.

"It is the number of your Swiss bank account."

"Pardon?"

"The one you opened with the Winterthur Union Bank, the account where you hide money from the tax authorities. A tidy sum, I can tell you. There is enough in this account to give all your staff a pay rise or buy up half the competition."

Jules prided himself on his reflexes, but this was a highly unusual situation, one that was disturbing and potentially dangerous.

"How do you know . . . ?"

"The important thing is not *how* I know, but *what* I know. And I know everything. Dates of deposits, withdrawals, annual interest, everything."

Although Madeleine spoke in a calm, determined voice, she was wary because the only thing she actually knew was that the name Jules Guilloteaux appeared in Monsieur Renaud's notebook.

But he did not know this.

Someone who knows the name of your bank and the number of your private account might reasonably know everything.

"Now, I must leave you, my dear Jules."

Madeleine was already at the office door, her hand on the handle. She nodded to the slip of paper.

"There is another number . . . Just turn over the paper."

"My God! You certainly do not do things by half!"

"Nor do you, to judge from your account."

"But what guarantee do I have that this will be the end of it?"

"You have my word, Jules. The word of a Péricourt, assuming you still believe that is worth something."

Guilloteaux looked reassured.

"I hope you will not mind if I emphasise the urgency of my

request. You can leave an envelope for me at reception, say, tomorrow morning? Now, I shall not bore you any longer, I have already taken up too much of your time."

"I think perhaps you can leave us, Robert."

Robert looked startled.

"What's that supposed to mean?"

Madeleine liked the young man. He did not have an ounce of common sense, and he reacted to everything with the impulsiveness of a seven-year-old, it was refreshing. The problem was that this meant he needed to have everything explained. On this occasion, Madeleine did not feel inclined.

"Go and play billiards, Robert, do whatever you like, but leave us to converse in peace, please."

Robert had always been impressed by Madeleine. She was an imposing presence. He got to his feet, shook hands with René Delgas and shuffled out of the room.

"So, this is your headquarters?" said Madeleine with a smile.

"If you want to put it like that."

A handsome boy, you'll see, Léonce had told Madeleine, he is bone idle, he sleeps all day, and I have no idea what he does with his nights, but he is reputed to be one of the best forgers in Paris. Madeleine looked at Léonce anxiously, is this something Robert told you? No, rest assured!

"I need some manuscripts, shall we say, reworked?"

"Anything is possible."

The change in the boy is astounding. He walked in with the languid gait, the candid face, the supercilious charm of a man who knows he is attractive. Now he is grave and focused. Now they are discussing business, it is a very different matter, there is no longer the hint of a smile, he weighs every word carefully. René Delgas instantly realised what sort of woman he was dealing with. If Madeleine sent Robert away, it is so that he will not know the terms of their agreement and so cannot ask for his commission. A clever ruse, and one that makes René nervous.

Madeleine, who needs to be sure that René is as clever as people claim, hands him a letter from André that she received on her return from Berlin.

Dear Madeleine,
The information that you provided has proved to be entirely correct, thank you. I look forward to further inside information.
I hope that your time at the spa has been beneficial for dear little Paul.
Yours very sincerely,
André

Delgas does not even deign to glance at the letter.

"One hundred and twenty francs per page."

A little expensive, Madeleine thinks, and it shows on her face. René sighs. Under normal circumstances, he would get up and leave; however, a profitable deal with some people from Marseilles has just fallen through, a deal he had been counting on. He will have to prove himself. He bends down, opens a little leather briefcase, takes out a blank sheet of paper and a fountain pen, sets André's letter in front of him, and copies:

Dear Madeleine,
The information that you provided

Half of the text will suffice, he thinks. He hands the sheet to Madeleine who manages to suppress her admiration. The similarities between the two are absolutely fascinating.

Delgas has already put away his pen. Gently, he takes the forgery he has just created and tears it into little pieces, he deposits these in the ashtray and folds his arms.

"I need a copy of this."

She hands him the Swiss banker's notebook and Delgas carefully thumbs through it. Then hands it back.

"Eight thousand francs."

Madeleine is puzzled.

"There are fifty pages here, at one hundred and twenty francs, that would make six thousand francs, not eight thousand!"

"The notebook is at least three or four years old. The man who wrote it used different pens over that time, in different places. We must first find an exact duplicate of the notebook."

"Not an exact duplicate. Something similar will suffice."

"Very well. Even so, it will need to be aged, to be copied out using different pens, different coloured inks, I will need to simulate the different times of day when it was written and how such things can influence handwriting. That will cost eight thousand francs. To say nothing of the fact that you intend to ask me to change certain lines, am I right?"

"Just one line. To be added near the beginning of the notebook. Seven thousand francs."

Delgas does not hesitate for a second.

"Agreed."

"How long will it take you to do the work?"

"Two months."

Madeleine briefly panics, then she smiles. He really is very clever.

"I assume that if I need it in ten days' time, it will cost eight thousand francs."

Delgas returns her smile. He does not trouble to answer. Madeleine pretends to waver, but it is a good deal, she had calculated the work at ten thousand. She takes out an envelope.

"Three thousand francs down payment, not a centime more."

Delgas pockets the envelope, carefully slips the notepad into his briefcase and gets to his feet. Madeleine can pay for the drinks, she is the client.

"What is your relationship with Robert Ferrand?"

"Irregular. He is not what I would call a friend. Something of a brute. We keep in contact, nothing more. Why do you ask?"

"Because if you should lose the notebook, or if you should attempt to use it to your own advantage, I would instruct Robert Ferrand . . . to get in contact with you."

René Delgas nods; that makes sense.

39

André had encountered him once or twice at society dinners, an obsequious man with pale, expressive hands and a voice so soft he had to listen attentively. He had spent his entire career working at the Department of Justice, where he held a very senior position and was intimately familiar with its workings. It was for this reason that André had chosen him, the man seemed best placed to deal with such a delicate matter.

A few days earlier, Madeleine Péricourt had offered him the head of Gustave Joubert on a silver platter. André Delcourt's reputation as the best-informed man in Paris had grown, and so, whenever a scoop was in search of an obliging ear, it invariably found his.

Here was another story that would not grace the pages of *The Lictor* – he would need to publish it immediately – but it nonetheless confirmed that, when the time came, his newspaper would be one of the best informed and consequently the most influential.

"There are rumours of a new daily newspaper," said the magistrate. "We know very little about it, but even so . . ."

André raised a hand. This was a good sign. The corridors, the lounges were all buzzing with the news. In recent weeks Guilloteaux had been sulking; that, too, was a good sign.

Now that they had dispensed with the preliminaries, the magistrate gave Delcourt a wide-eyed look to signal his interest, highlight his discretion and emphasise that, while he was delighted to receive André Delcourt, he did not have all day.

"It is a delicate business . . . A letter."

"Let me see it," said the magistrate, extending his hand.

André did not move.

"It contains an accusation."

"We are accustomed to such things; the French love to write to the police."

"I am not a police officer."

"Senders are not very particular, anything that will eventually lead to the police will work for them. So, who is being accused this time?"

"It is a list of French clients of a Swiss bank guilty of tax evasion. More than a thousand names."

The magistrate blenched. Gingerly, he reached out a hand and abruptly closed the right-hand desk drawer that sat slightly ajar.

"Come, come now," he said, like a schoolmaster remonstrating with a pupil.

"One thousand and eighty-four, from what I have been told. The list I was sent has only fifty names, but they include merchants, artists, two bishops, several high-ranking military officers, including a general, a police commissioner, three magistrates, I'm sorry to say, a member of the Court of Appeal, and a lot of double-barrelled names."

"If this can be proven . . ."

"Not to mention a celebrated industrialist. Someone very much in the news. A model of patriotic virtue. Together it paints a pretty picture of the cream of French society. If we had a search warrant, we could seize the complete list from the offices of the bank."

"And your source?"

"I have no idea. Doubtless someone with a grudge. I can give you what I have been sent to help with the investigation. In exchange, I want to be the first to publish the results of your investigation."

The magistrate took a deep breath and leaned back in his chair.

"That is not something we are accustomed to doing," he lied. "You must understand that justice is . . ."

"Or I can simply publish everything I have today, with a liberal sprinkling of the word 'allegedly'. If the accusations are true, the bank's headquarters will be closed up, its agents will be on the train by nightfall, and the headquarters in Switzerland will shield its records, claiming client confidentiality. The article would doubtless cause a considerable uproar, the judiciary would be asked to undertake an inquiry but would no longer be able to do so. And I will publish a verbatim account of our conversation today, explaining that you did not think the matter worthy of your time."

As he showed Delcourt out, the magistrate felt it necessary to reiterate his scruples for the sake of form, these are truly exceptional measures, André smiled, of course, of course. All he need do now was hope that it was all true and could be proven.

The list, together with a letter signed "a true Frenchman", had arrived in a large manila envelope. Two hours later, it was in the office of the public prosecutor, in the hands of the head of the fraud department ("My God, what a business . . ."). By evening, he had finished writing the indictment and an examining magistrate had been appointed to lead the investigation, and the following morning, at about seven o'clock, an unmarked police car from the Sûreté de la Seine was parked on the corner of the rue de la Tour. Waiting there were a security officer and three plain-clothes officers tasked with shadowing people as they left the building specified in the anonymous letter.

Charles got to his feet, went over to the window and peered out onto the rainy boulevard.

"Is this your idea of a joke?" roared the minister. "Do you not think we have enough trouble with these idiot protesters without you proposing legislation that is nothing less than sheer provocation!"

"But, but, but—"

"But, but, but what? Have you even stopped to consider what will happen if we debate this cretinous proposal? Half the population has already taken to the streets, do you want the other half to join them?"

The minister tossed the document that represented Charles' pride and joy onto his desk.

"I plan to bury this legislation and you with it. Two days from now, your parliamentary commission will cease to exist. Now, get out of my sight!"

"What are you saying?"

"We set up the commission because, at the time, it was necessary. That time has passed, and with it the commission."

At this point Charles had bellowed. An unusual gambit in the ministerial office, but these were trying times for everyone.

"What gives you the right . . .?"

"Oh, the law . . ."

"By law, this commission is scheduled to sit until it delivers its full and final conclusion!"

"Consider it done. You submitted a report last month, in August, that will serve as a conclusion. The commission has admirably completed the task assigned to it, in a day or two you will be congratulated. And thanked."

For Charles, it was back to square one. To carry on as a mere member of parliament having chaired a commission was almost unthinkable. His prospective son-in-law would fly the nest and make his future with a family other than the Péricourts. Charles had assumed that half his problem – the half named Rose – was settled. Now the problem was once again whole.

All this was extremely unfortunate, but what most upset him was that the government was about to strip him of his purpose. His mission. His struggle. Don't laugh, this is how he saw it.

The commission had been the apex of his career, he was not

about to let anyone take it away, but he could not think what to do to avoid it. For all his chin jerks to the admiring and amazed Alphonse, and his declarations that he would not yield an inch, he felt utterly alone and could not help but wonder how it would all end. He thrust his hands in his pockets. Buck up, man, he told himself, I—

"Papa?"

A worried Rose popped her head around the door.

"Yes?"

"It is Maman, she is not feeling very well."

Charles sighed and got to his feet. Hortense was lying on the sofa, clutching her belly as she had been doing for days, Charles could see nothing out of the ordinary. Except perhaps that she was complaining more. Yes, perhaps her abdomen looked a little more swollen than usual, but even so . . .

Rose and Jacinthe were clinging fearfully to one another.

"I think perhaps I should see someone," Hortense said with what she hoped was a winning smile. "Go to the hospital."

Good God, it was past eight o'clock in the evening . . . Charles summoned the driver and slipped on his overcoat while the girls got their mother dressed, and they headed to the Hôpital Pitié-Salpêtrière, where Hortense had been treated in the past and where her records were kept.

"Thank you, Charles," Hortense said, squeezing his hand.

She was undressed in a dimly lit room and laid on a bed with sheets as stiffly starched as wing collars.

"There is a little soup in the kitchen," she said, still clutching her stomach.

"Yes, yes," said Charles, "we can think about that later."

By rights he should go home and take care of the girls, but actually all he wanted to do was run away. He was very worried, he could not get the problems with the legislation out of his mind.

Over supper, Rose and Jacinthe whispered to each other like nuns. Charles read the papers, but the news was not good. The knight in shining armour was being attacked from all sides, the papers were pessimistic about the future of the commission, and the rest of his career. He pounded his fist on the table. His was a noble fight, God damn it!

The girls looked up. Charles had not realised he had spoken aloud. He tried to seem sociable.

"You haven't told me what the two of you got up to with Alphonse on Saturday."

The twins giggled. Once again, they had swapped places, and that charming young man had not noticed a thing. From this was born the idea that one of them would marry him, and the two would share his bed alternately, it was thrilling. But it was a sad laugh because they knew that this was the moment when Hortense would have said:

"Surely you'll have a little more soup, girls, you can't let it go to waste!"

Charles worked late into the night, rereading a statement to the committee drafted by Alphonse whose terms he felt he should revise, even though they were not incorrect.

The following morning, he rose early and drove to the hospital before going to the office.

When he arrived, the nurses had just discovered that Hortense had died during the night.

40

The officers from the Surêté de la Seine had experienced more difficult surveillance operations. The building was visited by three, perhaps four, people a day, rarely more. One officer stayed in the car, driving off every two hours to change it for another that he parked nearby to avoid arousing suspicions, while the other officers tailed the people coming out. A routine operation.

Those who visited were quiet, confident, unsuspecting individuals. They came from well-heeled neighbourhoods. The officers trailed them to government ministries, expensive restaurants, once even to Notre-Dame cathedral, but mostly to houses in Passy, in the eighth arrondissement . . . For officers earning a minimum wage, it was a little frustrating, but not unexpected.

On the other hand, they had not yet seen a woman like this. Firstly, because few women visited (she was only the second since the operation began), secondly, because there could be few women as ravishing in all of Paris. When the officer in charge of the surveillance saw this willowy figure appear on the rue de la Tour and go into the building, he felt a little peculiar.

As did Monsieur Renaud.

He had been reluctant to meet her since he did not recognise the name and "Madame Robert Ferrand" sounded like a pseudonym; he had not returned her telephone call, but she had called back. She had a charming voice. He had given in, precisely because of her voice. Besides, he was a past master at selecting his clients; those he did not wish to take on did not hang around. Before he revealed any of his cards, he engaged in a little trivial conversation, though he did not shrink from the occasional indiscretion. He needed to know exactly who he was dealing with. Especially since this unfortunate assault on him. Nothing had come of the matter, the police had done nothing as he had not filed a complaint, he had heard no rumours, this confirmed his theory that it had simply been a robbery, and he was able to sleep once again.

The woman was beautiful, but her name, Ferrand . . . He had skimmed through the *Bottin Mondain*, the *Who's Who* of the Paris beau monde, but could find no mention of it anywhere. The wife of a diplomat? Of an army officer? No, she wore no wedding ring, so she was not married. She had no private fortune, if she had he would have found it. He took things cautiously.

She had not given him a passport or a visiting card, but a marriage certificate. Casablanca, April 1924. It was an uncommon thing to do, as though the young woman were desperate to prove her identity, to prove something, the action of someone with everything to hide.

"I wish to – to invest some money, you understand."

She removed her veil. My God, what a woman.

"Your own?"

"Yes . . ."

Her pink blush brought a lump to his throat.

"Some money . . . A private fortune, perhaps?" he ventured.

She flushed from pink to red.

"Money . . . that I earned."

He was as tense as a drawn bow.

"Friends . . ."

Monsieur Renaud was speechless. His first whore! He felt quite moved.

How much would she charge, a woman like this? A considerable sum, no doubt. He felt completely reassured. To the Winterthur Union Bank a top-class whore was as trustworthy as a general or a member of the Académie Française.

In a low-key state of euphoria, he explained the services offered by the bank, oh, how he desired her, now that he knew what she was. Her questions demonstrated that she had a good head on her shoulders. Unsurprising, hers was a profession that required fine judgment.

She drank her tea in tiny sips, even her fingers were magnificent.

An appointment was made to open the account. She planned to bring the money in cash.

"How much are we talking about?"

"One hundred and eighty thousand. In the first instance."

My God! Renaud instantly revised his estimate upward, this woman clearly charged a fortune.

"Do you think it would be dangerous to travel with such a sum?" she asked.

A sudden flash of inspiration led him to suggest:

"Would you like me to come to your home? To avoid any . . . I can . . . personally, if you would like . . ."

"Well, well, Monsieur Renaud," Léonce simpered. "I would not say no."

His mouth dropped open. He was finding it difficult to decide what she meant. To visit her at home? To collect the money, of course, but perhaps she wanted to include him in her intimate circle, a banker who could advise her, support her, maximise her returns?

"Perhaps you could come next week?"

Monsieur Renaud picked up his diary, dropped it, picked it up again, opened it upside down, come on, come on.

"Shall we say Tuesday? Around noon? I'm sure you won't refuse a little something . . ."

Monsieur Renaud was speechless. He tried and failed to swallow.

She gave him an address in the seventh arrondissement. If he were to visit, Monsieur Renaud would find a dog-grooming emporium.

Before she left, Léonce idly asked if she might use the . . .

"But of course!" said Monsieur Renaud, pointing to the corridor that led to the ladies' lavatory.

He watched her walk away. Dear God . . .

He had to sit down.

Léonce went into the lavatory, looked around, hesitated, then put on a pair of gloves.

Monsieur Renaud heard the toilet flush. The young woman reappeared, a picture of elegance. When he thought of what she did for a living, it seemed incredible.

Once outside, one of the officers shadowed her. She led him to the lingerie department of Bon Marché, an embarrassing place for a man to be seen loitering, a place filled with visual distractions, suddenly he lost sight of her, she had disappeared.

On September 23, two officers took up their usual positions, one on the rue de la Tour, the other on the rue de Passy, and waited for the first appointment.

A man of about fifty in an elegant grey coat appeared shortly before eleven o'clock. Ten minutes later, a team of six officers raided the building, including an investigator from the fraud department of the Sûreté de la Seine.

When he saw the search warrant, the clerk took a step back as though he had seen the devil himself, which was not entirely inaccurate.

Hearing a commotion in the hall, Monsieur Renaud apologised to his client, looked around the door and instantly knew what was happening. Two officers were guarding the door, a third grabbed him while the others rushed in. The customer stood up and took his coat, prepared to leave, he did not want to get in the way.

"If I might ask you to stay for a few minutes," said one of the officers.

"I'm afraid that's impossible, I am in a hurry."

He took a step forward.

"Then you will be late."

"You do not seem to know who I am, monsieur!"

"That was to be my first question. Your papers, please."

Villiers-Vigan. Sprawling vineyards in Bordeaux, a vast family fortune, the company exported a third of its production to the United States.

"Might I ask you the reason for your visit?"

"I . . . I was visiting a friend. Monsieur Renaud. Surely a man has the right to visit his friends?"

"Bringing one hundred and forty thousand francs in small denominations?" said the officer.

Villiers-Vigan turned, the officer holding his coat had just taken a large wad of banknotes from the pocket.

"That is not mine!"

It was very foolish statement, as everyone knew, even Villiers-Vigan, who bowed his head and slumped into a chair.

Monsieur Renaud, for his part, said nothing. His mind was racing.

Since the theft of his notebook, the only existing list of clients was at the bank's headquarters in Switzerland. Obviously, the police would discover receipts, but it would be impossible for them to connect account numbers to names of individuals. It is in the most difficult situations that the wisdom of a system can be judged. In hindsight, he was happy that he had been robbed. But for the attack, his notebook would be in the safe, which a court order could force him to open . . . Ugh, just thinking about it . . .

His visitor agreed to sign a short statement acknowledging his presence in the building and the cash found in his overcoat.

Granted, Monsieur Renaud had probably just lost a customer, that would be the price for Monsieur Villiers-Vigan's scare, but the business was in no way compromised. Monsieur Renaud turned back to the officers.

"May I ask whether . . ."

"Here!" called a voice.

The commissaire appeared. A colleague handed him the records.

"These are the records of accounts! They list the securities deposited with the bank."

The two men looked at each other. All they needed now was the cross-referenced list of customers they had been assured was on the premises, a document without which no court case was possible.

The officers set to work, they ransacked the office and the opulent meeting room, they searched through the filing cabinets, under carpets, behind chests of drawers. Monsieur Renaud sprawled languorously on the large sofa, would you care for some tea, gentlemen, leafing through a magazine, feigning interest in advertisements for great railway journeys.

By one o'clock, the atmosphere had soured.

Officers from the Fraud Squad began to leave, taking with them a mountain of paperwork that would lead nowhere, since they still did not know whom to charge with opening accounts with a Swiss bank. The bank was untouchable for as long as it could not be proven that it had been paying dividends that avoided taxation on French soil.

"Leaving so soon?" Monsieur Renaud said.

Boxes and cartons were loaded into the police van. The commissaire was sick and tired of this case, he preferred to deal with real criminals.

"Well, I'm going for a piss!"

"You do that!" said Monsieur Renaud, disgusted by such vulgarity, the officers of the Sûreté Générale were poor losers.

As it turned out, they were not losers, poor or otherwise, since a moment later the commissaire reappeared holding a notebook.

"I found it behind the cistern. Is it yours?"

Monsieur Renaud was staring at the notebook. No, it was not his . . . Well, it was *almost* his. A notebook that looked very much like his but was not his. He took it, opened it, there was no doubt that it was his handwriting, these were the lines that he had written, he recognised the names and the account numbers, when it came to such things his memory was like a magnet . . . it was inexplicable. He was being entirely honest when he said:

"Yes, I mean no, this is not my book . . ."

"This is your handwriting, unless I am mistaken?"

On this point, there could be no doubt. How could the notebook have ended up here? And in such a curious location?

Suddenly, it dawned on him: the strumpet!

She had gone to the lavatory. He had watched her go. Oh my God!

Her remembered the sway of those buttocks now! He had seen it before, on the street, the girl who had broken the heel of her shoe . . .

"It's a fake!" he roared.

"If it is, it now has your fingerprints on it."

Monsieur Renaud dropped the book as though it were a viper.

"We shall see whether there are others," said the officer.

The banker signed his statement like an automaton, his mind a blank.

This story was truly astounding. It would trigger a blistering scandal. The Winterthur Union Bank would be pilloried.

For a brief moment, Monsieur Renaud contemplated suicide.

Two weeks earlier, Paul had said in passing:

"I was thinking, Maman, might there not be workshop space available at Pré-Saint-Gervais?"

The lease was very affordable, the previous tenants, the Aeronautics Atelier, had hurriedly vacated the property and the landlord was eager to rent it.

"It's huge!" Paul said.

He loved this vast space where he could easily move around in his wheelchair. On the long tables on the ground floor, Monsieur Brodsky had laid out all the equipment he had shipped from Germany. The remainder of his tools were still in crates.

Superstitiously, Madeleine had forbidden Robert Ferrand from setting foot on the premises.

Dupré uncorked a bottle of champagne and removed the white linen napkins from the plates of canapés, everyone stood around, feeling rather moved. Paul was disappointed that Dupré poured him only a small glass.

"You need to keep a clear head, my boy."

When Dupré spoke in this tone, no-one dared contradict him.

It was agreed that Monsieur Brodsky would begin production of the first three hundred pots on Monday, which gave him just enough time to set up his equipment. Vladi and Paul would help with the more monotonous tasks.

The labels and the packaging were to be delivered within two weeks.

The publicity campaign would not begin until the laboratory (the sign above the workshop door read: LABORATOIRE DES ÉTABLISSEMENTS PÉRICOURT) had sufficient supply to meet demand. Although everything would initially be fulfilled by mail order, as was usual with such products, Paul was considering sounding out pharmacies as the product became better known, he was constantly dreaming up ever more impossible plans.

The laboratory closed shortly before eight o'clock that evening. "Come on, everyone, time to close up," Dupré said. He suddenly seemed to be in a hurry. They drank up their champagne, eagerly looking forward to work starting the following day.

"Paul will stay here with me," Dupré said when the taxi arrived.

"It's just that . . ."

"Don't worry, Madeleine, I have just a few practical matters to settle with him, I shall drive him home as soon as we are done."

Caught unawares, Madeleine reluctantly acquiesced. There was something she was not aware of, and she did not like the fact, she vowed to tell Monsieur Dupré as much the following day.

They did not speak during the drive. Paul could not tell whether Dupré was angry, but his face was even more inscrutable than usual. What mistakes had he made in his preparative work that Monsieur Dupré should urgently wish to speak to him alone, and at his home?

Dupré effortlessly carried Paul up four flights of stairs without panting, without stopping, without a word.

"Right, then," he said as he sat Paul down.

On the bed.

Despite the fact that Paul could see a table and chairs.

But from a corner of the room, he could also see the ravishing smile of a sixteen-year-old girl.

"Paul, may I present Mauricette? She is very sweet, as you will see. Right . . ."

He patted the pockets of his jacket.

"What a fool I am, I've gone and forgotten the keys to the laboratory. Never mind, I shall go back and get them, I'll leave the two of you here, I'm sure you will find something to talk about."

He picked up his duffel bag and was gone.

Hortense had had stomach troubles for a long time, on several occasions she had been hospitalised, many doctors had visited her bedside and Charles had never worried. For as far back as he could remember, his wife had had some complaint, sometimes it was her womb ("It feels as though it is rotting," she would say), sometimes her bowels ("If you knew how heavy they feel . . ."), but in this tournament of complaints, her ovaries invariably won out. This was something Charles found excruciatingly embarrassing, since it evoked a reality that was altogether too feminine, too organic. He considered her aches and pains to be a peculiarity, a trait, something that he had simply to endure. Something that had seriously affected their sexual relationship after the birth of the twins.

Seeing her on her deathbed, she was almost a different person. Whereas he had thought his brother looked old in death, Hortense looked surprisingly young, she reminded him of their first meeting, when they were twenty years old. She had been a delicate, ethereal creature, like a porcelain figure. They had flirted passionately during their courtship, but Hortense had always refused to "go all the way", a phrase that had made Charles laugh, since Hortense saw no harm in it. They had spent their wedding night in a hotel in the centre of Limoges, where Hortense had relatives. Although it was the largest room in the hotel, it was no better than the others – the floors creaked, the walls were made of cardboard. Hortense had let out shrill little cries, *please, please*, but her whole body said the opposite. They had fallen asleep in the early hours. Charles had lain awake for hours, watching her sleep, a tiny figure in the vast bed . . .

It was curious how these memories resurfaced, in no apparent order, memories he had long thought lost. Yes, he had loved Hortense very much, and she had worshipped him and him alone. She had always thought him a hero. It was foolish, of course, her blind faith in him, but this was what had kept him going. She could be infuriating, that much was true, and he had brushed aside her complaints.

Though he hardly realised it, he was crying. For himself, like everyone. It was not the tears that surprised him, he had always been sentimental by nature. He was weeping for a woman he had deeply loved. A love that, for many years, had been little more than a memory, but the only love that he had ever known.

Hortense had died on a Friday. On Monday, the coffin would be brought to their home, from where the funeral procession would set off.

Charles had been terrified of how the twins would react, and had been very surprised. They had cried, but solemnly, something that was not really in their nature. They looked uglier than ever. Alphonse came to offer his condolences, he asked if he could do anything to help, the twins had welcomed him, but like a cousin, thank you, they said, tucking their handkerchiefs into their sleeves. When he saw their calm, their profound grief, the maturity with which they assumed responsibility for the household, advising him on funeral arrangements, it occurred to Charles that they would never marry, that they would never leave him, and he found the prospect of that future terrifying.

The rest of the family were informed. Madeleine did not come to pay her respects, but sent a rather formal letter of condolence, she would attend the funeral.

*

If it was to have any chance of success, the "Swiss Notebook" case had to remain completely confidential, something that would prove extremely difficult.

"Just imagine . . . More than a thousand people . . ."

They struggled to describe it. The Winterthur Union Bank was capitalised at five hundred million francs, but probably had more than two billion in French deposits in its vaults.

Having consulted his colleagues at the Ministry of Justice and the Ministry of Foreign Affairs, the examining magistrate issued a warrant for the commissaire of the Sûreté Générale to launch a series of dawn raids on September 25.

At precisely the same moment, groups of two or three officers pounded on the doors of almost fifty people in Paris and the provinces, the biggest tax raid in the history of the Third Republic.

In the Haut-Rhin, the elected senator from Belfort was dragged from his bed, a viscount and his mistress were rudely awakened. Monsieur Robert Peugeot, the automobile manufacturer, Monsieur Levitan, a cabinetmaker, Maurice Mignon, a financial advertising director, were respectfully requested to open their doors, their homes, their offices, their safes, their books. A military general attempted to shoot himself, only to stop short and burst into tears. Bishops were more dignified, the Bishop of Orléans behaved as though welcoming members of his flock and offered coffee. The managing editor of *Le Matin* laughed, but his wife hung her head in shame. Henriette-François Coty, the former wife of the famous perfumier, shrieked that she had nothing to do with her former husband, presumably calculating that this would let her off the hook. Monsignor Baudrillart, a member of the Académie Française, stood on his dignity.

The operation began at six in the morning. By nine o'clock, it was burning like a powder trail through well-heeled neighbourhoods filled with well-heeled citizens; those who did not receive a personal visit learned about it from the newspapers.

At that moment, the bier carrying the coffin of Hortense Péricourt was entering the Batignolles cemetery.

Madeleine was regretting bringing Paul with her. The moment she saw Monsieur Dupré standing on the pavement next to the line of cars, she was gripped by doubt. But it was too late. In less than a minute, he would open the car door, discreetly set the package on the passenger seat, and it would all be over. Madeleine took her son's hand and squeezed it, Paul assumed that she was grieving, which, in a sense, she was.

The funeral procession wound its way through the cemetery to the family vault. The throng of mourners were walking slowly behind Charles and his daughters when the word began to spread. At the end of the cortège, there was a commotion. What? How? Who? Where did you hear such a thing? Like a pneumatic telegram, the news travelled through the crowd until it reached the front of the procession and the ear of Alphonse, who did not know what to do. He vacillated, but as everyone began to mutter, he realised that to hide the truth would serve no purpose. He stepped forward and touched Charles' shoulder. Rose mistook this for a gesture of compassion and gave him a grateful look.

"What are you saying?" asked Charles.

The interment in the family vault was about to begin. Charles, impatient and exasperated, said:

"What do you mean, a search warrant?"

"It was served on your home an hour ago. We have been speaking to the examining magistrate, the commissaire, the Ministry of Justice, trying to find out, but . . ."

Charles was overwhelmed by thoughts and images, his daughters hugging him; through the coffin, he saw Hortense smiling at him, he was sobbing but no tears would come, and now this news, breaking like a devastating wave, in the midst of his grief. A search warrant? But why? Just after the funeral procession had left the house? It was so unbelievable that he felt the need to talk to Alphonse, but there was no-one nearby – the mourners had moved on, to show their respects in the final minutes. At the cemetery gates stood several shadowy figures who should not have been there.

Madeleine said to Paul:

"Let's go home, my darling."

But in the time it took to manoeuvre the wheelchair, to try to make their way through the crowd, Charles had already come back, followed by his daughters.

Knowing what was happening, the crowd parted. Charles felt like a cuckold: the last person to know. He was greeted by three plain-clothes officers.

"What is the meaning of this? Can a man not bury his wife in peace?"

"I apologise, monsieur. If you need time to pay your respects, we can wait, we have all the time in the world."

"No! No, get this over with! What is it about?"

The people standing in front of Paul's wheelchair cleared a path and Madeleine stepped forward. She was standing directly behind her uncle when the investigating magistrate said:

"Monsieur Péricourt, following the discovery of your name in a ledger at the head office of the Winterthur Union Bank, I am arresting you on suspicion of tax evasion. I must ask you to come with me."

A shout went up from the mourners, this situation was not merely grotesque, it was a scandal!

"What on earth are you talking about?" Charles roared.

Had he been imprudent? Not in the slightest. Had he ever sought to hide his money? Quite the contrary, every centime he earned was spent on his electoral campaigns, his constituents had bled him dry, he did not have a sou to his name! Rose and Jacinthe clung to their father like limpets to a rock.

"It would be for the best if you came with us and answered our questions, Monsieur Péricourt, if we find your answers satisfactory, you can go home. Believe me . . ."

"This is utterly preposterous! I have no money, how could I deposit it in a Swiss bank?"

"That is precisely what we hope to clear up as swiftly as possible, Monsieur Péricourt."

"But you must surely have an authorisation, a warrant?"

The examining magistrate sighed. It was a large crowd, he had hoped to keep things discreet, but he had his orders: "Péricourt is a priority. Arrest him as soon as possible!" An example needed to be made. Charles was that example. The judge took out the warrant. Charles did not take it or attempt to read it. The fact that there was an examining magistrate present, that a warrant had been issued, that he, Charles Péricourt, was being compelled to go with the police officers, all these things began to coalesce in his mind. He groped for a word. He found one: "conspiracy".

"Now I understand! The government is trying to silence me!"

"Come now, Monsieur Péricourt," said the magistrate.

"Oh, I understand! You have your orders! The government finds the commission's results troubling!"

The magistrate was a plain-spoken, honest man of forty who had been entrusted with a delicate mission by his superiors, one that he was attempting to carry out diplomatically. But Charles Péricourt would not let him. The crowd had already begun to chatter and comment, and these were no ordinary people, there were politicians, lawyers, doctors, luminaries . . . One of them was already advancing, swaggering, excuse me, monsieur . . .

He needed to take action.

"Monsieur Péricourt, we have carried out a search of your home, and—"

"You found nothing! Ha! Absolutely nothing. What on earth were you thinking?"

Charles called the crowd as witness:

"Ha, ha! They searched my home!"

". . . and of your automobile. In the process of this search, we uncovered two hundred thousand Swiss francs in large denominations. I need you to explain yourself. In my office. If you please."

The money had a serious effect.

The examining magistrate held up a brown-paper envelope and, as discreetly as he could, showed Charles the thick wad of Swiss banknotes.

This cut short Charles' tirade and the barracking of the crowds; there was a deathly silence.

"If you please," repeated the magistrate calmly.

For some reason, perhaps an intuition, Charles turned around.

His eyes fell on Madeleine.

On Paul, in his wheelchair.

His mouth fell open.

"You . . .?"

The crowd thought he had suffered a fit of apoplexy.

His friends rushed to his aid.

And Charles Péricourt, after a final wave to his daughters, who had already begun to howl like damned souls, walked out of the cemetery, flanked by two police officers and led by an examining magistrate.

Madeleine stood, petrified, her hands gripping the wheelchair.

She had wanted to flee, but the desire for her uncle to see her had been overwhelming; now she felt foolish, spiteful. Her father would not have approved. She looked down at Paul and felt a familiar pang of emotion as she saw the nape of his neck, his bony knees pointing from beneath the blanket: no, she was not foolish nor spiteful. Had her father been there she would have said: "Don't meddle, Papa! Let me do things my own way!"

Without a word, Paul reached over his shoulder and gently laid his hand on hers.

41

No, not this time, it was out of the question! Léonce crumpled the piece of paper and tossed it on the floor. She felt like trampling it underfoot, but that would have been ridiculous. She resolved herself to say no, absolutely not. She was so angry with Madeleine that suddenly the prospect of prison seemed less frightening. First, she would appear before a judge, she would make herself look beautiful, she had always managed to be persuasive where men were concerned.

Her means were such that for more than two weeks she had been obliged to live in a seedy hotel, where Robert would have been in his element were it not for the fact that he spent his time complaining about not being able to go to the racetrack. She had hoped they would be freed as soon as Madeleine came back from Berlin, but no, it was "not the right time". "Soon, Léonce, very soon," Madeleine kept saying, only to constantly postpone the date. Going to see little Paul was one thing (God, how the boy had grown! Seeing him like that had been even more upsetting than she had feared), but then Madeleine had forced her to play the whore for a Swiss banker and hide a notebook behind the toilet cistern, very entertaining, thank you! Now, Madeleine had left a note for her at the hotel: "Meet me at four o'clock this afternoon at Ladurée. Without fail."

No, thought Léonce, as she got dressed, this time it was over, she would tell Madeleine to go hang. She would remind her of everything that she had been forced to give up for her sake. She felt like slapping the woman.

"Where are you going, my dove?"

Robert, too, was beginning to get on her nerves. There could be no question of making noise in the hotel since they were supposed to be in hiding, so they were forced to sit around politely, and Robert was hardly the most entertaining conversationalist.

Truth be told, everything was going wrong. By the time she sat down at the table in Ladurée, Léonce was exasperated, livid, even. She did not give Madeleine a moment to catch her breath.

"Enough is enough, Madeleine!"

"I agree with you, Léonce. You are a free woman."

"Excuse me?"

"You are free to go. Leave Paris, leave France, go where you please, I no longer have need of you."

Madeleine's tone was unambiguous, she was dismissing a servant. Léonce flushed.

She wanted to weep, knowing that she was now free . . . and utterly helpless. With no money, no papers and Robert hanging around her neck, she barely had enough to pay for the seedy little hotel room, from which they would probably have to do a moonlight flit . . .

Suddenly, freedom seemed the worst possible fate.

Madeleine calmly studied her, as though she were watching her pack her bags and patiently waiting for her to close the door behind her.

Léonce did not move. So, there would be nothing, not a word, not a mention of all the things they had come through together.

"Well," Léonce stammered.

She rose from her seat. In this moment when they were to part forever, there was a terrible emptiness between them.

Madeleine was a seething ball of resentment, driven by a vengeance that was icy. Inhuman.

Léonce stood, she looked from the table to Madeleine's face, then turned to the door. Still nothing came. She did not know what to say. She resented Madeleine for turning this punishment into a humiliation.

"I bear you no ill will anymore, Léonce," Madeleine said after a moment. "As I know from my own experience, a woman rarely has much choice in her actions."

Would she extend the hand of friendship?

Madeleine did reach out her hand. She proffered an envelope. "This contains fifty thousand Swiss francs. Be prudent."

Already Madeleine had got to her feet and stepped around the table, Léonce opened her mouth to say something, she turned . . .

Madeleine had already left.

With barely a month to go! It was maddening!

Had the tip come a month later, the first issues of *The Lictor* could have published this sensational story, a perfect illustration of the decadent society André intended to denounce!

He had resolved to give the scoop to *L'Événement*, a major right-wing newspaper known for its seriousness and the quality of its political analysis, but not afraid to publish more spectacular stories.

A MAJOR SWOOP ON TAX EVADERS

A major Swiss bank has been running a series of clandestine branches in Paris, paying out benefits while withholding taxes. The fraud is estimated to run into tens of millions . . .

The previous evening, André had visited his employer's office at *Soir de Paris* to tender his resignation.

"In a few days, you personally will be in the spotlight. A major story about tax fraud is about to break and you will be at the very heart of that story, for weeks to come. I shall be writing that story, I will have the scoop because I flushed out the story. Given the circumstances, I hardly think the pages of *Soir de Paris* would be an appropriate place to publish . . . the details. So, I hereby tender my resignation."

Jules Guilloteaux was outraged. Not simply by André's smug vindictiveness, but by Madeleine Péricourt's betrayal.

"How much do you want?" he asked André.

"It is too late, Jules, the case is already in the hands of the police.

I only mention it to you now out of a sense of loyalty. And because I need to free myself."

"I paid you for your silence!"

Without pausing to think, Guilloteaux had immediately called upon Madeleine unannounced, he had mounted the stairs, had pushed Vladi out of the way, where is your mistress, had forced open the door, and had seen Paul, who was listening to music, and next to him his mother. He did not waste his breath on pleasantries.

"You promised me!" he roared.

"That I did, Jules," Madeleine said with a smile. "And I lied to you. I had no intention of keeping my word. I hardly think your scruples are such that you can afford to reproach me."

He choked back an insult, for the sake of the boy, though Paul could read it on his lips.

Guilloteaux sprang into action, he telephoned everyone in his address book, friends, acquaintances, but the scandal was about to break, there was nothing anyone could do now.

From among all the offers he had received, André Delcourt had chosen *L'Événement* because it appealed to his own image, nationalist and anti-parliamentary. He gave the editorial team all the information at his disposal so that the scope and detail of the case would be clear, while he squatted in his ivory tower and penned the analysis and the commentary:

A SHINING EXAMPLE

Swiss bankers are extremely obliging. They are happy to come into our country in order to help our fellow citizens evade taxes.

The suspects will doubtless justify their actions: why should anyone be surprised that the public would attempt to defraud a larcenous taxation system? But while it is true that it is the ordinary taxpayer who has been made to pay for

Republican mismanagement, can one reasonably argue that it is not the thief who is to blame for the theft . . . but his victim, that the miscreant cannot help it if the victim was fool enough to possess a wallet?

The list of thieves – more than a thousand names – offers an edifying cross section of our national decline. Chief among them, obviously, is Charles Péricourt, chair of the parliamentary commission responsible for battling . . . tax evasion. No laughing, please! Two hundred thousand Swiss francs were found in his car on the day of his wife's funeral, a sum he has been unable to explain away. Perhaps he thought he had to pay for the funeral concession in cash . . . He has been charged but released on bail. He has loudly protested that he is the victim of some great conspiracy. It is an ignoble end for someone who bears such a prestigious name.

After such a scandal, can it truly be surprising that the country is clamouring for more stringent institutions, more virtuous leaders, for simpler and fairer laws? That the public are crying out for someone who can restore order?

Kairos

42

"This looks promising, I think . . ."

Madeleine quickly turned her head.

"A Ceylon tea, please, mademoiselle. No, perhaps it is a little late for tea – just a glass of Vichy water, please."

Dupré was jabbing his finger at an article at the bottom of a page in *L'Intransigeant*:

MURDER IN RAINCY
VICTIM WAS FOUR MONTHS PREGNANT

It was only by the purest chance – a visit to the property by a gas man – that the body of thirty-two-year-old Mademoiselle Mathilde Archambault was found late yesterday. She had been dead for two or three days. The young woman died from multiple stab wounds – as many as a dozen – after a fierce struggle with her attacker. No weapon was found at the scene. That the victim was "four to five months" pregnant makes this a particularly heinous crime.

There was no sign of forced entry, suggesting that the murderer was known to the victim.

The murder has baffled police. Mademoiselle Archambault had moved to this address two years earlier, following the death of her father in the family home on the impasse Girardin in Raincy. Neighbours and local shopkeepers described her as a quiet young woman, but admitted that they had seen little of her in recent weeks.

Following their initial investigation, the local police contacted the Forensic Science Unit in Paris. The body of the woman has been taken to the morgue for a post-mortem. The dearth of information about the victim has meant that police are uncertain about the outcome of the investigation, which is to be led by Judge Basile, an investigating magistrate at the Seine Public Prosecutor's office.

The location of the article at the bottom of the page said as much about the meagre information available to *L'Intransigeant* as about the scant hope that this murder might become one of the juicy criminal cases increasingly popular with newspapers and magazines.

Madeleine looked up.

"Yes. Perhaps . . ."

Her back to the wall, she was preoccupied. She reread the article slowly, attempting to project herself into the life of this young woman.

"Mathilde," she murmured.

"I can't see any other solution."

André Delcourt led a monk's life, which meant that they had no hold over him.

"If you were to decide . . ."

"I know, Monsieur Dupré, I know!"

She nervously drummed her fingers on the table. Dupré waited.

She had not touched her glass of Vichy water, besides, she no longer felt thirsty. She angrily folded the newspaper.

"Well . . . we need to finish this once and for all," she said, her voice barely audible.

"It is entirely up to you, Madeleine, but . . . Perhaps you would like some time to think it over."

Rather than feeding her doubts, this suggestion seemed to galvanise her. She gave him a bitter, ugly smile.

"Think about Paul, Monsieur Dupré. You'll see, it helps."

Her tone was still bitter, she had not relented, the family trait of obduracy rising to the surface.

Dupré felt she was accusing him of indifference and, hence, of cruelty, which he found unfair because he truly understood what Madeleine was feeling. His sense of justice had not been offended by the fall of Gustave Joubert, nor that of Charles Péricourt. André Delcourt deserved no better than the others; it was only the means that they planned to use that troubled him.

"I'm sorry to have to insist, but you need to be sure, this is a serious decision."

"One that, clearly, you question . . ."

Dupré did not look away. Madeleine found herself faced with the Dupré she had encountered earlier that year, plain-spoken, insensitive, stony.

"I might."

"On what grounds, Monsieur Dupré?"

"You hired me to do a job. This," he nodded to the newspaper, "was not part of the contract."

To regain her composure, Madeleine picked up her glass and took a sip, then turned back to him.

"If your conscience so dictates, you can walk away. And you are quite right, our agreement did not anticipate our going to such lengths."

"And your conscience tells you that this is permissible?"

"Oh yes, Monsieur Dupré," Madeleine said with a fierce candour that pierced his heart. "It tells me to do the most terrible things."

Sadly, reluctantly, she added:

"And, as you can see, I am prepared to do them."

Dupré found himself faced with a choice, though, in his heart of hearts, he had already made his decision.

"So be it."

Madeleine did not get up. Dupré understood her, but he did not approve of what she planned. Their relationship had taken a grave, unexpected turn.

Soon, they would no longer see each other. They needed to find the words, but nothing came.

"Very well," said Madeleine. "I must respond to Monsieur Delcourt's generous invitation. Dinner tonight, perhaps. Would that suit you, Monsieur Dupré?"

"That would suit me perfectly."

He got to his feet. There was nothing more to say. He bid Madeleine goodbye and made to leave.

"Oh, Monsieur Dupré!"

He turned.

"Yes?"

"Thank you."

For a long while, Madeleine sat staring at the table, at her glass, at the newspaper. She was already shattered by what she was about to do. Her every moral qualm and scruple opposed it, while all her anger and resentment urged her on.

As always, she surrendered to the bitterness.

"Madeleine?"

A cry from the heart. Half surprise, half fear.

"I trust I am not disturbing you?"

"Not in the slightest!"

In recent months, André had been practising such expressions, which he found elegant and refined.

He disappeared suddenly as though an unseen hand had tugged at his collar. Madeleine stepped inside. Monsieur Dupré had often described André's apartment, which he visited regularly. Madeleine could not help but glance at the chest of drawers, the second drawer, where the bullwhip was kept.

"We just got back from the spa yesterday, I was in the neighbourhood and I thought I would take the opportunity to respond to your kind note."

André was overwhelmed by the torrent of information. Madeleine, here in his home, her enigmatic telegram, the consequences that had ensued for Gustave Joubert, the former senior executive of the Péricourt Bank. And now, to find himself with her, in private, in an ambiguous situation that reminded him of their erstwhile relationship.

The shelves were stacked with so many books, so many piles of paper, that the scene resembled a painting entitled "The Humble Apartment of the Great Writer André Delcourt as a Budding Journalist".

"Would you perhaps be free for dinner this evening, my dear André?"

She hoped that he had a prior engagement, it would be easier, but he did not.

"Um . . . yes, that is to say . . ."

"In that case, I will not take up any more of your time. Shall we say half past eight at the Brasserie Lipp?"

Things were going from bad to worse. An invitation he could not refuse, a brasserie where the cream of Paris society would see them together.

"Yes, good, the Brasserie Lipp . . ."

"It has been an age since I last went there."

"Well, in that case . . ."

She left behind a trail of perfume; André threw open the window.

As he had during their previous encounter, René Delgas set his face into a mask of inscrutability as soon as Madeleine began to discuss business.

"Here is a sample of his handwriting. This is the text of the letter. And the paper you should use."

Something had changed. This time Delgas was wearing spectacles, an occupational hazard, thought Madeleine. He set them down on the table after he had read the letter. He opened his mouth to say something, but Madeleine forestalled him:

"How realistic is a forgery . . . of the kind you . . . ? I mean, the police . . ."

"To be honest, the police have an increasing array of tools to detect forgeries. And there are very few men in Paris who can produce documents that are virtually impossible to distinguish from the real thing."

Even indirectly, everything always came down to money.

Madeleine did not respond; she merely folded her hands on the table.

"In the first instance," Delgas said, "there would be no doubt. The police would accept the document as genuine. As would the investigating magistrate. The trouble begins much later, when defence counsel demands an independent expert. At that point, it is impossible to know which way the decision will fall."

For Madeleine, this was long enough.

"For this letter, I would want fifteen hundred francs," he said.

"Are we to do the same little dance? I offer three hundred francs less, you agree, then I ask if you can do it by this evening and you increase the price by three hundred francs?"

"No, not this time. I did not charge a fair price for the notebook I did the time before."

"Are you attempting blackmail? Have you embarked on a new criminal career?"

"No, I simply underestimated the work involved."

"That is your problem, not mine. I paid the price you asked."

"I agree. But now that you wish me to take on another job, I feel compelled to make up a little of the deficit."

"A little?"

"A thousand francs. It is the least I can do. Which brings the cost of the letter to fifteen hundred francs."

Madeleine wondered whether the game was worth the candle, and this thought suddenly plunged her into doubt.

Delgas interpreted Madeleine's silence as a misstep in a negotiation she could not hope to win.

"On the other hand," he said, "I will not charge extra for the rush. Tonight. Eleven o'clock. Here."

"Very well," said Madeleine. "Oh, I did not bring enough to pay the advance . . ."

Delgas raised a conciliatory hand.

"No matter. We trust each other."

Dupré watched as André Delcourt got in the taxi and guessed rather than heard the young man give the address of the Brasserie Lipp.

It was still possible that he had forgotten something, that he might return unexpectedly. It would be safer to wait for half an hour, by which time the taxi would have reached the boulevard Saint-Germain.

*

"I took the liberty of booking the table in your name . . ."

André nodded, yes, of course.

They crossed the room to the large window bay on the left, where the plants painted between the mirrors seemed to grow out of the diners' heads.

It was not the table André would have chosen; a corner table would have been more discreet. But it is what Madeleine had requested since it would be all the more embarrassing for him. A waiter pulled out the table to allow Madeleine to settle on the moleskin banquette.

"I'm sorry, André, but would you mind if I took the chair? I find these banquettes so uncomfortable. I feel much better after my rest cure, I would not want to injure myself again."

"But, of course," André said. He would have preferred to sit with his back to the room, which was precisely why Madeleine was forcing him to sit on the bench.

"Will you excuse me for just a moment, my dear Madeleine?"

She made a brief gesture, by all means.

André embarked on a tour of the neighbouring tables to greet his acquaintances, a member of the parliamentary opposition, the managing editor of *L'Événement*, Armand Chateauvieux, an industrialist sympathetic to the fascist cause who was vacillating as to whether to support André's newspaper.

In passing, he ordered a carafe of chilled white wine.

"You are a much sought-after socialite, my dear," said Madeleine admiringly when André returned to the table.

André feigned modesty. Sought-after, socialite . . .

"Do tell, this newspaper of yours, is it to be launched soon?"

Madeleine knew how terribly superstitious André was.

"Rumours . . ."

Madeleine set down the menu, having made her choice, and folded her hands in front of her.

André's attention was drawn to Chateauvieux. Had he just subtly raised a glass in his direction? André contented himself with a grateful nod. My God! If Chateauvieux had finally decided to support him, the deal was in the bag!

"Pardon?"

"You seem distracted, André. On the one evening you dine with your old friend, it is hardly polite."

"I'm sorry, Madeleine, I . . ."

She laughed.

"I am only teasing, André!"

She glanced over her shoulder and saw Chateauvieux, whose face she recognised from the newspapers.

"I sense that something of importance is at issue for you this evening, or am I mistaken?"

The waiter brought the carafe of chilled white wine and served them. Madeleine raised her glass.

"To the success of both our plans this evening . . ."

"Thank you, Madeleine."

André's building comprised a large number of apartments. Dupré stealthily climbed the four flights of stairs. Picking the lock was easy, he had already let himself in on seven or perhaps eight occasions. This would be his last visit.

"So, this rest cure of yours?"

Madeleine set down her fork.

"Marvellous. As a man who is constantly overwrought, you really should try it, André. I can assure you, these people work miracles."

"What do you mean 'overwrought'?" André smiled.

"I think so. I have always thought of you as nervous, indeed skittish. Granted we have seen little of each other lately, but tonight you seem positively distraught."

"Perhaps you are right. My work . . ."

Madeleine concentrated on her platter of fruits de mer, with which she was engaged in hand to hand combat.

"One of the doctors at the spa told me that certain remote tribes treat nervousness using a whip, can you imagine?"

She looked up.

"It's true, I assure you," she continued. "Apparently they whip themselves until they bleed. They really are barbaric, don't you think?"

André was no fool. He greeted the anecdote with disquieting coldness, as though every word had to be parsed and placed in the column of things to be redressed.

"Where was it, this spa?" he asked tersely.

"Bagnoles de l'Orne. I can give you the address if you like."

The uneasy silence hovered. Could the mention of whips be sheer coincidence? André could think of no other explanation; nonetheless he was on his guard.

"I read your article about my Uncle Charles."

André sensed no reproach in the comment, which was just as well as he would have found it disagreeable to have to defend himself.

"Yes . . . I am so sorry."

"As am I. I feel terrible for poor old Charles. There he was, leading a virtuous crusade only to be brought down by a nasty little scandal, I'm sure you agree."

There was a sardonic tone in her voice that André had never heard before and a malicious glint in her eye. Why had she sought him out? A doubt insinuated itself into his mind, one that he could not put in words.

"You were rather harsh on my poor uncle, André, but I understand. You have your job to do. And, as they say, he would have had nothing to fear if he had not cheated!"

André decided to steer the conversation to the reason for their dinner, to see whether or not it had merely been a pretext.

"I wanted to thank you again for the information you sent me concerning Léonce Joubert . . ."

Madeleine put down her cutlery.

"And working on behalf of Gustave, too! Who would have thought? Even you, in your columns, wished him every success! Such an ambitious project . . . And as though it were not bad enough that he brought the company to ruin, he had to go and sell his ideas to our sworn enemies. Really, I ask you, André, who can we trust?"

"But what about you, Madeleine?"

"Yes?"

"Where did you come by such . . . confidential information?"

"Sadly, my dear André, I am not in a position to tell you that. What is it that you say in journalistic parlance? A confidential source. I found out through someone who would be in grave difficulty if I were to give you his name. This is a man who has done an invaluable service for France, he does not deserve to be pilloried, surely you agree?"

Perverse. That was the word, there was something perverse in the way Madeleine was steering the conversation, in her implications. And now here she was refusing to answer his question using the very argument he himself might have used. He sat back on the bench. He had lost his appetite. He felt as though the situation was spiralling out of his control.

Dupré crept to the kitchen, a tiny space that Delcourt scarcely ever used. More often than not he was invited out to dinner, his one meal of the day. For the rest, he nibbled on something from the meat safe, a small icebox beneath the window that opened onto the balcony. Dupré looked around for utensils but found only cups, spoons, two plates, all immaculately clean.

"What a career you have had!"

Madeleine, in turn, sat back in her chair and studied André as though he were a painting of which she was particularly proud.

"I can still remember the young man I introduced to Jules Guilloteaux."

Their shared past was the one subject André really could not bear, but the mention of the name Guilloteaux put him on his guard. First Charles Péricourt, then Gustave Joubert, now Jules Guilloteaux . . .

André thought quickly. His article would appear the following day, there was no longer any need for secrecy. In such circumstances, it was logical for him to tell her what he knew. Otherwise, she might blame him, how could you have known and not told me?

"There are serious troubles ahead for Monsieur Guilloteaux."

Madeleine looked at him, wide-eyed.

"His name appears on the same list as your uncle's. He will also find himself facing the justice system."

"Jules Guilloteaux? Are we talking about the same man?"

Once again, her tone seemed to belie her words. As though she were feigning surprise at something she already knew.

"And how do you know this, André? Oh, I apologise, your source is confidential, no doubt . . ."

Could he say that it had come to him via an anonymous letter?

André was convinced that Madeleine's airy prattle about her uncle and Jules Guilloteaux masked something else. Behind this display of false naivety, what was she actually trying to say?

"I think I shall have a little dessert, André, what about you?"

Using his handkerchief, Dupré picked up a glass from the desk, held it up to the light, then slipped it into his duffel bag. He opened the second drawer of the chest of drawers and slipped the bullwhip into the pouch he had brought with him.

Then he left as he had come, silently closing the door behind him.

Madeleine finished her sorbet and delicately dabbed the corners of the mouth with her napkin.

"Since I have you here, might I ask your advice, André?"

"I am disinclined to give advice . . ."

"If you cannot ask a future newspaper editor for an opinion, who can you ask?"

Had she raised her voice slightly as she said these words?

"It is about Paul."

André froze at the mention of the name. He was convinced, utterly convinced, that the other names she had mentioned in the course of the evening had but one goal: to lead to this. The blood drained from André's face.

"Ever since the unfortunate incident when you came to visit and Paul suddenly woke from a terrible nightmare, you remember? Well, not only has he continued to have those nightmares, but, with hindsight, it occurs to me that they started before then, though I cannot say precisely when. Were you aware of him having nightmares when you were living with us . . . I mean, when you were around?"

André felt a hard lump in his throat. What could possibly happen? Paul's nightmares . . . The years he had spent with Paul seemed so far away now, what did he have to feel guilty about? How old was the boy now? Was it possible to talk of a time long gone?

"I'm in no position to . . . I mean, I . . ."

"I ask you, André, because you knew Paul well."

Madeleine gave him a broad smile and looked him directly in the eye.

"You were his tutor. Nobody knew Paul more intimately than you did, André."

She left an almost imperceptible silence between these sentences.

"You were fond of him, you took care of him, you were kind, objective, disinterested, that is why I am asking for your opinion, but if you have nothing to say, so be it. But since the time has come for us to part (thank you for a charming evening, by the way), I feel that I should tell you that I know all the things you were to my son. All the things you did for him. And I just wanted to reassure you," she gently took hold of his wrist, as though they were still lovers, "that such care never truly fades."

Dupré took a taxi to the town hall in Raincy and made the last leg of the journey on foot, although the fog made it difficult for him to get his bearings. Visibility was good for about forty metres, after which everything became a blur. According to the newspaper article, the forensic officers were not due to arrive until tomorrow at first light, and he thought it unlikely that the Raincy police force would have the manpower to station guards at the front and rear of the house all night.

Four steps led up to a glass-roofed porch. The house itself, a burrstone building, had been sealed off, and a police sign stated that all entry was forbidden on pain of imprisonment. Dupré nimbly scaled the railings and went around to the garden at the back of the house. The back door had also been sealed. He studied the upper floor and decided to enter via a circular window. He took a stepladder from the garden shed, climbed up, and, using a length of wire, set about opening the window lock. Twice, he almost fell from the ladder. Eventually, the lock gave way with a loud crack. Dupré put his tools back into his duffel bag, which he slung over his shoulder before hoisting himself over the window ledge.

He landed on the tiled floor of the bathroom. He paused warily and listened for several minutes before taking off his shoes, slipping on his gloves and making a tour of the house.

Two of the bedrooms smelled musty, it was clear that no-one used them, but the drawers had all been opened and searched. In the hallway, he carefully avoided the smears of mud and dried blood.

There had clearly been a struggle in the young woman's bedroom, the bedside table had been overturned, the lamp lay shattered on the floor. Had the murderer pursued the woman with the kitchen knife? Had she thrown anything that came to hand in an attempt to fend him off? Was she already injured?

Here, too, the drawers had been emptied; the clothes and underwear in the wardrobe had been searched. In the cramped bathroom, there was no shaving soap, no razor, no deodorant. Dupré took a fountain pen and an old ink bottle from his duffel bag and dropped them into the scattered objects from an upturned drawer. He hung a dressing gown with a crumpled piece of paper in the pocket in the wardrobe.

He turned on his torch, went over to the chest of drawers and studied the surface. There were streaks where someone had wiped it with a duster. This was good; the killer had cleaned up after himself, meaning Dupré would not need to do so. He checked the doorknob: clean. The door frame: clean. The banister: clean. He went back to Mathilde's bedroom, took a glass from his duffel bag and gently rolled it under the bed, then headed downstairs, careful to avoid the blood spatter on the steps.

In the living room, the location where the body had been found was clearly marked. Dupré knelt and studied the wooden floor. There were footprints, but they were not those of the killer. A murderer who takes the trouble to wipe away fingerprints does not tramp through the victim's blood; the footprints had been made by police officers. Despite the constant reminders from newspapers that nothing at a crime scene should be touched, it made little difference. The forensics officers would have to do the best they could, as always. The local forces were none too fond of "lab rats" who gave orders to the officers who actually pounded the beat all year round. It was obvious that they never had to interrogate low-life thugs. That required officers with brute force and brawn, officers whose working tools were not tweezers, camel-hair brushes and microscopes.

There was a door that led down to the basement. Hanging along the wall were small wooden crates containing tools and sundry pieces of hardware. One of the crates was empty, Dupré opened his duffel bag, took out the pouch containing the bullwhip and emptied the contents into the box. Then he checked the clean-up operation.

The table: clean. The chair backs: clean. The surface of the dresser: clean. The cupboard doors: clean.

Still moving on tiptoe, he crept back upstairs. The bed was a common model, an iron bedstead with brass globes at each corner. He unscrewed one, rolled up the letter he had been given by Delgas, slipped it into the bedpost and screwed the brass ball on again. He hesitated. Should he screw it tightly or not? Yes, tightly, the way Mathilde would have done. But not quite all the way.

Dupré slipped his shoes back on, climbed through the window and pulled it shut. With the length of wire, he managed to rotate the clasp a quarter turn; it would have to do. He glanced at his watch. Just gone four o'clock in the morning.

In an hour, the first labourers would be setting out for work.

For Dupré, it was time to go home.

The scene of the crime was thronged with people by the time the investigating magistrate arrived just before noon. Maître Basile was a thickset, plump, but powerful man with an expressive face and keen eyes, who demanded answers to his questions. He had the reputation of being an awkward magistrate. His career had been marked by an impressive number of arrests, more than one death sentence and eight of life imprisonment. He was efficient.

The forensic officers had succeeded in identifying two different sets of fingerprints.

The magistrate was led out into the garden, where the body of a six-month-old baby had been found buried.

"From the level of decomposition, we calculate that death took place some eighteen months ago."

"That's not all . . ."

The police officer looked exasperated. He had good cause.

The magistrate bent over the table, and, without touching it, read the letter that had been smoothed out.

"Where did you find this?"

"In the young victim's bedroom. In one of the bedposts."

Most exasperating.

The magistrate decided to consult his superiors.

"Dear God! We shall have to proceed with the utmost caution!"

There could be no scandal, no premature disclosures, no statements that would later have to be disavowed. The magistrate knew that he would have to deal with the case by himself, that he would have to get the result without rocking the boat, and without getting anyone wet besides himself, which, if he were to fail, would not trouble anyone.

The presence of two sets of fingerprints complicated the scene, but the magistrate focused on a set that had been found in four different places, and which, unlike the other set, was backed up by other evidence.

All things considered, the investigating magistrate decided to make a partial statement to the press, thereby evading the first obstacle:

A letter, written in a man's hand and found in the frame of the victim's bed, corroborates the hypothesis that the murder resulted from the young woman's refusal to have another abortion. In the letter, doubtless hidden there by Mathilde Archambault in case the situation should turn to tragedy, the suspected murderer pleads with her not to keep the unborn child, he begs, he threatens, he appeals to his mistress. According to investigators, the letter is well written, indicating a man of above-average education, though one who is not above plagiarism, since one of the sentences is borrowed word for word from an article by the respected columnist André Delcourt published last August in *Soir de Paris*: "the love that should prevail over all things, over fate, over destiny, over misfortune . . . That love which is the sacred gift of all God's creatures."

In Paris, the early editions had been on sale since dawn, but André did not read them until late in the morning. He claimed that a well-regulated life was not only a guarantee of longevity, but the symbol of a well-ordered mind. He often cited the story of the philosopher Kant, who forewent his morning constitutional only once, when he learned of the French Revolution (Delcourt, Kant – the reader could connect the dots).

"What do you mean, plagiarism?"

It was on the front page of *Le Matin*: "MURDERER PLAGIA-RISES FAMOUS COLUMNIST"; the story also appeared in *Le Petit Journal*: "In a letter to his victim, the murderer stole a quote from a column by Kairos."

"Extra, extra!" called the newsvendor.

For him to be associated with such a heinous crime, and only weeks before the launch of his newspaper.

Why had *L'Événement*, which would obviously be as well informed as the other papers, not called him? He went straight to the offices without troubling to go home.

The editor was not in Paris, but a telegram from him was waiting for André: *Bad publicity – STOP – make it cease – STOP – do not respond to questions – Montet-Bouxal.*

What could he do? Who could he call? The story was already in the newspapers. A retraction in the afternoon editions, that was what was needed.

And still the editor did not come.

In his stead, there came a police officer.

What had been a minor news story swelled, it spilled over the borders of Raincy and reached the capital. To lead the investigation, the magistrate appointed one Commissaire Fichet. The reader is already familiar with Commissaire Fichet from his role investigating the burglary of Gustave Joubert's house. An older officer, hunched and wrinkled, dressed in a beige trench coat, whose breath reeked of stale cigar smoke.

"I . . . I don't see how this case concerns me."

"I believe it does not concern you, Monsieur Delcourt! That is precisely why I have come to see you. Can you simply confirm that you do not know Mathilde Archambault?"

"Of course I can confirm it!"

André glanced around him.

"Come this way."

They were standing in the corridor of the newsroom, with people coming and going, overhearing a snatch of conversation and passing it on. André knew too many journalists not to be wary. He led the commissaire into his office. The officer did not remove his trench coat, why bother, he would be there no more than a minute.

"This business is utterly insane!" said André. "A man has only to copy a line from a column before murdering someone and then suddenly the police show up at my newspaper. And while we are on the subject, why am I being questioned?"

Fichet's grim expression clearly signalled that there was a problem.

"I must confess, monsieur, that there is no reason. It is what you might call an 'operational precaution'. The murderer could be anyone, as I am sure you understand."

André was aghast.

"Are you saying . . . it could be me? Am I a suspect?"

A secretary appeared with a tray of coffee, as she always did for visitors. Not a word was spoken until she had left. André's hands were trembling, his face was pale as tallow, he was deeply disconcerted. The cup made a terrible, glassy noise as he set it on the saucer. Commissaire Fichet, who had faced many hardened criminals in his long career, would have staked his pension that this man had had nothing to do with the murder, some indications do not lie. But he had to do his job.

"A letter quoting your words was found at the scene. Put yourself in our shoes. What are we supposed to think? We must do everything to ensure that it is clear you are above suspicion."

"Very well," said André, his voice hoarse with dread. "Let us get it over with. What do you want to know?"

Despite his unease, he was beginning to think that, if the police could immediately rule him out, the evening editions would publish the fact and the subject would be closed.

"So, you say you did not know the victim."

"Not at all."

"She lived in Le Raincy."

"I have never set foot in the place."

"The suspect left a handwritten letter."

The commissaire pensively scratched his head with a pencil.

"What I am wondering, monsieur, is whether all this might not be quickly resolved if you were to give us an example of your handwriting."

André was dumbfounded. He sat in his chair, unable to move.

"A simple visual comparison," said the commissaire. "And we need say no more about the matter. But it is entirely up to you, you are not obliged."

André's mind was working in slow motion.

"What do you want me to write?"

He got up, went over to his desk and got his pen. Instinctively, he picked up a sheet of paper, but was now so flustered he did not know what to do.

"Whatever you choose, monsieur, it makes no difference."

André stared at the blank page. The prospect of writing a single word gave him the dizzying impression of writing a confession, this was a nightmare. He wrote: "I have nothing whatsoever to do with this crime and I demand that the police immediately relay this information to the press."

"If you could sign it, too, please? For the sake of form."

André signed.

"Right, I shall be going. Thank you for your cooperation, monsieur."

"You will publish the results as soon as possible, I take it?"

"Oh yes, of course."

The commissaire looked down at the paper and, satisfied, neatly folded it in four and slipped it into the inside pocket of his coat.

"Oh, just one more thing, monsieur . . ."

André froze; this whole situation was an ordeal. Fichet gazed out the window, scratching his chin, engrossed by some minor niggle, but he said nothing more. André could cheerfully have slapped the man.

"The fingerprints . . ."

"What fingerprints?"

"I do not want to bother you with technical details, but hand-writing analysis is not a fully recognised scientific method. It is what, in police jargon, we call 'circumstantial'. Fingerprints, on the other hand, are one hundred per cent reliable."

André was familiar with the concept, but could not quite see what was being suggested. He had provided an example of his hand-writing. It slowly dawned on him. The commissaire was asking for . . . his fingerprints?

"What exactly are you asking?"

"Well, if we compare your handwriting to the letter found at the scene, and everyone is agreed that they do not match, the magistrate will inform the press that you have nothing to do with the case. But if someone should be hesitant, if he should say, 'I am not entirely sure, I would not swear to it,' then I will be back here in your office in a couple of hours. Whereas if I take your fingerprints now, then as soon as the forensics laboratory has compared them with those found at the crime scene, we will publish the results, and there can be no argument, the method is completely scientific."

Twenty minutes later, the commissaire left the offices of *L'Événe-ment* with André Delcourt's fingerprints.

André was in shock.

Fichet had gripped his forefinger with uncommon strength and pressed it onto a sheet of paper, rolling it right and left, then, without warning, he had done the same with his middle finger and his thumb. André stared down at his ink-smudged fingers. When giving his writing sample, André had imagined himself as a suspect. When giving his fingerprints, he saw himself as guilty.

He had allowed himself to be outflanked by a policeman . . .

He should have called a lawyer. He left his office and walked along the boulevard to catch his breath, or at least regain some semblance of composure. In the end, his handwriting and his fingerprints would definitely rule him out.

All he needed was for this fact to be published, and quickly.

He considered telephoning Montet-Bouxal. No, he would do that when he had the exoneration in hand.

He walked quickly, his resolve strengthening, the police were obviously well intentioned, but a case like this could drag on, and time was the one thing that André did not have. He needed to speed things up.

For the first time in his life, he was about to do something he had always managed to avoid: ask a favour of a friend. But the clock was ticking. He hailed a taxi, went to the Ministry of Justice and asked to speak to the chief of staff.

"You have done the right thing, my dear André. We cannot sit idly by. I will personally telephone the magistrate. At what time did the police officer visit you?"

"About an hour ago."

"That is more than enough time to compare fingerprints. By noon, this will all be over. I will insist that the ministry release a statement. First thing this afternoon."

"Thank you. You, at least, understand the situation."

"Of course, of course! Moreover, just between the two of us, I cannot see on what basis the police felt it was acceptable to bother you in such a manner. To be quoted or even plagiarised is not a crime, as far as I am aware!"

408

Late September. The weather was clement. The fog that had been hanging over the city for days had dispersed. The boulevard exhaled a last breath of summer. The trees were beginning to shed their leaves. André was relieved.

The refutation would be published in the early afternoon, at two o'clock, three at the latest.

He went into a post office, where he asked to be put through to a number.

"This business is most annoying," Montet-Bouxal said.

"A statement will be issued within two hours, I have the word of the Ministry of Justice."

"Good, we shall see."

"You do not seem to realise that I am the victim here."

"I know, but . . . This is a question of image, you understand. Just have a copy of the statement from the ministry sent to me as soon as it is released."

This conversation rekindled André's sense of dread. Was the battle lost before it could be won? He could not believe it.

What could he do?

Nothing. Wait.

Returning home to find everything as he had left it, he weighed up the gravity of what had occurred in a single morning. He felt profoundly depressed. He was angry with himself, though he did not know what more he could have done.

He was not hungry.

He took off his shirt, he felt like weeping.

Before getting on his knees in the middle of his study, he opened the chest of drawers.

His heart lurched: the bullwhip was not there.

43

There came a knock at the door.

André, panicked by what he had just discovered, hurriedly grabbed his shirt and pulled it on, who could possibly be knocking? What time was it? He was disoriented, his fingers fumbled with the buttons, a cold shudder coursed through him, leaving him completely numb. Another rap.

"Who is it?"

His voice sounded as though it came from the depths of a cave, the echo mingled with another.

"It is Commissaire Fichet, monsieur!"

André turned back to the drawer. He knew that he had never stored the whip anywhere but there . . .

"I have a document for you."

Sweet Lord! An exoneration from the police. He was safe. André raced to open the door.

"You have it?"

"Here."

It was an official document, André could not make sense of it, they really should make such things simpler. Article 122 of the Code of Criminal Procedure. Investigating magistrate Judge Basile. He scanned the text of the document but could not find what he was looking for.

"Where is it?"

"There," said Commissaire Fichet, jabbing at the middle of the page. "This is an arrest warrant, the magistrate would like to see you, I will take you to him."

*

André found himself unable to collect his thoughts. He bombarded the officer with questions. Why do they want to see me? Has the formal retraction been published? Is there some problem? Commissaire Fichet stared out the window and did not answer, as though he were alone in the car, or stone deaf.

A wooden bench. A hallway. Busy officers coming and going. Take a seat, André was told, someone will come and fetch you. But no-one came. He was being treated like a common criminal. He tried to calm himself, to still his heart, which was hammering so hard he felt nauseous. He had demanded that the police issue a formal statement, now they were trying to make him pay. The authorities did not like taking orders.

But the bullwhip . . . That was a mystery he could not resolve. When had he used it last? A week ago, when he came home from Square Bertrand.

He froze.

". . . certain remote tribes . . . they whip themselves until they bleed . . . barbaric, don't you think?"

André retched, and only just managed to avoid vomiting, he wanted to spit, he glanced around for someone, anyone.

Was he allowed to move? A uniformed agent stood at the end of the hallway. Was he allowed to go to the bathroom? He raised his hand, as though he were at school. From a distance, the officer shook his head. André choked back the acrid taste of vomit.

A door opened, and an official appeared.

"Monsieur Delcourt, if you would please follow me."

André stepped into the office of the magistrate, who did not trouble to stand up. Turning around suddenly, André saw that the door had already closed.

"Take a seat," the magistrate said curtly, by way of greeting.

In this place, André Delcourt was no-one. He felt terribly afraid.

He glanced to his right, the shutters were open. He felt the urge to jump out the window.

At length, the magistrate put on his spectacles.

"I shall not beat around the bush, Monsieur Delcourt. You are suspected of murdering Mademoiselle Mathilde Archambault between—"

"That's impossib—"

The magistrate pounded his fist on the desk.

"Hold your tongue! Right now, I am the one who speaks and you answer only when I ask a question. Is that understood?"

Without waiting for an answer, he continued:

". . . of murdering Mathilde Archambault between the hours of seven o'clock on the evening of September 23, and six o'clock on the morning of September 24."

"September 23, when exactly was that?"

"Saturday last."

"Ah! I dined with Madame de Fontanges, there were at least twenty guests. I cannot have done it. I have witnesses."

"Are you suggesting the dinner went on until six in the morning?"

"Well . . ."

"Is this your handwriting?"

The judge handed him a letter:

My beloved,

It was his handwriting.

Very soon, as you know, we will be able to declare our passion. I know the torments that you have suffered.

It was his handwriting, but he had never written such a thing.

Now, we face our last terrible ordeal. Once again, I implore you to heed my request. Do not sully our pure, untainted love with something that can serve only to defile it.

This notepaper, on the other hand, was his.

As I have told you, in a matter of months, perhaps weeks, we will be able to proclaim to the world that nothing and no-one will ever part us again.

He would never have written such a letter, so crude, so clumsy, never. It could not be him.

I beg of you, my dearest love, do not force me to take matters into my own hands . . . You know that I am as resolute as I am loving.

André's hands were shaking so hard that he found it difficult to focus on what he was reading.

Have faith, as I do, in the love that should prevail over all things, over fate, over destiny, over misfortune . . . That love which is the sacred gift of all God's creatures.
Your devoted André

"I did not write this letter."
"Is the notepaper yours?"
"It is no more mine than anyone else's. Anyone can buy it."
"Is it the same as yours?"
The magistrate handed him a page like the previous one, on which he recognised his own hand:

Dear Sir,
~~I respectfully write to you in order~~
~~I am taking the liberty of writing to you~~
As you doubtless know, thorough our ~~mutual~~ friend
I am writing to you,

"Did you write this letter?"
"Where did you get this?"
"It was found in the pocket of a dressing gown."
The judge rose from his chair, stepped over to the table on his left and held up a dressing gown that André instantly recognised.
"I threw that out two months ago."

"Then how do you explain that it was found in Mademoiselle Archambault's house? We also found this pen, and this bottle of ink."

"But surely they could belong to anyone?"

"With your fingerprints? I think not."

"Someone stole them! From my apartment! Someone broke into my home while I was out and stole them . . ."

"Did you file a complaint? On what date?"

André froze.

"This is a conspiracy, monsieur le juge, and I know who is behind it."

"Your fingerprints were also found on a glass beneath the victim's bed."

"This is a conspiracy intended to . . . On Tuesday night, at the Br—"

He was stopped in his tracks as the magistrate held up a bullwhip.

"Traces of blood were found on this. The blood group is not that of the victim. Could it be yours? Forensic examination will doubtless reveal whether it matches yours."

The charge of murder was being further tainted by odious insinuations.

"If that proves to be the case, you can hardly continue to deny that you did not know the victim."

It was foolish, but André felt more ashamed about the whip than he did about the other allegations. He shook his head vehemently, no, that is not mine . . .

"Your notepaper, your handwriting, your fingerprints found in four separate locations, almost certainly your blood. André Delcourt, I am charging you with the murder of Mademoiselle Mathilde Archambault, without prejudice to any further charges, including infanticide, which may stem from it."

44

Madeleine was drinking seltzer water. Dupré was slowly sipping his coffee. For more than an hour, they had been sitting, staring at the steps of the Palais de Justice.

Dusk was gathering.

Six o'clock, according to the clock on the embankment.

"Here they come," Dupré said.

Madeleine immediately got up and went outside.

On the far side of the street, André Delcourt, flanked by two uniformed police officers, was walking down towards a Black Maria whose doors stood open. His face was haggard and exhausted, his tread heavy, his shoulders slumped.

He saw her. He stopped dead.

His mouth fell open.

"Come on, now," said an officer, pushing him into the police van. "Shift yourself!"

The scene did not last more than a minute, the van had already driven away. As she watched it disappear, Madeleine suddenly felt terribly old.

Was it regret? No, she had no regrets. Why then was she weeping? She could not say.

"Did I . . ."

"No, no, Monsieur Dupré, thank you, it is nothing, it is . . ."

She turned away to wipe her eyes and blow her nose.

"Let us go," she said, recovering her composure.

She tried to smile.

"Well, then, Monsieur Dupré . . ."

"Yes?"

"I think we can say that our work is done."

"I think we can."

"Have I thanked you sufficiently, Monsieur Dupré?"

He considered the question for a while. He had thought about this moment, about this parting of the ways, but still he was not prepared.

"I think so, Madeleine."

"What will you do now? Find a job?"

"Yes. Something a little more restful."

They smiled at each other.

Monsieur Dupré got to his feet.

Madeleine held out her hand and he shook it.

"Thank you again, Monsieur Dupré."

He wanted to say something affectionate, but he could think of nothing, and it showed.

As he left, he stopped at the bar to pay for their drinks, then walked out without a backward glance.

It was five o'clock when the taxi dropped Madeleine outside the gate. She looked up at the sign, then slowly strolled through the car park, climbed the concrete steps and pushed open the door.

Although it was now fitted with long tables covered with distillation flasks, condensers, pipettes and test tubes, the Pré-Saint-Gervais workshop was so vast it seemed almost empty.

Vladi, Paul and Monsieur Brodsky were all wearing lab coats, and, at the pharmacist's insistence, all were wearing caps.

The workshop was pervaded by a miasma in which the scent of tea tree oil was overwhelmed by others redolent of glue, turpentine and hot fat. It was difficult to imagine that such a place could produce something so sweet-scented.

"Ma-ma-maman . . . Y-you don't often c-c-come here."

"I shall be able to come more often now. My, my, but the place has changed in no time!"

Madeleine wanted to know everything, and Paul explained, sparing her no detail of the process. Meanwhile Vladi and Monsieur Brodsky chattered in German.

"That's very good," said Madeleine.

Paul paused.

"A-a-are you f-feeling al-alright, Maman?"

"Not especially, my darling, I think I shall go home."

"Wh-what is it?"

"It is nothing, honestly. A minor upset, nothing more, I think perhaps I need an early night. Everything will be back to normal tomorrow."

She bid everyone goodbye, then kissed Paul.

As she went back down the steps, she felt fragile, there was a void in her chest. All that remained was for her to contemplate the ruins on which she would have to build her life.

She looked up.

A car was idling in the yard.

When she reached it, she stopped and peered through the window at the driver.

"I thought perhaps I might drive you home, Madeleine. It's getting late."

She gave a fleeting smile and climbed into the car.

"You are quite right, it would be much safer to drive home. Thank you, Monsieur Dupré."

Epilogue

The fascist newspaper whose launch was stalled by the arrest of André Delcourt never recovered.

The investigation into the "Delcourt affair", led by a team of handwriting experts, lasted more than eighteen months, following which the Seine assizes (where the experts once again did battle) sentenced André to fifteen years' imprisonment.

On January 23, 1936, Madeleine was distraught to learn of the arrest of a man named Gilles Palisset for assault under the influence of alcohol; his fingerprints perfectly matched the second set found at the home of Mathilde Archambault.

Palisset, a pathological liar and pervert who worked as a clerk for the Crédit Municipal and lived with his parents, immediately confessed to the charges and also confessed to the abortions and to the murder of Mathilde Archambault. It was decided that Mathilde Archambault had had two lovers: Delcourt, who had left too much evidence at the scene for anyone to doubt his involvement, and Palisset, who had eventually murdered her. Rather than denouncing a miscarriage of justice, the press praised the skill and efficiency of the police forensics laboratory.

André Delcourt was immediately released.

Madeleine followed the aftermath of this case with a fury that Monsieur Dupré could do nothing to appease.

Less than a month after his release, the press was mired in speculation about the circumstances of André Delcourt's death.

On February 20, 1936, his naked body was found, the hands and feet lashed to the bedposts. According to the post-mortem, Delcourt had ingested a considerable dose of a common sleeping draught, but the actual cause of death had been a large amount of quicklime poured over his genitals. The death had probably been slow and agonising.

The precise circumstances of his death were never discovered.

The saga of Gustave Joubert's trial was long and complicated. At the time, the charge of high treason was a rather vague concept, more useful in patriotic speeches than in a court of law; the fact that the charge was preferred had much to do with the rising tensions with Germany. Some who deeply mistrusted the Nazi regime felt inclined to demonstrate France's determination by making an example of Joubert. Others, who felt the country had to make its peace with a Third Reich whose warlike intentions, they believed, were no more than posturing, argued in favour of acquittal as a sign of peace.

The status of Joubert lent the case a particular gravity that further stimulated debate.

The trial quickly descended into a long, confused legal battle that perfectly reflected the troubles of the government, the diffidence of its leaders, the vagueness of its foreign policy and, in retrospect, the lack of moral clarity that pervaded the country's elected representatives. In lieu of a charge of high treason, the government preferred the notion of a secret agreement with the enemy, deeming it more prudent. In 1936, Joubert was sentenced to seven years in prison, although this was commuted and he was released in 1941, only to die the following year of a virulent cancer. "Faster than his jet engine", according to one vituperative journalist.

This leaves only Charles Péricourt. The scandal that had led to his downfall was quickly hushed up. The eighty-eight magistrates appointed to investigate were not helped by four certified accountants – an ingenious and effective method of slowing the investigation until the hue and cry had died down.

In the face of invective from the right-wing press, the authorities refused to disclose the identity of any other offenders, thereby depriving the general public of names on which to vent their anger. A section of the press preferred to pass over the matter, and alluded to the scandal in a few short articles of astonishing discretion. Other newspapers launched a counter-attack, and once again penned jeremiads against the tax system, whose voraciousness had stirred up the public in the first place. In short, the scandal gradually faded, and within a few brief months it was as though it had never happened. British and Swiss banks continued to ply their trade, while modest taxpayers continued to pay disproportionately more than their wealthy compatriots.

Charles Péricourt no longer needed to worry, but he was a man crushed by his failure. He never recovered from the death of Hortense. As he foresaw, his "two flowers" never married, and instead followed a curious path that led initially to them joining a convent, but they were not happy there. In 1946, they set sail for Pondicherry, and insisted that their father join them there. In March 1951, he finally agreed. It was here, surrounded by his "virginal bouquet", that he died the following year.

Paul's precocious talent for publicity, supported by a clever campaign of radio advertisements, made his balm a staggering success. The slogan "Gosh!" became popular, used in all manner of situations. Women loved it, since it allowed them to use a minced oath and pass it off as a joke. The Péricourt laboratory increased its range of products. An article about Paul Péricourt in *Le Petit Journal illustré* thrust him into the spotlight. The public adored this bright, enterprising, modest young man in a wheelchair, who spent most of his interviews with the press trying to explain (provided one had the time to listen) how the great Solange Gallinato had gone to Berlin shortly before her death to *defy* the Reich, how her last recital had been flagrantly anti-Nazi and how

421

the German authorities had fabricated a tissue of lies that needed to be scotched since it did a great disservice to the diva's legend, *et cetera*. When he launched into the story, it was impossible to stop him. All contemporary encyclopaedias include the version Paul managed to impose.

He joined the French Resistance in 1941 and was arrested by the Gestapo in 1943. He was not taken out of his wheelchair while being interrogated.

In Paris, in August 1944, he did not leave his chair, his window or his sniper rifle for almost seventy-two hours.

Paul accepted the decorations – the Médaille de la Résistance, Croix de la Libération, Légion d'honneur – but he never spoke of the war and never joined a veterans' association. He refused to see his father, who tried to use his own war record to reconnect with his son. The two men had chosen very different camps.

His penchant for pharmaceuticals did not survive the success of Calypso Balm. What interested him was not the products themselves, but the means of selling them. He devoted himself to advertising, founded the Péricourt Agency, married Gloria Fenwick, heir to a rival American agency, went to live in New York, moved back to Paris, and sired children, profits and slogans, the last of these being his strong suit.

Although she had plenty of options, Léonce Picard chose to return to Casablanca. She wanted to go back to the start, like a girl playing hopscotch who lands on the wrong square and starts over. She did not take Robert Ferrand – much to his surprise, though he quickly found consolation.

She never attempted to explain why she adopted the name Madeleine Janver. She fell back on the rank opportunism she had first employed in Paris, but instead of looking for a wealthy bourgeoise for whom she would be a dame de compagnie, she met and married an industrialist from Normandy to whom she bore five children, one each year. After her last pregnancy, Léonce gained a lot of weight, you would not have recognised her.

Oh, Vladi, let us not forget Vladi.

She married the young conductor who worked for the Compagnie des Chemins de Fer de l'Est, became Madame Kessler and settled in Alençon, but never learned a word of French. Her eldest son, Adrien, as everyone knows, was awarded the Nobel Prize in Medicine.

As for Madeleine and Monsieur Dupré, they continued their formal but cordial relations, they would do so for the rest of their lives.

He addressed her as "Madeleine". She addressed him as "Monsieur Dupré", like a shopkeeper's wife in the presence of a customer.

Roudergues, July 2017

Acknowledgments

The French title of this tribute to my mentor, Alexandre Dumas, is taken from *The Count of Monte Cristo* (1844) and the story is loosely inspired by a number of real events.

Gustave Joubert's "Renaissance Française" obviously owes much to Ernest Mercier's Redressement Français (1925–35); the practices of the Winterthur Union Bank are based on those of the Banque Commerciale de Bâle (1932); the actions of *Soir de Paris* are based on "the appalling venality of the French press" (a series of articles by Boris Souvarine published in *L'Humanité*, 1923). The character of Jules Guilloteaux is inspired by Maurice Bunau-Varilla, the editor of *Le Matin*.

Those I would like to thank here bear no responsibility for my deviations from "actual history", for which I, alone, am to blame.

Camille Cléret (whom I met thanks to Emmanuel L.) kindly offered her talents as a historian, her resourcefulness and her knowledge throughout the writing of this novel. When I stretched historical truth, she alerted me to the fact. When I decided to ignore her advice, she made me weigh the risks. Our collaboration was a pleasure.

I owe a great debt to the historians of the period, especially Fabrice Abbad, Serge Berstein and Pierre Milza, Olivier Dard, Frédéric Monier, Jean-François Sirinelli, Eugen Weber, Michel Winock and Theodore Zeldin.

L'Argent caché by Jean-Noël Jeanneney, a fascinating book about business and politics, furnished crucial elements, as did *Les Batailles de l'impôt* by Nicolas Delalande, from which I drew most of Charles

425

Péricourt's ideas on tax enforcement. These were supplemented by the work of Christophe Farquet ("Lutte contre l'évasion fiscale: l'échec de la S.D.N."). The idea of tax evasion I owe to Sébastien Guex's excellent article "1932: the tax fraud affair and the Herriot government".

On a completely different note, Germaine Ramos's novel *La Foire aux vices* proved an excellent source of information regarding the venal practices of the press; Robert de Jouvenel's *La République des camarades* did the same for parliamentary cronyism.

Reading the newspapers of the period was of invaluable help, especially the articles of certain columnists (B. Gervaise, L. A. Pagès, P. Reboux, C. Vautel, J. Bainville, G. Sanvoisin, *et cetera*) and the articles penned by François Coty for *Le Figaro*, together with the daily columns in *Le Matin* and the columns written by Monsieur de La Palisse for *Le Petit Journal*. "Does France need a Dictator" was the title of a long article published in *Le Petit Journal* in March 1933. For these and many other things, I am grateful to those who maintain the extraordinary database Gallica de la BNF; I only wish they had greater resources.

Translations in Polish were provided by my wonderful translator, Joanna Polachowska; those from (South) German, I owe to Laura Kleiner.

Jean-Noël Passieux provided a useful introduction to the fortunes and misfortunes of jet engines. I am grateful for his patience, as I am to Gerard Hartmann, who turned a blind eye to my technical approximations. Hervé David kindly helped me to allow Paul to indulge his passion for the phonograph, and the enchanting Phono Museum in Paris completed my initiation. Jalal Aro, at the Phonogalerie de Paris, that Aladdin's cave of the gramophone, perfectly completed my education.

In the course of writing this book, I was often visited by things that came from elsewhere; nothing that we write is truly our own. For example, when it came to explaining that, at a certain point,

Solange Gallinato would have to sing sitting down, I remembered how Victor Hugo describes the mysterious fate of Charles Myriel ("What took place next in the fate of M. Myriel? The ruin of the French society of the olden days . . ."). To list all such synchronicity would smack of pedantry, so I will simply draw up a rough alphabetical list: Louis Aragon, Michel Audiard, Marcel Aymé, Charles Baudelaire, Saul Bellow, Georges Brassens, Emmanuel Carrère, Ivy Compton-Burnett, Henry-Georges Clouzot, Alexandre Dumas, Albert Dupontel, Gustave Flaubert, William Gaddis, Alberto Garlini, Jean Giraudoux.

I am grateful to my attentive readers: my long-standing partner in crime Gérald Aubert, and Nathalie Camille Trumer, Perrine Margaine, Camille Cléret, Solène, Catherine Bozorgan, Marie-Gabrielle Peaucelle and Albert Dupontel.

A very special mention to Véronique Ovaldé for her wise advice and her generosity.

And Pascaline, from beginning to end.

PIERRE LEMAITRE worked for many years as a teacher of literature before becoming a novelist. His crime fiction includes the award-winning Camille Verhoeven trilogy, and standalones *Blood Wedding*, *Three Days and a Life* and *Inhuman Resources*, which is now a Netflix series starring Eric Cantona. He began his historical trilogy with *The Great Swindle*, which won the Prix Goncourt in 2013, and has since been adapted for film. *All Human Wisdom* is the second volume of this trilogy.

FRANK WYNNE is a translator from French and Spanish. His previous translations include works by Virginie Despentes, Javier Cercas and Michel Houellebecq. He has been awarded the Scott Moncrieff Prize and the Premio Valle-Inclán, and his translation of *Windows on the World* by Frédéric Beigbeder won the *Independent* Foreign Fiction Prize in 2005. His translation of *Vernon Subutex I* by Virginie Despentes was shortlisted for the Man Booker International Prize.